Looking for Romance

with

Steve Davis

a story of
Northern Soul
# DOWN SOUTH

First edition

All rights reserved. The contents of this book may not be reproduced in any form, except for short extracts for quotation or review, without the written permission of the publisher.

Copyright © Ben Summers 2018

The right of Ben Summers to be identified as author of this work has been asserted by him in accordance with the Copyright, Designs and Patents Act 1998.

Print Typeset by Electric Reads
www.electricreads.com

# 1

'Soul Sam is dead!'

Romance didn't know what to say. Another soul death. There was no reason for him not to believe it. It was one of those occasions on which he knew he should say something and it was one of those occasions on which he knew he should feel something, but he didn't say anything and the main thing he felt was a dizzying mix of guilt and confusion for not feeling more. Soul Sam was his hero.

'He had a stroke. He died in the night.'

Immediately, ashamedly, Romance was aware that he resented his friend for having this inside knowledge. But he liked Spaghetti. He loved him.

'I ain't sure I'm gonna be able to make it Saturday, mate.'

Now Romance was overflowing with feeling and it was a feeling like some Brummie twit had just turned off the turnable midway through a record and time had resoundingly crashed to a halt. This was terrible news. Spaghetti was supposed to be DJing on Saturday. Of course, Soul Sam's death was terrible news too, especially for Soul Sam, but surely Saturday could still be Saturday. And Saturday mattered. Saturday was the memorial do for Demetrios.

Immediately, ashamedly, Romance found himself more worried about Saturday than he was worried by the thought of a world without Soul Sam. And he loved Soul Sam. Soul Sam was his hero. But a world without Soul Sam was a long-term proposition; it had only just started. Saturday was on Saturday. And it was for his friend.

'I know it weren't totally unexpected like, but it's knocked me for six a bit, mate. We're gonna bury him in the garden.'

At that, Romance just waited. When someone said something so disorienting – like when Catford Keith told him that he (Catford Keith) was growing younger every year because his old cells were continually being replaced by new ones – he reckoned he just had to wait until they said something he could say something back to. And what did Spaghetti mean it wasn't totally unexpected? Romance hadn't even known Soul Sam was sick. Did everyone know but him?

Romance was familiar with the garden. It was at the back of Spaghetti's semi in Birmingham, where he lived with Annie. There was a square of grass and a washing line and wooden fences around, and beyond the fences were the gardens of other Birmingham semis. It didn't seem fitting as the final resting place of the world's leading cultural icon. Surely there was somewhere with a little more gravitas – a gravesite with a little more soul. Somewhere in Cleethorpes.

Or Great Yarmouth, maybe. Or Detroit.

And, if it was to be a garden, Romance's was better anyway. It was longer and more coffin-shaped. It wasn't Detroit or Chicago, but surely the London Borough of Brent had as much soul as Birmingham?

'Annie says it's barmy, but I think it's what he would have wanted. I've had him ever since he was a babby.'

A babby. Since he was a babby.

'You stupid fucking Brummie twat,' Romance thought but didn't say. (What he said was 'Oh, I'm really sorry.') The stupid fucking Brummie twat was talking about his stupid fucking Brummie dog.

Romance knew that Spaghetti loved his dog more than was normal even for a dog lover, and because Spaghetti loved his dog so much Romance loved Spaghetti even more than he would have done anyway, which would have been a lot. And Romance could hear that Spaghetti was upset.

'Sorry about Saturday mate, but I just don't think I'll be in the mood.'

'Don't worry, Spag-man. Just come down if you feel like it on the day,' Romance said, hopefully, and he thought, bitterly, about being blown out because of a fucking dog: an ugly, old, crippled Brummie dog that had been blind in one eye and had lost control of its bladder. But Romance loved Spaghetti, and he loved Spaghetti loving his dog, and he loved that he had called his dog after Soul Sam. And, when he thought about it (which was after the phone call but before *Countdown*), he came to the conclusion that the kind of DJ he wanted DJing at the memorial do for Demetrios Demetriou was just the kind of DJ who would cancel because his dog had died. And so he was pleased with himself for asking Spaghetti in the first place. The whole episode had simply confirmed his excellent judgement.

# 2

Sam Cooke was the original Soul Sam, although he was never known as Soul Sam and neither the human nor the canine Soul Sam to follow was named after him. But he was one of soul music's originators and there has never been another Sam in soul music to rival him. He was the first well-known singer to make the move from church to rhythm and blues… and to soul. And he was one of the first to die.

The official Los Angeles Police Department record states that Cooke was shot and killed by Bertha Franklin, the manager of the Hacienda Motel. Cooke had checked into the motel one evening and Franklin claimed that in the night he broke into her live-in office in a rage, wearing nothing but a shoe and an overcoat, demanding to know the whereabouts of a young woman who had accompanied him to the motel. Franklin denied any knowledge of the woman, but the enraged Cooke didn't believe her and violently grabbed her. According to Franklin, she grappled with Cooke, the two of them fell to the floor and then she jumped up and ran to get her gun. She said that she fired at Cooke in self-defence because she feared for her life. She shot three times. Cooke exclaimed, 'Lady, you shot me,' before falling, mortally wounded.

According to Franklin and the motel's owner, Evelyn Carr, they were on the phone together at the time of the incident. Cooke interrupted them and then Franklin dropped the phone in the struggle, but her boss continued to listen. Carr then called the police, saying that she thought there had been a shooting. 'A guy just broke through the door... I think she shot him, I don't know.'

Whenever Spaghetti heard the Sam Cooke song *You Send Me* (which was as little as possible as he considered it a sorry example of the pop schmaltz that Cooke fell into), he heard the words 'Lady, you shot me' in place of 'Darling, you send me'. And he wondered at the coincidence of the two female protagonists, Bertha Franklin and Evelyn Carr, sharing surnames with two of the greatest soul voices of all time: Aretha Franklin and James Carr. The world of soul music leaves many unanswered questions. But that's what it is to be human, Spaghetti concluded (even though the Franklin/Carr coincidence was clearly just a coinicidence and not a particularly remarkable one at that).

## 3

Soul Sam's funeral was a sombre affair. Spaghetti oversaw proceedings and Annie attended. Spaghetti had managed to squeeze Soul Sam into a record carrying case before he had gone too stiff and it made a good coffin and was a loving touch because Spaghetti loved his records. He loved his records and he loved his dog. (And he loved Annie, but that was a different kind of love.) He *had* loved his dog. Now his dog was gone. He still had his records. And he had Annie.

'So what records were in that box?' little Annie asked when she saw Soul Sam during the wake.

'Just some old reissues. Nothing special.'

'And where are they gonna go now? You're not having any down here you know.'

The records had a habit of creeping down and Annie was always on her guard. Spaghetti had a record room, but it wasn't big enough.

'They're just on the floor of the record room. Don't make such a fuss.'

Annie suspected that Spaghetti was planning on taking

advantage of the death of Soul Sam by sneaking some records down, thinking that concern and sympathy for his loss would stop her from intervening. The sight of Soul Sam in the open record box heightened her suspicion. But Spaghetti would never have taken advantage of the death of Soul Sam in that or any other way, and that was just one of the reasons Romance had wanted him to DJ at the memorial do for Demetrios Demetriou. The man had soul.

'That dog had soul,' said Spaghetti to himself, as Annie tried to wrestle Soul Sam from the box. But he was stiff now and had jammed fast.

Romance had met Soul Sam a few times – on his only visit to Spaghetti's house, when Soul Sam had lain dutifully on the landing as Romance and Spaghetti had sat in Spaghetti's record room playing Billy Stewart flipsides, and, of course, at various soul dos – but he hadn't known the dog was called Soul Sam. When talking to the dog, Spaghetti simply called him 'mate' or 'Sammy boy'. But the funeral was a formal affair and Spaghetti felt it right and proper that Soul Sam be called by his right and proper name.

'Soul Sam was so beautiful, like flowers full bloom in May. His kiss was like the summer breeze; it left me speechless, with nothing left to say. I loved and I lost. It happens to the best. I loved and I lost. I might as well confess.'

When spoken by a mourning Brummie at a dog's funeral, it isn't immediately obvious that those are the lyrics of a classic Impressions song (with the little addition of a new name and a subtle switch of gender). But even Annie was moved.

'That was beautiful. Poor Soul Sam.'

'Curtis Mayfield, init. He must have gone through what I'm going through now.'

And for Romance and Spaghetti that was the beauty of the music. When their hearts were broken and they felt as if they were broken as no hearts had ever been broken before, it reached out to them and showed them that others had been there, that it was a part of being human and that they were among many and a part of the whole. And because they were a part of the whole, they still had a place in the world. And it didn't just tell them as pop music did; it showed them. The pain resonated through the music.

Spaghetti had dug a hole in the grass about two and a half 45s wide, a couple deep and about a 150 (upright) long. He picked up the record box containing Soul Sam and lowered it in. He threw a handful of earth on top of it.

'Ashes to ashes, dust to dust… How does it go, bab?'

Annie shrugged.

'Ashes to ashes, dust to dust, here lies Soul Sam, in dog we trust.'

'What does that mean, *in dog we trust*?'

'I'm not sure. It just came out.'

Spaghetti was the officiator. Annie was a mourner. They hadn't invited anyone else to the funeral. They had thought about it, but Soul Sam didn't really have any close dog friends as he didn't get out much and few humans seemed appropriate, other than the human Soul Sam. Spaghetti had asked him, but, once the human Soul Sam realised that the voice on the phone belonged to Spaghetti Weston and wasn't that of a Brummie St. Peter informing him of his own demise, he decided to say that he was already booked on that afternoon to DJ at a donkey wedding in Blackpool. He had never DJed at a dog's funeral and wouldn't know what to play, and he wasn't able to grasp that he didn't have to play anything because, in the twenty-five years since he first stepped up before the soul masses of the Wigan Casino, no one had ever asked him anywhere to do anything other than play records.

Spaghetti was wearing his dressing gown. He had told Annie that he thought the priestly effect befitted the occasion. He was trying to keep a candle alight too, but the wind kept blowing it out.

'Does *Ashes to Ashes* mean you should burn him? Shouldn't we have a dog cremation?' Annie suggested, as Spaghetti was already covering the record box with earth.

'Burn Soul Sam? I don't want to burn Soul Sam. I want to give him a grave and a headstone.'

'A headstone? You never said anything about a headstone! I don't know if I want a headstone in the middle of the lawn.'

'He's gotta have a headstone, bab. How can you bury him and not give him a headstone? I'm going to make it out of vinyl and put an inscription on it from one of his favourite records.'

'Well as long as it's not *In Dog We Trust*.' Annie shook her head but wasn't going to press the matter.

'It wasn't going to be *In Dog We Trust*,' Spaghetti muttered to himself as he kept filling the hole, although he did think that had a nice ring to it. He didn't yet know what it was going to be, but it had to be something because Sammy boy needed a memorial and anyway the record box was metal and how could he burn that? Even if he were able to produce enough heat, which he wouldn't be, the box would just melt and form a globby mass of metallic dog, which they would then just have to bury anyway, and that wouldn't be a fitting end to a dog of Soul Sam's stature.

'Here lies Soul Sam, the most soulful dog in Birmingham.' Spaghetti would have to think about it.

Unlike Soul Sam, Sam Cooke had two funerals and, unlike Soul Sam's, both were national events. He drew the biggest crowds of his career.

In Los Angeles, for three days Sam's body was held in state in an open casket. It was then taken to Chicago for one funeral service and then back to Los Angeles for another. Two other soul luminaries, Lou Rawls and Bobby Bland, were among those who sang at the LA funeral. Strangely, Sam was dressed differently for the two funerals and, even more strangely, in LA his coffin was presented standing upright. 'Until the day break and the shadows flee away,' reads his headstone. 'I will get me to the mountain of myrrh and the hill of frankincense,' continues the Song of Solomon. It's all about the meaning of true love. It's all about soul.

# 4

*When you've got the trouble of the world on your shoulder*
*When each passing day, the sun grows a little colder*
*Your future doesn't look any brighter*
*Your load isn't getting any lighter*
*You're down*
*And push has come to shove*
*Now is the time…*
*To try my love.* [1]

'For fuck's sake, turn that fucking northern shite off.'

It wasn't shite. It was Troy Dodds. It was on a tape that had been copied for Jimmy by Mick the Twitch a few years before the death of Soul Sam (the dog) and a few decades after the death of Soul Sam (the singer). Jimmy knew it wasn't shite. Even Lee knew it wasn't shite. But it was Lainie talking and Lainie was bigger than Lee, even though Lee was a builder, and she was much bigger than little Jimmy from Bognor, and little Jimmy's littleness was accentuated now as he sat between the two of them in the front of Lee's van on their way back from the record fair in Southampton. It was the cold spring day that they were to meet Hippy John.

'What?' Jimmy responded, rhetorically.

'It's shite,' Lainie reiterated, 'and for fuck's sake, Lee, keep your eyes on the fucking road.'

'Hey Jimmy, did you end up getting that Steelers 45?' Lee asked.

'Yeah.'

'Cool.'

'Jesus fuck, what a pile of shite. I'm not fucking going back there again.'

'It was all right,' said Lee. 'You got that Luther thing. I got the Leon Haywood LP.'

'Fuck it. We could have them easy. A couple of fucking phone calls. We didn't have to drive all the way to fucking Southampton. Look at this fucking dump, and look where you're fucking going!'

'Glad you came, Jimmy?' smiled Lee.

Jimmy looked up at Lee and nodded.

They were glad. They were all glad. They'd had a good day.

The record fair had been quieter than normal and they had arrived early, so they'd had plenty of opportunity to go through the boxes. They knew the soul dealers and no one special did the Southampton fair, so it was a matter of wading through the unsorted records hoping something decent had slipped through the collectors' net, relying on the ignorance of the non-soulful, common folk.

There was a creeping excess of CDs and, as usual, there wasn't much soul, but then there weren't many soul people looking. Leeds Dave was there. Minimalist Mike. And Romance. It was fairly unusual to come across anything really rare at a record fair, but Lee picked up quite a few cheap LPs. He had most of them already, but he could sell them on or use them for trades. He was pleased with the Leon Haywood. It wasn't a hard LP, but he had just never felt compelled to buy it and he knew he would never phone for it. It was too obvious. And Jimmy was happy with his Steelers record. Once he had bought that he couldn't buy anything else, and he had to borrow some money off Lee for a cup of tea and a sandwich.

And yes, they could have done as well, if not better, sitting at home on the phone, but they all enjoyed the touch and the smell of the records and the excitement of looking.

'What a pile of fucking shite.'

Lee was approaching the Itchen Bridge. Neither Jimmy nor Lee knew if she was talking about Troy Dodds, Southampton or the record fair, but it made no difference.

'Romance found a Brown Sugar.'

'Did he? You know the twat moved down here cos he imagined records being unloaded at the port and he wanted to be first to get his greedy mitts on them? Thirty years too late. I think he heard that rumour about old 45s being used as ballast in ships and maybe he imagined the pubs full of American sailors with hold-alls full of rare soul records for sale. Instead he found Wigsy and Leeds Dave.'

And it was when Lee mentioned Wigsy and Leeds Dave – when they were half way up the long bridge that rises and falls over the River Itchen – that he noticed something that turned out to be Hippy John crawling on to the side crash barrier at the apex of the bridge. The river was a deathly distance below.

*On a pretty day you can't see the clear blue sky*
*Though you're looking up there are tears in your eyes*

Mick the Twitch had called the tape *Do the Twitch: Northern Soul to Make You Grimace.* It was a collection of his latest acquisitions.

*Now is the time…*
*To try my love!*

# 5

The term *northern soul* was first coined by the music journalist Dave Godin in the 1960s. He used it to describe the style of soul music that was being collected by soul fans from the north of England. While the fashionable clubs of London in the late sixties were tending towards fresher, funkier sounds, in the north a handful of DJs were unearthing smoother, rarer, more heavily beat-driven soul records. They were characterised by a driving uptempobeat, epitomised in popular music by the classic Motown sound of the mid-sixties. The music mainly emanated from the northern cities of the United States, particularly Detroit and Chicago, and was often the result of small, independent record labels attempting to emulate the successful Motown formula. Few succeeded, as the popular touch was hard to come by, but in the process a mass of music was produced, some of which was mundane, much of which was heavenly. If lucky, aspiring inner city youngsters were given a few hours in a recording studio to prove themselves and with such a once-in-a-lifetime opportunity they would sing as if their lives depended on it. When the moment favoured, there's an infectious energy about the music, even when unpolished and cheaply produced, and it's an energy that seemed to appeal to the white working class youngsters of northern English cities.

And it appealed too, years later, to Romance, Solomon and Demetrios Demetriou, and they would venture north to hear their favourite DJs and especially to The Ritz allnighters in Manchester to hear Soul Sam play records they couldn't hear anywhere else. 'Something for the sake of which it is worthwhile to live on earth,' said Solomon, quoting someone clever, as he raised his pint glass into the music-filled space. And it appealed to white working class little Jimmy from Bognor. He hadn't looked for it. And he wasn't looking to be different. He had just fallen into it. It was just him.

*Everything is dark and you can't seem to find the light*
*You're like a child lost, afraid, somewhere in the night* [1]

Little Jimmy mouthed the words as the music went in him and came out. Lainie shouted her words out loud.

'Lee, what the fuck do you think you're doing?'

Lee was coming to a stop at the top of the Itchen Bridge.

Lee didn't answer. Little Jimmy looked up at him.

'Lee, we're in the middle of the fucking bridge!'

There was nowhere to pull over. Stopping meant blocking one of the two lanes of traffic.

'Don't tell me it's this fucking van again. For fuck's sake, this fucking pile of crap. You said there wouldn't be any problem with it.'

'It's not the van. There's some nutter gonna jump off the bridge.'

Lainie didn't say anything to that. Little Jimmy looked up at her in wonder.

Lee stopped the van at the top of the bridge, opened the driver's door, stepped out into the bright coldness and walked round the van to the edge. Lainie stayed in the van and watched him. Jimmy didn't know whether to stay or go and as he was already sitting in the van he carried on doing that, which meant staying.

Lee had seen the figure clamber over the crash barrier at the side of the carriageway, and when he looked over the barrier he saw a small ledge that was the edge of the bridge and clinging to this was a man. Beyond the man was nothing but the faraway, muddy brown water of the River Itchen.

'What the fuck do you think you're doing?'

The man had heard the van stop, but he didn't know why it had stopped, and he heard Lee shout. He didn't look up. He hoped he hadn't been spotted. He hoped the shouting was meant for someone else.

'Oi! Beardy!'

The man had a beard. And he knew he had a beard. And he thought the chances of another man with a beard being in the vicinity with reason to be shouted at were worryingly slim. He slowly moved his head. He looked up and saw Lee looming over him, face glowering and body muscling.

'Yes, you, you fucking hippy twat.'

The man had a beard, that was true, but he had never considered himself a hippy. He could have been a hippy at the time of hippies; he was of that age. And now he had a beard, but lots of people had beards and it seemed natural to him to have one. He had not chosen to grow his hair long or to grow his beard; he had just not chosen to have them cut, just as little Jimmy had not chosen to like northern soul or to get out of the van.

'What the fuck do you think you're doing?'

The man was clinging on and he hoped this gave him an excuse not to react.

'Get your fucking hairy hippy arse off this fucking bridge!'

The man had come across aggression before. He wasn't aggressive himself, but he had come across it. Young men had shouted at him in the street. He had been pushed and spat at. He had been kicked awake. And there was the one time he had been beaten senseless for no reason other than for just being who he was. He didn't understand such acts and he had long since given up trying to understand them. He seemed to offend people. And now he was offending this man who had stopped and looked for him and hated him so much that he had gone out of his way to be offended.

'I'm sorry,' the man said. He wondered at his power to offend and he thought that he had excelled himself in this case. He couldn't even do this one last thing without the world stopping to spit at him.

'I'm sorry,' he said. 'It's your bridge.'

His voice was soft and he was well spoken.

'What d'you mean, it's my bridge? It's not my fucking bridge. Why's it my bridge? I don't know whose fucking bridge it is – probably some posh twat like you, although yeah, probably not such a fucking basketcase – and no one owns bridges anyway and it's just a fucking bridge. What would I want a fucking bridge for?'

Lee left this last question hanging in the cold air and waited for an answer. The man was looking into the brown, murky space. He hadn't expected this. He hadn't expected a conversation. He hadn't had a conversation for a long time. He hadn't expected someone to be putting questions to him – questions like why one would want to own a bridge.

The man remembered the bridge being built – he and this bridge had history – but he didn't know who had paid for it and he didn't know who owned it, but before the bridge was built, in the space that his body was filling now, there was nothing. He knew that. And below him there was nothing because no one had built anything there. And, right then, nothing is exactly what he wanted.

'I don't know,' the man said. He didn't. He didn't know why this towering young man would want to own a bridge.

'You don't know much, do you? You don't know how fucking cold I am stood in the middle of this fucking bridge. You don't know the lip I'm gonna get off my mental woman. You don't know what a fucking traffic jam there is cos I've stopped my van in the middle of the fucking Itchen Bridge.'

Lee hadn't been fully conscious of the traffic jam until he mentioned it, but then he heard the horns and when he turned his head he could see the jam and he could hear Lainie, who must have had her head out of the driver's window because she was shouting and swearing at the cars stuck behind.

No, the man didn't know any of that. The older he grew, the less he seemed to know.

'What the fuck do you think you're doing anyway? If you're gonna fucking kill yourself just fucking get on with it cos there's a right fucking mess up here and I want to get home to watch *Final Score*, don't I?'

'I do want to kill myself,' the man whispered.

'What?'

'I do want to kill myself! I do want to kill myself!'

'Jesus Christ, you fucking fucking twat. *You* want to kill yourself. You should see what I'm fucking married to. I'm the one whose best mate thinks modern soul is anything past 1967. Jesus, what the fuck do you want to kill yourself for?'

The man thought. 'I've no reason not to.'

'Yeah, and I've no reason not to fucking grow my hair and turn into a fucking hippy twat but doesn't mean I'm gonna do it. And what about Johnny Davis? Fuck. I don't suppose you know who he is, being a hairy hippy, but he fell twelve storeys and got splattered in the rubbish, didn't he? He was a good singer, you know, and was pushed. He was thrown off that building. And now you're choosing to jump. It's insulting to him. It's insulting to his life. It's insulting to Johnny Davis. It's insulting to fucking soul music. And listen, mate, you know what happened to me the other week? I got a mint copy of the Lyn Collins *Wide Awake in a Dream* and you probably don't know what the fuck that is but what it is is fucking brilliant and it's not rare or anything but I'd been after a decent copy of it for fucking ages, and it came on the day I was doing a guest spot on this soul radio show, so I thought, great, I'm gonna play that, aren't I? And I took it along and I hadn't even played it at home yet – hadn't played it once – and I stuck it on and played it and it was fine – played absolutely mint, beautiful – but this fucking radio station just had those annoying Technics middles that you put in the middle of 45s and they're always too bloody tight for old records and after I'd played it the fucking middle was stuck and I was trying to get it out and I was in a bit of a hurry and a panic cos I was live and I had to get the next record cued up and I forced it too much and the fucking record broke. Clean in half. What a bastard. And then I just had to forget it and put another record on quick and carry on all happy and enthusiastic like nothing had happened when inside I felt fucking sick and just wanted to fucking puke. Anyway, then what happens, two weeks later, Prestatyn weekender, going through Binsy's box, there it is – demo, mint – fifteen quid. Result. So you never know do you? The thing about topping yourself is there's no going back is there? What it is is yeah, you want to die now, so you drop into the river and then fuck knows what happens down there, or you live and put up with a load of shit and who knows you'll probably stay miserable for fucking ages – weeks, months, years, who knows? I don't know how long you've wanted to die for. It's not like "Oh let's get off this bridge cos everything'll be all right" cos it won't, but what it is is one day – one day in the future, whenever that might be and it might be years – you'll feel OK and things will be better, because things change. Everything changes, mate – unless you're Johnny Davis and dead in a pile of rubbish in some Chicago back street – and if things change for the worse like they have with you then things can change for the better too and then you'll look back at this moment and think thank fuck I didn't top myself then because now things are all right.'

Lee looked at the man. He hadn't moved a muscle.

'Listen geezer, take a hold of my arm.'

Lee reached down to the man. The man clung on to his ledge. He was now beginning to shiver.

'Just take hold of my fucking arm before I climb over and kick your hippy fucking arse into the river!'

The man pushed one arm up and Lee grabbed it.

# 6

At New Bern, North Carolina, there is a new bridge over the Neuse River that closely resembles Southampton's Itchen Bridge. It has a similar trajectory and a spread of bold, concrete uprights. Both bridges have a waist-high, concrete protective barrier and both barriers are more than adequate to prevent any accidental drivings-off but neither were designed to stop a determined jumper.

Unfortunately, in January 1970, when soul singer Billy Stewart was speeding towards the Neuse River he was not in the vicinity of New Bern. The bridge he was aiming for was upriver and small in comparison. His fancy new Ford Thunderbird struck the bridge kerbing and plummeted into the river and he was killed, along with three members of his band. (If he had been in New Bern, the result might have been the same, as the bridge there hadn't been built then and there was just a big stretch of empty space where it was to be. But then the chances are Billy wouldn't have been speeding towards it.)

And as Johnny Davis was falling through twelve storeys

of cold Chicago air, he was heading for a rubbish cart, but it seems that he was already unconscious, if not dead. He was a victim of organised crime. 'We may not be remembered when we're gone, but we have love,' sang Johnny (when he was alive and conscious), but it was Billy Stewart that Romance and Spaghetti were playing when they were sitting in Spaghetti's record room, and, when Spaghetti put on *What Have I Done*, Romance thought of Billy driving his car into the river.

'He drove his car into a river, didn't he? Wiped out half his band too.'

'Maybe the car sank too quick cos he was so fat.'

Maybe it did. Billy was very fat. Demetrios Demetriou, however, was getting thinner by the day. The chemo was eating away at him. And it wasn't long after Romance and Spaghetti were playing Billy Stewart records that Demetrios Demetriou was swept away.

'There is music in thy wave, calmest, purest river; in thy waters let me bathe, ever and forever,' sang a youthful, podgy Billy Stewart, who, like Sam Cooke and so many others, began his singing in the church.

# 7

Spaghetti felt bad about letting Romance down, but he felt worse about the death of his dog. After the official ceremony had ended, Annie went inside to watch the *Eastenders* omnibus. Spaghetti took a moment by himself at the grave of Soul Sam.

He had found Soul Sam in a dogs' rescue home. He wasn't the prettiest dog in the home – far from it – (missing an eye was the least of it) but then Spaghetti was far from the prettiest human visiting. When their three eyes met there was an immediate connection.

'All right mate?' asked Spaghetti, and Soul Sam looked at him, pointedly, and there was a knowledgeable, experienced depth to the dog's eye. That's what Spaghetti felt. The dog had soul. He didn't have a right eye, but he had soul. He might not have had a breed – he was a scruffy thing that looked like a cross between two other ill-bred scruffy God-knows-whats – but he had soul. He was about average dog size and average dog shape, with average dog-length matted, grey hair, which fell over his above-averagely watery eye and eye-place and thinned over his averagely-lengthed tail. He didn't jump up and he didn't bark, and he was neither happy nor cross to meet Spaghetti. The volunteers at the rescue home saw his lethargy as a sign that he was weary of life, despite his (estimated) tender years. No doubt he hadn't been looked after properly. But Spaghetti saw in Soul Sam a kindred spirit: a dog whose soul was deep enough for him to remain unemotional and unaffected by the ups and downs of everyday life.

'You look in a bit of a state, mate. I know, I ain't much to look at either.'

The home didn't know about the dog's background. Spaghetti didn't care. Soul Sam was the dog for him.

Spaghetti had to visit the home five times to take Soul Sam out on long walks to make sure they would get along. They got along fine. They walked around the park. Neither of them ran. Neither of them looked happy or sad and neither of them barked. They just looked like a unit.

'All right mate? I think me and you are gonna get on fine.'

They already were.

There was the home visit and Spaghetti showed the garden and the place under the stairs where he had it in mind for Soul Sam to sleep. And he pointed to Annie.

'That's Annie. She's all right.'

And then Soul Sam moved in and it was as if he had always lived there.

And now Spaghetti stood at the grave.

'All right mate?'

He wondered if he was all right. Spaghetti didn't have any strong religious beliefs and wasn't sure about heaven. He wondered if there was such a place and, if there was, whether it would take dogs. Too many places these days were banning dogs, he thought. Eyebrows were even raised on occasion when he took Soul Sam DJing with him.

'No more gigs for us, Sammy boy.'

If heaven did exist, it was supposed to be the place of perfect happiness, and Spaghetti couldn't imagine being happy without Soul Sam. So they would have to let Sam in, at least when Spaghetti died too, but maybe they wouldn't until then and Soul Sam would be held in some kind of dog limbo. He hoped not. That wouldn't be fair. There would be other dead owners who were only happy with their dogs, so there would be other dogs in heaven so Soul Sam could hang out with them.

'I hope you remember me, boy, when I come to meet you,' Spaghetti smiled. 'We did all right, didn't we?'

They had done all right. They had done well. Spaghetti loved Soul Sam and, because he did, Soul Sam loved Spaghetti, and this love was unconditional. It was an unquestioning, dog's love. It wasn't like the love between two humans, with all its strings and conditions. It was uncomplicated and unsullied.

Spaghetti loved Annie but that was complicated. He also loved soul music and that was uncomplicated. That was a pure and unsullied dog's love. He loved his records and when he looked at them and touched them they were alive to him, and when he listened to them they told him of love and loss and he felt their pain. But they weren't looking for a reaction. They were made solely to be listened to and Spaghetti was made to listen to them. It was a mutual, dog-like exchange and it was a satisfying exchange – one that was needed to feel whole. It brought contentment and gratification, and in his record room Spaghetti didn't feel that he was fleeing from the world but that there he was experiencing the world at some fundamental, dog-like level.

'I won't feel whole in heaven without me records, mate!' Spaghetti suddenly thought. If heaven was heaven then they would have to let them in. But he knew people who had died and who had loved their records as Spaghetti loved his and their records hadn't gone with them. They had stayed in the world to be sold or auctioned or given away. He had even been to see Demetrios Demetriou's records and no one of right mind could say that Demetrios Demetriou hadn't loved his records.

He hadn't been sure of the existence of heaven before and now its likelihood was suddenly looking decidedly less. But he kept these thoughts to himself.

'You'll be all right mate,' he said out loud. 'Don't worry, you'll be all right.'

# 8

'Don't worry mate. You'll be all right.'

The bearded, Christ-like figure clung to his saviour.

'Where the fuck is that stupid fuckwit?' Lainie muttered as another horn blasted at her rear. 'What?! Just come past then for fuck's sake!' The car passed. 'Yeah, yeah, yeah, whatever! Wanker!'

Lainie looked back and saw more cars queuing up behind.

'For fuck's sake, what the fuck's he doing? Has he fucking jumped as well? I should be so fucking lucky.'

She didn't bother looking to Jimmy for a reaction.

But Lee hadn't jumped. He was pulling the bearded man off his ledge.

'Help me for fuck's sake,' Lee uttered as he was struggling awkwardly, bent over the crash barrier. The man reached out with his free arm and grabbed hold of the barrier. Lee was pulling him by the other arm and, with a lack of hippy resistance, Lee managed to wrestle the hairy man up and over, who then collapsed in a shaking heap by the side of the road.

'Come on mate,' Lee said and held out his hand.

The man took it and Lee pulled him to his knees and the man was violently sick. The sick stank of alcohol and some of it splattered over Lee's loafers.

'You fucking hippy cunt!'

The man burst into tears.

'Oi! Get your fucking van off the bridge!' Lee looked up. A man was shouting from a car. 'It's not a fucking picnic spot!'

Lee held himself up straight and took a couple of steps towards the car.

'Piss off! What's your fucking problem?'

'You're holding up the whole fucking bridge!'

'Yeah? My friend's fucking ill isn't he, arsehole!'

'Tell your friend to fuck off and die somewhere else!'

Lee was heading over but he stopped when he saw that Lainie was beating him to it.

'Oi! Wanker!' she shouted, as she approached. 'You got a problem? Come on then! You fucking arsehole!' She was at the car and she slapped the bonnet hard. 'Come on then! Get out the fucking car! You're the one that's gonna fucking die!'

She kicked the side of the car and at that moment it jolted forward. There was a gap in the oncoming traffic and the driver took the chance and sped past.

'Yeah, fuck off! You fucking wanker!' Lainie shouted after him, but he was gone and wouldn't have heard her.

She walked to Lee and looked past him to the man who

was kneeling before her.

'Jesus Christ, what the fuck is this?' The man stared back at her, mouth open. 'It fucking stinks.'

He wasn't crying anymore. He was motionless.

'Yeah, what's your name mate?' Lee asked.

Stinking man looked at Lee.

'What's your name? You got a fucking name!'

'John.'

'John. John!' Lainie was first off the mark. 'What kind of a name's that for a fucking hippy? John the hippy!'

Now *she* was calling him a hippy. The man didn't know what to say. John was his name but no one had ever called him John the hippy before. He hadn't known he was a hippy. He hadn't really realised he was an anything.

'So where do you live mate?'

The man looked blank. Lee tried again.

'Where do you live? Where are you staying tonight then?'

It wasn't a sensible question. The man had been intending to spend the night at the bottom of the Itchen or possibly out in the Solent somewhere.

'Jesus Christ, Lee, you fucking twat.'

'Well all right, but I was just asking. I mean we can't really leave him up here can we?'

'Well if he does jump at least he'll get a bit of a fucking wash. And there'll be one less fucking hippy in the world.'

John imagined again the calm, soothing cold of the water. But, at that moment, he was able to stay where he was: on his knees, damp now from the sick, on top of the Itchen

Bridge. He wasn't happy – of course he wasn't – but he was enduring and it was because these two strangers were talking about him.

'Look at the fucking state of him,' Lainie continued. 'What a fucking loser. Fucking hell Lee, if I ever get like that remind me to fucking top myself quick.'

The traffic had begun to jam up again and a car blew its horn. Lainie turned and was on her way in an instant.

'Oi you fucking twat there was someone gonna fucking jump here!'

But she hesitated because she didn't know which driver to approach and, after she had paused and given them all a hard stare, she turned and saw Lee leading John the hippy to the van.

'Jesus Christ,' she said to herself. 'Jesus fucking Christ.'

# 9

The one time Romance had stayed at Spaghetti Weston's house and the boys had sat on a record box each in Spaghetti's record room playing Billy Stewart flipsides with Soul Sam listening on the landing was a consequence of Spaghetti asking Romance to DJ with him at his do in Birmingham City Centre. The Rik Tik Bar. It had been a good evening. There had been hardly anyone there; the music had been fabulous.

Three people that were there were the two Borelli brothers and the barmaid, Bettye. The Borelli brothers hadn't noticed Bettye and Bettye hadn't noticed the Borelli brothers. Romance had noticed Bettye. She was gorgeous.

Spaghetti was very drunk, as he always was whenever he organised his events. With Soul Sam, he would arrive at the venue early to set up the decks and, because he was nervous about the evening and whether anyone was going to come, he would always have a few drinks before anyone else had even arrived. So he was tipsy from the beginning and by the time of his final set he was invariably too drunk to work the decks. When a record ended, and with Soul Sam lying, resigned, behind him, there would be an awkward silence, broken by a drunken Brummie voice exclaiming, 'Why the fuck ain't this working?' One of the Borelli brothers would go to him and press the *on* button on the offending deck. And then the same would happen at the end of that record.

Because the Borelli brothers were furious at Spaghetti's lack of professionalism – which, to them, was thoroughly disrespectful to the music that they loved and took to be the highest art form ever created by humankind – they began to delay their helping touch in protest. The silence affronted them but they thought Spaghetti should be exposed as the disgrace that he was. The result was increasingly long silences and, as the old soul records typically run for between two and two and a half minutes, an interesting juxtaposition developed between the heartfelt exclamations of lost love in sixties black America and drunken Brummie cries for help.

Romance loved Spaghetti's music. He thought the music was wonderful. And he loved the lack of music too. He thought that was wonderful – certainly too wonderful for him to volunteer any assistance himself. And to Romance the silences were useful because they meant he could chat to Bettye.

Bettye was gorgeous. Romance was gaping at her.

'So is this music driving you mad yet?'

He thought it a good opening line. It was a sympathetic acknowledgement of her position. He had used it many times before, to no effect.

'No,' she said.

It was a straight answer. Things could have been going worse, although Romance couldn't see how. It was an answer Romance hadn't anticipated. The alternatives – 'Yes,' 'I don't know' or a total blanking – Romance hadn't anticipated either. He made a mental note to anticipate better.

'You're gorgeous,' he said.

She blanked him.

Another record started. After a few seconds, as the Borelli who had helped was walking away across the empty dancefloor, Spaghetti turned off the deck and the music stopped again. The Borelli refused to go back. He stood still, looking between Spaghetti and the other Borelli, shaking his head.

'Can I have your phone number?'

Romance was satisfied with his recovery.

'No.'

'Why not?'

'I've got a boyfriend.'

Romance hadn't anticipated this. Maybe she did have a boyfriend. Maybe she didn't. But maybe she did.

'How old are you?'

Romance remembered that it was good to show an interest.

'Why?'

'I'm just showing an interest.'

'24.'

'Well how long have you been seeing your boyfriend?'

'Why?'

'Because the chances are you've been seeing him for a few months or maybe a year or two, and maybe maybe you're really in love and will live happily ever after but the chances are you'll split up sometime, and even if you get married the chances are you'll either split up or at least have an affair, so you might as well at least take my phone number so if and when the occasion arises when you split up you can call me and we'll go out.'

Bettye watched Romance write his phone number on a napkin. The napkin was scrunching up under the tip of the biro and it took Romance longer than he would have liked to make it legible. He gave the defaced napkin to Bettye. She took it and looked at it and didn't say anything.

When his phone rang the next day and it was a withheld number, Romance knew that it was Bettye. He stepped out of the record room and stepped over Soul Sam so that Soul Sam couldn't see him without turning.

'Hello?'

'Hello.'

'Hello Bettye?'

'Hello.'

'Hello, Bettye.'

'Hello. My name is Jane.'

'Oh, hello.'

Romance had thought that the lovely barmaid was called

Bettye, but now that she had said her name was Jane he thought again. And he wondered why he had thought she was called Bettye and Bettye with an *e* at the end at that. He didn't remember asking for her name. But he did remember a Borelli playing *What Condition My Condition Is In* by Bettye Lavette. Maybe that was it. And Bettye Lavette was Bettye with an *e*, and he knew that he loved Bettye Lavette. She had the most anguished voice. And he was quite keen to marry Bettye Lavette. (Her and Debbie Taylor.)

'Hello. Good morning to you sir. I would like to ask what mobile network are you with right now?'

Romance couldn't remember. He wanted to tell her. He didn't want to hide anything from Jane but he couldn't remember, and why was Jane sounding as she was sounding? She wasn't sounding as she was sounding the evening before. It dawned on Romance that it was the wrong Jane.

'I'm sorry, Jane, but you've got the wrong number and I really have to go now because I'm expecting a very important phone call.'

He hung up. He stepped back over Soul Sam, who hadn't been in the least interested, and back into the record room.

'All right?' asked Spaghetti.

'Yeah.'

But it wasn't long before his phone rang again. This time he could see who it was. The letters popped up. JBP.

'Hi, you all right?'

'Yeah, all right.'

'What you up to?'

'I'm up in Brum with Spaghetti Weston.'
'Oh. I'll leave you to it.'
'What you up to?'
'Just at home, with Bella.'
'How's Bella?'
'Yeah, she's all right.'
'All right then.'
'Yeah, all right then.'
'All right, catch you soon.'
'All right, see you then.'
'See ya.'

Romance and JBP had lived together. They had been a couple. And they still loved each other very much and, even though Romance was living back in London again and was now excited about Jane from the Rik Tik in Birmingham, his eyes still welled up at the sound of JBP's voice. Billy sang 'What have I done, to you my baby, to make you want to leave me this way,' [2] and Soul Sam listened and it sounded as fresh as the day it was recorded (which wasn't long before the fast car, fast road, bit to drink, calmest purest river).

To Romance, Soul Sam showed a disappointing lack of emotion. But Spaghetti explained that Soul Sam was a dog who didn't show his emotions in an obvious, outward way.

# 10

It's quite a fast road, the A27 from Southampton to Chichester. It's motorway to Portsmouth and then dual carriageway the rest of the way. Hippy John had been along it before, when the line dancing man had given him a lift to his new job and his new life. He remembered looking down on the River Hamble and seeing the yachts and he saw them again now and he knew that they belonged to other human beings, but such people were an abstract concept to him and it was like looking at carefully constructed animal habitats. Beehives. Wonders of nature. And the cars on the motorway floated by like weird space age capsules in a sci-fi film.

'Romance has got a boat,' said little Jimmy. It was the first thing he had said since before the bridge.

'What?'

'Romance has got a boat. A little rowing boat. *Soul Survivor*. He uses it to row to the Pigeon Club.'

Lainie looked at him but didn't comment. 'This van's a pile of shite,' she said instead. 'And now it fucking stinks too.'

The next glimpse of water was the sea and everyone in the van had more of a sense of being on the edge than normal, and above, to the left, on top of the ridge, were the red brick forts built to defend them all against Napoleon. Hippy John was an educated man. He knew about such things. But he didn't think of them then. He was looking straight ahead, fixed in his seat like an astronaut.

'Fucking Pompey. What a fucking dump.'

They left Portsmouth behind and Hippy John kept his eyes set on the dual carriageway. He hadn't been expecting to see this stretch of road again. The road to Chichester. He hadn't known in any detail what to expect the first time he was taken along it, but he had a general outline: gardening, lodgings, Chichester. Now he knew nothing. He didn't know these people or where they were going or why they had stopped and picked him up. Such questions entered the buzz of his head, but he couldn't process them. He just looked at the cars and felt himself still and moving at the same time.

When the spire of Chichester Cathedral came into view, he felt it rather than saw it.

'When's the next Chi-soul then?' Lainie asked.

Lainie had a soft spot for the do. There were only a couple a year and it was modern soul oriented and always featured a good number of seventies boogie and club tunes too. She and Lee always went, but it wasn't for Jimmy.

'Dunno,' Lee answered. The two of them thought about

the last one as they negotiated the roundabouts of the Chichester ring road. An alcohol induced modern soul love-in. They all drank in celebration of their love for the music and their fellowship. It was far removed from Hippy John's drinking. He drank in desperation and to forget, and the alcoholic stink in the van was as alien to its soul folk as an incence-smelling sound therapy healing workshop.

Both Lainie and Lee were smiling to themselves and thinking of the same thing: Romance collapsed in the doorway of the downstairs room. He always drank a lot when he was DJing, but at the last Chi-soul Dancing Derek and Geography Geoff kept slipping Tia Marias into his Guinness and as soon as his set finished he was gone. The adrenalin of playing records had kept him alert, but that rushed from him as soon as he had stopped and with the satisfied relief came the drunkenness. Making it to the door had been an admirable achievement. Lee had sorted Romance's records and ensured they were all in their sleeves and boxed up.

'This hippy fucking stinks,' Lainie said, and they continued round the last roundabout of the ring road. Lee took the A27 Littlehampton turning. Lainie collected her thoughts, and then she turned on him.

'I thought we were gonna drop him off in Chichester.'

'What?'

'I thought we were gonna fucking drop him off in Chichester! I thought we were gonna drop off stinking hippy man in fucking Chichester!'

'Why?'

'Cos that's what you said!'

'No I didn't.'

'That's what you fucking said!'

'I said he came from Chichester.'

'You said he came from Chichester, so that's where we were gonna drop him off.'

'I didn't say we were gonna drop him off in Chichester.'

'Well where the fuck are we taking him?'

Lainie looked at Hippy John. His eyes had been on the road, but when she looked at him he looked at her. He was wide-eyed, dog-eyed and without anything of an answer. He hadn't thought for a moment where these people were taking him. And even when the question was posed around him and he heard it, he still didn't even wonder. He had decided to end his life and then he had failed or had been stopped, and that one momentous decision – a decision so huge that he had been so proud to have taken it – had led to nothing (and not the nothing it was supposed to lead to). He couldn't think anymore. He knew he wasn't good at decision-making and now that big one was ruined and control of his life had slipped or been taken away from him and he was just going to sit and see. He was as much an observer to his immediate future as little Jimmy, who had spent the trip so far watching the traffic and listening to the *Do the Twitch* tape and not thinking about where they were taking Hippy John or even why he was in the van.

'This is a good 'un,' little Jimmy commented, as

the unissued Dynamics track started. 'It's an unissued Dynamics.'

Hippy John didn't know what the little one was talking about, but it made as much sense to him as anything else. Life. More life. The A27. A van. Unissued dynamics.

'Well I thought we'd just take him home.'

'Home? Home! Are you fucking joking? You just thought we'd take him home? Lee, what kind of fucking moron are you? Do you really think I want a smelly alcoholic hairy fucking suicidal trampy hippy in my house? Why the fuck would we take him home? What would he do in our home? And then what? And what about Ree? You haven't stopped to think about Ree have you? This mentalist just tried to top himself and now you're saying "Oh let's invite the nutter to stay in the same house as our baby." Believe it or not, I'm not really that keen. If he wants to fucking kill himself he'll kill himself and I don't want him doing it in my house and I don't want his stinking breath around my daughter. For fuck's sake, he's used to living on the fucking streets and Chichester isn't exactly South Central LA, is it? What the fuck are we gonna do with him?'

Little Jimmy hadn't heard any of this. He had really wanted to hear the Dynamics track. He had only heard it once before, when Hemel Hector gave it its first outing at the 100 Club. While Lainie had been talking, Jimmy had been concentrating hard on the music. It was quiet compared to her, but with a hushed determination he could make it the dominant sound in his head.

Hippy John hadn't noticed the music. He had heard the conversation that had been raging across him, but he wasn't retaining much and it was as if they were talking about someone else.

Lainie was staring at Lee. Lee glanced at her, made a nod towards Hippy John and frowned.

Lainie sank back in her seat. 'Jesus Christ. Jesus fucking Christ.'

# 11

*Until the day break and the shadows flee away*

Romance wasn't the first to ponder on these words. Until the shadows of darkness, ignorance and unbelief disappear. It wasn't obvious why such a half-thought was an appropriate epitaph for Sam Cooke.

*I will get me to the mountain of myrrh and the hill of frankincense.*

What the bloody hell is a mountain of myrrh? A great big lump of aromatic gum resin. Or a great big lump of beautiful woman, as some Biblical scholars would have it. The church, others say. A place to commune with God. A communion of flesh or spirit. That there are such differing interpretations spills some unintended light on to Sam Cooke's flat, grass-enclosed gravestone, Romance mused.

In life, the man's heavenly voice carried itself from the church to the dancehalls and, on the day of his death, Sam went from the arms of his loving wife to the fragrant embrace of Elisa Boyer. He was a man governed by temptation and he had the voice of an angel.

Romance wanted to make a film. It would be a documentary. It would be called *Looking for Romance (with Steve Davis)*. It wouldn't be about looking for romance with Steve Davis. Romance certainly did not want to have a romantic involvement with Steve Davis. It would be about looking for Romance Watson, singer of *Where Does That Leave Me* (Coral Records, 1965). It had been one of Romance's favourite records ever since he had first heard it in the bedroom of his dead friend Demetrios Demetriou, and it was the reason he was called Romance. But Steve Davis would be with him on the journey – at least for some of it. Romance thought that Steve Davis, as a celebrity, would give the documentary popular appeal. He knew that television executives liked celebrities. He didn't know much about television, but he knew that much.

Romance hadn't picked Steve Davis at random. If he were to have picked a random celebrity, he would have hoped to pick someone else. He picked Steve Davis because Steve Davis liked soul music. He really liked it. He collected records and once even bought a record off Romance. That was at the Soulful Reflections soul weekender in Great Yarmouth. When that weekender started, one of the regular DJs was Bob from Crewe, and Bob edited a soul fanzine that was financed by Steve Davis. So Steve Davis was at the weekender and looked through Romance's sales box and, after some pretty tough haggling, bought a record for £12. Romance remembered the record. It was the Lost Souls *It Won't Work Out Baby* on Glasco. He couldn't remember if it was a red or a blue one. (The red one has some extra female vocal harmonies, which give it a slight edge over the blue, but they are both about the same price.)

Even before seeing Steve Davis at Great Yarmouth, Romance had been thinking about *Looking for Romance (with Steve Davis)*. And when he saw Steve Davis he knew that he should talk to him about it. He realised that Steve Davis might not be interested in finding Romance Watson, and he didn't think *Where Does That Leave Me* was really a Steve Davis kind of record. It was a bit early for his taste and possibly too lush/soft. But he thought Steve Davis might go along with the idea for the good of soul music. And anyway, the film would not only be about looking for Romance Watson. It would also be about Romance and Steve Davis looking for records along the way (particularly, in Romance's case, looking for the Romance Watson record) and that was something Steve Davis might well have been interested in doing.

But there was a subtext to the film that in Romance's mind made it something special. The subtext was Romance's search for love and romance. The quests both for soul records and for Romance Watson were metaphors for the quest for romance, and Romance could even sneak away from Steve during the trip to try to find romance. He could talk to American girls along the way. Surely they would like his accent and, even if they didn't, he reckoned most of them would do anything to be on telly. Maybe Steve Davis would be interested in finding romance too, and then they could look together.

Romance was unaware of Steve Davis's marital status. Even though he was a top celebrity, Steve Davis wasn't one to feature heavily in the gossip columns (and Romance wasn't one to read them anyway). But even if Steve Davis wasn't interested in finding romance, he might still be interested in finding records (if not Romance Watson). He would be given a free trip to America, paid for by a television company, and even though he was mega-rich Romance assumed that by the way Steve Davis haggled for the Lost Souls record a free trip would be a significant incentive for him. And anyway, soul music would be publicised in an original and enlightening way.

Romance already had the first shot of *Looking for Romance (with Steve Davis)* worked out. It would begin with a close-up of Romance's eyes. Then the camera would slowly spin and as it did so draw back to reveal Romance lying on his back on the floor, surrounded by records. Then the camera would keep going around and back and Romance would be lying in the middle of a room stuffed full of records – all over the floor and on shelves – floor to ceiling. There would be some clever, subtle commentary over this shot, which he hadn't written yet.

After that dramatic beginning, the film was less clear in

Romance's mind. There was one other shot he could visualise and that was a shot through the windscreen of a moving car, driving along a typical American highway. It would be a fixed shot with a wide angle, looking straight ahead as some of America passed by. The only sound would be the music track and that would be *Where Does That Leave Me* played in its entirety. This would be a seminal cinematic moment. Romance was already preparing himself for the argument with the television executives, who would consider such a shot as *arthouse* and unsuitable for primetime viewing, and he hadn't yet decided whether or not he would compromise if that was what it would take to have the film shown on Channel 4 (its natural home). He thought that he probably would, for the good of soul music. Perhaps the shot could cut away to something else half way through, but he couldn't think what.

Another year and another Soulful Reflections weekender and Romance saw Steve Davis again, and he felt sure enough about his idea to approach him with a view to getting him on board. But Steve Davis didn't fully appreciate the subtleties and depth of meaning. In fact, the conversation was a little awkward and didn't even stretch as far as the subtext. Steve Davis's idea was to approach *Holiday*. He then surprised Romance by offering him a signed photo. Romance would have to think more carefully about Steve Davis's involvement. Perhaps once a television executive was interested Steve Davis could be talked into being cooperative. After all, it would be for the good of the music. But then JBP came along.

Romance had the idea of *Looking for Romance (with Steve Davis)* before he met JBP (and long before the death of Demetrios Demetriou). And then he met her and he found romance. This complicated things. The documentary needed its subtext for it to achieve classic status. Perhaps he could make it anyway and then explain to her that it was poetic license. It was television and not real, and it was all for the good of the music. He wondered how she would take it. Then, when she started throwing bottles of wine at him, he thought that the relationship might be ending and that if it did end he could then make the film and it would be true art, without the need for any poetic licence. He thought of this as another bottle went by and was pleased that he was able to take the positive out of the situation. Of course, there might only be a narrow gap in his life before he found romance with someone else, so he would have to work fast to exploit this gap, for the good of art and for the good of the music, so as soon as he moved out he began working on his letter to the head of Channel 4.

# 12

Spaghetti Weston, too, had experienced the end of a romantic relationship, years before he met little Annie. And Soul Sam was not the first dog to be a part of his life (although Spaghetti had now come to think of him as the dog of his life). There was Rufus, the dog of his young childhood, and there was Tamla, the dog of his young adulthood. Tamla had come with Karen Carstairs, his first serious, live-in girlfriend. He had met them together and they had moved in together. They were a package and he took them both on. And from the beginning, he loved them both.

Karen Carstairs was married – she had been for years – but she had separated from her husband before she met Spaghetti and it didn't bother Spaghetti at all. But the husband loved Tamla too. In fact, Karen Carstairs and her husband had bought Tamla together, when she was a puppy. It was reasonable that he should maintain contact and Tamla went to stay with him for a couple of days every week. It was an amicable arrangement. Everyone involved made an effort to be cordial, for the sake of the dog, and Tamla loved them all and enjoyed her two homes. It was only when Spaghetti Weston and Karen Carstairs split up (records, allnighters, lack of attention relative to dog) that the situation became awkward.

Tamla went with Karen. That was fair enough. They had come together and they went together. But when Spaghetti asked if he could visit Tamla, Karen Carstairs refused. She didn't want anything more to do with him. He was a nice guy but had driven her mad, and she thought it best that they had no contact. And so the healthy, loving relationship between Spaghetti and Tamla was destroyed from without. This was made even more difficult for Spaghetti to bear by the knowledge that the relationship between Tamla and the husband was maintained. In all the time Spaghetti and Karen Carstairs were together, Tamla had spent by far the majority of her time with them. For years, Spaghetti had been more a part of Tamla's life than the husband had been. Spaghetti was like a father to that dog, even if a stepfather. There was something not right about the situation and Spaghetti didn't like it. He would never begrudge the original father his visiting rights, as these were right and proper, but should he not be granted such rights of his own? And even years later, when he was with Annie and then Soul Sam and Soul Sam had become the dog of his life, he would think of Tamla and be cross about the situation, not because he wasn't totally satisfied in his relationship with Soul Sam but because of the principle of the thing. So when he saw on the news men scaling the Palace of Westminster dressed as Batman and Robin, demanding the right to see their children, Spaghetti was inspired. He would form a new group to fight for the rights of ex-dog-stepfathers. (Or was it ex-stepdogfathers?) All he had to do was think of a snappy name for the group and an appropriate costume.

# 13

Dogs are barred from the cathedral in Chichester (other than guide dogs). If Spaghetti had known this, he wouldn't have been happy. He believed that Soul Sam had a soul and, if there was any nourishing of souls to be had, Soul Sam's soul didn't deserve to be left out.

Still, it's a lovely town. Officially, it's a city because it has a cathedral, but it didn't feel like a city to the man Lee was to call Hippy John or to anyone else from a big city. The cathedral is beautiful, and around it are the cathedral green and the old town, and around the old town are the old city walls. The shopping streets have their share of high street chains, but there are also local boutiques and craft shops and other smaller streets with family-run shops, old-fashioned pubs and a few old guesthouses. A small river, the Lavant, runs around the centre and through the walls and gives the place a pretty, postcard appeal. It isn't Wigan, or Warrington. And it isn't Detroit or Chicago (the original Chi-town). But twice a year, in the basement of a pub just off the main high street, is the soul bash, and people come from all along the south coast and some down from London. It's a good do and has a good reputation, but all but a handful of Chichester's residents are oblivious of it.

Round the corner from the pub where the soul happens is a lane, and next to the lane there is a patch of grass that is squeezed by the old city walls. It is here that the man Lee was to call Hippy John slept. This little area of lane, grass and wall was his home.

Of course, it hadn't always been his home. Hippy John was a Brummie, like Spaghetti Weston. But, unlike Spaghetti, Hippy John had been brought up in a nice house in a nice neighbourhood, and he'd had posh friends (a few), having been sent to a posh school, and he'd never had any trace of a Brummie accent. And his father was a doctor who worked in Sandwell General Hospital and who would spend his working time seeing to injured Brummies – Bunky, for instance, when he had his emotionally charged dancing accident at These Old Shoes – and who would then return to his nice house in his nice neighbourhood and beat his nice wife and beat the young, beardless Hippy John too. He wasn't even one of those doctors who drink too much. He was just a bastard.

Hippy John was scared of his father, and he never grew out of being scared. When he was a child it was a simple, straightforward kind of fear – a fear of being hit, a fear of being hurt, a fear of seeing his mother being hit and hurt – and then when he grew and became too big to be hit, instead of going away, the fear just became more complicated. It was a fear of the past and a fear of the future. A part of this fear was for himself – he was afraid of never having had a loving father and he was afraid of never having one – but most of it was for his mother because his mother was a lovely woman, and when Hippy John was older he looked upon his mother not just as a woman being bullied but as a woman whose past was being bullied and whose future was to be bullied. But she wouldn't leave his father and Hippy John thought that one of the reasons she wouldn't leave him was that she didn't want Hippy John to come from a broken home, because she loved Hippy John. And even when he had grown up and left home, she still wanted to give him the security of a family (she hadn't given him any brothers or sisters) and she didn't want to do anything that would draw attention to his less-than-ideal upbringing. She couldn't see how that would be good for him. Hippy John was her life (her own life having long since been knocked out of her).

There was nothing Hippy John could do for his mother, and then there was the altercation with his father and he had to get away and he really didn't much care to where. It seemed more usual to head south than to head north and he went as south as he could, and directly south was Southampton. He had enough money to rent a room, and he set about looking for a job, and he found one fairly readily as a casual labourer working on the building of the new bridge across the Itchen. The bridge was to link Southampton city centre with Warsash and was easily the largest and most important civil engineering project in the area. It was to be one of those bridges that rises and descends from a central point so that boats of a certain height can still pass underneath. Hippy John was proud to be involved, even though his job was menial, and he knew that it was good to keep himself occupied, and putting himself under such physical strain seemed to ease the tension in his head. He didn't have much to say to the other workers and they didn't have much to say to him, but pushing a wheelbarrow of sand across the site of the Southampton bridge-end meant that he could live one step at a time, and he might think of his mother and of his father and sometimes even cry at what he remembered, but the sand forced him on; the rhythm of his work carried him forward. On his days off he was tired and this was good too because it meant he could sleep.

Hippy John had loved his mother but had always been shy with women. Unlike Romance and Spaghetti, he had no romantic relationships to reflect upon. He had never longed for such a relationship but the lack of one accentuated his feelings of inadequacy. And he became aware that he was existing rather than living, but the despair wasn't to the same extent as the despair that plunged upon him when he heard his mother had died. And he didn't hear until after the funeral. He had abandoned her and hadn't been there for her and then she was gone. And then, when he was sacked, he felt the full suffocating weight of his mother's death; it pressed on him hard, not only because she died and he hadn't been there but also because in dying suddenly her life could be evaluated, and as best he could tell the net result of her selfless and sacrificial life was a pathetic, unemployable, talentless, friendless, assetless, womanless, familyless waste of space.

Then, just as his money was running out, a relentlessly friendly neighbour in the flats where he lived called Mr Quinton – who dressed as a cowboy and went line dancing – told him that he (Mr Quinton) knew a fellow line dancer who lived in Chichester who was looking for someone to help him in his gardening business. Hippy John had never dressed as a cowboy or anything else but did quite fancy the idea of being a gardener, so off he went. He worked for a week, staying in a B&B, didn't get paid and wasn't asked back. This wasn't because he was a bit slow and feeble (which was why he was sacked as a builder and which he was now even more so due to his worsened mental condition) but because he wouldn't or couldn't listen to instructions properly and was just in too much of a state to chop, prune and cut the right things. He did too much damage in too short a time. He hadn't been able to see the bridge grow and he hadn't been able to see a garden grow. In all of his forty-odd years the only thing he had ever seen grow was his mother who grew old, too soon, and died, too soon. And when he spent his first night on the grass by the walls, he first thought it a good thing that his mother wasn't alive to witness what had become of him, but then he thought that maybe being dead meant that she was able to witness it as she wouldn't have been able to if she had been alive and in Birmingham. Still, it was just a night, he told himself. But by the time Lainie walked across the green from the car park on the other side of the walls, with Lee following and carrying his record boxes, it was years later and the green was no longer just a place for Hippy John to spend the night in an emergency; it was where Hippy John spent every night that there wasn't a place for him in the hostel and, even when there was, it was where he came to drink.

'Get a fucking job,' Lainie said casually, not slowing, as Hippy John was settling himself down to another can. Lee didn't look. The boxes were heavy. He didn't want to think about anything other than getting to the club as directly and efficiently as possible.

# 14

As usual, Romance was at Chi-soul in Chichester to hear Lee DJ, and he was at the Pigeon Club in Southampton too the night that Lee DJed there. That was when Romance met Johnson's Babe Power. Lee was Wigsy's guest DJ. It was in the days when Lee played northern. (Lainie was there supporting him, but not approving.) And it was in the days when Romance wasn't so forward with women. (Romance suddenly started approaching women after his break up with Johnson's Babe Power. Then he talked to them as if he had nothing to lose, because he didn't – he'd lost it.)

Romance did talk to JBP when he met her, but he was on home territory in the Pigeon Club and it almost would have been rude not to talk to her. And Romance wasn't one to be rude. She was a new face when she strode in and her pink *Johnson's Babe Power* T-shirt was a new T-shirt in the club too. The pigeon fanciers didn't notice her particularly as to them she was one of the strange soul people with their weird, musical hobby, but the soul people couldn't take her for a pigeon fancier.

Wigsy knew her. It was his do and he knew everyone, even the pigeon folk. It had just been a long time since she had been out, and Romance hadn't been in town that long. And she knew Wigsy and she knew his records – they hadn't changed.

Lee put on Darrell Banks *Somebody (Somewhere) Needs You*. Lainie cringed. Nutty Casper leapt forward, arms aloft.

'I haven't seen you here before,' Romance ventured.

Years later Romance would use the same line with an ironic smirk, but in the Pigeon Club that night it really was the best he could manage. But it was true – he hadn't seen her there before – and he was interested.

'That's because I'm just visiting from another planet,' the strange woman replied.

Romance doubted this and decided to press her.

'What planet's that then?'

'The planet Babelicious. You wouldn't know it – it's a long way away. I came by inter-stellar pigeon.'

Already, Romance was madly in love, and he began looking at the woman curiously.

The woman he was going to spend the rest of his life with had a blond bob. The woman he was going to spend the rest of his life with wasn't too young but wasn't too old. The woman he was going to spend the rest of his life with had small but not too small breasts, a pretty nose, and beautiful, not-too-perfect teeth. She had sparkling eyes and a cheeky, confident, feminine voice. All these things were of great interest to Romance. It isn't every day one meets the woman one's going to spend the rest of one's life with.

'And do you have a name?'

'Yeah, this is my name,' she replied, pulling her T-shirt down tight over her breasts. 'On Babelicious we always wear T-shirts with our names on. It cuts down on unnecessary small talk.'

Lee played his classic songs, Nutty Casper did a spin and fell over (perhaps unbalanced by his mismatching footwear) and the pigeon fanciers drank their cheap beer and talked of pigeons. JBP left to go on somewhere else, but before she did she handed Romance a phone number. Romance was surprised. He was even more surprised when he phoned it the next morning and got through to the Thai massage parlour on Shirley High Street.

'Johnson Babe Power no. Many nice girl for you.'

'No. I want Johnson Babe Power.'

'You want babe. We have babe. Many nice babe. Johnson I don't know. Who she? Thai girl?'

'No. She from planet Babelicious,' Romance tried, in desperation.

'She from which planet?'

'Babe-lic-ious.'

'I no know that planet. Solly. Fucky fucky?'

Romance was wary of Thai massage parlours. In fact, he was wary of all massage parlours, streetwalkers, escorts and women of the night. This wasn't for any high-minded moral reason. He was simply scared. He considered Sam Cooke's

*A Change Is Gonna Come* to be one of the greatest records ever and he knew that this angelic, gospel imbued voice was undone by physical temptation. By loveless lust. By the prostitute, Elisa Boyer, who stole his clothes with all his money in them and ran from the motel room, prompting Sam to run after her and to the manager's office where he thought she was hiding and pound on the door and force his way in. Two of the shots missed but the third went straight to his chest. He was killed by a punctured lung and heart.

(Nobody could say for sure, but it was generally believed – it was the vet's considered and professional opinion, on sensing that 'He's dead' would not suffice - that Soul Sam had a stroke.)

Romance received a phone call. It was JBP. It hadn't been difficult for her to find his number. Wigsy probably had it and if he didn't he would know someone who did.

She went over to his bedsit and found a path through his records to the window and didn't mention them, which made him love her even more. She looked out over the industrious river and soon Romance was rowing her upstream in *Soul Survivor* and he felt that he was taking them both somewhere wonderful from where they wouldn't return. The river was theirs, *Soul Survivor* was theirs and life was theirs, and that night they held each other and wondered how things were before they met.

They spent the summer walking by the river and going to the coast, and when she left him Romance was sick as a hippy and couldn't eat properly for a week.

'There's no such thing as love,' she said, to his bewilderment, as he sat there, loving her. But it was because she had never had it and was scared of it and had no memory before the age of eight.

JBP was sectioned because she told her doctor that she felt like stabbing her clients in the neck with her scissors. She cut hair, but she felt like cutting throats. She came out of the hospital and Romance tried to look after her, and when she cried he would put her to bed.

JBP wondered how anything could be because of her childhood because she didn't even remember it. She remembered, later, what her father made her mother do for money and then what her father did to her, and Romance wondered how such a childhood could result in someone so lovely, lovable and loving. From something horrible comes something beautiful. From social deprivation comes sweet, sweet music.

# 15

*Somebody (Somewhere) Needs You* was Darrell Banks' second and last release on the Revilot label from Detroit. His first, *Open the Door to Your Heart,* which he co-wrote, was the first single issued on the label and – astonishingly for a decent soul record – it crept into the top thirty as well as reaching number two in the R&B charts. Over twenty more 45s were released on Revilot but strangely only the one other with Darrell. This fared less well, but it rarely failed to have an outing at the Pigeon Club in Southampton in the 1990s. Wigsy could play it knowing that Nutty Casper wouldn't be able to resist. (Guaranteed dancefloor action of some kind.)

In 1967, a deal with a new record label, Atco, led to new material for Darrell and an album was issued, *Darrell Banks Is Here*. A couple of singles were released but they failed to chart, and Darrell was then drawn to Memphis to work with the hugely talented producer, Don Davis. The result was the wonderful *Here to Stay* album and a couple of superb singles, *I'm the One Who Loves You* – which eventually became massive on the northern scene – and the ever so soulful *Beautiful Feeling*. The music was exquisite – and it bombed. But *Beautiful Feeling* was in Romance's playbox. He had the idea to play it early on at the memorial do. He knew that Demetrios Demetriou had shared his love of the record. It was too slow to dance to, but Romance reckoned he could get away with playing it as people were drifting in.

'Yeah, I'm all right mate, no problem, looking forward to it. Still got fucking Hippy John hanging about so he might come along if that's all right.'

'Yeah of course. No problem. You can bring who you want.'

Romance was happy he had phoned. He was relieved to hear that Lee was still on board. If neither Lee nor Spaghetti had shown, he would have been in trouble. It would have looked as if he had lied about the DJs.

'Lainie and Jimmy are gonna come along, and then maybe smelly hippyman, and I think the Brighton lot are coming up. I've been digging out some stuff – some classic seventies things, a bit of Philly – and it's all right to slip in a few newer things init?'

'Lee, do you what you want. But it's gonna be a soul crowd. It's in London. And it's all Demetrios Demetriou's soul mates. So it's gonna be mainly a northern crowd. So just nothing too alienating.'

'Yeah yeah, what you mean is nothing too banging,

you fucking retrograde northern gobshite. Well you're not getting any fucking northern shite. Demetrios Demetriou might have been into all that but I can tell you something for sure and that is that he'll want me to do my thing even if he hates it and makes him thankful he's not there. So if anyone fucking requests *Open the Door to Your Heart* from me they can fuck right off back to fucking baggy trouser land the sad fucks. Jesus.'

Lee cared. Romance didn't like much of the more modern stuff that he played. But Lee cared and that's why Romance had asked him and he was pleased he had.

'Bye Lee. Keep the faith.'

# 16

*If someone you'd give your life for*
*Walks out on you*
*And you feel you have no one*
*No one else to turn to*
*Open up your heart*
*Stretch out your arms*
*Remember somebody else somewhere*
*Somebody, somewhere*
*Remember somebody else somewhere*
*Needs you*
*Right now*
*They need you*
*Right now.* [3]

When Romance first heard those words, he had never had anyone walk out on him. And he had never met anyone he would give his life for. But the song affected him then no less and no more than years later when his heart was broken. The soul of the record was beyond personal experience.

Romance had always considered himself a creative type and, like the Borelli brothers, he viewed soul music as the ultimate form of human creativity. It was the peak of creativity: the pinnacle of human development. There had never been anything like it and there never would be again. He couldn't imagine his life without it, and he wondered at those who had not yet accepted it and at the vast bulk of humanity who existed Before Soul. In this way, he felt about soul music the way Christians feel about Christ. Soul music was the end of art as Christ was the explosive, divine end to a long line of prophets. But it was subtler than a religion. It was a clever, subtle art form, which required a mastery of technique and yet simultaneously was pure emotion. Its beauty didn't lie in its notation but in its performance. It lay in the deviation of the exact. It lay in expression. The music held within it the key to life: knowing when and how to break the rules without producing anarchy. The meaning was not in what the music indicated but in the manner of the indicating. It required both open-mindedness and discernment and incorporated something of the joy of being alive. It gave a community with others and elicited a wonder at the capabilities of others. It was something of religion and science combined and therefore, to Romance, seemed to point to the answer to everything. But it was a pointing that couldn't be articulated. 'Not too indefinite to put into words – too definite,' his friend Solomon (who was in the habit of quoting other people) had once said. If it were explainable, it would be something less. Perhaps the soul understood it but couldn't translate it. If it didn't count as the answer, it was at least proof of the total inadequacies of any other answers, whether religious or scientific. The universe has soul. There is a soulful dimension and we can only feel it. We're not clever enough to do anything else but feel it and we're stupid to pretend otherwise. Perhaps, when we die, we lose our restrictive individuality and revert to being part of the soulful universe and in doing so we suddenly know and understand everything. Romance wasn't sure if he actually believed that, but he was sure he believed it more than he believed anything else. And when it came to matters of faith, he strongly believed that it was wrong to believe anything too strongly. The only thing he believed in totally was soul because that had nothing to do with faith – or reason. That, he felt. When Bettye Lavette sang *Let Me Down Easy*, he felt it. The pain resonated through his body. The beautiful pain. So he believed in it totally. He was a soul fundamentalist. For the first time in human history, an art form encapsulated the beautiful pain of existence and gave a clue to the meaning of it all by humbling all before it. Romance was aware that others could argue that other art forms had as much to offer and along similar lines. He had heard people rave about sculpture or paintings and harp on about the beauty of them and the subtleties and the inner truths. But they were all wrong. They had to be. Compared to good soul music, it was all rubbish. Nothing could compare. Soul music was on a different level. Nothing could compare to music and no musical instrument could match the emotive power of the human voice, and it was through soul that the human voice was at its most emotive. Soul music alone was some of the beyond – the other, the more – given to us; it wasn't a sign or a window or a portal but the thing itself. Other art forms equated with other kinds of music and were of the perceived world. There was music and then there was soul music.

*Remember somebody else somewhere*
*Somebody, somewhere*
*Remember somebody else somewhere*
*Needs you*
*Right now*
*They need you*
*Right now.*

Romance knew the song hadn't made Darrell Banks rich, and he knew that riches rarely came the way of the true soul artist. And years later Romance was to discover that Darrell had died in poverty and obscurity and was buried in an unmarked grave in Detroit. Demetrios Demetriou, who hadn't been wealthy and was not a great artist, still ended up with a granite headstone and a grave solid enough to foil the maddest of graverobbers. Even Soul Sam (the dog) was in line for a memorial of some kind. Clearly, being a conveyor of something of the beyond didn't lead to financial reward; any money that was made tended to go into the pockets of the record company executives. And if Darrell and the rest could sing for the sake of soul alone, then Romance thought the least he could do was make his art for the sake of art. Only soul was capable of capturing that otherness, and so his art had to be about soul. (In fact, without soul, he would have had no inspiration, so he wouldn't have been looking to do art in the first place. It probably wouldn't even have occurred to him.)

# 17

When Romance was a teenager, he had an LP by the wonderful sixties Hammond organist, Jimmy McGriff, called *Looking for Mr Jimmy*. (At that time, he hadn't appreciated the depths of soul music and listened to other types of sixties black music too.) This LP moved him. The music was tight but mad. It was seriously brilliant but laughed at itself.

He decided to make a film called *Looking for Mr Jimmy*. (He already considered himself a creative type.) It would be about a man searching for meaning, as represented by *Mr Jimmy* and the music of Jimmy McGriff. Romance might not have known much about soul then, but he had lived just enough to realise that the combination of artistry and cheekiness was the sign of something great. He would film someone knocking on doors and asking for Mr Jimmy. Whoever answered would look confused and say that there was no Mr Jimmy there. These little interactions would be cut together quickly and interrupted by shots of the main character walking the streets, looking. Eventually he would knock on a door and the person answering would say 'Yes, he's here,' and lead him inside. The man looking would follow this person into the living room and there would be a sofa with two men already sitting on it, one at each end. Our main man would sit down in the middle. All three would sit in silence, looking ahead, while the man who answered the door would put on a record. It would be *All About My Girl* by Jimmy McGriff. The three men would wait, stony-faced, listening. One shot, from straight ahead. A slight movement of the head. A little fidget. Towards the end the music stops, and the three look at each other then begin to stand up. But it's a false ending and the organ kicks in again, so they sit back down and resume their listening. When it stops again they're not sure what to do, and that's the end of the film.

Andy Warhol with added mod. Romance thought this would be brilliant. In fact, it would probably win the Turner Prize. Really he wanted to play the lead role himself, but he couldn't do that and be behind the camera. This was just one of the many reasons the film was never made.

A few years later, Romance was intrigued to see in the South East London and Kentish Mercury an article about northern soul artist, Thelonius Tripp. By this time, Romance had lived the length (and breadth) required to realise that just as the anguish of love is the only subject worthy of soul music, so soul music itself must be the only subject worthy of honouring by any other art form. And in the honouring is a tacit admission of the inferiority of the art of the person honouring. Romance phoned the South East London and Kentish Mercury and a kind woman gave him a phone number for Thelonius Tripp. Romance imagined that he and Thelonius could be kindred souls – tortured soul poets together. Romance thought he might even make a film about his relationship with his fellow soul devotee: the painter and the film-maker in subjugation and reverence to the art that was beyond art. (This was a long time before his much better idea for a film, *Looking for Romance with Steve Davis*.) And before he had even met Thelonius Tripp, Romance had already decided that, like Darrell Banks before him, he would not compromise his art for the sake of the commercial market. He had to be true to the music.

# 18

*Stretch out your arms*
*Let the lovelight shine on my soul*
*And let love come running in.*
*Open the door to your heart*
*And let love come running in.* [4]

When Romance met Thelonius Tripp it was in Thelonius Tripp's studio in New Cross. Thelonius Tripp showed him his paintings. They were of northern soul dancers dancing. All of them. Rack upon rack, absorbing most of the confined space. They were dark and tortured. This was good, because it meant that Romance could talk to Thelonius Tripp about the tortured nature of soul music and how it was the most profound and greatest art form ever. But it was bad because it meant that Thelonius Tripp never sold any paintings. The northern soul art market is limited. Spare income is spent on records. Even Romance viewed spending money on anything else as frivolous, and he considered himself a creative type. He was happy talking to Thelonius Tripp about the tortured nature of soul music, and he wanted them to be tortured poets together, but he wasn't going to buy any of the paintings – not even one of the small prints. But Thelonius Tripp didn't mind. He wasn't even thinking of whether or not Romance would buy anything, because he was happy talking about the tortured nature of soul music too. He was quite good at art – better than he was at anything else – and he wanted to express his love of soul music through his painting. He wasn't doing it for the money (which was lucky).

'I painted this one at the allnighter in Blackburn.'

It was a view looking down at the dancefloor from the circle of the ballroom. Dancers were spread evenly across the floor in anguished, fixed poses. The painting was dark. Light from one spotlight illuminated the DJ, who was facing the dancefloor and high at the centre of the painting. He was cueing up the next record. He was a priest and the dancers were dancing as an act of worship. They didn't look as if they were enjoying themselves; they were demonstrating their appreciation of the message, as delivered by the DJ.

'It's like a cathedral,' Romance ventured.

Thelonius Tripp was excited to hear it.

'Yeah, a cathedral!'

'A celebration of soul.'

'Yeah, it is!'

Despite believing that soul music was beyond religion, Romance was deeply interested in the religiousness of the music. Soul had come from the church and the passion with which its adherents held the music was akin to a religious passion. They were a people apart: the chosen few. It stirred the soul as only religion can, but there was no soul god and no set of moral codes. The soul folk tended to share a sympathy for the disadvantaged – soul principally being a music of poor, black youth – but the music was about love: at once the most human of emotions and the most divine. It didn't provide an answer; it expressed a predicament. Humankind trapped between the earthly, animal kingdom and something else – something spiritual and intangible. Souls lost in limbo. Thelonius Tripp felt that loss too, even if he had failed to articulate it to himself, and it was something bordering on that loss that he tried to capture in the faces of his subjects. Whatever it was, it wasn't a sad loss, because the dancers were appreciative of knowing they were lost. It's better than thinking you know where you are when you don't. That's when you're bound to take a wrong turning. Better to know you're lost. Better to be a tortured, lost human than a deluded one or a happy animal.

'I remember saying to my mother when I was little that I wished I was a dog,' Romance said to Thelonius Tripp. 'Dogs have such an easy life. They don't have to go to school – they just laze about all day and get fed and have fun. Or a lion, maybe. She tried to explain that humans have an appreciativeness of things that sets us apart and is worth having above happiness or having an easy time. Obviously she was right, but I didn't really get it at the time. But I do see it a bit in your paintings.'

'Yeah, that's it!'

And, the paintings being paintings, time was fixed in them too. They were static representations of dancing. And in the physical but unconscious worlds of Thelonius and Romance, dancing was as close as they could come to an exploration of motion for the sake of motion and so had something of the meaning of life about it. The hopelessness of Thelonius Tripp's motionless artistic endeavour was just one of the reasons the paintings were so ugly.

The beautiful and the ugly. Unearthly beauty by way of earthly ugliness. Ten years after Romance met Thelonius Tripp, Goldmine/Soul Supply issued the first ever Darrell Banks compilation LP: *Darrell Banks, 'The Lost Soul'*. Thirty-two years before this, on a cold Tuesday morning in February 1970, Darrell Banks drove to the home of a barmaid, Marjorie Bozeman, in the west side of Detroit. He waited outside in his car. At about eleven o'clock another car pulled up and a couple stepped out. It was Marjorie and the man who was dropping her off, Aaron Bullock. According to Marjorie, Darrell then jumped from his car, stormed up to them, grabbed her and tried to pull her away, saying they had to talk. Aaron intervened and identified himself as an off-duty policeman, at which point Darrell pulled a gun and pointed it at Aaron. Aaron ducked, drew his own gun and fired at Darrell, hitting him in the neck. Darrell was taken to New Grace Hospital where he was pronounced dead. Marjorie told the investigating officers that she had been friends with Darrell but had been trying to end the relationship. Darrell was buried in the Detroit Memorial Park Cemetery in the unmarked grave.

# 19

*Remember somebody else somewhere*
*Somebody, somewhere*
*Remember somebody else somewhere*

*Needs you… Right now… Needs you… Right now…*

The soul of it pulled Romance along and it didn't take long for them to pass shadow-like under the railway bridge and soon JBP could see the balcony of the Pigeon Club. She had never been in a rowing boat before, but more importantly she had never been in love and she was more concerned about that than any boaty mishap.

Romance had no such concern. The water slipped by and, with the invisible and unknown depths of the river below and the visible world above, Romance delighted in their condition and his mind floated in the delicate balancing of it. It was a musical experience, being awash in some loving dimension that was of this world and not of it, caught between the inner and the outer, and the electrical messages zipping about his brain – without which he knew he would feel nothing – no more explained the love he felt than the constituent wavelengths of sound explained the beauty of music. The rhythm of his rowing was the force of his love, and time was captured, massaged and squashed to everything and nothing, as it was whenever he heard a decent record. An urging onwards. Each beat, each note, each anguished phrase a force, a pointer – each possessing a will to pass beyond itself. Music was the melody not only of his life but also of life itself, and it flowed like a river. It was pure motion – motion without the movement of objects – and its meaning was in the movement, and so in music Romance heard the flow of life. He rowed and he kept rowing, and it didn't matter a hemidemisemiquaver to where and, when he looked into the face of the woman facing him, he saw that the force that gives meaning to a musical moment is the same as the life force of a human face. It's rooted in the physical but transcends the physical. Needs you. Right now. Needs you. Right now. The little pauses between the strokes were filled with meaning as the moments of quietness in music remain filled with the dynamism of melody. There is music in thy wave, calmest, purest river. And just as nothing can be filled with meaning, so their *right now* would always be right now because it was beyond the now of the physical world and, feeling this, Romance smiled a timeless smile and gratefully glanced up at the Pigeon Club which was gliding by and then looked back to his pigeon girl who was sitting majestically like an eastern princess.

'Where shall we live?' asked Romance.

'Anywhere but your pokey little room,' she replied, and it was the perfect answer.

# 20

But it was in Thelonius Tripp's pokey little studio that Romance's first idea for a proper soul film began to develop. He admired Thelonius Tripp for using what talent he had for the benefit of soul. Now he should do the same. Meeting this fellow creative-type had inspired him. Somehow he wanted to capture the essence of soul on film, and then other people could watch it and begin their own soul journey. If other people could sense the passion he and Thelonius Tripp felt for the music, then surely they would be intrigued enough to investigate further. It wasn't enough – perhaps it wasn't even a good idea – to hear the music, because Romance already knew that most people, for reasons that were beyond him, were not moved by the music. They had to see the passion to be drawn in.

Thelonius Tripp had a record player in his studio. He would play records for soulful inspiration. He didn't have a great record collection because, being a northern soul artist, he never had much money to spend on records, but what he had was good. He picked out The Precisions *If This*

*Is Love*. Romance smiled in recognition. Classic northern soul. Thelonius put it on the deck, pressed play and placed the needle. The record crackled a bit. Then the punchy introduction resonated through the two young men and they felt it in each other like two witnesses to a miracle.

*If this is love*
*Then I'd rather be lonely.*
*If this is love*
*Then I'd rather be free!* [5]

The Detroit soul beat drove the record forward and forced a path through the anguish. Looking at Thelonius, Romance saw a fellow soul traveller and the idea for his new film sprang upon him. It was brilliant in its simplicity. It would be, simply, to capture that moment. One shot: the two of them listening to that one record. The viewer would have to witness the profound effect the music had on them and for that – and here's the brilliance – the music would be taken away. It would start and then be taken away. At first, Romance thought the viewer could watch in silence. But on further, deeper thinking, he realised that might be too much to expect from the modern viewer, and he also realised he could be missing an opportunity. He could introduce some other element to the soundtrack to reinforce his message. Something universally recognised as beautiful.

Romance wasn't a great fan of classical music. Most of it was a load of tosh. What was it about? But he had heard some tracks that even he could recognise as really pretty good and one of these was Beethoven's *Moonlight Sonata*. It wasn't an orchestral piece, where the soul is lost through a plethora of session musicians playing what they're told to play (he thought of the accompanying band at Cleethorpes), but one musician at least attempting to bare his or her soul (within the confines of the instrument and the prescribed notes). There was no singing in it, and usually Romance was disdainful of instrumentals, but that made it the perfect soundtrack. It would be recognisable to a western audience and it would say, 'Look, you think this is beautiful, but look, whatever these guys are listening to is at least as beautiful.' There was nothing not to like about it, and it would draw in the audience and not alienate them (as soul would) and that was the idea. It might be lost on a Chinese audience, but you can't have everything.

## 21

Walk right on in. Stretch out your arms. Let the lovelight shine. Open the door to your heart.

Demetrios Demetriou was beautiful in a bedraggled, hairy way. When he was alive Romance loved him because there was nothing not to love, and so when he was dead Romance loved him too. His funeral was a sombre, giggling west London affair.

The hairy Greek came from an Orthodox, church-going family and was destined to have an Orthodox funeral, as long as he died before the last of the older generation. This gave him considerable incentive to live and might well have prolonged his life. But in the end the cancer, and then religion, got him.

Romance arrived at the church pleased with himself. By coincidence, he had bought a new suit not long before (he had been anticipating an important meeting at Channel 4) and it fitted well and afforded him some funereal gravitas. He wouldn't have bought a suit especially – he would have thought that silly and any surviving spirit of his good friend

Demetrios Demetriou would have thought that silly too – and so he would have had to make do with trousers, shirt and raincoat.

Outside the church there were two groups of people. Standing near the door were the Greeks – family and friends of the family. Romance walked past them. They had the funeral attire off to a Greek T. (Evidently, they were well practised. Perhaps the sneaks had had some instruction.) The women were all in black, the older women with shawls, and the men wore unfashionable but purposeful broad-lapelled black suits with white shirts, black ties and polished shoes. And then there were the soul folk, about equal in number, spread along the pavement beyond. They shuffled about in trepidation and had a distinctly unpractised look of casual clothing feebly masquerading as something formal: ill-matching dark shades, plain but coloured shirts, dark but patterned ties.

Normally, Silky from Enfield was the smartest of the lot. He was one of the few who regularly attended soul dos in a suit (curious young mods aside). His clothes were never ostentatious, but they were precise. Now he was in the funeral ensemble wearing an old pair of jeans and a T-shirt.

'Yeah, it's for Demetrios,' he explained. 'When did you ever, ever see him in anything other than jeans and a T-shirt? I reckon it's what he would have wanted. He hated all this formality.'

'He could well be right,' Romance considered. But little of this affair was about what Demetrios would have wanted.

Actually, Demetrios probably wouldn't have wanted any of it. He was embarrassed by the conservatism of his family and the Greek Cypriot community. He was a Londoner and a soul boy. And his ego was so lacking that he would have been embarrassed at even the soul folk gathering to remember him. For Romance that was part of the point and he had to disguise a smile. Mates were supposed to embarrass each other. He felt good in his suit. Demetrios was his mate – perhaps his best one.

Demetrios Demetriou arrived and everyone outside the church and along the pavement turned to face him. No one could see him because he was dead and lying inside a coffin inside a hearse, but they all knew he was there. The funeral men chatted to the family and then chatted some more, and then they carried in Demetrios. The Greeks followed, knowingly. The soul folk followed the Greeks and as they went in they were each handed a lit candle and holding these they filed into position in the pews. All remained standing, with candles burning, and the church filled with the noise of a chanting priest who was standing at the front, facing the candle-holders. Because of the nature of the filing in, the Greeks filled the front half of the church and the soul folk, the back. Romance, Silky and all the others were waiting for the chanting to stop so they could sit down.

The priest stood centre stage, aglow in his Orthodox garb, with a little Orthodox beard and wide Orthodox eyes. He looked slightly stoned, but maybe that was a consequence of spending so much time standing, looking into nowhere, chanting. Perhaps it was the look of blind faith. Or soul-gnawing doubt.

None of these soul people ever went to church. Romance had been taken as a child but stopped going when he was old enough to say no. But they shared a sense of spirituality as they shared a passion that they couldn't explain and that transcended the material world. And it stemmed from the gospel churches too. And of course they all had a biblical mountain of respect for Demetrios Demetriou, otherwise they wouldn't have been there. And so they stood respectfully. Or at least they tried. For as long as they could.

The problem was that the glowing man-doll doing the chanting wouldn't stop. He just went on and on. And everyone had to just stand there, still, waiting, holding their candles. Greeks in front, soul folk behind.

In the front soul row, Romance was standing next to Solomon and Tony Davis Two. Romance and Solomon had been observing the priest and had whispered to each other that it was remarkable how little he moved his lips. They had seen ventriloquists on telly who weren't as proficient as this priest.

Then Tony Davis Two turned to whisper to Romance.

'I got an Occasions yesterday. *There's No You* on Big Jim – the one with the American football design on the label.'

Romance tried to look uninterested, but Tony Davis Two was undeterred.

'He was an American football player, Big Jim, that's why. It's their only record. But apparently they did backing for some of the Way Out artists. If it was rare it would be huge. 1967 from Cleveland.'

If ever there was an occasion not for The Occasions. Romance marvelled at Tony Davis Two's one-track mind. At least he didn't have his little sales box with him. In fact, Romance was fairly sure this was the first time he had ever seen Tony Davis Two without his little sales box. Romance couldn't think of anything to say that wouldn't encourage him to carry on, so he said nothing and looked back to the priest.

Beyond the world of soul, Romance was rarely sure about anything, and he couldn't be sure that ventriloquism wasn't a part of the Greek Orthodox tradition. However, he was sensible enough to know that it was really very unlikely. He was not a part of the Greek Orthodox tradition himself, and he knew that there might well have been beauty and subtleties in the chanting and in the service that were lost on him, but clerical ventriloquism... why should that be? There seemed no logical reason for it. But he supposed there might have been some reason unknown to him that wasn't in evidence during this particular service. Priests and holy men across the globe engaged in all manner of peculiar activities. Perhaps he would see it on the Discovery Channel that evening. Admittedly very unlikely, but he couldn't be sure.

Churches made him think like that. In fact he thought like that for much of the time, but churches conferred a more serious tone upon his thinking. Suddenly he felt guilty about equating the likelihood of the existence of God with the likelihood that somewhere in west London existed a secret school that trained Greek Orthodox priests in ventriloquism. He didn't think there was. He knew that his very existence and the fact that he was thinking such silly thoughts – and the very existence of West Acton, the universe and everything – could be taken as evidence of some sort of divine goings on, if one chose to look at it that way. The whole priestly ventriloquism matter could be investigated and was more provable, one way or the other, but there wasn't any point if that wouldn't help with the whole God matter, which it wouldn't.

A sizable chunk of chanting time went by before Solomon pointed out the little man standing to the side, on the right, at the front, lips most clearly moving and in perfect sync. with the chanting too. The priest wasn't a ventriloquist after all. That particular music hall talent wasn't a part of the Orthodox priesthood. At least, there was no evidence for it in that service.

The soul folk were all presuming that when the chanting stopped not only would they be able to sit down but also the service proper would begin, and the priest, freed from his ventriloquism supposition, now looked as if he was waiting too, but it was impossible to guess for what.

There were many older people in the Greek contingent and many of them were little women. Intermittently, one of them would suddenly drop to her seat. Apparently, it was acceptable to give in to the chant if one couldn't stand anymore. As the chanting went on, and on, the little Greek women, and now men, proceeded to drop, one by one.

Solomon and Romance could sense each other's feeling of the absurd. Another old woman succumbed in front of them.

'Perhaps he's not going to stop until the last person's dropped,' Solomon whispered.

That was it. That was the straw that broke the camel's back. Those were the words that broke Romance's front. He got the giggles. Badly. He couldn't control them. He was desperate to remain inaudible. He bowed his head. He bit his lip. He turned to see if anyone was looking at him and behind him French Freddie was looking straight at him, the most appropriate kind of tears streaming down her face. He hoped, vainly, that his own tears would be mistaken for her kind. He turned to the front again. Strange noises kept leaping from him. An old Greek woman heard and turned and saw him and threw him the filthiest of looks. He sat down. He wasn't old enough to sit down, but he sat down and put his head to his knees. Perhaps he could be praying. Perhaps his uncontrollable shaking could be due to his uncontrollable grief. Bastard Solomon.

Romance consoled himself with the knowledge that if the spirit of Demetrios Demetriou existed and was somehow witnessing the occasion, he/it would be laughing too, delighting in Romance's predicament. In fact, Romance thought, perhaps the Demetrios spirit had orchestrated the whole episode to embarrass him. He/it could have been working through Solomon. It's just the kind of mischief he/it would do and the event could even be viewed as evidence that such a spirit did exist. He/it would be pissing him/itself. Ha ha. Bastard Demetrios.

# 22

Romance hadn't had much contact with organised religion and so he hadn't had much contact with vicars, and so when he was at Demetrios Demetriou's funeral, gazing into the wide eyes of the Orthodox priest whom he suspected first of being stoned and then of being an accomplished ventriloquist, he couldn't be absolutely sure that at least one of his suspicions wasn't justified. But in his adult soul life there was one vicar he had met before and this was the soul vicar, and it wasn't long after Romance met Thelonius Tripp for the first time that the two new friends both met the soul vicar for the first time. They were on their way to an allnighter in Staffordshire with Demetrios Demetriou. Romance had spoken to the vicar on the phone sometime before, because he thought the vicar might make an interesting subject for a film. Perhaps Channel 4 would be interested. The northern soul vicar-DJ. It would be called *Keeping the Faith*. (He hadn't forgotten about his film in the studio with Thelonius Tripp and the *Moonlight Sonata* etc., but that was more art-house, whereas *Keeping the Faith* was definitely for television.)

The soul vicar lived in a vicarage in a little village in Berkshire and, when he showed the three young men in, they each looked about and supposed that it was a typical vicar's house. None of them had been in a vicar's house before but, if ever they'd had to imagine one (which they hadn't), they would each have imagined one much like this vicar's. It was clean (he had a cleaner), understated, a little twee and, to the boys, remarkably uninteresting. There was exposed wood, wooden furniture, carpet and tablecloths. And on the walls hung pictures and drawings of churches and cathedrals. It seemed appropriate that they all sat down for a cup of tea.

'I often get mistaken for a policeman, because of the size of my feet,' boomed the vicar. And he did boom. He couldn't have been more of a typical booming vicar. He was a big man with big feet and little hair and rosy cheeks. He could easily have been described as hearty. Booming and hearty.

'I can walk into a do and those who don't know me look at me with panic on their faces. I never take anything myself, but if popping pills means they'll stay and dance for my set then I'm all for it.'

Romance, Thelonius Tripp and Demetrios Demetriou all looked up from the vicar's feet. The big man was delighted to have an audience and quite fancied the idea of being on Channel 4. He knew these were soulies, but he presumed Romance had connections in telly. By the way Thelonius

Tripp enquired about his etchings, he thought that perhaps he was what they call an art director. And the quiet, long-haired one? Perhaps he helped them with all the equipment.

There had been a few things on telly before about northern soul. Apart from the Granada film about Wigan, none of them had been much good and anything in the media was usually met with derision by those immersed in the scene. How could these media people understand if they didn't have soul? Anything they made was bound to be superficial. (Clearly, there was a gap there, which Romance was eager to fill.) But still, the vicar wanted to be on telly. He delighted in his own eccentricity and thought it about time that others did too. And it would all be for the good of the music.

The vicar thought his best chance of creating a suitable televisual impression was to keep talking and to try to be controversial.

'There's too much fuss made about sex and drugs. As for rock and roll, of course, there's not enough fuss made about that – it should be banned. Soul is the music of heaven.'

Romance thought of Sam Cooke and all those other gospel singers of the fifties who had been ostracised by their churches for turning to secular music – to soul.

'Although I have to say, I am rather partial to a bit of Bach too. Some nice organ music. And bell-ringing of course. I'm a very keen campanologist you know and even though I'm a vicar that has nothing to do with fiddling with young boys.'

He was rather camp though. They had all noticed that.

'Plato said something good about music. I can't remember what though. Soul of the universe or something. And I've been all round Europe ringing bells. I go through phases – sometimes my bell-ringing is to the fore, sometimes northern soul.'

The three friends didn't have much to say. There wasn't much they could say. But Romance thought he had come across another creative type and this one with a hotline to God too.

'I suppose my two lives are quite separate, although the bishop did find out about my DJing and, when he realised it involved being up all night and dancing with the kids, he thought maybe my "street credibility" could be put to good use by the diocese. He asked me to change parish. He wanted me to be the vicar of an inner city church in some run down part of Reading where I could work with young people from deprived backgrounds. I told him no way. Sod that.

'But I do get roped into the odd bit of vicaring on the soul scene. I had a young couple come staggering up to me at the end of an allnighter wanting me to marry them there and then. They were clearly off their heads on something. I was actually quite tempted. We could have played *With This Ring* by The Platters and it would have rounded the evening off quite nicely. But I don't carry around that kind of paperwork.'

Romance wasn't a great fan of *With This Ring*. It was poppy northern soul and not soulful enough for his taste.

He could see that it would have been fitting, but he hoped that by the time of his own wedding he would have found a better record to announce the union. He hadn't yet met JBP and he hadn't been to Southampton, let alone the Pigeon Club, but he still imagined a Pigeon Club-style social club for his northern soul wedding. And he had now met the vicar. This vicar could do it. That would be cool.

The problem for Romance was that it was easier to find a northern soul vicar than it was to find a northern soul wife. There weren't many women on the soul scene and those that there were tended to be coupled up and in happy, long-term soul relationships. (Romance looked on enviously at these matches made in soul heaven.)

Thelonius Tripp wasn't much bothered by this. He really only cared about his paintings. He appreciated the female form but his ambitions in that direction ended at capturing womankind sympathetically on the dance floor. Demetrios Demetriou just let things happen. If a woman came along, that was fine. If one didn't, that was fine too. When he went out, he went to dance.

The vicar led the three boys into his record room. A couple of trestle tables ran the length of one wall and on them were a series of wooden record boxes. There was a record player at the far end, and otherwise, apart from the etchings of churches framed and hung on the walls, the room was bare.

'I've had the floor specially laminated for dancing. Normally after the allnighters there are always a few that want to come back and carry on. But I have to chuck them out when it's time for church.'

Having opened all the boxes, the vicar stood back and delighted in the awe of his new, young disciples.

They had never seen a record collection like it. Row upon row of original, rare northern soul 45s. They had to look through them but didn't know where to start. Romance placed his flat hand on a random section of a random row, and then on another, feeling the texture of the back-to-back card covers as if he were trying to get a sense of which bunch was ripe for the picking.

'Of course, sometimes it's a struggle to get them out and I might let them stay if I know them well, and there was one occasion with these lads from Newbury who wanted to carry on playing records, so I said to them, "Well, you have to leave but you can come back later," but they had nowhere to go, so they jumped in with me and came to church. I don't think they'd ever been before, but they sat at the back and behaved themselves, but I did find myself unconsciously addressing them during the service. I can't remember what the sermon was about – probably the eternal soul or something – and then, when I had to announce the next hymn, I said, "And now the next record is…" '

The boys wanted to listen, but they were struggling because they had started flicking through the records and were mesmerised by them.

These old 45s were the embodiment of all that mattered. Identical in shape and size but every one with a unique face – a tribal label, which to the knowledgeable gives a suggestion of date, style and place – and every one holding within a unique, individual story of life and love. Each record was silently crying to be played, as the shoppers in Oxford Street or the commuters on London Bridge or the fans walking to the match in Southampton silently cry out for their own story to be told, too contained to make a song and dance about it. And as the boys flicked through those titles – *Gone with the Wind Is My Love, If You Ever Walk out of My Life, I Never Loved Her Anyway* – it was as if they were flicking through the photos of prospective life partners in the office of an ever so soulful dating agency. A life and soul in every one, but an instant judgement made on a whim. Playing God.

'I suppose something similar could happen at a soul do,' the vicar continued. 'I could say "All stand for the next hymn" when introducing the next record, but it hasn't happened yet. I don't wear my dog collar, but maybe I should. And that might save some confusion. All that sudden scurrying and hiding of substances when I go to the gents. Because of the policeman thing. Because of the feet.'

The three boys had each picked out a couple of records and laid them flat on top of the others as a sign that they wanted to hear them. The vicar picked up one of Romance's.

'Johnny Maestro. I've been pushing this record.'

He began to sing as he moved towards the record player. 'Heartburn! You make my heart burn!'

Romance didn't know the record. But he had on tape

something else by Johnny Maestro that he loved (*No more will I sit at home and wait for you! No more will I let my poor heart break for you!* [6]), so he thought this might be a good one too.

Romance knew very few of the records he looked at. He loved this music but was feeling out of his depth. He wanted to know everything and was less patient about it than his two friends.

'But then maybe it would be worse if they knew I was a vicar! Maybe they'd rather be nicked for drugs than left alone in the gents with a randy old vicar! Ha!'

The record started.

*Heartburn! You make my heart burn!*
*You're the one who sends my heart a-reelin' baby!*
*You're the one who gives me strange feelin' baby!* [7]

It wasn't Keats and it wasn't the heart-achingly soulful *Stepping out of the Picture* either.

'Parkway Records, Philadelphia. Founded by that pesky old Quaker, William Penn. I mean Philadelphia. Not Parkway. That would have been odd. Nothing to do with Didcot, you know. Kicked the bucket just up the road, William Penn. Trying to do the likes of me out of a job!'

*Heartburn* was an uptempo northern soul dancer – full production, driving beat and rich vocals – and it had the vicar moving his big feet clumsily over his specially laminated floor as he sang aloud to it.

*I get a feeling I can't explain*
*And it's a feeling that's driving me insane*
*And it's you, you, you, yeah.*
*You know you make my heart burn baby.*
*You make my heart burn baby.*

Romance smiled. Soul gave him a feeling that he couldn't explain. But he wanted to try to explain, even if it was only to explain that it was inexplicable. He looked at the dancing vicar. 'Surely there's a film in here somewhere,' he thought to himself.

## 23

JBP wasn't a soul girl through and through. Not really. But she had an affiliation. An affinity. She was a regular at Shelley's in Southampton in the 1980s, where she danced to classic modern soul sounds (more Johnny Bristol than Johnny Maestro) and she met Leeds Dave and Minimalist Mike and Wigsy and they were all into sixties northern soul too. She didn't fall as deeply into the soul underworld as the guys around her and she kept herself up and open to other influences and experiences. She wanted to grasp the given world and all it had to offer, but she appreciated that there was a wonder about soul music and her own soul was as deep as any. She was underage at Shelley's but had already taken a heavy blow of abuse, responsibility and deprivation, and it was because she felt that life was to be embraced despite her heavy blow that her eyes and her soul were as deep as they were.

By the time Romance met her, it was as if she had lived a few lives already. He didn't mind that she had married the first man who showed her any genuine affection or that the guy was from the modern soul scene or that the marriage ended not because she didn't love modern soul man enough (which she didn't) but because MSM found some consolation from her lack of love in the arms of another woman – or two. But when she sat in that armchair – that grand, heavy, enveloping, cream, regency armchair – and told him not to be so ridiculous as to talk about love because there was obviously no such thing, the ache in his stomach that came at that moment was such as would be expected were an alien about to pop out.

She fought against him but he couldn't give in, and he fought harder, and in the end she succumbed but only to push him away again, and, when she told him on the phone that it was all no good, he went to her anyway and tried to kiss her and it was then, when she said the words she said, that he knew he had to walk away. When he said goodbye it was as if he had never said goodbye to anyone ever before. Every breath was an effort and every step away was a step away from life itself. But he loved her, and for her he had to go.

One week. Two weeks. Of waking up, forcing himself to live. Of going to the bathroom and kneeling at the toilet, waiting to be sick but not being sick. And then an evening of drinking after work and being sick and collapsing and sobbing and hoping the drunkenness would disguise it.

Three weeks and a phone call, and he met her in The Stokers Arms, and he could sit there, next to her, and be composed, and he could converse politely, and he was as proud of himself for that as he ever had been for anything and he told her so. Then he walked home and his insides vibrated with every step.

*Baby, baby, baby, my heart's not in it anymore*
*Oh, the feeling that was there*
*No, it's not the same anymore*
*It's nothing like before.*
*Baby, baby, baby, please don't ask me to stay*
*Oh, I got to break away*
*You'll be better off without me.*
*Baby, baby, baby, my heart's not in it anymore!* [8]

The song incorporated her words, and the rhythm of his walking incorporated her words and the song. The music was with him as he walked away and that was something, at least.

It was a few weeks later that Romance found himself kneeling at the bedside of JBP as she was crying uncontrollably. He couldn't understand why, but through the tears she was muttering a few words and among the ones he could pick out were 'I'm scared of how much I like you.' How odd. How odd that this woman, who had torn him into little pieces, would be declaring these feelings for him when he had loved her as much as it was possible for anyone to love anyone and she had told him that her heart wasn't in it anymore. Where did this leave him?

He didn't understand it, but he knew he had her. She had torn him into little pieces and now he had her. He didn't understand it but he didn't care because now she was his.

She didn't think it would last. She was worthless. It would last a couple of years and then he would dump her. Ha.

What a strange way to think, he thought. Life is for living, he thought. Who knows what will happen? If it feels good, go for it. They both loved each other. It was obvious.

It was an explosive relationship. It lasted a couple of years and then he dumped her.

# 24

After JBP told Romance that her heart wasn't in it anymore, Romance could listen to Romance Watson sing *Where Does That Leave Me* and relate personally to the pain of the song. But strangely, when Romance dumped JBP he could still listen to the record and relate personally to the pain of the song. In fact, when he heard the record for the first time, he hadn't dumped or been dumped in any serious, life-changing way, but he still heard the record as if it was speaking to him personally and he still felt the pain of it as if he was living it. But that's music for you; at least, that was soul music for Romance.

He was sitting with Demetrios Demetriou, the first time he heard the record, in Demetrios Demetriou's bedroom on the edge of the bed. Demetrios Demetriou was playing Romance a selection of his records. Demetrios Demetriou's mother was downstairs watching *Strike It Lucky*. Romance loved all the records his soul friend played him, but he loved some more than others and when he heard Romance Watson he loved that one the most. In fact, he loved it more than anything he had ever heard before and the love was instant too, in the way that normally only heartbreak can be. He loved it so much he couldn't stop laughing.

'Bloody hell. Who's this?'

'Romance Watson.'

'Fuck me.'

Demetrios Demetriou knew what he meant. Music could affect him in the same way.

They had both fallen into soul music in the same way too. It had crept up on them, embraced them and pulled them in. It took them out of their world and it filled their world. It was of the world and it wasn't. Like being in love, floating down a river, it was beyond the within and the without of the mind and the world, and the boys were carried along on the wave of it. When Romance heard Romance Watson, the sound surrounded him and lifted him. Romance could hear a force, and it was a force that obliterated the boundaries between within and without. Everything else he sensed from the outer world was the consequence of forces – all those tangible things that the human senses sense – but here was a force with no lasting evidence, with no material effect. It was made up of physical bits of sound and the character of the bits was something psychic, but the driving force he heard was neither. To a religious person, something that was neither physical nor psychic would be something divine. Similarly, for Romance, the force of the tones, beats and anguished phrases had to exist because soul existed, not the other way round. It had a dynamism that pointed beyond itself to some greater purpose, knowing its place in the whole, every piece of it demanding its own replacement for the sake of some greater completeness. And because soul existed Romance knew that the tangible and the visible couldn't be all that was. It was something to do with the meaning of life itself, even if it was impossible to know what exactly. There was soul because there was soul, and Romance didn't just hear it, he was a part of it, and as a part of the music he lived the heartbreak as much as the singer. It was as if he had an extra, super-sensual sense. If others couldn't feel it, that didn't negate it. He could, therefore it was.

This was soul music and, in Demetrios Demetriou, Romance had found a fellow soul traveller. They were young and stupid but they had soul, and when Demetrios Demetriou died Romance was slightly jealous, because he thought that now, at last, it might all make sense to his friend. Perhaps Demetrios Demetriou was now living in soul itself. Perhaps he was a part of it. Perhaps soul on earth was just a taste of what was to come – a heavenly tease – or a tantalising clue to a reality that was beyond knowing. Perhaps he was laughing at Romance's pitiful and sporadic experiences of it. Bastard Demetrios.

They were interrupted by Demetrios Demetriou's mother asking if they wanted tea.

'Tea? You want tea?'

Demetrios Demetriou was embarrassed by the interruption. It didn't sit well with them being in the midst of soul greatness.

'No, thank you, I'm fine,' said Romance, knowingly. (It was nearly thirty years since Mrs Demetriou had boiled her first kettle on that strange, unorthodox British cooker and made her first weak, lukewarm, milky mug of foreign tea and she still hadn't got the hang of it.)

# 25

Soul music didn't get off to an explosive start in Britain. There was no soul scene Big Bang. But perhaps that accounts for its durability.

The simmering mix of rhythm and blues and gospel made its way across the Atlantic and on to British dance floors by way of the American pop charts, and it was the less intense, more easy-listening and poppy soul sounds that first hit the decks in the UK. But by the time Nutty Casper was spinning himself to the floor of the Pigeon Club and JBP had become clinically depressed and was sectioned for the first time, what had become the northern soul scene was alight and well established. The soul fanatics of Britain had a wealth of knowledge and appreciation of the more soulful, underground music that had scorched the hearts and feet of young, urban black America in the sixties.

In those early soul years, every American city had its own distinct sound, as countless black youngsters threw their hats into the ring and put their hearts on the line by recording one or two songs on small fly-by-night record labels for local distribution, and it was into this bottomless pit of gospel-inspired seething lyrical abandon that Romance found himself falling – twisting, turning and out of control – a couple of decades after those young black voices had used the raw emotion of their church music to tell their heartfelt messages of lost love.

There were events all over the country and, with regular trips across the Atlantic in search of rare soul vinyl, some of the more adventurous had established themselves as rare soul record dealers and were posting weekly lists of records for sale. Knowns and unknowns... £5... £50... £500... Detroit... Chicago... Philadelphia...

The sound of the postman. The recognition of the list. The scramble to open it. Every weekend, days lost to travelling and nights lost to dancing and flicking through sales boxes, desperate to see something familiar, wanted and affordable. Dancing in delight and appreciation. Talking, listening, learning.

'It came out on Coral and is pretty rare, but this is some weird test pressing thing. I picked it up at the Audio Arts record fair from that old Austrian bloke, Victor. It was just in a box of cheap stuff. Cos he mostly does classical and he didn't know what it was. I went and showed it to Diamond Jim and he said he'd never seen one.'

Romance Watson. *Where Does That Leave Me*. Romance was jealous of his friend, obviously. He would love to have owned that record and to have been able to play it whenever he wished, weird test pressing or not. He would love to have owned the record just to know that he had it, that he had captured it, that he had reached out and grasped it and saved it, that he had captured its soul and imprisoned it like a ladybird in a matchbox saved from a dangerous world and with a soul that was now his. But mostly he was simply in awe that such a dramatic demonstration of artistic perfection should exist.

## 26

The first soul do that Romance organised was a demonstrably undramatic affair. It was in the basement of a Chinese restaurant in Shepherd's Bush. The restaurant was unlicensed and the Chinese owner had decided it would be a good idea to open an illegal nightclub. Romance had some flyers printed on rice paper and, as food was available, they said, 'Authentic Northern Soul, authentic Chinese cuisine,' in both English and Mandarin.

The only two punters were Nutty Casper and Demetrios Demetriou, the long-haired Greek Cypriot from Acton. Thankfully, they each brought a box of records, so when Romance had played all his – and many of the flipsides too – the evening could still continue. No one bought any food.

The Chinese owner viewed the evening as a great success – so much so that he wanted it to become a weekly event and to charge £5 on the door. Romance was worried this might drive the punters away. He had a discussion with Nutty Casper and Demetrios Demetriou. They said they were unlikely to pay £5 for the privilege of playing their own records, to each other, in the basement of a Chinese restaurant. The owner was mortified. His dream was at an end and, without the support of the West London Soul Scene, the restaurant closed and he went back to China. (There may have been others factors too.) But that was all long before JBP became suicidally depressed. And before Demetrios Demetriou was diminished by cancer too. And long before a battered builder's van from Littlehampton stopped at the apex of the Itchen Bridge causing a tailback of cars all caught nervously between a reassuring forward movement and a terrifying slipping, down and back.

## 27

Lee and Lainie were a lovely, ugly couple. He was a bruiser and she was more so. He was a solid, stocky builder; she was bigger than him. And they had a lovely, ugly baby, Aretha, who was to grow up to retain both her ugliness and her loveliness in a way that so many other babies don't. And when Lainie, Lee, little Jimmy and Hippy John were travelling along the A27 towards Littlehampton, baby Aretha was eight months old. She was at her nan's.

Aretha's nan was Lainie's mother, and she lived in a well kept flat not far from Lee and Lainie's. From the outside, Lee and Lainie's house looked well kept too: a two up, two down end-of-terrace. But inside it was a building site and it had been for years. Lee was a builder, but the last thing he wanted to do when he flopped in from work was work. The floors were untreated, bare boards and all the walls needed plastering. Lainie hated it. 'When are you going to sort the fucking house out?' she asked, once or twice a week.

Lee, Lainie and baby Ree had one bedroom, the records the other. Lainie was expecting the record room to be turned into a bedroom for Ree. And she had said as much to Lee, numerous times.

And now Hippy John was standing in the doorway of Lee and Lainie's living room, but he wasn't looking into it. He could see, but he wasn't capable of looking. It was a plain room and there wasn't much to look at, so he wasn't missing much. The old plaster was cracked and flaking – the white paint faded and dirty – and the bay window uncurtained. But there was a sofa, a TV on a coffee table and some boxes of records. Hippy John didn't notice any of that. He just stood there.

'All right then, what are we supposed to do with him now?'

Lainie hadn't wanted to let him in the house. But then she thought she had to, at least until they had decided what to do with him.

'Well offer him a seat for a start.'

'Oh for fuck's sake. Oi, hippy, sit down. And don't puke on my sofa.'

Hippy John sat down and didn't puke on the sofa. He could do what he was told. In fact, he couldn't not do what he was told. That's all he could do. Decision-making was a thing of the past – a thing of his previous life.

Lee and Lainie carried on talking and Hippy John could hear but the talk wasn't directed at him and it didn't register. He just sat there and stared at the wall opposite. (Jimmy quietly browsed through one of the record boxes.)

Hippy John felt alive but not alive. He had never felt like

this before. He was confused and all he could do was accept that and wait. He couldn't reason his way out. If he was to pull through this it would be as a result of an exterior force – Lee, Lainie or God perhaps.

Perhaps he was dead. He certainly felt strangely divorced from his body. He didn't fit it anymore. He was rattling about somewhere inside it. Before he had arrived at the bridge and as he was clambering out on to that ledge, he had imagined the deep, dark peace of the water, his entire being surrounded by a comforting nothingness, his body released from the world he knew back into a womb-like security, free of any obligation to himself. That would be a halfway house and, if that imagined place was a sign of what was beyond, he wanted to go there. But now he was here. Perhaps he had jumped. Perhaps his memory of imagining the aftermath was his memory of the aftermath and now this was the beyond. The patterns of the plastered wall stared at him as if they were equations to the meaning of life pummelling his head. 'How can such an imbecile be a son of mine?' his father used to shout, as he slapped John as hard as he could.

'Well we can't have him here, can we? Not with Ree in the house. I mean we don't know anything about him. He could be a complete lunatic. I mean he obviously is cos he was gonna top himself – that's not exactly normal, is it? Maybe he'll wanna take one of us with him next time! When someone gets into that state they don't know what they're doing anyway. Jesus f.... Why the fuck did you stop in the first place? Lee, you're such a dipstick! It's like when you wanted to take that fucking fox to the vet! Fucking smelly old fox. Yeah, great. Let's rescue the smelly fox so he can go out and kill more cats or whatever. Great. The fucking van stank for fucking ages and that's even more than it usually fucking does.'

Lainie paused and they both looked down at Hippy John, who was still staring straight ahead. Jimmy had picked out an early Marvin Gaye record on Tamla that he didn't know – he had thought he knew them all – and he had taken it out of its sleeve and was examining it.

'Lee, get on the phone and see if you can't work something out. There's some hostels, isn't there, for people like him. I mean, what the fuck are we supposed to do with him? He needs a good fucking wash but I ain't fucking touching him. Look in the phone book or something. And Jimmy, you could fucking do something couldn't you? What you looking at that pile of old fucking crap for anyway? And Lee, I thought you said you were gonna get rid of these ones or take them upstairs at least. It's bad enough having a smelly old trampy hippy smelling up my house. A box of crusty old northern crap doesn't really help does it? For fuck's sake. I'm going to get Ree. You two get this mess sorted. Jesus.'

And she left.

Lee had met Lainie at a soul do in Brighton. Or rather Lainie had met Lee. She saw him dancing and even though she wasn't really into northern, there was something about the way he moved that she found attractive. There was nothing effeminate about him. He wasn't one of the grown up mod soul-types. He was a grown up tattooed skinhead, with both muscles and rhythm. When she first saw him, he was in the middle of the dancefloor, dancing to *Girl Don't Make Me Wait Too Long* by Bunny Sigler. There were just two others dancing, both grown up skinheads too, and the three were friends. The boys moved about the floor, at all times managing to keep a respectful distance from each other. Clearly, their dancing was strictly between themselves and the music. The dancing was in homage to the music, not for its own sake, let alone for the sake of a woman.

Bunny screamed and pleaded, his voice overcome with sexual tension. The men were expressionless. But their feet felt the soul. Their glistening loafers slid across the wooden floor in recognition of Bunny's heartfelt plea, and the grace with which these muscle-clad men moved was an affront to gravity – two fingers up to the laws of nature – and a celebration of the human soul. Their sublime art was concentrated in their feet, as their feet bore their weight and were their interface with the world. Through their feet they could express their most tangible defiance. Any expression of rhythm through the movement of any other part of their bodies was meaningless in comparison. And they didn't simply dance on the beat; they felt the dynamism of the music and constructed their own sophisticated and ever-changing rhythms, true to the metre, falling in and falling out with the music. They were in direct dialogue with the music, out of respect for it. If Romance had been there he might have said that meaning was in the act of communication itself – the movement – and it was a creative act never to be repeated. If Solomon had been there he might have grappled with some quote by someone clever about polarity and intensification and how those are the two forces that govern life and that together they reside in the relationship between the overlying constituent parts of music and that it's they that propel music along and that it's they that can be seen too in the relationship between music and dancer. (However, that might have been a quote too far, even for him.) If Deptford Dave had been there he would have said something about how stupid it was that Bunny Sigler was called Bunny and it wasn't even his real name anyway so why did he pick it? Did he look like a rabbit? Was it his teeth? No wonder the girl was resisting him.

Lainie liked the look of Lee. He wasn't the tallest and he wasn't the shortest. He was of medium height. His features were hard but not bruised. He danced with purpose; he knew the song. There was no movement wasted. And the combination of elegance and masculinity appealed to her.

Lee was there with his girlfriend, Moira McLaughlin, but it wasn't clear that they were there together. Moira didn't dance and spent most of the evening sitting on the floor against the wall, watching. When Romance arrived with Wigsy from Southampton, he saw Moira and liked the look of her, but it was in the days when he didn't know how to talk to women, and he spent the evening trying to work out what he could say to her and then trying to summon up the courage to say anything. He spent the journey home being cross with himself for failing miserably on both counts, and it was a long journey because Wigsy took the wrong road out of Brighton and set off towards London and they ended up going back to Southampton via the M25.

It was only at the end of the do that Lainie approached Lee, gave him a piece of paper with her number on it and said, 'Call me.' It was more of a demand than a request.

'Lee?'

'What?'

'What? What d'ya mean, what?'

'What?'

'What... !?'

Lainie had come back with baby Ree, and Hippy John was still on the sofa. Lee and Jimmy were sitting either side of him. They each had a cup of tea in their hands and they were watching the football results on telly.

'What? It's Saturday. We spent ages calling round, didn't we Jimmy? But it's Saturday, init.'

'So?'

'Well, it's Saturday. We found some numbers. But, you know. It's Saturday.'

'And?'

Lee shrugged.

'So what's your big idea then?'

Lee shrugged.

'Lee. He can't stay here. What are you thinking? He's used to the…' – she stopped herself from swearing – '… outside anyway.'

Lee looked at her.

Lainie rolled her eyes and mouthed a few of the words that she had been avoiding saying.

'I'm taking Ree upstairs. And yes, she's fine, by the way. Good you take such an interest.'

Hippy John had never been one for football. He hadn't had any brothers and when he was a child for some reason he had found it difficult making friends and so didn't play it much and when he did he really wasn't very good, which just put him off even more. His father never played with him or took him to matches either.

His father was strange like that, because he did take him to some places, but he would take him to places that he didn't want to go to. The young John thought this odd at the time and, in fact, still did, because he wasn't just dragging John along with him through necessity. He could have left John at home or allowed him to do his own thing. And he wasn't punishing John, making John do things he didn't want to do. It was more complicated than that.

They used to have days out, the three of them – sometimes just the two of them – at National Trust houses or gardens, museums or art galleries. If his mother was there, she would try to make it interesting for John by fabricating stories or showing him things she thought a child might be interested in, but his father was oblivious to what interests a child. He was the arbiter of good taste and so if it interested him, John should be interested in it. Not just should be, but would be.

In the morning his father would come up with a great idea for an outing and he would expect it to be met with due enthusiasm. John would try desperately to wriggle out of it. He would be asked, did he want to go. He would say no, he would stay at home. He would be asked again, and this time his mother would give him a look. He would despair. And then, somehow, it would be settled.

And then after hours of all the dreary tedium of a refined middle class excursion and being constrained in the exercise of some weird adult pretension, his father would turn to him smiling and say, 'Well, aren't you glad you came?' Everything in him wanted to shout out 'No!' But he knew what the consequences would be and the effect of those consequences on his mother too. So he would grimace and say 'Yes' and the worst of it was that his father would believe that *yes* and take it as verification.

It wasn't that he deliberately wanted to inflict boredom on his child. His selfishness was more profound than that. If he liked something or wanted to do something, he simply presumed others would like it or want to do it too. Why wouldn't they? He was a human being and they were too, even if, in John's case, they were a little one. So if they said 'No', it couldn't be because his idea didn't appeal to them. They must be lying. The only reason they would say no would be to deliberately insult him. To get at him. To ruin his day. They would be putting themselves out, denying themselves enjoyment and fulfilment, simply to deprive him. And for him that was inconceivably mean-spirited. They would quite rightly be hated for it. And they would quite rightly be punished. Severely. Physically.

And now here he was watching the football results. At least, his eyes were on the telly; he wasn't really watching. He was just staring. Lee was making the occasional comment ('Ha, wankers!'), but Hippy John wasn't hearing them. His mind had yet to catch up with events in his life. So he wasn't thinking about his father either, or anything else. His feelings of otherness were now too deep-rooted and profound to be thought about, extending, as they did, to the whole physical world. Thinking itself entailed something of the physical world. For the moment, he could just be, and that was weird enough.

In Southampton, somewhere, there was a sad and angry man getting drunk and preparing himself for a random act of violence. But for Hippy John, the fact that Southampton lost, again, was lost.

## 28

Marvin Gaye had a difficult relationship with his father, to say the least. And it wasn't made any better when he moved back home at the age of 43, hopelessly in debt (having made millions), addicted to cocaine and pornography, with two failed marriages behind him and convinced that someone was out to murder him. His father, Marvin Sr., was a failed preacher of a small but largely-named sect – The House of God, the Holy Church of the living God, the Pillar and the Ground of Truth, the House of Prayer for all People – which mixed elements of Orthodox Judaism and Pentecostal Christianity ('We don't drink no wine, we don't eat no swine, we keep all the saying of the Lord Elohim, commandment keepers are we. This is the church of the living Yah!') He had a penchant for vodka, cross-dressing and, like his father before him (and as he was to bequeath unto his son) beating his wife. He thought it a good idea to beat his children too and Marvin Jr. in particular. He didn't love young Marvin and didn't want his wife to love him either. Playing sport and going to the cinema were forbidden. Television and popular music were banned from the house. The children were drilled on biblical passages and beaten for incorrect answers. With enough idiosyncrasies of his own to deal with, Marvin Sr. was in no mood to empathise with those of his son, world famous soul superstar or not.

On tour, Marvin surrounded himself with bodyguards and, other than when on stage, insisted on wearing a bulletproof vest. At home, he installed an elaborate security and surveillance system and he kept a lively assortment of guns, including a machine-gun under his bed.

It was the day before his 45th birthday when Marvin pushed his father out of his bedroom and knocked him to the floor. Marvin Sr. returned with a handgun and shot his son in the chest. He walked up to him and shot him again.

'He shot my son!' screamed the long-suffering Alberta Gaye.

When the paramedics arrived Marvin Sr. was sitting on the porch. His son was dead.

Marvin Sr. had said repeatedly and publicly that if his son were to lay a finger on him then he would kill him. Marvin Jr. was well aware of it. And he had given his father the handgun as a Christmas present the year before.

Marvin's funeral was led by the Chief Apostle of the House of God etc. Over 10,000 people attended.

There are not many soul artists who achieved commercial success and yet retained the respect of the enthusiastically critical British soul fraternity. But Marvin Gaye was one.

# 29

The first bullet was enough to kill Marvin Gaye. It pierced his heart. He died of a broken heart, literally and quickly.

But the cancer that killed Demetrios Demetriou crept up on him, slowly, as soul music had. It wasn't a sudden thing – it rarely is with cancer and it rarely is with soul music. It wasn't explosive. He had a bit of a cough, and then the cough worsened, and when it worsened still he went to the doctor. Some tests were carried out and then he had to wait for the results, and when they came they showed he had a cancerous growth in his chest. He had to go to hospital and have chemotherapy, and when Romance went to see him in hospital for the first time he didn't recognise Demetrios Demetriou. He walked straight past him. His friend was in a bed in a cancer ward and Romance looked at him and moved straight on. Demetrios Demetriou muttered an 'all right?' and Romance had a second look and then tried not to look shocked. The long hair was gone and in place of the rounded, red-blooded, warm dark face was something thin, pale and empty-looking. The young but ancient Greek eyes were fighting to remain true and it was the warmth of them that caught Romance.

Demetrios Demetriou had been one of the first people Romance had met on the soul scene: his first true soul friend. For two to three years, Romance had sat at home listening to Kent compilation LPs without even knowing there was a soul scene – without knowing there were places to go that played this music. He had been listening to soul music since his mid-teens and every Friday evening he would record Peter Young's *Soul Cellar* on Capital Radio. Sometimes one record would stand out from the others and then Peter Young would say that it was on a new Kent compilation LP, so Romance would scour the shops for Kent LPs and buy any he could find. And this was his introduction to northern soul. Then one day he noticed in the *Time Out* listings that there was northern soul in the function room of a pub in Clapham, so he went. It was a small place and there were only a handful of people, but he felt like a reincarnated child returning to his original, lost family. He sat and listened and was amazed to hear the music he loved being played in public. And then some guys danced and he could see they felt it as he did, and then a record came on that he knew and loved – *Open the Door to Your Heart* – and for the first time he saw others mouthing the words, as he had been doing for years... *Open the door to your heart, let my love come running in*... and when the break came in the middle of the record, two of the guys dancing clapped in time to the irregular beat, as he had been doing for years.

Someone put fliers on the tables for a northern soul allnighter at the 100 Club, so Romance went to that too and he was shocked to his core. There were a couple of hundred people in there and the dancefloor was full. Record after record thrilled him, but he didn't know any of them, despite having all the Kent LPs he could find. The DJs were playing 45s and at the back there were guys at tables selling 45s – hundreds of them, thousands of them. He began to look at them but didn't know any of them and was astounded at the prices. He began to long to see something familiar, or to hear something familiar, just to give him some grounding. And all these people seemed to know each other. He was floundering and alone and overwhelmed, and it all seemed so wonderful but so beyond him that he felt as if he had met the love of his life but that she was already married.

The tables were littered with fliers for other northern soul nights and Romance left making sure he had one of each, and at those events there were more fliers, and Romance went to every event that he could. He went by himself and stood and watched and listened, and he began to recognise people, and the person who was most recognisable was Demetrios Demetriou.

Demetrios Demetriou had long, dark hair, almost down to his waist, and his dancing set him apart too. He danced from side to side in long, sweeping movements and then, at a break in the record, he would pause and drop to the floor and then spring up into a frantic spin.

At a small venue in east London, Romance spotted Demetrios Demetriou and approached him and said hello, saying that he recognised him from the 100 Club. They had been friends ever since. But in the hospital Romance hadn't recognised him. He had walked straight past him.

Demetrios Demetriou had cancer and he was just 32: the same age as Darrell Banks when he was shot dead in Detroit (and Billy Stewart when he plunged his twelve-day-old Thunderbird into the Neuse River).

Marvin Gaye had a long, fruitful career compared to many of them.

## 30

Spaghetti Weston went to Demetrios Demetriou's funeral with Mick the Twitch. They both travelled down from Birmingham especially. It was obvious why Mick the Twitch was called Mick the Twitch. He twitched. He had a nervous tick. He twitched his head when he was speaking and often when he wasn't speaking too. Nobody knew why and nobody asked and Spaghetti had never even wondered. The only time Mick didn't twitch was when he liked the music being played.

When they were standing in the pew holding their candles and waiting for the chanting to stop, Mick was twitching (because even if chanting counted as music, he didn't like it) and Spaghetti was feeling guilty. He wasn't feeling guilty about Mick twitching. Why should he? No, he wasn't thinking about that. He was feeling guilty because he wasn't feeling as upset at Demetrios Demetriou's funeral as he thought he should have been. So his main feeling wasn't sadness but guilt – guilty at not being sad – and he was beginning to feel sad about that. He could see that French Freddie was crying and, even though Spaghetti could only see him from behind, Romance was clearly crying uncontrollably. And Mick kept twitching and to Spaghetti that felt more befitting of the supposedly moving occasion than his own nothing-of-a-reaction (even if he didn't think about it).

Spaghetti was finding it difficult to be sad in the appropriate way because he kept thinking of Soul Sam and what his funeral would and should be like. Soul Sam wasn't dead then but he was a doddery old dog and, even though Spaghetti didn't like to think about it, he knew that Soul Sam wasn't going to live forever. Perhaps he shouldn't have left him to go to Demetrios Demetriou's funeral. Now that was something else to feel guilty about. But then how guilty would he have felt if he had missed his friend's funeral? He wondered if he should have allowed Annie to dissuade him from taking Soul Sam.

'You can't take a dog to a funeral!'

'Why? People go to dog funerals.'

'No, they don't! Dogs don't have funerals! They're dogs!'

'Well Sam's gonna have a funeral.'

'If you take him he might get depressed by getting an accentuated sense of his own mortality. He is, after all, a very sensitive dog.'

There were times when Spaghetti wasn't 100% sure if little Annie was being sincere. But, either way, she was right. He might. He was a very sensitive dog.

'And anyway, they won't let a dog in, you twat.'

Demetrios Demetriou's was a professional affair; Spaghetti could see that. These people were experienced. The chanting was peculiar but atmospheric and the candles were a nice touch. The man in robes was good too and that made Spaghetti wonder if he should wear something special for Soul Sam's funeral. And it was in a church. Everything suggested that this should be the occasion for enhanced emotion, but Spaghetti was left curiously unmoved.

Spaghetti knew that he was responsible for Soul Sam in a way that he hadn't been for Demetrios Demetriou, and so perhaps that excused his thinking about his dog rather than his friend. But he also knew that Demetrios Demetriou had been human – like him – and that, even though Soul Sam was quite intelligent for his species, his species (dog) was a less intelligent species than that of Demetrios Demetriou and Spaghetti, and so really he should feel sadder at the loss of a fellow human than at the mere thought of a dog-loss. Although what about a nice dog (Soul Sam/Tamla) and an intelligent but evil human (Hitler)? But Demetrios Demetriou was a nice human so, whatever the answer to that, it didn't apply here. And the point was he didn't feel sadder. Everyone else was sad – especially Romance, by the look of it – but Spaghetti felt numb. But then he saw that not everyone else was sad. The man in robes with a beard didn't look at all sad. He was just standing there. If anything, he looked a bit stoned. In fact, he reminded Spaghetti of Donald Sutherland in *Kelly's Heroes*. Maybe Demetrios Demetriou's coffin was full of gold. Maybe

Demetrios Demetriou wasn't dead after all. Something odd was going on and this was an elaborate set up and that's why he wasn't sad, because Demetrios Demetriou wasn't dead; he had been kidnapped or maybe he had masterminded this whole bank robbery business. Or it could be Greek church gold or diamonds like in *Diamonds Are Forever*. But even if any of that was true, Spaghetti surmised that he wouldn't know about it and so that couldn't be why he wasn't sad. He wasn't stupid.

The chances were that Donald Sutherland was a genuine priest who believed in God and such. Perhaps that's why he wasn't sad: because he believed. And so he knew that Demetrios Demetriou had gone on somewhere (such as heaven) and was OK. So maybe deep inside Spaghetti knew that too and that's why he wasn't sad. Maybe God was telling him. But then the fact that he was sad at the thought of the demise of Soul Sam must mean that Soul Sam, as a separate dog spirit, didn't live on, and when Spaghetti thought about that he was sad. Poor Soul Sam. It wasn't his fault he was a dog. (Was it?)

And why weren't the priest's lips moving? That was odd. Spaghetti could hear the chanting but couldn't see the expected degree of lip movement. He could hear what should have been visible but wasn't, and it made him wonder if everyone else could hear it too. He looked at Mick the Twitch, who was twitching, and wanted to ask him but didn't want to look an idiot.

Spaghetti then wondered why, if his theory was true and

he wasn't sad because somehow God was letting him know that somehow Demetrios Demetriou – or whatever he now was or was a part of – was OK, then why was God somehow letting him know this and not somehow letting everyone else know, especially poor Romance who was clearly in a right old state. And then there was the chanting too; either only he could hear it or somehow he was able to see beyond it. There was only one conclusion. He had, for whatever reason, been chosen. And it was at that moment that Spaghetti decided that he was to become a Greek Orthodox priest and he was so, so happy.

Eventually the chanting stopped. And when it did, it came as quite a shock. In the silence of the church everyone looked at the Donald Sutherland character and in retaliation he looked back.

And then he spoke, but it would have been better if he hadn't.

'The one certain thing about death is that it is not the end. It's the beginning of a new life.'

'Isn't that birth?' whispered Solomon.

In the silence after the chanting, Romance had managed to compose himself a little, but that birth comment didn't help.

'As our Lord told us, "Most assuredly, I say to you, he who hears my word and believes in him who sent me has everlasting life and shall not come into condemnation but pass from death to life." '

'Well that's Demetrios fucked,' thought Romance, but didn't say it.

' "Most assuredly, I say to you, the hour is coming, and now is when the dead will hear the voice of the Son of God and those who hear will live. The hour is coming when all who are in the graves will hear His voice and come forth – those who have done good, to the resurrection of life, and those who have done evil, to the resurrection of condemnation." And St. Paul tells us, "The Lord himself will descend from heaven with a shout, with the voice of an archangel, and with the trumpet of God, and the dead in Christ will rise." '

Romance had only to hear mention of trumpets and he couldn't help but hear in his head the Kurt Harris song *Emperor of My Baby's Heart*. He loved strings and he loved trumpets, because he loved drama in his music. And now the record came to him in the rhythm of the talking priest:

*When I'm walking down the street, I'm just another guy. No one pays attention, anytime I'm passing by. But when I'm with my little girl, I'm something special in this world... the bugles play... oh, the trumpets start... cos I'm the emperor, of my baby's heart.* [9]

' "And the Lord Jesus, intent on denying Death yet another victim, marched to the tomb of Lazarus and looking on that blocked-up cave, He beheld not just the buried corpse of His friend, but the corpse of the whole world." '

*When she says that I'm her only one... I rule the earth, I own the moon and sun.*

' "If you are sick and tired of death stealing away people that you love, strike back. Strike back at Satan. Strike back at Satan through prayer. Keep praying, for prayer pushes back the darkness." '

*Let the other guys be famous men, or millionaires. They can have that kind of wealth and glory, I don't care. Cos when my girl says she's my own, I take my place upon my throne...*

' "Through our dear Lord Jesus Christ. Now unto him be all glory, and praise, now and ever, and unto the ages of ages." '

*The bugles play... oh, the trumpets start... cos I'm the emperor, of my baby's heart.*

Romance wasn't the only one finding it difficult to concentrate. In fact, the biblical quotes about death proved so endless that at least half the congregation lost the will to live. When his head wasn't filled with bugles and trumpets, Romance had to put all his efforts into muffling his chuckles. He didn't mean to be irreverent, but he had known Demetrios Demetriou well and the idea of his body rising to meet his soul again somewhere in the troposphere wasn't an easy one to take. He had always been scared of flying. And what would he be wearing? And would he manage to keep his change in his pockets?

Spaghetti wasn't listening because he was dreaming of his own priestly robes. In fact, none of the soul people were aware of how long the priest talked for as their minds were elsewhere, but when he stopped they looked to see what would happen next, and what happened next was that all the Greeks in the front started filing out of their pews to make a queue in the central aisle. They then began to shuffle past the coffin, kissing a framed photograph of Demetrios Demetriou that was resting on top of it.

Romance, Solomon and Tony Davis Two, being in the front row of the soul folk, were the first of their ilk to join the queue and when they did the others fell in behind.

'Roosevelt Grier,' Tony Davis Two whispered to Romance.

Romance looked at him, irritated, not wanting to be distracted. What had Roosevelt Grier to do with anything?

'He was an American footballer too, you know. As well as a singer.'

Romance turned away. He didn't want to think about that. His immediate concern was the immediate future.

Romance was first to make it to the coffin, behind the little Greek woman who had given him such a stern look. He watched her bend forward and give Demetrios Demetriou a smacking big kiss, full on the lips. When she stepped aside the glass of the picture still bore her moist mark.

Romance had never been one for blokey physical affection. All this man-hugging that was going on these days. And he had spent the previous ten years or so avoiding any close physical contact with his very good friend Demetrios Demetriou, even though he loved him very much. Demetrios Demetriou was a goodlooking chap, by all accounts, but Romance wasn't going to go there. And there was no way he was going to start kissing him now, just because he was dead.

Maybe Demetrios Demetriou had stopped being a man when he died and was now just an asexual spirit thing, but that didn't hold much appeal to Romance either and, anyway, it was that hairy man-picture that was being kissed. And the hairy priest was standing there, watching, wide-eyed in anticipation.

Romance gave the Demetrios Demetriou man-picture a friendly scowl and walked past. The priest, who had a constant look of bewilderment about him anyway, now looked more bewildered still, and this was taken a notch even higher when, after a stream of other non-kissing non-Greeks had followed Romance's lead (and then one who seemed to be throwing kisses at Demetrios Demetriou with violent flings of his head), there came a small, excited one who gave the startled priest a knowing wink and a smile as he processed by.

# 31

Romance hadn't had much contact with organised religion and the only vicar he had met and had tea with was the soul vicar, and so when he was at Demetrios Demetriou's funeral, gazing into the wide eyes of the Orthodox priest whom he suspected first of being stoned and then of being an accomplished ventriloquist, he couldn't be absolutely sure that at least one of his suspicions wasn't justified.

The Orthodox priest hadn't encountered such an unorthodox congregation before, whereas the soul vicar, naturally, knew these people. But the soul vicar hadn't always been a soul vicar. In fact, he hadn't always been a vicar. His was a life marked by two revelatory moments, which, whether by co-incidence or not (and he thought not), occurred within a week of each other shortly after his fortieth birthday. The first came as a consequence of him making a phone call to see if his sheepskin rug was ready and, when he looked back on it, he couldn't help but wonder at how the simple act of phoning the dry cleaner's on Greenwich Park Street could have had such a profound effect on his life. (The second involved speaking to no one – just listening.)

The soul vicar had moved to London from Chatham, Kent, where he had grown up in the flat above the family pub. It wasn't a lively pub; it wasn't a lively part of town. The surrounding streets wouldn't have been out of place in the Kentish suburbs of London. He couldn't remember an age when he wasn't helping in the pub – in some minor way, at least – but to him the Rising Sun was distinctly dull and grey. When he was old enough and wanting to find his own way, he left the pub and found a job in a local bookie's. Eventually, however, he tired of having sawn-off shotguns pointed at his face and he fell back into bar work. But he tired, too, of the small town intolerance – he was an increasingly flamboyant character, marked not only by his foot size – and by the time he had reached his mid-thirties, he was managing a vibrant pub in the middle of 1970s Greenwich, which catered mainly to passive tourists and rough old locals whose fighting days were behind them. Here, his jovial character and naked good nature proved themselves inoffensive, at least. There was a function room upstairs, a cigarette machine in the corner and a signed photo of Michael Caine behind the bar, none of which in any way seemed likely to increase his chances of one day becoming an English country vicar.

There was no accommodation for him at the pub and at first he rented a room nearby, but soon he found something bigger and better, and he had only been in his new bachelor-pad-of-a-flat for a few days when the need to phone the dry cleaner's arose.

On the morning of the phone call it was raining hard, but to make the call he had to venture out of his flat, as a phone line had yet to be installed. And that empty space on the parquet flooring in front of the white leather sofa was crying out for the fresh, rejuvenated sheepskin.

He had an umbrella, but it didn't take long for his lower half to be soaked through, so it was with considerable relief that he reached the phone box, although getting into it meant taking down his umbrella in the doorway and a quick wetting of the rest of him.

'Hello? Greenwich Clean Time?'

'I'm sorry?'

'Clean Time?'

There was a pause. Then the voice came again and it was the voice of an old woman.

'Is it Tuesday?'

'Um, no. It's Thursday.'

'Well someone normally comes on a Tuesday. I don't need anything done today, thank you.'

It wasn't the response he had been expecting and the noise of the rain was making him doubt what he was hearing.

'Is that Greenwich Clean Time?'

'It's Mrs Meredith. And who are you, young man? You have a lovely voice.'

'It's Terry Gibbs. I was calling about my sheepskin rug.'

'Oh I don't have one of those. Sheepskin rug, you say. We

did used to have one of those, me and my George. Ooh, wouldn't you like to know! Well why don't you bring it with you? I'm game!'

'This isn't the dry cleaner's, is it?'

'Dry cleaner's? No it is not! And if you don't get off the phone now and stop harassing me I'm going to call the police!'

'I'm sorry. I must have the wrong number.'

'Oh yes, that's what they all say. Phoning up a dying woman as she's lying in agony and making fun of her with all kinds of indecent propositions!'

'Are you OK? Is everything all right?'

'The Cutty Sark is burning down.'

'What?'

'The Cutty Sark is burning down. I can see it from here. It must have got struck by lightning. I've got to go.'

And with that Mrs Meredith put the phone down.

Terry put the phone down too and looked out at the rain falling on the pavement. Could the old ship really be on fire? There had been some thunder, but he hadn't noticed any lightning. And would it stay alight in all this rain? He looked in the direction of the ship. There was no glow in the sky. The mad old woman was probably imagining it or making it up. But he wanted to know for sure and, if it was true, he wanted to see it. It would be quite an event and on the news. He picked up his umbrella, half-opened it, held it out in front of him, pushed the door open with his shoulder and stepped out into the absurdity that was all that water gushing from the sky. He then hurried north up Greenwich South Street.

The nearer Terry was to the Cutty Sark, the less he could imagine it being on fire. The lack of any fiery glow became more noticeable, as did the never-increasing number of people about. With each step he couldn't help but feel a little disappointed. He didn't actively wish fire and damnation upon anyone or anything, but he was excited at the thought of seeing it. Perhaps when he turned the corner of the High Road, round and past the church of the martyred St. Alfege, he would suddenly be presented with some towering inferno.

But he wasn't. There was still nothing unusual, apart from the more than reasonable amount of rain. He walked on towards the ship, past his still sleeping pub, and turning into the dry dock he saw the solid darkness of it against the sky. If he had never seen such a thing before, it would have been a wonderful sight, but perhaps that was true of everything. To Terry, it was boringly normal. In fact, it was so normal he reverted to thinking about his dry cleaning. He had been diverted in his mission by some uncalled for silliness. He looked about, saw the row of phone boxes at the edge of the pedestrianised area and checked in his pocket for another 2p. Then, in the dryness of one of the boxes, he looked at the Greenwich Clean Time card and wondered where he had gone wrong. He dialed again and someone answered and whoever it was wasn't mad, and he was free to collect the rug at any time, and with that chore done he hung up, picked up his umbrella again, pushed and then held the door open with his left hand, took one step out and that's when it happened. His world changed forever.

## 32

For Romance, meeting JBP wasn't quite like being struck by lightning but almost. The love was sudden and painful. It was all embracing and life changing, and they were very happy together, for a while. After she succumbed, they moved in together and lived quite an idyllic life, cuddled up at home or going on little excursions into the New Forest and into Dorset. They went to Over Wallop, and then through Middle Wallop to Nether Wallop, and they went in search of the long lost Wallop-on-the-Wane (which Romance made up especially for the occasion). They came across a village in Hampshire where the villagers were racing plastic ducks down the stream, and they stayed in a B&B near Weymouth run by a woman they remembered as Mrs Bumblebee. And they cuddled up and snuggled up and watched *Changing Rooms* and *Midsomer Murders*.

It was all lovely, for a while.

But then JBP was sectioned when she told the doctors about wanting to stab her clients. She didn't like all their chitchat. She just wanted to get on with her job.

She was only put away for a couple of weeks and the treatment she received inside was good, but then she was let loose again and things reverted. Unfortunately, the whole episode was symptomatic of some fairly deep problems, and those cosy nights in of cuddling and snuggling became tense and alcohol-fuelled, and then one evening JBP picked up her bottle of red wine and hurled it at Romance. It missed him but smashed against the wall, which remained stained and splattered like the scene of some grisly massacre.

Romance had known all along that JBP had a few issues, what with her childhood (not being able to remember before the age of eight) and all this being scared of love business. And JBP knew she did too, what with all this depression and despair. But he wanted her to succumb and then she did succumb because they each felt that a loving relationship might be the answer to her problems, what with all this love conquering all business. (*Love is... Love is the answer, babe. Let's try it! Let's try it!*)

Watching the plastic ducks. Looking for Wallop-on-the-Wane. Slowly it became apparent to both of them that their love wasn't curing JBP of her low self-esteem, her depression and her despair, and that made her despair more and her depression deepen (which, no doubt, lowered her self-esteem), and it made Romance despair and be depressed too because there was no end in sight, and the upshot was JBP talking about stabbing people and drinking a small boatload of cheap wine (and throwing some of it at

Romance).

Romance moved out.

'I can't imagine my life without her,' he told MSM (Modern Soul Man) (JBP's ex-husband).

'Have you told her that?'

'No.'

He hadn't. He couldn't. He didn't think he should.

Romance had left JBP in misery and feeling abandoned, and he hadn't told her that he couldn't imagine life without her. What he could imagine was a few months apart, during which she would be forced to confront her issues (low self-esteem etc.), to stop drinking and to pull herself together, and during which he too could overcome his own feelings of depression and despair (if not low self-esteem). And he hadn't told her that he couldn't imagine life without her because he thought that their time together had shown that as long as he was there for her she used him as a crutch and wouldn't face up to her problems. Their relationship hadn't made her better and now she had to be forced to make herself better, by herself and for herself, and if he told her that he couldn't imagine life without her then she might rely on that and not do it. He thought this was obvious and when MSM (Modern Soul Man) (JBP's ex-husband) asked him if he had told her that he couldn't imagine life without her Romance thought that MSM must be of the same mind and was just checking that Romance hadn't said such a thing. But he wasn't of the same mind and he wasn't checking. He thought that Romance should have told her and then she might not have been so despairing etc. But he didn't say that to Romance because he was a nice guy, and anyway he thought that it was obvious.

'No, I haven't,' Romance continued.

MSM (Modern Soul Man) made some tea, put on a CD and they watched *Match of the Day* with the sound turned down and that was the end of it.

*Love is…*
*Love is the answer, babe.*
*Let's try it, let's try it.*
*Love is…*
*Love is the answer, babe.* [10]

Romance knew his plan was a risky one, but he couldn't see any other way and, anyway, he didn't think that she could sink any lower. But she did. She went down, deeper still. She drank more. She drank herself into a stupor every evening. She ate lots too, but mainly she just drank. She had never had love and then she had it and now she would never have it again and Romance had left her because she was such a horrible person. She had never really been interested in life, until she met him, and now she hated it.

Sometimes Romance would go to see her, and the quickest way was to cycle over the Itchen Bridge. But it was quite a long rise up to the middle of it and he would have to step off his bike and push it, and when he reached the apex he would pause and look down into the river far below.

Looking into the deep, dark beyond he would imagine continuing his journey and walking up to what was now JBP's door and knocking on the door and no one answering. He would try again. Nothing. He knew that if the light was on then he could peer through the window into the living room, and the light was on and he peered through and there was JBP – the woman he had loved and still did and had abandoned – lying dead on the floor. He couldn't imagine the way in which she had done it, but she had done it. And looking down into the water, he imagined how he would feel at that moment of discovering her.

Obviously it would be horrible. Traumatic. Yes, very traumatic. He would hate himself. He would probably never get over it. It would haunt him for the rest of his life. And it would confirm that he was not a good planner of things, if any more such confirmation were needed. But there would be something final about it that he imagined would be quite appealing. That would be it. It would all be over. He wouldn't have to tear himself apart anymore trying to decide what to do, as nothing could be done. A line would be drawn. There would be some less of life's awkward movement to wrestle with. He knew that he would never do such a thing himself, as however low he sank he wouldn't sink that low, and so there would be nothing for it but to move on. People would feel sorry for him ('Oh, what an awful thing to happen') and that might be quite gratifying because, as it was, he felt that others didn't really appreciate the desperateness of the situation. So he wasn't entirely sure how he would feel and how it would affect him but, in some horrible, horrible way, he was curious to find out. And he didn't feel very good about that.

Freewheeling down the Itchen Bridge through the cool, dark evening air. Then peddling along, legs up and down, and feeling the rhythm of it in his muscles, breathing hard, in and out, and feeling the rhythm of that, and with every breath feeling the cool air fill his lungs. Ploughing his erratic groove through the streets, as people living their lives move around him, walking by and driving by. Knocking hard on the door. Knocking harder, as if trying to beat some life force into the house. Seeing that the light is on. Taking more breaths and hearing them. Peering through. Registering first the peripheral things, such as the wine bottles and the plate of pasta, and then focusing on the woman on the sofa, lying still, eyes closed. Quiet. Chest rising, ever so gently, and falling. In, out.

## 33

When Hippy John woke up on Lee and Lainie's sofa, he wasn't sure about anything. He wasn't even sure that he had woken up. Since the bridge, his awake life had been so dreamlike and his dreaming that night had been so awake-like that distinguishing between the two was tricky. Normally, by remembering his dreams, he would know they were dreams and, by remembering the day before, he would know he was awake, but on the sofa that morning he was struggling. Tentatively, he opened his eyes, and without moving his head he could see the wall opposite and the little marks and lines on it and, slowly, spasmodically, memories of the day before came back. He closed his eyes again.

He wanted to drift back into sleep, but his mind was too much of a quiver. It was shaking with fear. He wished he could dream some happy dream, and he thought about how he used to fly in his dreams, gliding effortlessly, soaring above the house of his childhood, studying the land below. And sometimes he could leap down a flight of stairs or even an escalator on the underground and, instead of coming to ground, the leap would go on and on until it became as stable as something in orbit, and he would feel at one with the movement of the earth and the cosmos, and then he could glide up and hover at will, looking down on the grounded people, totally relaxed, assured and smug in the knowledge of his uniqueness, lapping up their wonder.

'All right?'

Hippy John opened his eyes again. Lee was standing over him. He didn't know how to respond, but it didn't matter. It wasn't really a question and Lee didn't seem to be expecting an answer. He had walked straight past the sofa to the window and opened the curtains and had then walked back and picked up a handful of 45s from the box on the floor. Hippy John looked at him as he flicked through them.

'I'm going to work. Lainie'll be here.'

Hippy John had sat up now. He tried to think of what he should say. He hadn't expected his eyes to open to another day and now that they had he knew that something had to be done with that day – that was the trial of living – but he had no idea what; he hated having to decide what, so what he decided was that he was still incapable of deciding, and he was right enough. He couldn't say anything. He would be talked to and be told what to do and, if either of these two told him to leave straight away and to go out into the middle of the road and lie naked and spread-eagled on the tarmac until he was run-over, died of thirst or was sucked into the earth by the devil, then that's what he would do.

'Later' was all Lee said, and then he left the room and

Hippy John heard him leave the house.

Hippy John was finding it hard to think straight because of the buzzing in his head. It wasn't an audible buzzing, but more a feeling of buzziness – like the kind that arises through stress or depression. It felt to him as if it were some kind of life force that had risen up in him to plague and persecute him. It wasn't a new feeling and to relieve it was one of the reasons he had gone to jump from the bridge. But he didn't feel driven to jump now. He would jump if he was told to, but he didn't need to. He could live with the buzz, for the moment. There were new people in his life and they had brought him to a new place, both physically and mentally, and this newness was enough to live with the buzz. It also marginally increased his pitiful sense of physical awareness. Enough to realise he had pissed himself.

When Lainie came down with baby Aretha, Hippy John was still sitting on the sofa and in his own dampness.

'All right?' she said, and she stopped in front of him and looked at him, and this time it did feel as if it was a genuine question. She was holding Aretha in her arms and gently bouncing her up and down, and this regular movement was enough to distract Hippy John from any answer. Then she noticed the dark wetness of his trousers and on the sofa too.

'Oh... bollocks' was the expletive that spilt out as she stopped bouncing the baby. (If she hadn't had Aretha with her, it would have been a stronger one, but she considered 'bollocks' to be mild enough to be used as a baby-fallback option, along with 'prick', 'twat' and 'arse', all of which she saved mostly for Lee.)

Lainie swore like a builder. She swore like a football fan who is ever disappointed but whose commitment never wanes. Hippy John didn't swear. He didn't swear, even though he had worked as a builder. And he had never been a football fan; he had no loyalties and was aware of it, and so was just left with his own pathetic self.

When Hippy John worked on the building of the Itchen Bridge in Southampton, sometimes he would find himself working on a Saturday and, even though it was a few miles to the ground from the building site, he could hear the roar of the crowd and he knew whenever Southampton scored. And before the match he would see people travelling to the ground. Large groups of young men would offload themselves from the river ferry and they would walk past the site and often they were shouting and singing. Hippy John looked at them and listened to them and it reinforced his feeling of otherness. He didn't look down on them, as his father would. He envied their passion, their camaraderie… their stupidity. He stopped himself. That was his father in him, thinking they were stupid, and he hated that. What's stupid about being happy and belonging and having friends? Was he too intelligent for those natural things? Was his intelligence more than a thing of nature itself? Maybe he was the stupid one because he didn't know how to live and that was despite his good education, which made him doubly stupid. But he was clever enough to know that he could never be a part of that. He wasn't loud or brash, let alone violent, and even if he were allowed to be a part of it he would never feel a part of it. He didn't understand the meaningless of it. He would love to be lost in it, like those others, but it wasn't him, and he didn't know anything like it that was him, and that troubled him. He hated his own class and he hated who he was. He was doomed to be lonely and apart and what's so bloody clever about that? And now he had pissed himself in somebody else's house.

With Aretha in her walker on the landing and the baby gate at the top of the stairs closed, Lainie had Hippy John outside the bathroom and was taking his clothes off.

'You fucking stink. Jesus.'

The hairy man stood, silently, and when Lainie told him to lift an arm he did it, and when she told him to lift a leg he did it, and soon he was standing naked, pale and scrawny, bruised in places, and he felt no more or less self-conscious than he had at any other time since the bridge.

Lainie ushered him into the bathroom and stood him in the bath under the shower. She took the shower hose from its hook and turned it on and tested the temperature, and then she began to give Hippy John, from the feet up, his first wash since neither of them knew when. She couldn't bring herself to touch him, but she held the shower close and she went over him thoroughly and repeatedly, and he moved when and whatever as requested. Aretha bumped in her walker and seemed to be making encouraging noises, and when Hippy John felt the water on his neck and hair he closed his eyes and then it streamed over his face, and if it wasn't washing away his sins it felt as if it was washing away something, and when he opened his eyes the colours and shapes did seem brighter and clearer.

Lainie turned off the shower and left him standing in the bath to drip a little, and then she told him to step out on to the bath mat. She handed him a towel, which he managed to hold, but his attempts to dry himself were pathetic, so she took it back and dabbed at him from a step away and when Hippy John felt the pressure of those dabbing movements he felt Lainie's shame and disgust, but at the same time he felt a caring human touch the like of which he hadn't felt for years, and it was this confused mix of feeling that set him off. It began with a quiet, child-like snivel as he would catch his breath trying to withhold it, but then it was out and he was sobbing uncontrollably and Lainie had to allow him to fall to his knees.

She put the towel over his shoulders and rested her hand on one of them.

'You daft twat.'

And in a minute Aretha was off too, wailing in baby sympathy, and Lainie left Hippy John to go to her and pick her out of her walker. Then, clasping her baby daughter to her shoulder, she went back into the bathroom and sat herself down on the edge of the bath with the two sobbing creatures either side.

She sighed heavily, but the 'Oh for fuck's sake' she kept to herself.

In the late afternoon Lee returned from work, and Hippy John was sitting as he had been, in the middle of the sofa. But he wasn't as he had been. He looked different and he looked strange. His hair fell flatter about him and he was wearing jeans that were none-too-faded and that scrumpled in his lap. His thin, pale shins were comically exposed and he sat barefooted, but it was the sweatshirt that made Lee first scowl and then laugh. It was grey and had red and black writing on the front: *Soul. If you have to ask, you will never understand.* Lee recognised it immediately as his own. Lainie had given it to him as a present once and he wore it about the house.

'You cheeky git.'

Hippy John didn't understand, but he didn't worry about it.

Lee could hear that Lainie and Aretha were upstairs. He walked into the hallway. 'All right?' he shouted, and then he stepped back into the living room and stood admiring Hippy John's new outfit. Lainie came down holding Aretha and Lee kissed the baby fully on the forehead.

'All right,' Lainie answered softly.

They both stood, looking at their guest. There was no talk of Lee's day at work, but then there rarely was. He was a builder and when he was at home he didn't like to talk about it and Lainie wasn't interested anyway. Normally he asked her about her day because he was interested in the baby, but now they just stood, looking.

'You still here then?' Lee jeered, and it was meant more for Lainie than for Hippy John.

Hippy John looked confused, but it was a confusing situation for him, compounded by seeing Lee standing before him dusty and dirty and in grubby old clothes while he sat so fresh and clean. It was a curious reversal.

'I thought you were gonna get rid of him,' Lee said to Lainie, while continuing to look at Hippy John.

'Yeah, well, he pissed himself, the bugger, and while you were pissing about at work I had to bloody sort it all out. By the time I'd done all that I had to sort out Ree.'

'So... what? Is he gonna stay tonight then too?'

'I suppose so.'

They looked at him some more and Aretha squirmed awkwardly in Lainie's arms.

'Hippy, put your left arm up,' Lainie suddenly said.

There was a pause and Hippy John looked at Lainie, but then he raised his left arm.

'Hippy, put your left arm down.'

He put it down.

'Hippy, put your right arm up,' and he did what he was told.

'Hippy, put your arm down.'

Lee smiled and looked at Lainie and shook his head.

'You twat,' he sniggered.

She was wide-eyed and enjoying herself.

'Hippy, put both arms up.'

Hippy John obliged. Lainie laughed and baby Aretha looked at Hippy John too and broke out into a gurgling smirk. Then Hippy John smiled too. It wasn't a big smile, but it was definitely a smile, and it was the first smile he had smiled since God knows when.

## 34

Demetrios Demetriou's mother was an old, lovely, small Greek mother and when Demetrios Demetriou was alive she looked after him at home, stroking his hot, sweaty forehead when his drugs were making him sick, and when he was a child she looked after him at home with his brother and her husband too. She moved to London with her husband when they were teenagers, and then Demetrios Demetriou and his brother bounced into their lives, and eventually Demetrios Demetriou's brother married and moved out, but Demetrios Demetriou stayed at home with his soul records. And Mr Demetriou died, so then it was just the two of them.

And now Demetrios Demetriou was dead and the small Greek mother was distraught. At the funeral, it was cryingly clear how distraught she was. There was the classical chorus of ancient Greek women, weeping and wailing dramatically, but the mourning mother at the front had the lead role. As the soul queue filed past her, between coffin and exit, she cried and pleaded and every recognised face was a catalyst for a new, invigorated outburst. Mick's twitching increased with his proximity to the old woman but Spaghetti was ahead of him, and when Spaghetti stood in front of her he found his faith being tested for the first time. He placed his hand on her shoulder. He couldn't think of anything to say. 'Open the door to your heart' nearly slipped out, because Spaghetti felt it was the kind of thing a priest might say, but he was just sensible enough to keep it in. He moved away. Perhaps a gentle touch alone was the best thing. Yes. And she would feel the power of his faith and that would strengthen and comfort her more than any words could. He was happy with that and walked on reassured, leaving the wailing woman to a barrage of devilish Brummie twitching.

'My son! My son!' she cried, which was confusing for Mick the Twitch, as he had never known his own mother and he thought for an instant that this was his *Surprise, Surprise* moment.

By this time, Romance was at the door to the church, and there he easily recognised Demetrios Demetriou's brother, standing, receiving the exiting nods. He was a slightly older, slightly plumper, shorter-haired version.

'Please call me before you get rid of his records,' Romance said to Demetrios Demetriou's brother. 'It's a very special collection. Call me and I'll help. I know about these records. They were very special to Demetrios.'

Demetrios Demetriou hadn't made a will. Romance didn't know that but he guessed it. He didn't have to guess what Demetrios Demetriou's records meant to Demetrios

Demetriou. He didn't have to guess because he knew what his own records meant to him.

Romance hadn't made a will either. Other than his records, he didn't have much, but by the time of Demetrios Demetriou's funeral he had thousands of quality soul records and their combined financial value must have been equivalent to that of a small house. When he thought about his own death, his biggest fear was that his records would be sold by someone who knew little about them: any member of his family, for instance. If they took them to a record shop, they would receive a tiny fraction of their true value and be sold by numpties who knew next to nothing about soul. Just the thought of it made him sweat and need his brow wiped. Classic soul masterpieces like *The Drifter* being handled as if they were just any other record. His record collection was a carefully constructed entity that had taken many years to build. It was unique, just as he was himself. It emdodied him better than anything else did or could (other than his body). It was his creation and his mark, and he found it as difficult to imagine life without it as a parent might a child. There were days when he didn't play any records, but they were there, with him, and his greatest wish was that they would be treated with respect after his death – with at least as much as his body. In fact, perhaps they should play as important a part in any post-death ceremony. In fact, perhaps he should write a will saying as much: his body was to symbolise his earthly presence and his soul music, his soul.

Before the funeral, Romance had never met Demetrios Demetriou's brother – mainly because the brother wasn't into soul music – but he seemed to be a nice guy. Romance had brothers too and they weren't into soul music either. And there were numerous other brothers of soul people who weren't into soul music. There were the Borelli brothers, who both did have brothers who were into soul music (each other), but they were the exception. The brothers not being into soul music trait was strong enough to show that a soulful predisposition was nothing genetic. It came from neither nature nor nurture and couldn't be explained by environment or peer pressure or other such stuff to which the faux-explainers were forced to resort.

Romance had tried to educate himself on the subject. He was curious. There were people who wrote about the philosophy of music or the sociology of music and they seemed to think they understood it. They prattled on about how one's taste in music was determined by what one was introduced to at a certain age, or the importance of who introduced it, or how certain music appealed because it summoned up certain memories. Of course, for Romance and the others, it was all nonsense. None of it applied. Perhaps such theories held some truth for people who listened to music without any real involvement and whose tastes didn't evolve. But none of it came close to explaining the feelings that arose in him when he listened to good soul music and his own experience showed such theories to be untrue. Perhaps it was possible for Romance to explain why he liked Spaghetti Weston but not the man in the tool hire shop in Southampton, but could he explain why he had fallen in love with JBP? Of course not. And nobody could. Who can predict such a thing? It was a mystery then, where this love for soul music came from. His brothers didn't have it. None of the other boys at his school had had it. He'd had to search for others who had it, as they'd had to search too. And it was an evolving love. There was nothing static about it. His taste in soul music was constantly refining and there was no end to it.

Soul groups were riddled with brothers: The Fuller Brothers, The Smith Brothers, The Wilson Brothers, The Isley Brothers, The Admirations, The Esquires, The Five Stairsteps, The Mandells, The Valentinos, Little Ben and The Cheers, The Soul Brothers Six (but not The Brothers of Soul, The Soul Brothers or The Soul Children and only one of the four sixties soul groups called The Scott Brothers). And then there was Jerry Butler and Billy Butler, Brian Holland and Eddie Holland, Jimmy Ruffin and David Ruffin. Even Sam Cooke and Billy Stewart had soul-singing brothers. But then if soul music were a bottomless pit, even if soul-singing brothers were a tiny minority in the pit – as the Borellis were in the soul appreciators' pit – then their bit of pit would itself be bottomless. And they were of their time and of their culture, which was necessary for performance if not appreciation. And as well as sharing a time and a culture, more often than not, they shared a church.

*Therefore thou didst provide a flaming pillar of fire*
*As a guide for thy people's unknown journey,*
*And a harmless sun for their glorious wandering.*

Eli Ruffin, the brothers' father, was a Baptist preacher, and he was in the habit of quoting the Book of Wisdom. The degree to which his knowledge of the Bible informed the beating of his children is a matter of dispute.

# 35

Romance wasn't a violent man. He wasn't uncommonly scared of violence and didn't run away from it, but he didn't attract it and it didn't attract him. So when JBP became hysterical and began pummelling him about the face, uncontrollably and as hard as she could, he was confronted by an unfamiliar dilemma. What to do? He began by raising his arms to protect himself, which helped a little, but as the attack continued his defences weakened and it became clear that an alternative strategy was needed.

It was impossible to talk to her. She was drunk and hysterical. He could run away, but running would mean leaving her in the house or in the street in that terrible state and he couldn't do that. He could wait, because surely there would come a time when she would tire and calm down, but maddeningly that time kept not coming. So he hit her. Once. A slap.

It was a very calculated slap. It wasn't in anger or even frustration. Romance thought about it very hard and then did it, hard.

In old films he had seen the hero slap the hysterical woman and the shock of the slap brought the hysterical woman to her senses. She would collapse limp and sobbing into the arms of her man or, in that moment of her being startled, the man would kiss her hard on the lips and she would squirm and wriggle for a few seconds but then give in to the wonder of his manly embrace.

JBP didn't collapse limp and/or sobbing and she wasn't startled. She just carried on attacking Romance. In fact, all carried on as before. The slap had no effect. Romance suspected that she hadn't even noticed it. He thought of those Hollywood screenwriters and pondered on their capacity to mislead the public. Ultimately, a more realistic approach might have proved more useful to the viewer. Bastards. As the fists on the end of those flailing arms continued to strike home, Romance decided that this was the worst moment of his life, not because of what he was enduring but because every blow was a violent, horrible demonstration of the torment being endured by this beautiful, wonderful woman, for which he must have been at least partly responsible.

Eventually JBP did calm down. She exhausted herself. She collapsed on the bed, sobbing uncontrollably. And, as she sobbed, Romance sat down beside her, held her hand and felt both sick and empty inside. She began to mumble through her sobbing about what a horrible person she was. He stroked her hot, sweaty forehead. She was the most selfless, loving, wonderful person he had ever met.

'You're the most selfless, loving, wonderful person I've ever met.'

But her tormented mind was elsewhere and she couldn't hear him.

# 36

There was a flash and he was thrown backwards. After the shock of it, whatever it was, he presumed he would come to rest, somehow, somewhere, but, instead of ending, that sudden, bright lurch backwards turned into a floating forwards, back towards the phone box, and then there was some readjustment again as if he were something swinging to a stop, but instead of stopping he floated up until he was about ten feet off the ground, and when he looked down he saw himself lying there on the paving slabs, directly beneath, the rain splattering on his unprotected body. He watched it batter his face.

A woman in an orange kagoule appeared beside Terry's body and then a man in a green one, and they were talking loudly and anxiously in some foreign language. He wondered what it was. Something Scandinavian, he thought. And then a young man came – scraggly hair, dark jacket, tight jeans – and he heard the foreign man say, 'We must call for him the hospital!' and the young man, face wincing against the weather, hurried into the same phone box. The foreign couple were crouching down and touching the soulless body and the woman took his hand in hers and with that he floated up higher, and higher still, accelerating fast – not into the sky, but into somewhere – and instead of his lifeless body he now saw that fabled bright light and he was overcome by a feeling of calmness, tranquility and euphoria. Whatever was behind him was of no interest. He was enveloped by a longing for the unearthly wondrousness that lay ahead, and he succumbed to the purity of it with the core of his being.

Terry had never been religious. He hadn't been taken to church as a child and had developed no religious interests when he was old enough to think for himself. He was vaguely left wing, socially liberal and religiously tolerant but fundamentally agnostic. He thought of himself as a thinker, but as a thinker whose thoughts were rooted in the material world, and that was a good thing, he thought. But in that timeless moment of rushing effortlessly into the light everything changed, and when he woke with a jolt and green kagoule man was over him, hands about his head, he was furious. 'Leave me alone!' he wanted to cry out. 'Get off me! Let me be! Let me go!' But it was too late. He was back in the world and he could feel the hard coldness of it beneath him and the drizzle of it on his face. Before, the purity of the light was everything, but now, back in body, he was being persecuted by the baseness of his senses and by a tickling drop of water on the end of his nose and he couldn't move to get at it. He was taken to hospital and within a few hours had made what the doctors called a 'full recovery'. In fact, he had been transformed, and he was now to choose a life very different from the one that, until the phone call, he had been accepting without any serious question.

## 37

*I'm just a drifter*
*No place to call my home.*
*I'm just a drifter*
*Out in this world alone.*
*I see lovers pass me by*
*I watch them all with a tear in my eye*
*Can't help thinking how lucky they are.* [11]

Romance could only presume to what extent the violence inflicted upon Ray Pollard had affected the singer's life. Obviously, it must have affected his life in a practical way: he was missing an arm. It had been blown off. This was the organised and impersonal violence of war, inflicted at a distance, which exploded into the life of Ray with a crashing, limb-diminishing flash. But he must have battled on to survive the guns, tall buildings and speeding cars of America, because Romance saw him when he was an old man.

It was at a weekender in Great Yarmouth and the white-haired Ray had to have a stool on stage with him. He put so much of his soul into each song that he had to have a rest after each one. And when he sang *The Drifter* the effect on Romance was explosive, all-be-it in a loving, limb-affirming way. The richness of the man's voice rattled through him, and when the song reached its crying climax it filled him and overpowered his senses. It was a direct experience that was beyond the senses, as an explosion might be, or a religious awakening. It made his body feel whole and yet took him out of it. And as a beyond-the-senses, euphoric experience, it gave a taste of some kind of other reality, and to Romance it was like when he was with JBP that first time, when at the moment of ecstasy his earthly senses were so confused that he felt he must have been experiencing something of the hereafter.

For the duration of the song, Romance found himself at the centre of some placeless space. The music flowed through space and must have been made up of physical, spatial bits and yet it came from every direction and no direction and he was at the centre of it. This space flowed towards Romance, as if it had extension but no magnitude. He seemed to hear the flow of pure space – a directionless, matterless, immeasurable space that was an undivided whole, beyond any idea of place – and it filled his consciousness and, because it did the same to everyone else there, it was an inexplicable experience that bonded those present as witnesses to a miracle are bonded or people who have had near-death experiences.

*I see your face before me*
*It brings back a memory*
*Of days gone by*
*Of you and I*
*And then I cry*
*Oh how I cry...*

Romance wasn't listening to a story about a drifter. Romance was that drifter, as much as he was anyone. He had loved and lost and was so much at the centre of it all – a part of the fundamental whole – that he hardly existed.

And Ray wasn't inventing the music; it was coming from somewhere and was flowing through him. And Romance wasn't listening to the music; he was hearing with it.

It was years later when Romance wondered if the placeless place where it was coming from was the placeless place where the non-existence of Demetrios Demetriou existed.

# 38

*Cos once I had a girl by my side*
*A love so strong that money couldn't buy*
*But heaven called*
*And took her away…*
*Out of my arms and left me to wander.*
*I'm just a drifter*
*I go from town to town*
*Just a lonely drifter.*

Hippy John had never had a girl by his side. But he'd had a mother, whom heaven had called. Before her death, Hippy John had never considered how he would be affected were his mother to die, but, if he had, he would have been wrong about it anyway. He couldn't even have guessed it.

The day after Hippy John stayed on Lee and Lainie's sofa for a second night, Lainie was on the phone, trying to dispose of their hairy friend.

'Of course it's an emergency,' she found herself saying, to

one voice and then another, as she was passed from office to office, but mostly it was a number not being answered and she cradled the phone between her shoulder and her ear as she went about her day, washing, changing Aretha, feeding Aretha, sitting with Aretha and watching *Trisha*.

She had started with the council and with social services, and then she was put on to various hostels. But there was a problem. Hippy John wasn't living on the streets. He was living on their sofa. And, even if he were living on the streets, there were no beds available.

'But he's only been here two bloody nights and that's only cos if he weren't here he'd be at the bottom of the bloody Solent!'

And as Lainie persevered, she was in one room and then another and Hippy John sat on the sofa, hearing her (though when the talk grew heated on *Trisha*, the sound of those quarrelling telly people became dominant).

'Right, well listen, where do you live? We'll bring him over to yours and you can have a smelly hairy hippy sleep on your bloody sofa for the rest of your life. What's your address? What's your address? ... yeah, right. And the other thing is, we've got a baby – I'm holding a one-year-old baby in my arms right now. We don't know who this man is, do we? What if he does something to the baby? I'm gonna make a note of this call and if anything happens you'll be well and truly fucked... Oh, there isn't? Well, I think there is. Fuck you!'

She put the phone down.

She sat down on the sofa next to Hippy John. She was cross and upset that she had been driven to swear while holding Aretha. The adult eyes were fixed on the telly. Trisha was berating some young man about his lack of parental responsibility. There were a couple of others on the stage: a thin, gaunt young woman with long, lanky hair and a large, slouching, short-haired youth. Hippy John wasn't digesting what was being said. And he hadn't been consciously processing Lainie's words, but their broad impact added to his already highly developed stupefaction. Before the bridge, he had been persecuted by everything he saw, heard and felt, and the confusing mush of it all mixed with the mush of his thoughts to take him away to some horrible, hellish place; but sitting on the sofa the net result was close to nothing. To Hippy John it seemed an age before the next real words came, although it might not have been very long at all, and they came from the burly young woman next to him.

'Just leave him you… twatting stupid twat!'

Actually, Hippy John got along quite well with small children and, even if he hadn't, he didn't have it in him to intentionally inflict harm on another human being, of whatever size. Sometimes older children would tease him and there had been times when he had been on his patch of grass when teenagers had been out drinking and they had chosen that patch too, and then he had been the victim of some verbal abuse and he might have had an empty beer can thrown in his direction. And then there was the hellish occasion on which he was seriously assaulted. But the little children he liked, and they seemed to like him.

There was a bench on the path that ran across the grass and sometimes he would sit on it, and it wasn't uncommon for a mother to come by pushing a buggy or with a toddler ambling beside and, while the mother seemed to make every effort to avoid eye contact, the child would often look, curious and friendly, and Hippy John would smile in return, making the most of this touching moment too quickly ushered away.

'You're gonna have to go, you know,' Lainie said, without looking at him, as she walked back into the living room and stood in front of the telly. (Hippy John hadn't noticed her leave.) 'I mean, you can't stay here forever.'

She walked out again.

Hippy John was on the sofa and now there were other people chatting on the telly. He was still in Lee's jeans and sweatshirt. He wasn't sure what had happened to his old clothes, but he was settled in these new ones now. When he stood up, the jeans stopped well short of his ankles and Lainie had had to punch new holes in an old belt to hold them up. The top was short on the sleeves too, but Hippy John was as comfortable in his new outfit as he would have been in anything else.

Lainie went into the kitchen and the hairy man stood up. He walked obligingly into the hallway and opened the front door. He hadn't been out of the house since he had arrived and the brightness of the day, dull and overcast as it was, momentarily dazzled him. He paused, steadying himself, as Neil Armstrong must have done before taking that one small step.

'Oi! Where you going?' His pause was interrupted and that turned it into a stop. 'I didn't mean right now for fuck's sake. Where are you going? Come back in you twat.'

He turned and looked at Lainie, not happy, not sad, but ready to be instructed.

'You ain't even got any fucking shoes on.'

Hippy John looked down at his bare feet and, in doing so, he saw too his discoloured old plimsolls, placed neatly against the wall at the foot of the stairs.

'Get back in here. I'll make some tea.'

As he went back to his place, Lainie closed the door behind him.

Later that morning Lainie went out with Aretha, leaving Hippy John alone in the house. There was something about a young family moving to Australia on the telly. Hippy John was taking in more of it now. The man seemed happy with the move; his wife was missing her family and friends at home. It wasn't clear how their differences were going to be resolved, but then the man said that if his wife wasn't happy and nothing was changing, he would agree to move back to England, giving up the lifestyle of which he had dreamt. And, with that, Hippy John stood up and walked to the hallway, and this time he sat down on the stairs and put on his old plimsolls. He walked out of the door, closing it behind him.

Hippy John's first outside decision was whether to turn left or right. He turned left. That was the direction from which they had come when he had been brought to the house. He walked along the street slowly and deliberately, and he felt the light of the day around him. He wasn't happy to be out, but he wasn't sad either. It was something new – his first steps in the world post-bridge – and he faced it with the acceptance and subtle curiosity of a young child.

Lainie, his friend, had talked about hostels and the council, and he'd had experience of them back in Chichester, but not here. He didn't know anything about them here. No, he had chosen to turn left for a reason. He was going to head back.

# 39

*Dear JBP,*

*I don't know whether you wish to hear from me, so it's possible you will never read this. But I wanted you to know that I'm thinking of you and that the strength and courage you have shown is an inspiration to me as I try to tackle my own small problems.*

*I wish that I had some kind of religious faith so that I could at least pray for you. I would pray too that something good will come of all this and that the day will come soon when we can look back on our wonderful time together and smile and laugh instead of cry.*

*I would pray that all the love we have shared would serve to give you strength and hope instead of pain, and I would pray that, at last, now you are proud of yourself, as you so, so should be.*

*R x*

Hmm. 'My own small problems.' He hoped that didn't sound as if he was putting all the blame on her. But he didn't want to belittle what she was going through. Hmm. He would post it. By hand. He wasn't allowed to see her, but he would walk over to the rehab place and push it through the door.

JBP had lasted a year without killing herself, but the time came when something had to be done. She arrived at that place people on TV chat shows refer to as rock bottom. But she was repelled by the prospect of drawing attention to herself. She didn't care for over-dramatic acts. She hated who she was, but she wasn't one for throwing herself off a bridge or anything like that. She would like to have quietly slipped away in her sleep and she was cross every morning when she woke up. But morning after morning she kept waking up, and then when some horrible act of drama began to loom larger (even the thought of which made her hate herself more) she looked for help, and suddenly she found herself in St Bartholomew's House rehab clinic. She was there for six months and wasn't allowed out unsupervised. And she wasn't allowed any visitors without permission and she wasn't allowed to see Romance. But he could write to her.

Romance liked JBP being in St Bartholomew's House. Obviously he was pleased that she was seeking help and that she was receiving help. She had accepted that she needed help and she had opened herself to receiving it, and in doing so she was acquiring faith in some things that were beyond her. This was new. She was allowing herself to be guided by the knowledge and wisdom of other people, even though she didn't know them and even though she didn't know where this knowledge and wisdom came from. And they were telling her to have faith in her own inner strength and that this was a strength that could be nurtured by drawing upon some greater, more profound strength that lay beyond her that was something to do with God or the universe or a collective human strength. She didn't fully understand it, but she didn't care. She had nothing to lose and she was being given hope and – like a hippy sitting on a sofa staring at a wall – she was going to do what she was told. She was beginning to believe that she would be made better and that being made better would be wonderful. Romance already believed that it would be wonderful if she were made better and that she was a wonderful person who deserved to be happy. She was a good woman. But he knew that her being made better wasn't the only reason he was happy that she was in that place. Her being there, and him not being allowed to see her for six months, meant that he had six months free of tearing at his soul trying to trigger a decision on whether to get back together with her or not. Now he had six months during which he didn't have to think about it, because even if he wanted to have her back he couldn't. And it was a blessed relief. He was free as a hippy loose on the streets – to live, to think about nothing and, eventually, to think about other things.

# 40

*Dear* HEAD OF CHANNEL 4 TO BE INSERTED HERE,

*I am writing to enquire about the possibility of making a documentary for you, 'Keeping the Faith', about a very particular English vicar and his love of northern soul music.*

*The vicar in question is a typical country vicar, living in a small village in Berkshire. He has been there for over twenty years and has a loyal and dedicated congregation. But he has a secret passion of which they know nothing – a love of northern soul.*

*Northern soul is a style of sixties black American soul music, adopted by young people in the north of England in the early '70s. It is the rarer, earthier, more underground and more soulful side of '60s soul, and it has a fervent following in the UK. In his area, the vicar in question has one of the most impressive collections of rare northern soul records, and he is a regular DJ at local soul nights and allnighters.*

Romance paused at this point. Too much information about northern soul could become boring for someone who isn't interested in it. This film wouldn't be about northern soul. It would be about the vicar's love of northern soul. By showing the love – of someone as respectable and well thought of as the vicar – Romance could show that there must be something very special about this music, and thereby spread the word in some small way. It would be clear that the music has an uplifting, spiritual effect on the vicar. This could be compared to his religious faith. In fact, *Keep the Faith* is a northern soul slogan.

And Romance had decided not to reveal the name or precise location of the vicar. He was worried his idea might be stolen. He had heard of that happening to the best ideas. He would know nothing about it until one day, sitting down to watch telly, up it would pop, *Keeping the Faith*, his film about his vicar made by someone else. He didn't want to imply that the head of Channel 4 was in anyway dishonest or dishonourable, and he hoped that the head of Channel 4 wouldn't take offence at his reticence in giving too much away, but his letter might easily be intercepted or seen by someone of a lesser stature, and he knew that he had to protect his intellectual copyright.

> *My view is that the vicar would make an excellent subject for a documentary. He is a very engaging character and could become something of a television personality, like the man who climbs steeples. Northern*

*soul itself is a fascinating subject and hearing about it from a country vicar would be a truly memorable experience for the viewer.*

*The interesting juxtaposition of vicar and soul music would be reflected in the form of the film: there will be a static interview with the vicar at tea and then an imaginative use of hand-held camera to capture the actuality of the vicar looking through his records. GVs of the village and of the surrounding countryside will be treated with a soundtrack of hard, driving northern soul.*

Romance imagined the film opening with the village GVs. These were *general views* and meant general, unspecific shots used to set a scene. (Romance knew that the head of Channel 4, if he knew his job – and he had no reason to think that he didn't – would understand the term.) They would be simple, static, carefully composed chocolate-boxy shots. The village wasn't exceptionally beautiful – it wasn't the Cotswolds – but it was still very English and undemonstratively quaint. There was a village shop that was also the post office, with a post box outside, and there were grey stone houses and cottages, and a road with not much traffic. There was a cul-de-sac with some plain, unappealing council houses and at one end of the village there was a plain, unappealing church hall with a big, bare brick wall, but they needn't be in the film. (Any director should have the freedom to make such editorial judgements.) And Romance thought he would add some similarly highly crafted GVs of the countryside. He was aware that this might seem a bit boring, but he was confident that it would be brilliant because of his juxtaposition idea. Hard, driving uptempo northern soul over these GVs, as well as being original and brilliant juxtaposition in itself, would set the tone for the story: the fascinating double-life of an English country vicar.

After this startling introduction, the film became a little vague in Romance's mind. It would have to include an interview with the vicar – perhaps sitting down to tea in his living room. The vicar would talk about northern soul, DJing, drugs, the size of his feet, etc. And then the film would have to show the vicar's record room and all the records. It would be boring if these were just pictures (GVs); perhaps the vicar could be looking through them (actuality), picking some out, playing some and talking about them and, Romance hoped, dancing. If these shots (actuality) were all filmed with a hand-held camera, it would make for interesting juxtaposition with the interview. And then there could be close-up, static shots of the pictures of the churches and perhaps some record labels.

How long should such a film last? It was obviously going to be very interesting. Perhaps he should leave that decision to Channel 4. It might depend on their available slots.

Romance left the letter. He would return to it. He always thought it best to review these things with fresh eyes. Moreover, yet another idea for a documentary was beginning to take shape.

# 41

*In your eyes*
*Where the glow of your love used to shine*
*In your eyes*
*Where my lovelight used to be...* [12]

When Demetrios Demetriou's brother phoned Romance to talk about what to do with Demetrios Demetriou's records, it wasn't the first time he had called. The first time was when Romance was on the top deck of a 23 bus from Ladbroke Grove (Sainsbury's) to Liverpool Street, on his way to the Soul City Soul do. Andy from Southend was DJing and Romance had arranged to meet his friend Solomon in the bar upstairs for a drink beforehand.

Taking the bus had seemed a good idea. Romance had been quite excited to find that there was a direct one from where he was (Ladbroke Grove, Sainsbury's) to where he needed to get to (Liverpool Street), but naturally it went through the middle of London and, even at the weekend, the traffic was bad. As well as beginning to think that he may be late, Romance was beginning to think that perhaps the tube would have been the better option. Or perhaps Ladbroke Grove (Sainsbury's) hadn't been the best place to start from. After all, the reggae shop up the road in Kensal Rise would still have been there the next day and the chances of any other soul nut knowing that the shop had inadvertently received from America, amongst a big reggae collection, a stack of boxes full of seventies soul 45s were slim. Very slim. And, even if they did, what were the chances that they would be able to get at them before Romance could go there the following day? Even slimmer. And he had to return there anyway because he hadn't been able to look through them all, so perhaps he should have travelled straight to Soul City Soul that evening without the Kensal Rise diversion.

All of this, and more, had been running through Romance's exercised mind when he was sitting on the upper deck of the 23 to Liverpool Street but, at the moment his phone rang, he was looking out of the window and down on to the pavement and admiring the legs of a particularly attractive twenty-something girl. She was wearing tight-fitting jeans and as she overtook the bus Romance ran his eyes over her, contemplating sex, romance, marriage and happiness ever after. Perhaps he should run down and beg the driver to open the door so that he could jump off and run after her. After all, his future happiness was at stake, and possibly even hers too. The drivers weren't supposed to let people off between stops, but sometimes a driver would do so, Romance had found, if he explained about the future happiness thing.

But it was at the moment that Romance was looking at the girl and thinking that he would have to make his move – or his chance, the moment and the girl would all be lost forever – that his phone rang. He didn't like talking on his phone on buses because he thought it was rude, but there was only one other person on the upper deck and he or she was some way behind him and, anyway, when he saw who it was, he couldn't not answer.

'Yeah, Mr Demetriou.'

'Hi, this isn't Demetrios actually. It's his brother.'

Straight away, Romance knew. The person on the phone sounded like Demetrios but wasn't Demetrios. He had heard of this person but had never heard from him and he was using Demetrios's phone.

'Oh, hi,' Romance managed to respond.

'Is this… Romance?' He said it as if he had never said the word before.

'Yes.'

'I'm afraid we've got some bad news. We've lost him.'

It was a choice choice of words. Romance wasn't one for euphemisms, but it was gracious of the brother to imply that the loss was a shared one, as he had no idea who or what Romance was and was just making his way through all the numbers stored on the phone.

'Earlier this evening. Things came to a head a bit these last few days and in the end we were with him and he slipped away quite peacefully.'

That *we* was a family *we*, and so maybe the first one had been too. Never mind. We, the family. We the blood family, not we the soul family, nor we the extended Demetrios Demetriou blood family/soul family family.

The brother knew little of the soul family and the soul family knew little of the blood family, and only in Demetrios Demetriou's death was a connection forced between the two. Only in his *slipping away*. Only in his slipping and sliding out of this life, and for Romance a feeling of a memory of years before and the opening bars of Art Freeman's *Slippin' Around with You* and Demetrios Demetriou leaping from his seat and those slippy feet of his slipping and sliding themselves silly. It was the feeling of a memory, somewhere in his stomach, rather than an actual mind-memory. Demetrios Demetriou, slipping around. Demetrios Demetriou slipped away.

As soon as he was off the phone, Romance texted Solomon:

'He's copped it. The bugger's gone and left us.'

# 42

When Hippy John walked out of Littlehampton heading for Chichester, he was alive, but it had been a close thing. And the state of his mind meant that he was both more alive and less alive than most other people. He knew vaguely in which direction to head – at least if he was to stick to the main roads. Up to Arundel, and then left on the A27. It was simple enough for him to do without much thinking and his head was already feeling so cluttered with thoughts. Doing all he could to avoid adding to the clutter could only be a good thing. With thoughts and worries about life and the meaning of it all, the last thing he needed was the extra burden of worrying about whether to turn left or right, or so he thought. It's little things like that that push people over the edge – in his case, quite literally. He had been in tears that morning because, when Lainie had offered him a choice, he couldn't decide what breakfast cereal to have. Now he had to put one foot in front of the other and not think about it, and that all worked fine for as long as he was feeling his way out of the town. He liked pavements because they kept his walking within a narrowly defined path and they pointed the way to go. Left, right, left. In the past, as a young man, he was apt to sing to himself to keep going, to support the rhythm of his walking and to keep other more unsettling things from his head, but he wasn't really interested in music and often it was just a little rhyme – a little chant – that had fallen upon him from somewhere:

*John, John, you've got to carry on*
*You've got to carry on till you get the job done.*
*John, John…*

It was a simple chant with a steady rhythm, which he had found seemed to keep him focused on the job in hand, and as he walked out of Littlehampton he attempted to summon it up, but his feelings of alienation to the world around him were too strong even for that and there wasn't room for it in his head. It was easy to feel alienated and he knew it. The pavement beneath him helped him along, and it had been made by humans, like him, but he didn't know how they had made it, and ditto for the road next to the pavement and the houses and buildings around him. He wouldn't know how to build any of them. He wouldn't even know how to start. And he didn't know how cars worked, let alone know how to make one, and they kept going past on their way to somewhere else. He was a child in this modern world but plagued by an adult mind. The excitement of discovery was gone and what remained was the burden of not knowing and of knowing that knowing – truly knowing – was impossible. And knowing that others were grown up and OK with it all just made it even more depressing. He was ever impressed and depressed by the grown-up-ness of other grown-ups, and he knew that there was little solace to be found in the natural world or in what seemed to be an infinity of time and space – or some bending space-time – pressing down from above, so he didn't look up and wasn't tempted by the sound of an aeroplane; he had fallen into that flying metal trap before. No, he had somewhere to go and didn't want to be stuck by the side of the road like a weird hairy pillar of salt. John, John. You've got to carry on.

Hippy John's legs dutifully carried him on and out of the town and, beside the road, buildings succumbed to trees and bushes. But to Hippy John, as he was then, such botanic structures were no less oppressive. He was no more a part of nature than he was of modern man. So when he saw a sign coming up for a footpath – off to the left, in the direction he knew was right – the temptation to take it was nothing to do with the call of the wild. The confines of the pavement were gone and, being forced to walk on the road, he missed the restriction of it, and those cars going somewhere else buzzed by him like angry birds attacking out of nowhere. He turned on to the path to keep things quiet and simple.

He began to skirt the edge of a large expanse of manmade nothing that was a field and he had to hug a barbed wire fence to get round it. But then the path dropped down through some woodland and for the first time in a long time he felt he was somewhere that hadn't changed much for centuries, and it was this feeling of being somewhere more constant, rather than being a part of nature, that gave him some comfort, and for the first time since Littlehampton he felt comfortable enough to sit down.

There was no obvious place to rest. With some difficulty, he chose a little grassy incline in a little clearing. He picked up a leaf and considered the intricate design of its veins (although he didn't know if they were designed or if really they were veins). It looked like a map of a river and its tributaries, and the edge of the leaf was the edge of the river basin. He looked at it not with curiosity but with pure sadness because, even though he was trying not to think, it was sad knowing there was no point thinking about it even if he wanted to. After all, he didn't really know what leaves were or why leaves and trees even existed or why they were green and what did *green* mean? (Or brown, in this case.) What he did know was that no one really knows what light is – whether it's a wave or made of particles of stuff – and no one really understands anything fundamental about matter and energy, such as what these fundamental particles and bits of energy really are and where they come from, and he only had his eyes' and fingers' good-for-nothing word for it that leaves and trees existed at all. But no one except children seemed to care. Scientists were becoming better at describing things and processes, big and small, but there was no explanation for anything. Where did their laws come from? Whenever he heard anyone trying to explain anything, really they were just describing, not explaining. He had read something when he was a young man about the nature of photons (or rather our lack of knowledge of…) and about why light of differing wavelengths should appear to us as the colours they do (who the f*ck knows?) and about how all our senses are the result of electrical impulses in the brain and the world must be a very different place to a bat. His father had journals containing articles about such things and Hippy John used to dip into them when he knew he wouldn't be seen. (Showing an interest in anything remotely connected to his father would have caused him acute, if not chronic, embarrassment.)

He wasn't thinking in such detail when he was sitting in his little clearing, but he felt the oppression of not being able to take for granted the reality that confronted him. He knew that all he had ever experienced and would ever experience could be the result of sense data being fed to him by some super-powerful demon, or the result of a fiendish experiment devised by an evil scientist who was feeding Hippy John's brain electrical signals via some complicated computer programme while his brain was being kept in a vat. Alternatively, it could well be possible that some superhuman descendent of Hippy John's was reliving the experience of being one of his, her or its ancestors, by connecting his, her or its own brain to some similarly sophisticated computer programme. But why would they pick him? Had all the other ancestors been taken? Was there no escape button? Where was it? Sitting in his little clearing, he wasn't thinking about that either, but it was in his head somewhere. He had used to wonder about such things. Experience had kicked the wonder out of him, even before those young lads on the green in Chichester had kicked the shit out of him.

So he tried not to think and to take some comfort in the stillness and constancy that surrounded him, but then in trying to take comfort in that he found himself thinking again, about how everything he could see and feel was made up of tiny bits of matter that were whizzing about at ridiculous speeds and that the earth and everything big was whizzing about too and everything would change, utterly, sooner or later. No wonder his brain was filled with buzziness. He was being persecuted by this persistent motion. Where did it come from?

And then he heard a noise that rooted him to the ground in fear, as he seemed to relive those frightening moments before his assault. Something human-scale was moving towards him. The hearing before the seeing. It was a noise that was the type of footstep-type brushing noise that a person would make if coming down the path, and in those few seconds between hearing and seeing, as his feeling of alienation was surpassed by fear, his mind was unable to keep that awful memory at bay. But when the seeing did come, it wasn't like before, and it came as a shock.

A young boy emerged on the path, young and

unthreatening. He was probably no more than twelve years old, fairly dark in his complexion and with hair a little lighter than his skin tone would suggest. He was shocked too to see Hippy John, but not unpleasantly so, and as he confidently strode by he caught the funny-looking man's eye and showed that he wasn't afraid. When, a little further on, he turned to look back, it was not with any worry that he was being followed, but it was to give a sign that he wouldn't mind if he was, and Hippy John felt compelled to accept what to him was tantamount to an invitation. He put his palms flat on the grass and pushed himself up.

As Hippy John followed the boy down the path, the sound of casual, childish humming-cum-singing drifted back to him. When inclined, the boy looked back and gave a skip, happy to have something new in tow and something so rare and exotic at that. For the course of the short walk Hippy John was prized, and as such kept a respectful distance. For someone else it might have been like a dream, but for Hippy John it was no more like a dream than anything else, and the boy was young enough to feel the same; so the strange pair both looked upon their novel relationship with a simple acceptance.

Out of the little wood and round a little field, alongside a hedgerow they went. The further they continued, the more of a thrill it was for the boy, who was now smiling whenever he looked back. Hippy John was making the boy smile by just being himself and by putting one foot in front of the other and there was no one to stop him. To the corner of the little field and the boy dropped out of sight, and when Hippy John reached that spot on the path and followed it down and round a corner, he could see the path running away from him down across a scruffy, nettled green to a little church and its village beyond. He couldn't see the boy.

# 43

Romance was riding up an escalator in London the first time he saw the blond girl. He almost didn't see her because, as an experiment, he was standing still, looking down at the step in front of him, seeing how easy it would be not to raise his eyes until the step began to drop as it approached the top. Actually, it wasn't difficult. Really, he should have seen the experiment through but, having determined it wasn't difficult, he looked up, suddenly appreciated his place in the movement of everything, and then saw her going down on the other side.

It was like when he saw the girl from the bus but more so. These moments happened and some moments were more momentous than others: glimpses of people who might transform his life. And then regret at not leaping to the look. Love passing, beckoning, and if it wasn't love but just some girl in some jeans then the not knowing was painful and was an affront to love itself. The soulful thing to do would be to embrace the moments, whether transforming or not, and Romance was haunted by his failures to do so.

The blond girl had a striking, short, crisp haircut and her hair was almost white. She was beautiful and had big eyes and was standing, poised and elegant, and then Romance felt the drop of his step beneath him and he had to turn to step off the escalator. He stepped aside to let those behind him pass and he wondered what to do. He told himself he had to think quickly or the chance would be lost. Then he told himself the chance was probably lost already, just in the time it had taken to tell himself that he had to think quickly, and by then obviously it was even more likely to be lost.

He went to the down escalator and hurried down it. He would compliment her on her hair. At the bottom there was the choice of north or south platforms and he hurried from one to the other but couldn't see her. There was a mass of people on both platforms and she was probably on a train by then anyway.

## 44

'Men profess to be lovers of music, but for the most part they give no evidence in their opinions and lives that they have heard it.'

That's why Romance liked Solomon. He said things like that.

Solomon was taller and quieter than the others and, while most of these young, southern soul types (hairy Greeks aside) had a relatively smart, leftover mod look, Solomon was passionately and unconsciously non-descript. He hadn't found soul through the mod scene. He was a few years older and, if soul hadn't always been with him, it had been with him since he was old enough to walk out of his door, go to the youth club on Mirwood Road on a Friday evening and hear the occasional northern soul record added to the mix of seventies dance anthems.

'Henry David Thoreau,' continued Solomon.

'Eh?' said Romance.

'He was an American. He campaigned against slavery. He said that.'

'Oh.'

They were in the pub. Soul City Soul was in progress in the cellar bar.

Solomon was good at quotes. He had said one by Beethoven once, which had stuck with Romance, about music being the link between the spiritual and the sensual. (Ever since then, Romance had had a soft spot for Beethoven and thought he was probably the kind of tortured soul who would have been into soul music if he hadn't had the misfortune to be born Before Soul.)

It felt right that they were upstairs. They had been thrown into a state of mourning. So they sat apart from people enjoying themselves and above them and yet close enough to be in touch. If the spirit of Demetrios Demetriou was hovering about in the ether, eventually it would gravitate towards the soul music and would find them. And periodically one or other of the soul folk from downstairs would come up and sit with them.

'He had good taste, Demetrios. I remember watching him dance to *Lonely Girl*. He felt it, didn't he?' had been Tony Davis Two's personal tribute and possibly the first time Romance had heard him talk about anything other than a record he had just acquired. 'There's a record. I nearly had it, you know, a couple of years ago. I've got a Willie Pickett on the way. The one on Soul Spot. It's a bit more northern sounding than the Eastern one.' His little sales box was on the table between the beers. The boys steadfastly ignored the box and were silent until he went back down.

'Demetrios Demetriou. A man with long hair, some half-decent records and an idiotically good nature.'

'Demetrios Demetriou. Ridiculous name. True to his soul.'

'It's not easy being true to your soul. He did pretty well though, didn't he?'

'Yep.'

'The boy's gone. What a plonker.'

'He's up doing some fancy floorwork at the big allnighter in the sky.'

'Cloudwork.'

'The big foreverer!'

'Here's to him.'

They drank to their departed friend. It wasn't until the next day that the grief welled up inside Romance and he burst into tears.

# 45

Once the boy had gone, it was harder for Hippy John's mind to be distracted from the time and space within which he found himself. It was beginning to rain, growing dark and cold, and he found that he was tired and hungry. The path went to the church so that's the way he went too, and when he walked along the path, as when he had walked along the path into the wood, he was painfully aware of the thinness of the line he was treading, with all that eternity in front of him and behind him and all about him and now without the boy or anything else on which to concentrate. Even the scale of everything he saw was oppressive – it was all such a minute slice of everything that must be, even at that one moment – and he lived in terror of the smaller as well as the bigger. He would have been more comfortable in an age when such bigness and smallness was unknown and when the heavens turned but weren't expanding and time was as cyclical as the circular groove at the end of a record.

In the porch of the church it was dry, at least. He sat on the ledge in the porch that he thought was probably for sitting on (but wasn't sure), and his pale shins protruded in front of Lee's jeans and his old plimsolls protruded in front of them.

He hadn't reached Chichester and had nowhere to sleep, but he wasn't overly concerned; after all, some grass and a bench were all that awaited him there. Even if he was to sit in the porch all night, he didn't consider it any more of a problem than any other act of living. The physical distress was no more to endure than living itself – in fact, significantly less so. What was the worst that could happen? He would die of over-exposure? Well, he wouldn't mind if he did. It's true that he had felt the benefit of being alive while in the company of the boy, but in his experience that was a very rare feeling. There would be worse ways to depart this life than with the memory of that feeling fresh in his mind. So he sat in the porch, waiting for whatever was to happen to happen and feeling as at home as he did anywhere sitting on and within the aged stone. He didn't know how long he had been there when the woman came.

# 46

The Mount Sion Baptist Church is an old building, relatively (being in America). It has a well-kept lawn in front and is on a wide, sunny, palm-lined American boulevard. In December 1963, the week before Christmas, the gospel singer Bessie Griffin was close to performing there at Sam Cooke's second (LA) funeral but, when Lou Rawls sang *Just a Closer Walk with Thee*, she was so overcome that she had to be carried out of the church. With the encouragement of the crowd, Ray Charles stepped up to take her place. Apparently, his rendition of *Angels Keep Watching over Me* had men in tears and women fainting. It was eight days after Sam had driven his shiny, new, red Ferrari across the city to the Hacienda Motel (rooms: $3 per hour).

When Demetrios Demetriou's brother phoned Romance for the second time, it was a few weeks after the funeral. Romance wasn't on a bus. He was sitting, at home, thinking about what it would be like sharing motel rooms in America with Steve Davis. The brother was calling about the records.

'I'll go round and have a look through them,' Romance said, and the following weekend he was ringing on the bell with Spaghetti Weston, and the canine Soul Sam was at their side.

'This is all right,' Spaghetti said, looking about before the door was opened. 'Very nice, very nice.'

Romance looked at him. It was a small, dreary terraced house in a small, dreary terraced street in some small, dreary part of west London, but Spaghetti was a man who was easily impressed and that was just one of things that Romance found so impressive about him.

'Oh yes, this'll do for us, won't it Sammy boy?' Spaghetti continued, as if the purpose of the visit was to establish whether Spaghetti and Soul Sam were prepared to take the place of Demetrios Demetriou as son and dog-son to the elderly Mrs Demetriou.

The elderly Mrs Demetriou opened the door. She was all in black with a silver chain hanging from her neck and with a silver *D* hanging from the chain. As she opened the door with one hand, she was caressing the *D* with the other. She looked wretched.

'Oh, yes, oh, come, come,' she said, before she had noticed Soul Sam, and she began to say 'Oh my son, oh my son', which had become her mourning mantra, but in the middle of it the low and skulky movement of Soul Sam distracted her.

'Oh my son... ohhhhhhhhhh.'

She didn't like dogs, even the goodlooking ones, and the

ugliness and nonchalance of Soul Sam struck her devilishly. They all came to a pause half way through the door and while the old woman froze, fixing her stare on the ugly mutt, Soul Sam stood patiently, a step ahead of Spaghetti, as if he was so used to this reaction it simply bored him.

'It's a dog,' she said, questioningly.

Spaghetti had never grown accustomed to other people's reactions to Soul Sam, and it always took him by surprise that his lovely, one-eyed dog wasn't welcomed with adulation wherever they went. In this case, he was doubly surprised, as Demetrios Demetriou's mother had momentarily welcomed Soul Sam as her son. Perhaps she took Soul Sam to be the reincarnation of Demetrios. Yes, there was a slight resemblance. Demetrios was a goodlooking lad.

'This is Spaghetti,' Romance said, touching his friend on the shoulder and expecting that introductions would ease the situation. 'And this is Sammy.'

Romance bent down to pet the uninterested dog in an attempt to show the old woman that the dog was friendly. It wasn't something he enjoyed doing and the dog-eye viewed him suspiciously. Spaghetti looked at Mrs Demetriou, caught her two human eyes and smiled, and then he whispered earnestly, 'Soul Sam,' nodding as he did so as if the words were wonderfully revelatory.

Soul Sam. Mrs Demetriou had heard of Soul Sam. Her son had often talked reverentially about this icon of soul music.

Mrs Demetriou knew in an instant that any explanation

was beyond her, and she had already found that one of the advantages of being bereaved as well as Greek was that she could allow herself to be overcome by Hellenic grief, thus freeing herself from any need to partake in rational thought. In Greece, dogs were dogs. Here they were introduced as people, revered as soul icons and accompanied their owners to look at records. But the mere implication that there was some justification for the presence of the ugly mutt was enough for her to overcome her prejudice. And she trusted Romance.

She ushered them in. 'Oh my son, my son,' she said, to none of them, and a knowing Brummie glance caught Romance's eye and, with a wicked smirk, Spaghetti nodded from Soul Sam to the old woman. Romance gave a quizzical look in return.

'My son! My son! He gone! He gone!'

Mrs Demetriou had lived in London for thirty years and was secretly proud that her English had come along so well. She was able to express her grief at losing her son so much better than she had been at the loss of her late husband. When he had died, all she had been able to muster, in English, was 'Yeh, bye bye. Husband. Huh.' (The stream of Greek was between her and her maker.)

Romance was now worried that she was about to start wailing. He hadn't been expecting it and had never had to deal with a wailing Greek before, of whatever language proficiency. But it was Spaghetti who rose to the occasion.

'He is at peace,' Spaghetti ventured, in a voice calmer and

more serene than any Romance had heard emanate from him before. The bright-eyed Brummie had decided that, whether the old woman thought her son was dead or was his dog, it was the moment for his newly-found spiritual self to come to the fore.

'No, no. He gone!'

'He is in a better place.'

'No, no. He dead! Dead!'

Romance took a hesitant step towards the living room. He thought that the conversation might benefit from being moved beyond the hallway. The old Greek woman was thus spurred into more ushering.

It was a small room, the living room, of mismatching floral patterns – wall, carpet, sofa – and cold. There was no central heating. But the national lottery was on the telly and Dale Winton was emitting a warm glow. Soul Sam stood and watched as the humans, predictably, sat down.

'He used to go to Wigan, you know,' Spaghetti commented, looking at Dale.

'What?'

'He's an old soulie. I've seen him out a couple of times.'

Romance didn't reply but was momentarily saddened by this reminder of the lack of quality northern soul celebrities for media or creative types to call upon. (Apparently, that bloke with a moustache off *The Antiques Roadshow* was into it too.) Steve Davis was as good as it got – of that he remained assured. There could be no *Looking for Romance (with Dale Winton)*. No. Soul was a serious business.

He turned to the woman in black.

'We've come to look through his records. We thought we could help you decide what to do with them.'

'He gone. He gone!'

'He was a very good friend.'

'He was a good dancer too,' said Spaghetti.

'Oh, my son.'

Spaghetti nodded, raised his hand and made the sign of the cross as if he were the Pope.

'It was a wonderful funeral.'

'I no cry. I very strong. For him. The funeral, I feel like crying, very much. But no. I strong. Very good.'

Romance thought of all the weeping and wailing at the funeral and wondered what it would have been like if she had let herself go. And when Dale started talking about bonus balls he thought it time to move matters on again.

'Shall we go upstairs?'

'Ooh matron,' added Spaghetti.

'To look at the records?'

'Oh, he gone. He gone, my son. I no go. His room, I no go. I can no go.'

'Well, we'll go up there and have a look, and then we can talk about what can be done.' Romance rose to his feet. Soul Sam looked up at him and then to Spaghetti.

'Yes. Go, go.'

Spaghetti stood up too and, for some reason known only to him (and there could be some doubt about that), he bowed his head in a courtly manner.

The two friends walked to the stairs. Soul Sam followed them to the bottom and then watched them go.

Romance knew the way. He had spent many hours sitting with Demetrios Demetriou, playing records in his bedroom.

Soul Sam returned to the living room and lay down. The old woman and the dog waited, eyeing each other cautiously.

# 47

The woman who came to clean the church that Hippy John had stumbled across was fundamentally a good woman. She was about the same age as Demetrios Demetriou's mother but as English as can be, and she was good and confident through being so much a part of the landscape. She was the kind of woman who, if she came across a man in ill-fitting clothes sheltering in the porch of a church, would engage him in polite conversation as a way of tactfully and respectfully ascertaining the degree to which he was in need of help; so, when she came across Hippy John sheltering in the porch of the church that she regularly and voluntarily helped keep clean, that's exactly what she did.

'Oh, hello,' she said, when she saw Hippy John. 'It hasn't turned out so well today, has it?' referring only to the weather.

Hippy John looked at her, wondering if she was psychic.

'No,' he said.

'Why don't you come in? Have you seen the inside? It's a lovely little church, you know.'

She pushed the door open, which had been unlocked all the while.

Hippy John paused, wondering at the small, old woman and the large, very much older door that was bending to her will. As she went in, she turned round and extended him a reassuring look, as the boy had done, and he pushed himself up and followed her in.

It was a lovely little church and it had that dank, lovely little church smell that seems to come with centuries of shared worship. The high nave afforded space and gravitas, and the small, golden cross on the altar shone out through the simple starkness of it. It was old. Everything about it was old. Apart from the notice board inside the entrance:

*God is... warm.*
*Down in the mouth? It's time for a faith lift.*
*Kindness is difficult to give away. Because it keeps coming back.*

'Norman.'

Hippy John looked round, expectantly.

'Norman, mostly,' the old woman continued, 'but it's likely there was a church here even before that. Lovely windows.'

Hippy John had paused by the font.

'I was baptised in that font,' the woman continued. 'Ha! Imagine that! Well that's what I was told anyway. I doubt you'll find anyone around today who can vouch for it.

Dorothy Margaret. Ha! What were they thinking? Soul. If you have to what?'

She was trying to read Hippy John's sweatshirt. Hippy John looked down. He had no recollection of what it said. She looked closer.

'If you have to ask… you won't understand it.'

She paused in thought and then looked up into the face of Jesus. At least, in that instant, that's what she saw. A shiver went through her. She collected herself. It probably wasn't Jesus. It was probably an unkempt, lonely tramp with long hair, a beard and world-weary eyes. But she had been shaken and suddenly felt on trial.

'Right, I'm going to get on with my cleaning.' She was carrying a plastic bag, which Hippy John only noticed when she started to pull things from it. 'We take it in turns, you know. Although, between you and me, sometimes I think… well, let me put it this way, these pews seem a bit more dusty than they should be and let's just leave it at that. Here, you can hold the bag and follow me round.'

She had always been one for confronting her fears and, having taken out polish and a duster, she handed Hippy John the plastic bag. He watched her set to work. He didn't think to help more – he was quite overcome with the responsibility of carrying the bag.

The old woman didn't believe that Hippy John was Jesus. That would have been silly. But she did believe that he could have been, however unlikely that was. She believed in Jesus and in God, otherwise she wouldn't have been cleaning the church pews, but she didn't believe in them 100%. Maybe 95%. (The vicar seemed to believe in them about 99%, but she didn't understand that.) And in the same way, she was about 99% sure that this man wasn't Jesus. Why would he be? Maybe 99.9%. But that remaining fraction of a percentage was crucial. What were the chances that she, as a human being, should exist in the first place and be alive, there and then? So slim as to be almost unbelievable – she had seen it on telly – and yet there she was.

'So where are you heading? Where are you going to sleep this evening?'

Hippy John looked blank.

'It's getting on, isn't it? And it's not too pleasant outside. This village isn't really set up for visitors. It's a shame. It's not so much that there's no room at the inn but that there's no inn. Oh, and where I live is no good anymore. It's funny, isn't it? I mean, you come into this world with nothing and leave with nothing, we all know that, but when you're old you know it's like being like a child, not just because you might need looking after and lose a bit of the old grey matter but you end up in a small room with just a few things about you. It's the time in the middle when you have the space and things to offer.'

She regretted saying it at once, because this man plainly had nothing.

'Oh, but don't you worry. You'll be OK, one way or another. You can stay in here if it comes to it. I'll see you're OK.'

She had another quick look at his sweatshirt.

'I mean, it's me who's got the key, isn't it? The vicar likes me to lock up behind me but I do forget, you know, accidentally on purpose, shall we say. I mean, the church was never locked when I was young. Couldn't imagine such a thing. In fact, you know what, we used to have an old fella live in here. Gus he was called. He had nowhere else to go. He used to actually live in here – bed down at the back there every evening. I do remember there was this one time when everyone turned up on a Sunday morning as usual, for the service, and Gus wasn't quite with it that morning, and he got up and everyone was there and he said, "What are you all doing in my house?" I'll never forget that. The vicar was none too happy. Made me laugh though. Although it's not really funny is it? No, shouldn't laugh. Still, you have to sometimes. Anyway, it was his house, really, wasn't it? I think Jee...,' looking at Hippy John she struggled with the name, '...sus would have liked that. But I've got the key now. That's what I am – the key lady. It says so on the door if you'd noticed.'

Dorothy Margaret carried on cleaning and Hippy John carried on holding her bag for her and, when she finished, she said, 'That'll do.' She took back the bag and put the polish and the duster back with whatever else was in it.

'You just wait here. And if anyone asks, just tell them that Rose said so. There's a loo and a basin through there if you fancy a wash.' And with that she made to leave, but she turned again to Hippy John while she was still close.

'And what's your name then?'

It was the first question she had asked him for which she waited for a response, and she was quite frightened now to hear his voice. And, for some reason, he was frightened to use it.

'John,' he said.

And as Dorothy Margaret – or whatever she was called – walked to the door, she felt the eyes of John the Baptist upon her, as the last of the day's light shone through the sainted stained glass window.

Hippy John was left in the emptiness of the church, and he felt the reverend, old, three-dimensional space of it on him and around him. Scientists were now telling him that there were nine spatial dimensions, of which not only was he unaware but of which he could never conceivably be aware, and that the vast majority of matter in the universe was completely unaccounted for. He tried not to think about that. But it was difficult not to think. When he was a child, his mother had once told him to go and sit down and to try to think of nothing – to try not to think. He had tried very hard, but it was very difficult. Now the old woman had said to him to wait, so he would wait. He didn't know what he was waiting for, but, carefully, he didn't think too hard about it. He sat down on one of the pews. It had been a long time since he had sat in a church. He had a vague memory of childhood Christmases, but this church was more evocative of something deeper, beyond his memory, and he felt regret that his associations of being there were so limited.

Now another stranger had showed some concern for him. He was aware of that. But he wasn't clear whether such concern was due to the individual, the place, the time or something else. And any feelings of gratitude were bound to be suppressed for as long as death seemed even remotely appealing. And there was Jesus, dying, and there were saints all around, dying, and they were all Godly and saintly and noble. And there were worthy memorials to worthy dead people, and there were happy angels and the other good stuff of heaven, and all this was so old that it was easy not just to take comfort from it but to feel the appeal of it too.

He didn't know how long it took to come, but eventually he heard the door open. Before he turned, he had the terror of imagining the strange footsteps and what might be, and then when he did turn he was almost praying to see the old woman. But there was no woman. Instead, there was the angelic young boy who had met him on the path. The boy was looking at Hippy John and smiling as he walked in, and his arms were piled high with what Hippy John immediately recognised as bedding. Without seeming to take his eyes off Hippy John, the boy walked to old Gus's corner and deposited his load. Then he left in the same fashion. But before Hippy John had a chance to go to investigate the boy reappeared. Now he was carrying a Thermos and a plate of food – a thick sandwich and some fruit – which he laid carefully next to the bedding as though he were making an offering, and then he left, smiling excitedly.

Hippy John went over to inspect, nervously, all that had been presented. A couple of blankets. A sleeping bag. A pillow. A plate with a rim that was gleaming in the fading light and on it a shining apple, a radiant banana. A thick, high, hand-cut sandwich. He reached out and touched the warm Thermos. This was better than Christmas, as far as he could remember.

## 48

'This is a good 'un.'

'What is it?'

'Spencer Wiggins. *Lonely Man.*'

'There's a few here, isn't there?'

'The Turnarounds. *Can't take no more.*'

'You know I first heard that here. He loved that record. And the other side.'

The two friends had pulled out a couple of boxes and were flicking through records randomly. Demetrios Demetriou, being Demetrios Demetriou, didn't have them in any order, and there were thousands of them.

'How are we gonna do this?'

'Dunno.'

'We're gonna have to write them all down.'

Spaghetti was studying both sides of a rare Clarence Reid 45.

'I thought he was just into stompers, seeing him dance and all that. There's some good stuff here, in't there?'

'He's got that Icemen record on Ole-9 here somewhere.

And have you heard the other side of that? *What Would It Take to Get You Back* – version of The Manhattans. Brilliant. It might even be the original version. I dunno.'

'That's worth a bit, init?'

'There's a Kell Osborne here too somewhere.'

But there was one record Romance was most anxious to find and that was the Romance Watson. He wanted to buy that one himself. Maybe he couldn't afford it. They would have to have it priced somehow. But ever since first hearing it in that same bedroom all those years before, he had wanted a copy. He would be happy with the official release, but it would be weird and wonderful to have this curious test pressing, not just because it seemed that it was a mega-rare one-off but because it was his friend's find and it was the first one he had heard. He would give it a good, appreciative home. And it should be there – Romance Watson, on that strange do-it-yourself label – somewhere in that room.

The records were stacked high on shelves and were in an assortment of make-do cardboard boxes and small plastic crates. They were all in excellent condition.

'They're all in good nick. He was fussy like that.'

Romance paused and had a look about.

'Fuck,' he said, consideredly, and he wasn't one for swearing.

'Maybe we should put them in some kind of order.'

'Fuck.'

They heard some shuffling on the landing. The two friends stopped talking. And then there was a muffled voice.

'I can. I can go in.'

Romance deduced from the tone that she meant 'I can't'. He stepped through the doorway with a bunch of records in his hands. The old woman seemed to see the records before she saw him.

'Oh! Oh, those little ones! He liked those little ones so much!'

Romance was stuck for an appropriate response.

'Yes. We're just sorting through them. Just to see what's here. You mustn't throw them away.'

'Oh, the little ones! He liked the little ones!'

Spaghetti was now by Romance's side, trying to show him a copy of the Soul Communicators that he had just come across. The old woman was holding on to the rail at the top of the stairs.

'Oh yes, those little ones. When he go, I go see him. In the place. His coffin. He there, inside, my son. I put some in. I put some with him. I know he like very much.'

'In the coffin?'

'Yes, yes. In coffin. Some the little ones. He like very much.'

Romance looked at Spaghetti. Spaghetti looked at Romance.

'Fuck,' they both thought.

They spent the rest of the afternoon going through all the records then going through them all again. The Romance Watson wasn't there.

'Fuck, fuck, fuck!'

# 49

Helping Romance sort through Demetrios Demetriou's records wasn't the only reason Spaghetti Weston ventured to London that weekend. And DJing on the Saturday night at the D-Town Soul Club in Dagenham wasn't the only other reason. He had a third and most important reason. On the Sunday morning he had somewhere to go.

Spaghetti hadn't told Annie about his thoughts on becoming a Greek Orthodox priest. He was fairly sure that priests were allowed dogs, but he wasn't so sure about female partners. He knew that depended on the denomination, and so it was something he would have to look into, as well as whether there were strict rules about digging up dead people (in extreme circumstances). He hadn't yet decided on his course of action if he found one or both of these to be forbidden.

And it was a crisp autumn morning, that Sunday morning, and Demetrios Demetriou's mother was all in black, as she had been since her son's death, and her silver *D* was about her neck. She was a regular attendee of the Greek

Orthodox church in West Acton and, as a bereaved mother, the services had become more poignant for her. Late that morning, she walked out of the church and into the sun and was only half-aware of the courtesies and consolations being paid to her by the other elderly exiting Greeks. She had one thing on her mind and that was to get to the grave of her son; she visited it every day and she felt it fitting that on Sundays she go straight from church, and it was because she hurried herself away that she just missed the young Brummie and his age-unknown companion as they arrived at the church from the other direction.

Spaghetti had meant to make the service, but they'd had a late night. He had woken up at some indistinct time on a friendly soul sofa with Soul Sam on the floor beside him, and then they had taken the wrong bus. When they arrived at the church, there was a gang of elderly Greeks milling about on the pavement, and in the door of the church stood the tall, lean, bearded, wide-eyed, elaborately robed Donald Sutherland-looking priest. He was talking to a small, suited, heavily-bespectacled elderly gent, who was bending his head up to converse or perhaps just to keep his glasses on.

Because of the importance of the matter, Spaghetti wasted no time in approaching the priest, and he stood between the conversing Greeks like some kind of height-translator, with Soul Sam at his feet as if to take care of the lower ground. The Greeks looked at them both, rather perturbed by Spaghetti's smiling – a feeling enhanced in the priest by an uneasy notion that he had encountered this queer-looking fellow before somewhere. He wasn't Greek, that was for sure, and of non-Greeks he had long-since learnt to be cautious. In him, they saw something strange and eccentric, and he took those looks as evidence of their own strangeness, as well as Godlessness. And he was doubly suspicious now, ever since that visit by those two folder-wielding men from the Inland Revenue. They had suspected that, somehow, the priest had been supplementing his income. He would be happy, he had said to them, to give to Caesar what was Caesar's, but the Queen, as a constitutional monarch, had no right to expect such privileges. It was a clear point and well-argued but, by the looks on their official faces and the tone of their official voices, he had been expecting and fearing a return visit. But the one-eyed dog? Was he being physically threatened?

'All right?' Spaghetti ventured, in response to the confused and worried looks. The flowing Greek coming out of the small man with the resting glasses tapered away. Spaghetti didn't look like a man from the revenue, but the priest couldn't place him and he had come to believe they could be truly wily, if not devilish, in their ways. And even if the dog was not to be set upon him, it was a cunning psychological ploy.

'Hello,' the priest said, in his best English.

During the extended pause that followed, Spaghetti smiled upwards and downwards and was met by fearful, wide-eyed and goggle-eyed looks from each direction. Spaghetti being Spaghetti, he took these looks as a warm embrace.

'How's you doing? Y'all all right? Bit parky, init?'

After a little more looking, the tall, bearded one gave a slow nod. His pilled-up six o'clock in the morning face was nothing new to Spaghetti, who didn't give it a thought.

'I've missed the do then?'

The priest tried to smile, but he wasn't really the smiling type. He didn't know what Spaghetti was talking about.

Spaghetti leant towards the taller man as if drawn to the priestly authority of the beard.

'But I would like to talk to you.' He opened his eyes as wide as the priest's and gave a subtle nod that sent a shiver through the priest's long and holy bones. The smaller Greek slipped away.

'You probably recognise me from when I was here before. I felt we had a... connection.'

The priest was now as startled as he looked.

'Something happened to me that day. I found the whole occasion very moving.'

Spaghetti paused to reflect upon it. The priest thought he was being given an opportunity.

'It has been a very quiet year.' He looked round anxiously to ensure that none of his departing parishioners were within earshot. 'You know, the money we raised for the church is so little now.'

Spaghetti continued. 'I thought to myself, should I not be more upset? I mean, most people, in those circumstances, in that situation, would be very upset. That's just normal, init?'

The priest nodded, frightened by the degree of empathy implied. There was something menacing about it. It was as if the head of the mob were gently caressing a loyal servant before shooting his head off.

'So then I got to thinking... why wasn't I more upset? I mean, I get more upset,' and he began to whisper, 'just thinking about Soul Sam shuffling off his mortal tail.' There was a pause. 'I mean, you know... passing on. Deceasing this life, as we know it to be. Or not to be.'

Deceasing this life? Who was this strangely-spoken Englishman? Surely to speak in such sinister whispers wasn't normal for a man from the revenue. He must have gone bad. A corrupt one. And he's going to want paying. But can he really have so cruelly disposed of this Solsam man? Another priest, perhaps. Surely not Solon of Samos?

'Solon of Samos?'

Spaghetti nodded. After all, that could have been Soul Sam's Greek name.

Now the priest's long bones began to ache with fear. Was this the devil before him? Satan could have sensed some weakness in his faith as a shark smells blood and had come now to eat him up, a hideous Cerberus at his side. Or perhaps he was being tested – the strength of his faith tested by all that is great, pure and good. His creative accounting had seemed such a little thing at the time, but the subsequent elaborate water feature that had sprung up in the vicarage garden plagued him with guilt. The sound of the tinkling water, which was supposed to soothe his soul and remind him of the sparkling mountain village of his childhood, teased and nagged at him like a fiendish eastern torture and now, when he looked at this strange apparition of a man before him, he didn't know if he was looking at God or the devil.

'And then I realised,' Spaghetti continued, 'I was happy. Not ha ha happy but deep down happy. Because I knew that death wasn't the end. Although it might be for Soul Sam – I'm not so sure about that – but I knew there was more to this life than life, if you know what I mean.'

The priest didn't know what he meant. He hadn't the faintest idea. And he took his not knowing as an indication of his weakness and vulnerability.

'So now I want to be a priest. Like you.'

'You want to be priest?'

'Yes.'

The man who was a priest wondered how he might be expected to respond.

'I am priest.'

'Yes.'

'You are Greek?'

'No.'

'No?'

'No. I'm from Smethwick.'

'Smediks?'

'Yes.'

At that moment a car went past and with it a shout from

an open window.

'Ello love! Nice dress!'

Spaghetti turned, stood up straight and stuck two fingers up.

'Before I become a priest, I do have a few questions though.'

'Questions?'

'Yes. I mean God, who is everywhere, right, is everywhere, at once, but he can also come to you, can't he? Or is that what the Holy Ghost is? Or how do you know when a ghost is the Holy Ghost? Or is it just a head thing, so it's not actually seeing anything, just a feeling, like? Because, you know, I do get a feeling sometimes. I suppose that's why I'm here really.'

The priest looked at Spaghetti mournfully. He missed the certainties of his youth and the understanding he'd had then for all that was around him.

'And there is one other thing. When someone's buried, I know it's just the body, like. But they do get a cross and that. I mean, is the grave, like, a holy thing? If for some reason a grave needed to be dug up a bit and maybe opened, would that be OK? If there was something important in that grave that needed to be got out? Not the body though but maybe something else? Is there, like, rules about that?'

'Are you police?'

'No, no. Oh no.'

The priest had to think quickly. He had never been tested like this before.

'When a person be buried, he should be at rest. Rest in peace.'

'Hmm. Yes. And I wouldn't like the idea of anyone digging up Soul Sam, I know that, but what about on *Time Team*? They dig all kinds of people up and recover all the bits and pieces that were buried with them?'

The priest didn't answer. He didn't know what Spaghetti was talking about.

'Do you think if you're one of the ones in favour of digging people up, for a very good reason, like, like keeping alive the best of human culture and artistic whatnot, that that means you can't be a priest?'

'Perhaps.'

'Hmm. It's a dilemma, isn't it? Can dogs go to heaven?'

'Hm?'

Spaghetti was whispering again. 'Can dogs go to heaven?'

Donald Sutherland was fairly sure about this one. He shook his head.

Spaghetti looked startled. The priest looked more startled.

'And there's no exceptions to that rule? Surely God could make exceptions if he wanted to?'

'To go to heaven it is necessary to have soul. Animals do not have soul.'

The priest was on firm theological ground here, and he knew he should not be tricked into deviating.

But Spaghetti was alarmed. He knew that his dog had soul. That's why he had chosen him. And that's why he was called Soul Sam. Perhaps, he thought, if he was to become a priest, he could reopen this debate within the church.

'And what about the rights of ex-stepdogfathers to see their ex-stepdogs? Would the church have a view on that?'

Spaghetti took the blank expression as an expression of no view.

'So anyway, to take this further, how would I go about it, like? What's the next step? Is there lots of paperwork or something?'

'Papers? You want see papers?'

'It don't have to be now. Stick something in the post.'

Spaghetti gave him his card. *Spaghetti Weston. Keeping the Faith.*

'If I don't hear from you, I'll just come back and badger you.' Spaghetti tapped the priest on the arm and winked. The priest shuddered. 'We could come back next week, if you like, if you need time to get things ordered.'

'Hm?'

'We'll come back next week, won't we Sammy boy?' and Spaghetti gave Soul Sam a loving rub on the head. 'And we'll be earlier next week, so we can come to the do. We were only late today cos it was D-Town Soul last night and we got a bit lost too, but we know where we're going now. Soul Sam's got a very good memory, you know.'

The conversation had become no clearer for the bearded holy man, and he was none the wiser about the identity, human or otherwise, of the two beings before him.

'You come back next week?'

'Yes, if you like. And earlier. For the service, like. See how it's all done, proper.'

'No dogs in the church,' the priest said timidly. Perhaps the strange man before him would be less sure of himself without the devil dog by his side. And if this was a further test, he should stick to the church rules. No animals in the church.

Spaghetti looked at the priest. The priest stared back. Soul Sam did nothing.

The priest almost expected the devil dog to balloon into a giant, snarling, ravenous beast, looming over him, jaws gaping, so it was a huge relief to him when the nothing continued, and then continued to continue.

'You should think about that,' Spaghetti said seriously and after a long pause. He raised his eyebrows and nodded at the priest, as if to reaffirm the point.

To Spaghetti, this poignant moment seemed an appropriate one at which to depart.

'Anyway, I can see you're busy. I'll catch you soon. All right? Come on, Sammy boy.' The pair set off, continuing away from the direction they had come. 'Ta-ra then!'

The priest watched them go. Then he looked at the card again. *Keeping the Faith*. Solsam – horrifically badgered, no doubt, whatever that meant. He felt sick. And busy, the man had said. He looked about. All his parishioners had long since disappeared and the road and pavement were empty. But he knew that the man – or whatever it was – was right. He had a lot of thinking to do. He went back into the church, walked to the altar, knelt down and prayed properly for the first time in what had been too, too long.

# 50

Hippy John woke early, but then he was used to that. Sleeping outside, it's difficult to escape the natural rhythms of the day. And in the little village little church, the morning after he had met the angel boy and the old woman Rose – or whatever she was called – the morning light streamed through the high, holy windows, illuminating the dust-filled church-space and stroking Hippy John from his rest. He had dreamt but, in the confusion of this dreamlike awakening, he lost the dream and opened his eyes to a day no less strange. He was alone, but being in the old church he felt a part of something and the loneliness felt not unnatural. He lay awhile, thinking of whatever he could, but when he got up it was sudden and without thought. He folded the bedding as best he could and drank the rest of the tea, which still had some warmth to it, and on the stone slab that had supported his sleeping body, now free for the inspection of any hippy standing over it, was an aged inscription just a little bit younger than the ever-sleeping body beneath:

*For our time is a very shadow that passeth away*

And as a shadow himself, Hippy John slipped from the stone, and he went to sit on the rear pew, where he was aware of the kindness that had been shown to him and was appreciative of it, and by way of thanks he stood up and went to place the empty Thermos as neatly as he could on the empty plate, which was next to the neatly folded bedding. When he left the church he was curious enough to pause on the little path and turn and look back on it. The building looked absurdly lovely and it almost roused a smile.

Away, and down the small lane Hippy John tramped, and he was like a proper, traditional tramp, tramping from doss-house to doss-house. He knew that by one way or another he would arrive back in Chichester that day, but he also knew that nothing would be the same. He had wanted to die and had been stopped from dying and now, feeling the weight of himself on the road and the cool morning air in his lungs, he wanted to live. He wasn't happy – far from it – but now he was curious enough to want to experience what life had to throw his way, and one of the first things was the rumbling of a giant tractor looming at him through the still air, and when the monster machine came into view it was as much a marvel as anything. And an excited bird shot across the lane behind it.

Hippy John wondered about the angel boy – who he was

and what he was doing – and he wondered about the old woman – who she was and what she was doing – and by the time he reached the edge of Chichester he was wondering about Lee and Lainie too. And then he wondered what he would say if anyone else asked about what was written on his sweatshirt. He wasn't used to being asked questions, but now he would rather have an answer than not.

'It's a kind of music,' he would say, 'and it's about the soul.' That would do. But, if pressed, he could say, 'Some people like it but you wouldn't know from looking at them.' Hippy John felt comfortable that morning, wearing the sweatshirt, as it made him feel part of a family, even if he didn't really know what soul music was or what it meant to have a healthy, loving family.

# 51

Terry Gibbs had heard soul music before religion found him. Once a month, a young man who went by the peculiar name of Bobby Boogaloo hired the function room above the pub for an evening of what he called 'Vintage Soul and R&B'. There were several occasions on which Terry had been in the pub on one of those nights and twice he had worked behind the upstairs bar. Mr Boogaloo seemed pleasant enough and it was a good-natured crowd – smart young mods who were too cool to cause any trouble – and Terry found the music quite inoffensive too. He had been a young man in the sixties and, like all his peers, he was familiar with the classic Motown and Stax sounds. Many of the other records seemed less refined and there was nothing that particularly moved him, but then music wasn't an important element in his life. And he had never had any strange hobbies or obsessions; the closest he had come to that had been a brief flirtation with birdwatching on the Medway estuary, but that came to a sudden end when someone pinched his binoculars from the back of his moped on the A289.

But Terry's relationship with music changed abruptly and completely at the soul evening following the out-of-body experience at the Cutty Sark.

He was already a different man in a multitude of ways. He felt that he had been in the presence of God and what he regarded as a spiritual awakening had transformed too his relationship with the material world around him. He was overwhelmed by the intensity of his perceptions. *Seeing* that bright light didn't describe the experience he'd had properly; it was more that he had experienced the light, but then experiencing an experience didn't explain much at all. He was moving towards it and yet had been enveloped by it. It was beyond him and yet he was a part of it. The movement was everything but all was still. There was no way of explaining it. It was beyond our earthly perceptions and it was beyond explanation, and Terry took this confusion of the senses to be a glorious taste of heaven.

And being thrown into an acute awareness of the limitations of his human senses and now sensing a spiritual dimension – a further plane, an otherness – seemed to exaggerate the three-dimensional character (the reality/the unreality) of all that he now saw, as everything's place within time and space seemed nothing short of miraculous. Sounds, too, were more embracing and more vibrant. Perhaps this was something of the unknown world of the newborn baby before bitter experience thrashes out a difference between the perceived and the perceiver. Nothing was still; everything was moving and working towards some heavenly goal. And he was only just beginning to determine how he might fit into all this when the Vintage Soul and R&B night came round again and he heard *If it's All the Same to You Babe* for the first time.

He might have heard the song before. He hadn't really taken in any of this music on previous occasions. But this time it wasn't only as if he had never heard the song before, it was as if he had never heard music before. The sound of the opening violins resonated through his body, stirring something deep inside him, and he felt the rhythm with his whole being. When the richness of the vocals launched in, he was suddenly a part of the music. Passive listening was to this experience what standing in a church holding a candle is to flying through the ether into the light of God.

> *Got to have your sweet, sweet charm*
> *Take me in your loving arms*
> *I need you*
> *I want you*
> *Got to have you*
> *If it's all the same to you babe.*
> *If it's all the same to you babe.* [13]

The understatement overwhelmed him. The smooth, rough texture of the vocals. The sweetness of the music, the hardness of the beat. The pain of the man, the unadulterated joy of it all. The tension, the conflict – the resulting movement, the resulting oneness. How could something be so exact, so precise – have such a flowing order to it that was so blatantly right and correct – and yet be invisible, intangible and not a part of the material world? He had never been moved by music in this way before and it was a revelation. He seemed to hear it in three dimensions (at least) and, as when Romance heard Ray Pollard singing *The Drifter*, the singer was with Terry and a part of him and he had a sense of the space of the music as he'd had a sense of the space of God.

*I can't take these heartaches*
*I know I'm gonna lose my mind.*
*Understand, I'm a lonely man*
*And I need you all the time.*

Unlike Luther Ingram, Terry had never loved a woman. But he had now experienced what he took as God's love and he could empathise with the singer, as without God's love he could no longer live. There was a before and an after, and it was impossible to go back to the before.

When he woke up in his flat the next day, he had never been more excited about opening his eyes to the world. He couldn't remember walking home. He must have walked home, but he couldn't remember it.

Of course, at the time of its release, Luther Ingram's song sank without trace, and another young man from a gospel family remained destitute on the streets of the big city.

# 52

For days after he heard the news about Demetrios Demetriou, Romance was in a state of shock. Everything was different and there was nothing he could do about it. The rhythm of his life was broken. The rhythm of life was broken. It was as if he and everyone he knew – perhaps even the rest of humanity – were each notes in a melody and now one note had gone – one key on a piano – and the whole melody was ruined. Simply walking down the street was different. Everything was strange and he was divorced from it all. He always had music floating about in his head and now, as he walked, he sang it, quietly but aloud – simple riffs, random lines from random songs repeated and joined randomly together – forcing a constant rhythm, as if he was trying to reconstruct or recapture the life rhythm. And he walked determinedly, left, right, left, right, and when he wasn't walking his fingers tapped and his foot tapped. Everything had changed as much as it had changed when JBP had told him that her heart wasn't in it anymore. Some soul-love-life thing was broken. Everything was as different as a dream, in which things are recognisable but not the same. The lyrics of songs punctuated his thoughts; maybe there was no recapturing going on and it was the rhythm that was enforcing itself.

*The taste of madness that your lips placed on mine*
*Has turned to sadness in such a little time.* [14]

*If it's all the same to you babe.*

*I was born to love you*
*You were born to tear my heart apart.* [15]

And when he dreamt, he dreamt music too. He dreamt soul music and it was original, wonderful, perfect and pure. It came to him as he slept, but he had no musical training and no way of capturing it and, as with any dream, he couldn't retain it properly in his mind when he woke. But when he dreamt it, he listened to it intently, dissecting its components, marvelling at the unpredictability of the bass and the drums, the subtlety of the harmonies and the pure, rasping soulfulness of the vocals. This was original and brilliant music and it was spilling from his mind, complete and perfect.

'Heard melodies are sweet, but those unheard are sweeter,' said Solomon. 'But don't tell Soul Sam.'

'Bollocks,' said Deptford Dave. 'It's probably just a load of shit that you think's good when you wake up but isn't.'

But Romance knew that it was more than good. It was beyond good. And it was coming from somewhere very deep or somewhere outside, beyond him. It came down to the same thing. And if it wasn't proof of the existence of God, it was proof of something.

## 53

Terry Gibbs suddenly found himself believing in things that he couldn't explain, but he felt it better to be roughly right than precisely wrong. An awareness that there were forces at play seemed to be what was important, as well as a willingness to embrace the journey even if the destination was unclear. He was filled with anticipation for his spiritual journey and for his soul journey too.

Bobby Boogaloo informed him that Luther Ingram was northern soul and that if he liked northern soul he should join him on his next trip to a northern soul night. And that was the start of it: frequent trips around the country to hear this revelatory music. He was older than the other devotees but he didn't care. He immersed himself.

And he soon realised that there was a vast amount of this music waiting for him to discover, and the more he discovered, the more opened up before him. It was endless. He had more money than the others and could buy more records, and the more he knew the more he became aware of the depth of his ignorance. He was humbled yet excited by it, as he was by his religious experience. He came to appreciate that he could spend many lifetimes dedicating himself to soul music, and yet still not know it in any fundamental sense. And when he listened to a record, it seemed to poke fun at him for his not knowing. It played with him like a lover, challenging him to predict, toying with his anticipations – giving, withholding, giving, teasing. Giving enough to satisfy while still surprising. Delayed gratification. Suspense. And he loved it. And as he became more familiar with the various styles and the ploys of the music, the anticipation became all the greater and the relationship more intense. He looked back on his days before soul, when he heard the music but it meant nothing to him, and he thought of his old self as a savage hearing the word of the gospel but not hearing it, or as a Chinaman, divorced from all Christian cultural references, seeing the cross as a cross – as two bits of wood or metal or whatever – without any of the transcendental meaning that the symbol carries for even the most irreligious westerner.

Through his church, Terry developed a taste for medieval church music, which was designed to take the listener closer to heaven by delivering an auditory experience beyond earthly expectations. Chorus of heavenly angels etc. But it was through secular soul music that he was taken closest to heaven. It touched him as a saviour touches a sinner. It gave order to an intangible world. The juxtaposing, conflicting elements came together in perfect harmony. And the nebulous, immaterial space that had filled Romance's consciousness when he heard Ray Pollard sing now flowed into the vicar's unconsciousness and was given order by music. It was an order that depended on the dynamic qualities of the music and it was that sense of order that he felt. It was a pure order – a feeling and not a thought – and far beyond anything he could explain even if he had begun to think about it. And somewhere beyond his consciousness, somehow he felt that the placeless, ordered space could have been the same immaterial space within which he had found himself hovering, looking down upon his wretched, bloody body lying by the phone box.

# 54

*To be loved is my only destination, baby
And you're my every, every inspiration.
If it's all the same to you babe.*

Terry Gibbs was rosier and balder when he came to own that rare 45, and he was rosier and balder still when he came to play it at the Southside Soul Club anniversary night, as Terry 'the vicar' Gibbs. Among those on the dancefloor were his new, young soul friends, Romance and Demetrios Demetriou.

*I need you... I want you baby... Got to have you...*

Demetrios Demetriou span. He dropped backwards to the floor, one arm raised in praise. He bounced back up and launched into a handstand. Change from his pockets scattered across the dancefloor and it was only a little dancefloor so not much of it was spared.

It was a little dancefloor in the middle of an otherwise

carpeted social club in which chairs outnumbered people by about three to one. 'South Turbinton Rugby Club,' said the sign at the entrance. 'Nothern Soul Berks' said the handmade banner hanging behind the decks.

The vicar was the special guest DJ, and so Romance had been keen to attend. He had been reviewing his letter to Channel 4 about *Keeping the Faith*. The letter didn't seem long enough for such an important film, but he couldn't think of what else to add. So he had thought it might be a good idea to witness the vicar DJ in action. Thelonius Tripp had come along too and was at the side of the dancefloor sketching. (He didn't yet have any Southside soul paintings in his collection.)

Romance helped Demetrios Demetriou pick up his change before that particular event could be captured for posterity as a part of an original Tripp.

Luther Ingram, then Freddie Chavez. He was one for the stompers, this vicar, and Romance wasn't as fit as his friend.

'Bloody hell, I need to sit down.'

Demetrios Demetriou joined Romance at a table from where they could watch both the vicar and the artist at work.

'They're both fucking mad.'

Perhaps they both were, Romance thought. But then if the world's a mad place, maybe that's the only sane way to be. (He imagined Solomon saying that; it sounded like a quote.)

The other punters were local soul folk who all knew each

other, and there were only a couple Romance recognised from soul dos in London. As usual, they were 80% male and, as usual, there was a disproportionate number of balding heads and black loafers. There were a few women there, and there were a couple of attractive girls who seemed unattached, and there's nothing Romance would have liked more than to have a dedicated soul girl, but this was before he met and split up with JBP and so was before he became brash and bold about approaching women. And at northern soul dos it really wasn't the done thing. The women came out to dance and enjoy the music, not to be chatted up.

Demetrios Demetriou hadn't noticed the girls. But he had noticed a solitary male figure standing at the bar.

'You see that guy at the bar?'

'What?'

'You see that guy at the bar?'

'No.'

'That guy with the dark glasses.'

'Yeah.'

Romance did see the guy at the bar with the dark glasses. He had seen him as they had come in and had wondered why he was wearing dark glasses inside. He had presumed he was just a bit of a twat.

'He's blind, isn't he?'

'Is he?'

'Yeah. He's from round here somewhere. He was up at Cleethorpes. And you know what?'

'What?'

'He was looking through records at the record bar.'

Freddie Chavez finished. The vicar shouted something enthusiastically over the mic, but the mic was awful and no one could understand a word.

'Maybe he can understand, with his enhanced powers of hearing,' Demetrios Demetriou said of the blind man.

'Well not if he can see. He can't be blind to everything apart from records. He's trained himself to see them, has he? Or is it just anything small, round and black?'

'Yeah, records, and bowling balls. And Billy Stewart.'

On came *It's a Heartache* by Little Charles and the dancefloor was alive again. But Demetrios Demetriou was determined to continue.

'You know what I heard? Someone told me he can actually smell the records.'

'Well I can smell a record. A dusty old styrene one anyway.'

'No, I mean, he can smell what they are. Or where they're from – where they were pressed.'

'Fuck off.'

'And that's what he does when he flicks through records, cos he only collects Chicago.'

Romance looked at his dopey friend. He didn't know if he was being serious.

'The only ones he can't smell are the ones from Philadelphia. But that's how he knows they're from Philadelphia.'

'Who the fuck told you this?'

(He'd had a bit to drink and these were exceptional

circumstances – hence the swearing.)

'I can't remember. I think it might have been Fudge from Slough. I think that's where the guy's from.'

'For fuck's sake. Well he can't smell that well otherwise he wouldn't be living in fucking Slough.'

'Well maybe he can't smell Slough either. Slough and Philadelphia.'

The opening bars of Major Lance *You Don't Want Me No More* had the boys on their feet again and the blind man stepped on to the dancefloor too. Romance and Demetrios Demetriou looked at each other. Blind man started dancing. And he could dance. He did have his own style, but his balance was good and he wasn't bumping into anyone. Perhaps everyone else was subtly making way for him. In fact, there was another guy on the dancefloor who was being more of a nuisance. He wasn't blind, or at least not visibly so, but he danced with his eyes tight shut, his face scrunched up and contorted with emotion as he mouthed the words to the record:

*You don't want me no more!*
*That's what you're saying.*
*You don't want me no more!*
*I've got to keep on praying.* [16]

The vicar loved it and was singing along too. He was irritated that he had to interrupt himself to cue up the next record.

Terry had been happy to see the boys walk in. He took it as a sign that Romance was still interested in making the film and that he had performed appropriately at the vicarage. On arrival, Romance had had a quick word with the vicar about the film, but there wasn't much to say. He didn't have any news, as he hadn't posted the letter yet. He refrained from telling the vicar that he was on what is known in the business as a *recce*, as he didn't want to put the vicar under any undue pressure that might inhibit his DJing performance. However, the vicar, who was keen to become a celebrity – for the good of both his Lord and the music – saw that it was his opportunity to make a further impression, and he DJed with as much clerical panache as he could muster. He pictured himself as the DJing vicar equivalent of the man on telly who climbs up steeples.

When Major Lance finished, blind man easily found his way back to his place at the bar and eyes-closed man opened his eyes and walked away grinning. Romance and Demetrios Demetriou went to the bar for another drink, standing close to the sightless subject of their curiosity.

'You know some blind people,' Demetrios Demetriou continued, 'when they hear music, they see colours. I did hear that somewhere. So when they dance, as well as hearing the music, they dance to the changing colours.'

'Isn't that just called a nightclub?'

'No, you know what I mean.'

'And what if the sound system's crap?'

A record came on that Romance had never heard

before, but Demetrios Demetriou was straight on to the dancefloor. As much as the vicar was there to DJ and Thelonius Tripp was there to draw, Demetrios Demetriou was there to dance. Romance was there to observe and, anyway, he didn't like dancing to a record he didn't know. (He did so occasionally, when he couldn't help himself.) It was awkward not knowing the breaks and how the music was going to unfold, and he was also convinced that it took multiple listens to properly appreciate any decent record. But everything he had heard was inside him somewhere and when he danced he danced to that, and his musical memory – his own musical store – was growing rapidly.

Romance was glad he had made the effort. He always enjoyed soul dos anyway and it was especially exciting going somewhere new. The appeal of this music among these people never ceased to amaze and thrill him. The South Turbinton Rugby Club. The Southside Soul Club. Southside Chicago meets southside small town Berks. The vicar moved and enthused and Romance thought about the film. Really, it should include the vicar in action, DJing. Perhaps he could be filmed in a small venue like this, but one made to look busier and more atmospheric (for the good of the music). And the vicar could be filmed giving a church service too, and then the film could cut between him giving the service and him DJing. That would make for wonderful juxtaposition. Romance was excited by the idea and he determined to add it to his letter. And then all he would need to do for the letter to be ready for posting would be to find out the address of Channel 4 and name of the man in charge of it.

Demetrios Demetriou returned to the bar, slightly sweatier than when he had left it.

'What was that?' Romance asked.

'I dunno. I've got it on a tape somewhere.'

The vicar raved, unintelligibly.

'He's well into it. Look at him go. Alleluia!'

The boys watched the vicar finish his set and hand over to one of the balding, black-loafered types. He closed the lid on his record box but left the box by the decks, as he was going to be on again later. Then he stepped down awkwardly off the little raised platform.

'It's true. He does have big feet.'

Largely, Thelonius Tripp had been left alone to work on his drawing. No one had paid much attention to him. But the vicar was keen to see how the budding young artist was progressing. He was proud of his collection of cathedral etchings and so considered himself an artistic type. So, after accepting some enthusiastic accolades from what looked like a diminutive bank manager, he edged round the dancefloor to the shoulder of Thelonius.

'Yes, yes, that's really interesting. You seem to be capturing the spirit of the thing.'

The sketch was in charcoal and its stark, ethereal quality did give the work spiritual overtones. The room seemed bigger and grander – more like a ballroom – and the contorted dancing figures looked enraptured. Another observer might have seen something devilish about it, but the vicar tended to see the best in artwork as well as people.

Thelonius Tripp couldn't hear him. The music was too loud. But he had seen the vicar approach and had watched him try to say something.

'Hm?'

'You seem to be capturing the spirit of the thing! I like the pain on her face!'

'Yeah, she's really into it!'

At the back stood the man in dark glasses. Thelonius Tripp had picked him out because he looked symbolic, although he wasn't sure of what.

'Is it true you can smell where a record comes from?' Romance asked the blind man.

'What?'

'When you're looking at records, can you smell where a record was made?'

'What?'

The blind man could hear Romance well enough. He just didn't know what he was talking about.

'When you're flicking through records for sale, is it true that you can tell, by their smell, where a record was pressed?'

'I don't know.'

'Oh.'

So the issue remained unresolved and Romance retained his doubts, which were significantly heightened at the end of the night when he saw the blind man get into a car and drive away.

'How are we going to get home?' Demetrios Demetriou asked Romance.

'Fuck knows.'

It had been a fairly typical soul night out.

# 55

Hippy John found his way back to Chichester without any problem. He didn't feel that Chichester was his home (he hadn't felt at home anywhere since he was a child), and he didn't even truly feel that he knew where he was. He just knew where he was more than if he were anywhere else.

He had a night in the shelter and he had a night on his patch of green, and he queued at the soup run for a sandwich and a hot cup of Christian charity. He did all the things that he would have done before, but his relationship to them was different. Before, he had felt detached by an extreme sense of unworthiness. Now, he was detached too, but due to a feeling of being something more than this. Before, he wasn't grateful for the soup, because he didn't like the person it was feeding. And he hated himself still more for surrendering to the instinct to eat when really he just wanted to wither away. Now, he looked into the eyes of the young man serving him and not only was he grateful but he wanted to put his replenished strength to use. All it had been good for before was giving him the energy to climb to the apex of the bridge. Now he wanted to find a life worth living.

'Here you go, soul brother,' the young man said.

Hippy John knew the young man was making fun of him, but he didn't mind. In fact, he was happy to be noticed. And he wondered if the young man might be one of these soul people. A part of the soul family. He could be. You can't tell by looking at them. (He wasn't. He was a longhaired IT student who knew next to nothing about soul music.) So when Hippy John took the soup, it was with a degree of kinship. It was good to feel less anonymous, but it meant he couldn't hide as easily.

Before, he was ashamed and wanted to die. Now he was ashamed and wanted to do something about it. The green where he sat and slept hadn't changed, but it wasn't the same place. He was still belittled by the age of the walls and the natural wonder of the grass and the bushes, but now there was inspiration to be found in them. 'You're alive now. It's your time,' they said. 'Get out. Do something.'

So those days back in Chichester weren't comfortable ones, but Hippy John was excited by the change. Before, the buzzing in his head was the rhythm of life taunting him and he wanted to free himself of it. Now the buzzing was the excitement of life. He couldn't quite work out if he was depressed or not. He wasn't happy – that was sure. But he didn't want to die; he wanted to live. Perhaps he was still depressed. He was certainly still in a mess. But he was curious about it.

He didn't know what he was going to do. He didn't know what was going to happen. But he knew that it would be good.

# 56

Nearly dying, and then being rescued, and then being given a new outlook on life by someone or something inside or outside oneself is, probably, to most people, like being born again. (Hippy John wasn't a religious man. He was just a man. He was just a man called John, who to Lee and Lainie looked like a hippy.)

The soul vicar was a religious man – otherwise he wouldn't have been a vicar – and he had been ever since he had been struck outside the phone box. He had seen the light. And when he thought of the distant, pulling, within and without, enveloping light, he thought again of a newborn baby but this time newer still, because it occurred to him that his experience might have been like that of a baby witnessing light for the first time, and then he was happy to have thought of *witnessing* rather than the useless *seeing*. It really was as if he had been born again and he was a wondrous infant before the greatness of it all, and it was because his relationship to the world around him had changed so profoundly that he became religious and became a vicar, and it was because he became a vicar that he was handed overall responsibility for a church, and with the church came a church hall, and with the hall came a big, bare, exterior church hall wall. The big bare wall overlooked a little, grassy children's play area, which had been designed to make the village more child-friendly and thus to attract young families to the village. (The vicar's village wasn't alone in supporting an increasingly aged population. Ironically, it was the village's aged population that gave the play area its keenest adherent: Gerald, the village drunkard.)

There was some excitement when Mr and Mrs Pritchett moved into Tubbs Lane with a couple of small children in tow. And then there was some disappointment when their own climbing frame and slide appeared in their large, drunkard-free garden. Still, the little, grassy children's play area had something that the large Pritchett garden didn't have (apart from a drunkard) and that was the big, dark, imposing, bare-brick wall overlooking it. This gave the parish council an idea and an inspired one at that: a mural. They would commission a mural for the big bare wall that would draw the Pritchett children from their drunkard-free garden and into the village play area and thus into the view not only of Gerald but also of any passing young families on the look-out for child-friendly villages in the area. Thus the village would be rejuvenated and its decline declined. It was a grand idea, the mural, and the soul vicar was commissioned to commission it.

Naturally, the soul vicar delighted in the idea (partly

because there were very few ideas in which he wouldn't delight and partly because he knew just the man for the job).

'What?' Romance said.

'The vicar,' Thelonius Tripp replied.

'What?' Romance said again.

'The vicar,' Thelonius Tripp replied.

There was something overly-fresh and too dispiriting about stepping out of the 100 Club into the morning London light and going straight home, quiet, alone, having been lost to soul music for so many hours, so it was usual, after the allnighters, for the boys to go for a coffee in the nearby McDonald's to chat and wind down after the excitement of the night. And there were times when half the club seemed to be in there.

'The vicar. He wants me to do a mural.'

'You're joking.'

'No. He does. He phoned me up. It's for the church hall. A kids' thing.'

'Are you gonna do it?'

'Yeah.'

Thelonius Tripp was gonna do it. He was definitely gonna do it. No one had ever asked him to paint anything before, walls included. This was his first commission. The money wasn't great but it was a great deal greater than nothing, which is what he usually earned. And, more importantly, it would give him public exposure. It could be his big break.

Someone very well known in the art world might one day drive past the village hall and see it. Word would get about.

'What are you gonna do?'

'I'm gonna do it.'

'I mean, what are you going to paint? What's the mural going to be of?'

All the evidence so far suggested that Thelonius Tripp could only paint northern soul dancers, and in a rather dark, stark fashion at that. He had never tried to paint anything else. He had never shown any interest in anything else. What was the vicar thinking?

'Well, we talked about it. There's nothing finalised yet. I'm gonna sketch a plan of it and show it to him. But I thought maybe some people dancing, like they were dancing to the glory of God or something. He quite liked that. They could be dancing and there'd be this light coming down from above. He was into that.'

'Right,' Romance said. 'Bloody hell,' Romance thought.

'It'll be like a community project. I'd be in charge but other people could get involved – help with the painting and that. Kids.'

'And is he going to pay you?'

'Yeah.'

'With money?'

'Yeah. I told him I'd take records but he said it would be the council or something paying.'

'That would be like Michelangelo then, wouldn't it?' Demetrios Demetriou chipped in.

'What?'

'Well, cos he didn't do all his own painting. He had helpers. But it still counted as his work because he told them what to do.'

'Yeah,' Thelonius Tripp said, after some thought. 'A lot of those old painters were really good and as well as that their art was about something. It had a clear message. That's what I'm trying to recapture. A celebration. Celebrating the glory.'

'But you don't even believe in God.'

'How do you know? I might do.'

'Well, do you?'

'I don't know.'

'Right,' Romance said. 'Bloody hell,' Romance thought.

But the vicar was into it. He was into the whole idea. His own, original idea had been to put on northern soul dos in the church hall. This idea had been vetoed by the parish council, partly because they didn't really know what he was talking about and partly because they were worried by the little they did understand: records, music, noise and, potentially, youth. Everyone was in favour of attracting young people to the village, but preferably they should be very young. Prepubescent, in fact. And the right kind of prepubescent at that. The Pritchett kind. (The kind that didn't venture out of their own gardens.) That was the kind they wanted to attract. The village already had two youths and that was quite enough. It was children that were needed

– fresh, unchallenging blood. How these children were to become adults without passing through youth had yet to be determined. First things first was the attitude.

So a mural it would be, and so the soul vicar asked the soul artist, who was the only artist he knew. The vicar had liked what he had seen of Thelonius Tripp's work at the Southside Soul Club, but then he did tend to like everything he saw. The vicar took this open-mindedness as a sign of his rare ability to appreciate the visual arts in all their forms. If anyone were to apply the same argument to music, no doubt he would be with the soul cohort, denouncing such nonsense as a sign of a lack of taste. But then music was something else. Music was music. Music was bigger.

## 57

*For an angel went down at a certain season into the pool, and troubled the water: whosoever then first after the troubling of the water stepped in was made whole of whatsoever disease he had.* (John 5:4)

*Who's that young girl dressed in blue?*
*Wade in the water*
*Must be the children that's coming through*
*God's gonna trouble the water.*
(traditional spiritual)

For Terry Gibbs, finding soul and finding religion had gone hand in hand. God came first, with the blow to the head, but soul came close behind. The two were obviously connected. He was a changed man, and it was his newfound appreciation of these two things that gave them common cause in his mind and he had a profound feeling of anticipation for both. Whatever had suddenly made him appreciate one must have made him appreciate the other.

He started attending the services at St Alfege's Church, as it was the church he knew and it looked impressive from the outside, and he started going along as a punter to the soul dos in the pub. Some of the hymns he recognised, some he didn't. Most of the records he didn't recognise, but over the months he became familiar with more and, as a young Romance was to do a few years later, he began unearthing the occasional compilation LP in the occasional record shop.

The church people were mostly posh, friendly and well-meaning, and the soul people were mostly not posh, friendly and well-meaning, and he slowly grew to know more of each. They all loved something greater than themselves and this gave a feeling of communion absent from his life until then. He didn't talk to the God people about soul and he didn't talk to the soul people about God. In each case, he simply didn't feel the need. In fact, it was a relief to be free of the pressure to talk about oneself at all. There were other things that were more important.

He listened to the sermons and talked to the vicar and began to think that he might have something to contribute. He had been on an interesting journey and perhaps others could benefit from hearing about it and where it had led him. And he watched the DJs at work and he felt those 45s and saw others buying them and talking about them and was drawn into that whole record collecting world, and eventually Tom Tom from the Pied Piper Soul Club asked him to do a spot of his own.

He was more nervous about DJing for Tom Tom than he was when he read the lesson in church for the first time. He could practise the reading and he knew that people would sit and listen, but there was no way of telling how his set would be received.

He worked it all out. He decided what records to play – so that together they filled his allotted forty minutes – and in exactly what order, and he even thought about and practised what he would say between certain records. (It was customary, after all, for records to be announced, as the soul folk were always keen to know what was being played, and a bit of patter was needed as well to maintain the energy.)

He still had the flier for that do somewhere in the vicarage: the first with his name on it. He smiled when he thought about what he had put himself through. He hadn't been confident enough not to plan his set, but he would never plan it too much now. He was too experienced for that. A good DJ needs to be flexible. A good DJ needs to listen to what has been played already. A good DJ needs to sense what would be well received with that particular crowd at that particular moment, all within the boundaries of what he or she rates as the best music, and with the additional consideration of which of the more obscure records would those present most appreciate being introduced to.

Having been at it for years, the soul vicar was now pretty good at all that, and he had thousands of records from which to construct his sets. He had a reputation for traditional, uptempo northern soul and for playing with passion and for taking little interest in the soul fads of the day. And, within the church, he had progressed from the occasional reading in his local church to writing and delivering his own sermons in a church of his own.

None of it had been easy. The journey had been long and hard, but he was a driven man. London soul dos, allnighters up north, London Theological Seminary.

He lost himself in the otherness of it all. He revelled in the everythingness of it all. And wherever he played out, he thrilled in the sharing of it.

But when he DJed, as when he took a service, he was playing to the converted. Soul outreach was needed. The mural, as well as being an attempt to attract young families by brightening up the village, would be Christian outreach, but coming from a Tripp perspective it was bound to have soul and it felt like a start. And it might inspire him to further, more soulful endeavours.

# 58

Romance's soul outreach could have been going more smoothly. Steve Davis hadn't really grasped the film idea. Perhaps he could be persuaded to go along with it anyway. After all, it would be for the good of the music. He had been reticent, presumably because the project was too subtle for him.

But Romance began to wonder whether Steve Davis needed to appreciate the subtleties of the film for the film to work. Steve Davis had mentioned the *Holiday* programme, which was obviously inappropriate but, if his role in the film was simplified, perhaps the part of the film in which he would feature could resemble a travelogue, with looking for records providing the thread. And then Romance could go off chasing girls by himself. He could even film himself chasing girls after Steve Davis had gone home, and this layer of the film could then be intercut with the Steve Davis part by the magic of editing. (Romance made a mental note to be aware of issues of what is called *continuity* – length of his hair, etc.) The bigger problem was the crucial part of the film that was looking for Romance Watson. Steve Davis hadn't seemed at all interested in this, and so Romance would have to do the looking for Romance by himself too (as well as the looking for romance) and he wouldn't be able to look for Romance at the same time as any record-hunting travelogue (unlike looking for romance). He would have to hang about afterwards to do it.

Clearly, Steve Davis's role in the film would be diminished. Romance's hope was that, even if Steve Davis was to play this lesser role, his name would be a significant enough draw for the television executives. But he worried that they might want to limit the Steve Davis-free parts of the film and thus compromise the artistic integrity of the film. Romance had to use all his powers of creativity to think round this problem.

He considered that he could be less than explicit to Channel 4 in his intentions. He could go along with them. He could agree that the film would be primarily about Steve Davis journeying across America looking for records. And then he could surreptitiously sneak off and film himself chasing girls anyway and then think of some reason why he had to hang about afterwards too, during which time he would look for Romance Watson. The disadvantage of this clever but deceitful option was that he would be found out in the editing. At this point, the television executives might be persuaded to go along with Romance's vision for the film because of the remarkable nature of the footage. But Romance knew that even if, at this late stage, they were to appreciate his vision, it might well be too late for them to change tack, as it was probable that they already had some primetime slot put aside for the simple travelogue film.

So it was probably best, after all, for Romance to try to convince Channel 4 of the viability of his new idea, persuading them to accept a diminished role in the film for Steve Davis. Because, to Channel 4, Romance was an unknown, Romance thought that persuading them to accept less of a role for Steve Davis and more for the filmmaker (Romance) would be hard to do on paper. (For some time Romance had been trying to put to paper the idea of *Looking for Romance (with Steve Davis)* as it was and had been finding it very difficult – probably because of the subtlety of the idea.) Romance imagined that the only way to convince them of the viability of the new approach was to do it in person and to impress them with the force of his personality and thus his creative potential. But to arrange a meeting would mean letter-writing and thus putting the idea to paper. Romance surmised that the only way to escape from this Catch-22 would be to find out the address of the head of Channel 4 and surprise him.

To Romance, this potential solution had much appeal. His enthusiasm and energy would be obvious and, if the head of Channel 4 was as much of a creative type as he should be for a man in that position, then he would instantly be able to perceive Romance's creative potential and thus realise that he was being gifted an award-winning documentary.

But, there was a problem. When Romance had phoned Channel 4 before, having successfully put to paper his *Keeping the Faith* idea, he had been unable to find out the name of the head. The operator had given him a phone number but the Channel 4 telephonist had seemed confused and unclear about which name to give, so in the end Romance had had to settle for just the address of the main office. Consequently, the letter had gone awry – at least, that's what he suspected because he still hadn't received a reply. But then, if he was able to find out the name of the head, what were the chances of being given his address? Slim, at best.

It was depressing. Romance had faith in his idea, but he couldn't see how to get Channel 4 on board. He couldn't fund the project himself, as he didn't have any funds. And anyway, he reckoned he needed the kudos of a commission to get Steve Davis on board.

It was depressing, and it depressed Romance, even though he wasn't prone to depression. But still, he wasn't nearly as depressed as JBP when she was committed to a psychiatric ward in the Royal South Hants Hospital for the second time, for her own safety as well as that of those around her. But then she was prone to depression. She always had been.

# 59

Spaghetti was never depressed but was often sad, and he was sad when he left the church. But he determined not to show it to Soul Sam.

'Well, that's it for us then, Sammy boy. If they won't even let you in, then there's nothing for us there. This society is becoming increasingly doggist you know, and I think, of all places, maybe the church would be OK. But it don't matter and sometimes I think it's a good thing you don't understand, cos you'd be upset by all this doggy prejudice. I mean, they let kids in. There were kids all over the place when we got here. It's just like the George and Dragon in Warley, init? It gets on me wick. Well it's their loss, and just because you can't go to church and I can't be a priest, it don't mean there's no place for you in heaven boy. That's what I think.'

He was sad that Soul Sam hadn't been allowed in the church, but having Soul Sam made him happier than he would otherwise have been, so for him the best way to get over the disappointments that can come with having a dog was to have a dog.

They reached the end of the road and Spaghetti turned left, which was unfortunate.

'We'll walk to the cemetery. You'd like that, wouldn't you boy? I think I can remember the way. We'll go see our old mate Demetrios, Sammy boy. I mean, if I ain't gonna be a priest now, it don't matter about all that priestly red tape and rules and stuff, do it? Not that we're gonna go straight over and dig up poor Demetrios. Oh no. I'm not saying that. So don't get any ideas now. I'm just saying there's no harm in going and saying hello and paying our respects like, cos he was a top bloke, weren't he? He had a lot of soul, Demetrios did. Just like you, Sammy boy, whatever that half-soaked priest said. And just while we're there we'll just have a little look and just test the soil maybe to see how soft or hard it is, cos we'll be there anyway and there's no harm just seeing is there? I mean, that's all, but we'll say hello too to our old mate, cos we've got time, haven't we boy? We'll be all right.'

## 60

In modern times, dogs have not been allowed in churches and cathedrals but hippies have been. (Thankfully, Spaghetti didn't know this.) But despite living in the shadow of Chichester Cathedral through summers and winters and all in between, Hippy John had never thought to venture inside. Moreover, he had never thought why he had never thought to venture inside. But on his return to the city after the bridge/Lee/Lainie/angel-boy experience, when he was walking and drew near to the great, stone entrance, he paused and looked and felt the attraction of it.

He had been moved by his night in the angel-boy church. He wouldn't have said that it had been a religious experience, but that embracing old church seemed to embody the selflessness he had witnessed and the new life that had been bestowed upon him.

He had gone to church as a child because his parents had taken him. His mother had faith and, even though it wavered and she couldn't help but doubt, she was keen to instil in her young son a spiritual sense – a sense of the other. Hippy John had no idea what his father believed, beyond the maintenance of middle class (church-going) respectability.

Hippy John had even been confirmed and he remembered it. He remembered doubting then, because he was just old enough to do so. And he remembered confronting his doubt by looking into the flame of a candle on the altar. Somehow he felt the presence of God – or Jesus or whatever – in the flame.

And then there was more than one occasion on which, as an adult, he had sat with a fellow rough-sleeper before an open fire, finding sanctuary from a dark, cold night. And he would look into those heat-giving flames, miraculously sprouting from the cardboard and sticks and whatever else they had been able to find, and he would think of the candle of his confirmation. By then he had read somewhere that humans had developed an innate attraction to a fire – something to do with all those prehistorical nights that our ancestors spent sitting around open fires (much like the rough-sleepers of the West Sussex woods today) – and perhaps that explained the apparent ethereal quality of the flames. It wasn't enough to make him believe in God, but for better or for worse (and in the pre-bridge days, no doubt, it would have been for worse) it certainly did encourage him to question his place in the order of things.

Hippy John had been in a cathedral before. In fact, he had been in many cathedrals as a child. They were the kind of place (like the National Trust houses, museums and art galleries) that his father thought appropriate for a family outing. They were educational and inspirational, and boring as a Winfield Parker discography (Ru-Jac, Arctic, Wand, Spring, GSF, P&L Records, 1963-1979) to a young child. Family holidays were spent driving from one place of stony worship to another. As ever, his mother would try to enliven the occasion, by looking for amusing inscriptions or finding funny faces in the stained glass, but it was like trying to relieve hypertension with a cup of tea. Cathedrals, art galleries, museums, classical music: they were all associated in the mind of Hippy John with a feeling not merely of interminable boredom but of a boredom inflicted upon him by his father. Rather than imbuing his son with what he regarded as high culture, Hippy John's father did an excellent job of alienating his son from such things for life. But his experience in the little church in the little village with the little boy and the old woman had been entirely his own. It had been nothing to do with his father and he had been touched by it, and so when he felt the cathedral towering over him, as imposing as it was meant to be, he found that he had the will to face it. And it was through strength not weakness that he submitted to the draw of the huge and open door. He went inside.

# 61

*Precious Lord, take my hand*
*Lead me on, let me stand*
*I am tired, I am weak, I am worn.*
*Through the storm, through the night*
*Lead me on to the light*
*Take my hand precious Lord, lead me home.* [17]

As the rhythms of blues and jazz began to be incorporated into traditional gospel music, a novel and soulful component dropped from the ether into the sweet mix. In the 1930s a new style of gospel lyric developed, centring on the self and one's personal relationship with God.

One of the standard bearers of the new gospel music was Roberta Martin, a classically trained pianist from Chicago. For her accompaniment, she developed a rich sound of mixed vocal harmonies – a small group of male and female voices – encouraging individual voices within the group. She was known for her subtlety – her restraint – through which the heartfelt vocals would tear.

In 1949 Roberta recruited a young, local man to her group and, in 1969, Romance Watson was just one of the 50,000 mourners at her funeral.

On the last recording of the Roberta Martin Singers, Roberta sang the lead herself: 'I have hope. It's a beautiful hope, and it sets me free.'

By then, Romance had long since left the group to pursue his solo career.

*Hear my cry, hear my call*
*Hold my hand lest I fall*
*Take my hand, precious Lord, lead me home.*

*Precious Lord Take My Hand* was written by Thomas A. Dorsey in 1932. He became known as the father of gospel music. He wrote it on the death of his wife, Nettie, who died in childbirth, and the subsequent death, two days later, of his infant son.

# 62

While Terry Gibbs was born again and revelling in what lay before him, Romance, whose head was awash with soul music, was struggling to see the way. When he heard Soul Sam DJ, and Hemel Hector and Johnny Dells, he was overawed by their records and their knowledge. Romance was passionate about the music and yet felt woefully inadequate. And when he looked at all the records for sale at the allnighters and on the sales lists that dropped through his door, he was shamed by all those he didn't know. He wanted the end to be achievable – to have it all, to know it all, to feel at one with soul – and the very wanting seemed to hamper his journey. Soul lyrics swam around his brain as deranged sperm swim around in circles, backwards and forwards, without the faintest idea of what they are supposed to be doing. If Terry had thought he might have something akin to sperm in his head, he wouldn't have minded. (Actually, he probably would have liked it.) The swimming itself was the marvellous thing. But for Romance, it was a disorder and it was a nuisance, and there were times when it spilled out unfortunately.

*Dear JBP,*

*It was such a thrill to see you so well and I was proud as can possibly be. All I had wanted had come true, but a problem remained... with me. You were supposed to get better for the sake of us both, yet there I was, traumatised still. I should have been happy. Problem solved. But I didn't have the strength. I didn't have the will. Tears fell like rain and took me again to the worst of times when to make any decision was a river to cross – a mountain to climb. I walked away from love and now a year has gone by, and I want to try to explain the reasons why.*

Romance did want to try to explain why he walked away. But he put his pen down. He needed a break. He put the kettle on and made a cup of tea.

The problem for Romance was that as the time for JBP to come out of St Bartholomew's House had drawn closer, his mind had stayed in the same muddled place. He had been hoping that something would have evolved and that after six months he would have known what to do. But it hadn't and he hadn't. There had been no evolution – and no magical or divine intervention – and he was no nearer to knowing what to do than he was to knowing soul music. He was put into a panic, but he had one remaining hope: that on seeing JBP for the first time in six months all would be clear. It would be a transforming moment. It would be like when you die and in the instant of dying you become part of the universal consciousness and suddenly know and understand everything. But it didn't happen. And then nothing kept happening, persistently.

> *Day after day, decision delayed, and days led to weeks – too weak, too afraid. I missed you at Cleethorpes, but still I did nothing. When sad, doing nothing is the easiest thing. To be happy in oneself, to give us a chance. Together, forever. A soul-filled dance.*

The other problem for Romance was that he wasn't used to writing letters. Evidently, he was more used to listening to records.

> *After the break up I thought I should wake up and they've come and they've gone, as never before. Young, happy things, birds on the wing, but this short-term fix doesn't work anymore.*
> *Now our time together is but a dream, and life's been on hold since we've been apart. Faith, still, in our love, not wanting to move on. Refusing, choosing, staying true to my heart.*
> *To be never together – it's all in the past – but the past is so dear to me, ever so near to me, too much a part of me, ever may it last.*
> *You say it's no good to dwell on what's gone and that we've said farewell and it's time to move on. But my heart is*

*haunted – love never went away – by what I put you through, day after day.*

Romance found that his foot was tapping. And it was tapping to The Magnificent 7. His teeth were tapping too and he was rocking in his chair:

*So close, a breeze can't blow between us*
*So tight, you couldn't part us with a Tommy gun.*
*Standing in the need of one another*
*Like a flower... standing in the need of the sun.* [18]

*Ever a part of me. What would be left of me? To move on without you, yet keep you as well. To delight in shared memories. Don't leave me alone with them! I'd lose you twice over from heaven to hell.*

'And so I go on my way, back to the highway,' sang Ray Pollard in 1965, and he sang it again in Great Yarmouth in 1991 – his song about a lost love condemning him to drift from town to town – and when he sang 'Oh how I cried, Lord how I cried...' he cried it and it shook the souls of everyone who heard it.

The letter was already too long. Romance could see that. The problem with putting pen to paper is that there is no limit to it (providing one has plenty of paper and Romance had bought a new pad especially). The beauty of the 7" single is that it forced a concentration of concentration. In fact, Romance mused, as he studied his writing, it could be argued that the invention of the 12" single directly contributed to the death of decent soul music. It certainly coincided with the end of the classic era. All that needless stuff in the middle that didn't go anywhere.

*All this sentimentality is probably just what you don't want. Maybe it's even a bore. But I need to tell it, no less, no more, so thank you for reading if you've…*

And then his pen ran out.

He had wanted to go on to say something about not knowing what the future held but wishing her every happiness, and then something too about how she was the most wonderful person he had ever met. But nothing triumphed again.

## 63

*Dear Mr 'Romance',*

*Thank you for your letter regarding your proposed film, 'Keeping the Faith'.*

*I regret to inform you that the idea does not conform to our current channel requirements, but good luck with the project.*

*Yours sincerely,*

*Simon Spensely*
*Editor, Documentary Features*

Romance studied the letter. This was a blow. 'Does not conform to our current channel requirements.' Romance was a fan of Channel 4 and strongly believed that the channel was the natural home for his film. Wasn't it just the type of film that should appeal to them? Original, imaginative and working on many different levels. Surely no one else could have leapt in there first with an idea like his? They couldn't have, because his was so original. Perhaps the channel thought they could track down the vicar and make the film independently. But they wouldn't be able to do it justice, as they didn't have Romance's insight. He was the one with the inside knowledge. He was the one with the vision. And surely the vicar wouldn't agree to participate without Romance's involvement. Would he? (He did seem quite keen to be on telly.)

'Current channel requirements.' Perhaps the channel had finally succumbed and was dumbing down. Perhaps his idea was simply too subtle in this current, cut-throat climate. This was bad news not just for Romance and not just for soul music but for the cultural life of the country. This was just the type of film that Channel 4 should be making. They shouldn't be lowering themselves to the lowest common denominator in some mad, Thatcherite ratings war. Surely an insightful documentary such as this would bridge the gap between the intellectual and the popular. It would be deep and meaningful but would appeal to a broad cross section because of its fascinating subject matter.

Suddenly, Romance doubted his letter had ever reached the top. Who was this Simon Spensely? And what was 'Documentary Features'? He had addressed his letter to 'The Head of Channel 4.' Clearly, his letter had been dealt with by some less experienced and less creatively-minded underling. That was the problem with big media organisations these days: too many layers of bureaucracy. There were too many pen-pushers getting between creative types like him and the people at the top. Great ideas were failing to be recognised. And fresh creative talent was being wasted.

Romance was upset – upset with Channel 4 for losing its way and upset with himself for not thinking at the time to include something in his letter about his film appealing to a broad cross section.

# 64

Romance was curious about the mural. He was thinking about it in the 100 Club. He couldn't see it appealing to a broad cross section. Perhaps it didn't have to, as its target audience was more geographically defined. But then how could a little village in Berkshire contain enough of an appreciative section (it wouldn't be a cross section) for a huge Tripp? Surely it would be as alienating to the villagers as the 100 Club allnighter. How many of the villagers would be interested in dancing to rare sixties soul music till the morning light? The answer was probably none. The soul scene wasn't discriminatory against country folk; in fact, it was remarkably tolerant of all sorts, and Romance looked about him and saw the strange mix, united only by a love for the music. Most of the classes were there, and certainly the full range of mental health attributes. There weren't many rural types on the scene, but Romance reflected that the proportion of rural types in the general population was small and that, if the soul scene broadly reflected the general population, which, he reflected, it did – if with a bias to the mentally sensitive – then there wouldn't be, would there? There was big Jack from Ashford. The last time Romance had seen Jack had been at a do in Newbury when he had rolled up in his Land Rover with a pile of dead partridges in the back. But he was the only truly rural type Romance knew on the scene. (Big Jack was a gamekeeper or something similar.) There was the Dorset lot and their Dorset accents, but they weren't posh country villagers. Romance didn't think there was anything inherent in posh country folk that made them unable to appreciate soul music; it was just a matter of probabilities. Romance was all in favour of soul outreach, but it was the appropriately sensitive minds – those that experience the deepest of emotions and therefore are able to most appreciate the most emotional music – that needed to be lured in, and they weren't easy to find. In London, it was like looking for a needle in a haystack. In the countryside, it was like looking for a needle in a haystack but without the haystack (even though it was the countryside).

Romance had been upset by Channel 4's rejection of his own quasi-religious northern-soul-comes-to-a-little-village idea, but he felt he had learnt from the experience. It must have been difficult, if not impossible, for them to grasp the groundbreaking nature of the film on the basis of one short letter. To attain his *Looking for Romance (with Steve Davis)* commission, Romance had planned to use the strength of his character to impress, in person, the head of Channel 4, but he had failed to obtain the head's name and address. So now he decided to write to them again, but this time with a fuller exposition of the myriad of themes and concepts behind the film. He had been finding it difficult to put the idea to paper, due to its subtlety and complexity, but that's a challenge he now saw that he had to face.

It was the idea's subtlety and complexity that had led to the film's main protagonist, Steve Davis, failing to appreciate it. He didn't quite get it. This was a shame, but Romance thought that it needn't impinge upon the commissioning of the film. The subteties and complexities would reveal themselves with or without the awareness of Steve Davis, and Channel 4 should commission the film with or without an awareness of Steve Davis's lack of awareness.

Looking back on their conversation, Romance supposed that there was no particular reason why Steve Davis should have got it. The skill and judgement needed to be a good snooker player are quite different from the skill and judgement needed to appreciate an original and perceptive documentary idea.

That isn't to say that Romance didn't admire the skill and judgement of good snooker players. In fact, he admired their skills greatly. How they managed to hit those balls with such precision was truly amazing. He had tried once himself, when he was a child. His neighbour, Tommy Hestor, had a toy snooker table and it was difficult enough to pot anything on that. And then as well as doing the potting, Steve Davis and the others like him would work out all the angles of where to put the cue ball after the pot. It was astonishing, especially as it was such a contrived game.

Of course, it was possible that the intense development of such very particular skills could have an impact on other areas of the brain. Romance had seen something on telly (a documentary, in fact) about how some people could be incredibly good at some things and useless at others. They could perform incredible mathematical feats but be unable to tie their shoelaces. And it was because there was an imbalance in the amount of brain matter put aside for particular purposes. So naturally it was possible that someone as expert as Steve Davis in hitting balls with a snooker cue could have developed such an imbalance and therefore be less able than most to appreciate an original and perceptive documentary idea. Similarly, perhaps Romance's failure to compete to his satisfaction with Tommy Hestor could be put down to an abundance of filmic creativity in his brain, even if, at that time, it remained untapped. For this reason, Romance found it hard to be cross with Steve Davis for not really understanding the film. That would be like Steve Davis being cross with him for being bad at snooker. It was just a shame and Romance would have to use his creativity to get round the problem.

To Romance, in terms of luring, the Thelonius mural didn't seem to have the subtleties of his ideas. But it did have the veneer of religion and it had been commissioned by established religion. As with gospel music, the aim was to draw people nearer to God. And it was on the gospel journey that humankind found soul. Without being aware of it, perhaps Thelonius Tripp was going back to basics, and perhaps there was a lesson here for Romance to learn. The problem was that he couldn't really work out what the lesson might be. But then it was five o'clock in the morning and he was fucked.

## 65

A good sense of direction was just one of the things missing from Spaghetti Weston's brain, which was stuffed full of soul music, but eventually he and Soul Sam found the cemetery. It was much further from the church than he remembered and they only found it in the end because Spaghetti remembered what Annie always told him: 'If you get lost, ask a policeman.' They couldn't find a policeman but they found a traffic warden who couldn't understand Spaghetti's accent and pointed them in the direction of the tube station, which happened to be by the cemetery.

'Well you were right, Sammy boy, it was down here! Oh, and that's handy. We'll get a tube from here. You'd like that, wouldn't you?'

Spaghetti didn't know how long it had taken them, but he did know that his legs ached.

It was only on entering the cemetery that it dawned on Spaghetti that he had little idea how to find Demetrios Demetriou's grave. When he had walked to the cemetery from the funeral service and then on to the graveside, he had simply followed the crowd. He could picture them all standing around the open grave and the Greek priest standing there too, in all his priestly finery, talking over the gaping hole in the ground. He remembered looking into the hole as they all filed past and away, and seeing the coffin at the bottom and being shocked at how far down it looked and wondering why it was necessary to put quite so much earth on top of his friend just because he was dead. (And that was even before he knew about the Romance Watson being down there too.) But the space that had been a hole was no longer a hole and it could have been anywhere.

(What if he had known about the record then? What would he have done? He would have had to do something before the earth started being shovelled back on top. At least he could have had a discussion with the other soul folk so that the burden wouldn't have been all his.)

'Where do you reckon, Sammy boy? There's never a policeman when you want one. People could be robbing these graves of all kinds of valuable things. It could have been down here I suppose,' and they set off along one of the paths between the graves.

Being a Sunday, there were more people about than usual, and at first Spaghetti didn't pay any attention to the old lady in black who was walking towards them on their fifth or sixth path of random choosing. But when she was almost upon them, he glanced at her and they recognised each other and he was suddenly filled with panic and guilt.

'Ohh!' she exclaimed.

'Ohh!' Spaghetti exclaimed back.

'Ohh!' She couldn't remember Spaghetti's name. 'Oh! Sam!'

Spaghetti took his responsibilities as Soul Sam's master seriously and knew that he should answer on his dog's behalf.

'Oh hello, Mrs D. We were just out for a walk, weren't we Sammy?'

'A walk,' Mrs Demetriou replied, also on the dog's behalf.

'Yes. We were just going for a walk and we happened upon this place. It's nice init? Oh yes, very nice. A lovely place for a walk. I'll tell you what, I wouldn't mind ending up here. Oh yes, very nice. Very nice indeed.'

He paused, hoping that he had adequately explained their presence in the cemetery. Thoughts of opening graves and of Demetrios Demetriou's corpse were now scurrying about his head and he found it difficult looking the old woman in the eye.

'You come see Demetrios. Thank you. Thank you, thank you.'

'To see him? To see Demetrios?'

'Come, come. We go. Together.'

She turned to walk with them down the path, and it occurred to Spaghetti for the first time that he could have been there with Soul Sam simply to visit the grave of Demetrios Demetriou and to pay his respects and that was exactly what the old woman had reasoned. What a stroke of luck. What a perfect excuse. It was all so neat. And it was made all the sweeter when he realised, on reflection, that it was largely true. In the panic, he had just forgotten about that bit.

The three of them walked down the path and then, following the old woman's lead, they turned off along a row of graves.

'This is just like *The Good, the Bad and the Ugly*,' Spaghetti mused.

Demetrios Demetriou's mother made no effort to understand.

'You know, at the end, when there's the three of them and they're looking for the grave with the money in it. There was the three of them: the good, the bad, and the… Although, I'm not saying, you know, that we're like that, with those names.'

He paused.

'Or that we're looking for money, or anything like money. Like anything valuable or anything like that.'

She still didn't respond and Spaghetti was relieved that she seemed to pay no heed to his nervous ramblings.

The woman paused in front of a fresh grave.

Spaghetti hadn't previously considered what the grave might actually look like. He'd had in mind the coffin in the deep hole and the pile of earth waiting to be thrown on top, and now suddenly there was a lot to take in. The grave wasn't just earth. There were many other elements and everything was so precise and delicate-looking.

Around the grave was a little fence – a tiny, wooden picket

fence – which made such a neat little boundary between the wildness of the outside and what lay within. And the floor of the grave (or was it the roof?) was covered with a fine, light gravel – almost white – so evenly and carefully laid it shimmered like clear vinyl. And then on the gravel were several potted flowers, blooming bright gold and red and yellow. They were far too big for this tiny garden. Bonsai trees would have been sufficiently minimalist and Japanese to fit in naturally to this toy landscape, but instead these giant, garish flowers loomed over it and made it a landscape from another planet or from a dream and, as if they weren't enough, one of those child's toy windmills was stuck in the gravel-ground. The day was windless and the windmill wasn't turning, but Spaghetti wondered what would happen when it did – whether other things would come to life and little figures would start dancing in the glades or skating on the gravel-ice.

'My son, my son.'

'Oh,' said Spaghetti.

The cross at the head of the grave seemed to come from a different dream. Something of polished stone would have been more in keeping, but this was a cross of dark wood, fashioned at the ends with decorative twirls. A little gold plaque read 'Demetrios Demetriou' and gave his dates and below that, clinging on like a bird box, was a glass-fronted box containing a little burning oil lamp, a photo of Demetrios Demetriou and a few other little bits. An envelope. A postcard.

'Here my son. I can't believe. I come, every day. Every day, many time.'

The old woman leant down and twisted one of the flowerpots very slightly, making no difference to anything.

'It's very lovely,' Spaghetti said. 'Oh yes, a lovely...' – he didn't want to say *grave* – 'set up.'

'He gone. I can't believe. He in there, my son.'

'Yes. He was a good friend. But it is a lovely set up, Mrs D. It's a very nice place to be... in. And he is at peace.'

'He gone. My son dead. I can't believe.'

'But his soul lives on.'

'You think? Ohhh.'

'It's just his body that rests here, with the records you put in, at the statutory six feet so as to avoid the spread of the plague.'

Spaghetti pictured again the long drop that is six feet. That plague, he considered, as well as being so lousy to people at the time, continues to be a pest to this day. Six feet. Demetrios Demetriou didn't have the plague and records have never been known to carry it, although they can spread like the plague if played by the right DJs. Ha!

'Yes, it's a lovely set up,' he said, out loud. 'And this is his final resting place?'

'He dead!' was the answer.

Soul Sam let out a yap, which he wasn't prone to do. But it wasn't a response to the old woman's morbid assertion; his eye was elsewhere. He was on his lead and had been sniffing about at the feet of the odd couple, but something

– some people – had caught his attention. Normally he was very good with people – he simply couldn't be bothered to be riled by them – but the two approaching him now, zigzagging their way through the graves, had him perturbed. Spaghetti looked down and then followed the gaze of the awakened dog-eye, and then Nutty Casper and Bird's Nest Woman were with them at Demetrios Demetriou's grave.

'All right?'

'All right?'

'Hello.'

'Hello.'

Soul Sam was unsure whether to retreat behind the feet of his Brummie master or step forward to protect him, so he stayed put and awaited developments.

Nutty Casper was in full dinner dress mode: DJ, dicky bow, the works. Spaghetti knew better than to ask why. There would be no adequate explanation. Bird's Nest Woman was her normal, squat little self, in her immaculate sixties gear, her beehive hairdo winding its way up to Nutty Casper's chest.

'All right Mrs D.? You all right? We've come to see old Domestos. Oh, lookin' good. I like the old windmill. Does it go round? Yeah, it's good init?'

Mrs Demetriou didn't know who these new people were, but she liked them because they had come to see her son.

'Oh thank you, thank you.'

'Lookin' good, Mrs D., lookin' good. Yeah, shame he's not around to see it. Y'all right, Spag-man?'

Spag-man was all right but, like Soul Sam, he was suspicious.

Nutty Casper was nutty, but relatively harmless to everyone but himself (Bird's Nest Woman helped keep him out of self-harm's way) and he had been a good friend to Demetrios Demetriou – so good, in fact, that Demetrios Demetriou had consistently not answered his phone to him and not told him when he was in hospital in case he should visit. Casper was apt to find out anyway and to turn up with some bizarre and inappropriate treat – a kebab, a brand new game of Mousetrap – and Demetrios Demetriou, already sick from the chemotherapy, would be sicker still with the worry that his unpredictable friend was going to start fiddling with the equipment and pushing buttons on his drip machine. Things were better when Bird's Nest Woman was to hand, but she wasn't always.

And what were they doing at the grave? Was it just coincidence that they had come to visit Demetrios Demetriou the very day after Romance and Spaghetti had discovered that Demetrios Demetriou wasn't alone down there? Spaghetti couldn't help but wonder and the look in Soul Sam's eye confirmed that he was right to be concerned.

'Yeah, I'm all right. Just come along to pay my respects like, nothing else. Just pay my respects.'

'Coolio. Tell you what, it's a good thing you did. We was at the wrong grave! I thought it was over there somewhere. I don't know how you're supposed to know what's what. There should be signs or something.'

'Or, perhaps, names written on the headstones,' Spaghetti thought but didn't say. Instead, he exchanged a bewildered look with Bird's Nest Woman.

'Yeah, we was over there somewhere talking to some other silly bugger. Good thing we saw you, really. I told the other guy he could lump it! Oh, Mrs D., we brought something for Dommy.'

Nutty Casper turned to Bird's Nest Woman who reached into her disproportionately large vintage handbag. She took out a box of chocolates and a CD and handed them to Nutty Casper.

'It's a box of chocolates and a CD.'

Mrs Demetriou didn't understand the silly bugger. And she didn't understand the words *silly bugger* (nor most of the other ones). So there was a brief pause as the old woman considered whether these gifts were for her or for her dead son and, if for her son, whether or not she was supposed to accept them on his behalf. Nutty Casper was also considering whether he should present his offerings to the mother or directly to the departed (although, in Nutty Casper's case, *considering* is probably too strong a word). It was only Spaghetti who was contemplating the nature of the gifts.

Before the pause forced him into an inconsiderate amount of considering, Nutty Casper stepped up to the little fence and placed his offerings on the gravel. They didn't look out of place at the feet of the flowers and the windmill. It was a small box of M&S *Luxury* chocolates and Spaghetti could now see that it was the latest Kent CD, Eddie and Ernie *Lost Friends*.

'Ooh, thank you. Thank you.'

Nutty Casper had placed the CD face-up on the gravel but, on looking at it, he bent down again and turned it upright and dug it in, the upper half protruding. Spaghetti noted the ease with which the gravel gave way. The CD now looked like a mini-gravestone of its own, but then if it were a mini gravestone, it would have been a mini-gravestone to the two young, black faces, Eddie and Ernie, lost to their friends and buried together in an eternal, soulful embrace. It wasn't out of keeping in the surreal little landscape: a grave in a grave.

Nutty Casper hadn't considered the suitability of the title, *Lost Friends*. That was a coincidence. But he knew that Demetrios Demetriou would have been interested in this new offering from Kent. (Eddie and Ernie were a soulful pair.) Spaghetti knew that too, but he also knew that Demetrios Demetriou was a dedicated vinyl man and he doubted that he'd even had a CD player.

'I know he was a record man, Mrs D., but I thought, you know, it wouldn't be right to stick a record in the ground, and also, well, cos he's moved on now, maybe a CD might be more convenient, you know.'

'Oh thank you. Thank you.'

The old woman didn't understand. She barely knew what a CD was.

And Spaghetti, who had known Nutty Casper for years,

was struggling to understand. The implication seemed to be that it wasn't possible to take records to heaven, and perhaps there wasn't even anything there on which to play them, but that somehow it was possible to access digital music. Spaghetti fully appreciated the magic that was being able to hear music by means of a digital disc, but this one was still in its cellophane wrapping. Nutty Casper seemed to be living up to his name with gusto. Then it suddenly occurred to Spaghetti that it could have been a ploy to test the firmness of the ground.

'So how you keepin', Mrs D.? You all right? I missed the funeral, didn't I? I wanted to come as well. I went on the wrong day. I got the days muddled up. I went to the wrong funeral. Some old geezer from Northolt or somewhere. Nice family though.'

Nutty Casper pointed across the cemetery. 'He's over there somewhere. But you all right, Mrs D.? He was all right, weren't he, Domestos.'

'He gone. My son, he gone.'

'It looks lovely, dunnit? Yeah, lovely.'

Bird's Nest Woman rarely spoke, but Soul Sam kept her in his sight anyway. She was closest to his level and, to his experienced dog-eye, the most queer-looking.

'You all right, Mrs D.? I'll come round sometime if you fancy. I could bring some cake or something. I was always saying to Dommyman I'll come round. It's no problem. I've got me car now, in' I?'

Bird's Nest Woman nodded to confirm it. Soul Sam

raised his head a tad.

'How you gettin' home, Mrs D.?'

'What?'

'How do you go home? Car? Bus?'

'Bus. I get bus. 4-4-0. Bus 440. Then change to home.'

'Well I'll drive you back, won't I? When you wanna go?'

'Yes, I going.'

'She was on her way out when we arrived,' Spaghetti chipped in.

'You want go now? I drive. Me driving.'

'Oh!'

'We'll go in a minute then. In a minute. I just wanna say hello to nutjob.'

Nutty Casper stepped to the head of the grave and stood stiffly. He raised his arms as if he were a crucifix and shut his eyes. His head seemed to vibrate with the concentration. Then it was all over.

'Wanna lift anywhere, Spag-man?'

Spaghetti had been in a car once before with Nutty Casper and had vowed never again.

'No, we're all right. We're gonna get the tube. Sammy's never been on a tube before.'

'Yeah? You sure? Well we'll be off then. All right, Mrs D.? I'll run you home. Me drive you – home.'

'Oh, thank you. Thank you.'

She turned to Spaghetti.

'I stay a little,' he said.

'Oh, thank you, thank you.'

'Bye.'

'Bye. Bye bye.'

She gave Soul Sam a look goodbye but his eye wasn't to leave Bird's Nest Woman until they were a safe distance.

'She'll be all right,' Spaghetti thought aloud. 'She's not in a fit state to be scared. You all right, Sammy boy? We'll be off soon too. I just want to have a little word with me old mate, Demetrios.'

# 66

'So did you do that mural?'

'Yeah.'

'How did it go?'

'Great.'

'Yeah?'

'Yeah.'

The boys didn't have their usual table in McDonald's because there was a group of eager Chinese tourists making an early start to their day in the West End. The tourists hadn't danced the night away at the 100 Club and they weren't going to go on to the record fair in Kilburn either. They were intent on seeking the essence of Englishness elsewhere. (McDonald's, Madame Tussaud's, Les Mis., etc.)

'Yeah. It did. Great. I think it went down well. The vicar said he really liked it.'

'And was it what you said? People dancing?'

'Yeah. Dancing. People dancing, with a light coming down, like it was coming from a high window. It looked good. It worked well on the wall. It took a few days, all in all.'

'By yourself?'

'No, cos it was supposed to be a community thing. There weren't really any kids about but there was this old trampy guy who got quite into it and these couple of teenagers who lent a hand once they could see it wasn't gonna be all twee and lovey dovey. We did it once and then it rained and it all got washed away, but that was like good practice really cos I'd never done one before either, so then we did it again with this other paint and it's even better and it's there now, whatever.'

'And what do the people in the village think of it?'

'I dunno know really. The vicar likes it. And that old trampy guy, and the teenagers. I didn't really meet anyone else.'

The vicar did like the mural. And Gerald liked it. And Oli and Caitlin, the village youth. The vicar liked it because it was art and he was an art-lover. Gerald liked it because he liked Thelonius Tripp, and he liked Thelonius Tripp because Thelonius Tripp had said it was OK for him to paint on the wall of the village hall. And Oli and Caitlin liked it because it wasn't twee and lovey dovey. In fact, if you looked at it properly and thought about it really hard, it was actually quite deep and meaningful, in some weird way that they weren't quite able to express, which probably made it even deeper. They had no idea it was anything to do with the church.

Everyone else in the village hated it, but they were all

too polite to say. They thought it dark and depressing. The members of the parish council told each other that it was a good thing, because it had been their idea. The fact that the Pritchett children hadn't come running or that, as yet, no passing motorists had unloaded their children for a spontaneous play was inconsequential. Such an ambitious project deserved to be judged only from a long-term perspective. In fact, short-termism was much that was wrong with modern times. The village had been there for a thousand years and it was their intention that it should be there for another thousand. (Hence the need for children etc.)

McDonald's hadn't been on Oxford Street that long, but it had been there long enough for the boys not to remember it not being there and, like the 100 Club and Cleethorpes and The Ritz in Manchester, it was giving rhythm to their lives. Of course, the background music was, as a rule, poor and uninteresting but, while they were sitting there chatting about Thelonius Tripp's mural, the rule was broken by the first few chords of *Just My Imagination* by The Temptations.

'Oh,' the boys all said, smiling to each other. They would have hated to hear the record in the 100 Club (except, perhaps, Demetrios Demetriou), as they would have viewed it as a waste of precious rare soul minutes, but to hear it in McDonald's was a joy. If Nutty Casper had been there he might even have danced, but he had the dates muddled and wouldn't roll up to the 100 Club until the following Saturday. (He waited alone on the pavement outside, wondering why there was no one else queuing, and only gave up when all the aged jazz twits had gone home after their evening concert and the staff had begun to lock up.)

The mural talk was over as the boys concentrated on the song and the wistful tones of Eddie Kendricks:

*But it was just my imagination*
*Running away with me.*
*It was just my imagination…*
*Running, away with me.* [19]

And when David Ruffin's husky voice punched through, a discussion about the respective merits of the two rival singers was inevitable.

*Every night on my knees I pray*
*Dear Lord, hear my plea*
*Don't ever let another take her love from me.*

The Chinese didn't notice the change in the quality of the popular music. They were busy being excited and planning their day, but then they wouldn't have noticed anyway and, apart from the soul boys, no one else did either.

Unfortunately for Mr Ruffin, it was his drug addiction that ran away with him, and he collapsed and died in a Philadelphia crack house in 1991. He is buried in Woodlawn Cemetery, Detroit, together with a string of other Detroit soul luminaries, including Barbara Randolph, Richard

'Popcorn' Wylie, Billy Henderson, James Jamerson, Erma Franklin, Marv Johnson, a Miracle, a Pip or two and (at the time of writing) three Four Tops.

## 67

'All right, mucka? All right, Double Diamond? All right, Don Davis? D.D. and The Derelicts, that's a good 'un. The Dynamic Deadbeats. Hey Demetrios, what the bloomin' 'eck is this windmill all about? I don't suppose you like any of this, do you? And the cross and that box thing. At least you ain't got your photo stuck on as part of the cross. I thought your mum might do that. That's a Greek thing, init?

'It's all for your mum really init? She's nice, in't she? She comes here every bloomin' day. And she put those records in there with you, didn't she? I can't believe she done that. I bet you're bloody pissing yourself. Well it seems like Casper thinks you can't play records where you are, so if that's true the joke's on you, Greek boy. Romance Watson test pressing. Jesus. What we gonna do about that then? I thought maybe Casper was after it, what with all that fiddling about with the gravel. Yeah, I can just see him now, back here in the night with a pick and shovel and all dressed up like a matador or something. Maybe I should hang about a bit just in case.

'You've met Sammy boy, haven't you? Yeah, course you have.

'You all right, Sammy? It's Demetrios down there!

'*Lost Friends*, that's a good 'un. I mean, that is a good 'un. Poor old Ernie, though. Life can be a bit of a bummer, can't it? All that talent, then what happens? Don't need to tell you that though, do I? Not that you had the talent of Ernie Johnson. Fuck no.

'D-Town was good last night. Yeah, you'd have enjoyed it. Maybe you did! Yeah, maybe you did. Maybe you were there, with your heaven money scattered all over the dance floor. You twat.

'I don't suppose you have money in heaven, do you? Everything's probably free. You can have any record you want and they're all in mint condition. But they'd have to be special heaven records that you can play up there.

'We're gonna sell your earth ones, mate. Me and Romance. We've been going through 'em. We'll give your mum the dosh. Hopefully she'll put some bloomin' central heating in the house. It's bloody freezing in there!

'There's a few missing though, in't there! One especially, you sneaky bugger. I wonder if you managed to wangle that yourself. Maybe you came down and made your mum do it, or you magically sneaked it in when she was putting the others in. I wonder what the others are. Probably some rubbish. Yeah, you're laughing now. You won't be laughing when Casper comes back with his pick and shovel. Actually, you know what, he won't be able to find the place without Bird's Nest Woman and if she was with him she wouldn't let him do it.

'I hope they'll get your mum back OK. Bloody hell.'

Spaghetti had watched the CD slip in surprisingly easily, but that was just the top layer. Six foot was a long way. Spaghetti had seen just how long. It must have been possible, as Victorian graverobbers did it all the time. But Spaghetti wasn't a Victorian graverobber. He wasn't practised in it. He would still have given it a go, if he hadn't become increasingly perturbed by his graveside deliberations.

Looking at the grave, with its little fence and carefully laid gravel, he knew that if he tried to dig it up he wouldn't be able to refashion this lovingly crafted little grave-scene. He would make a mess of it. And even though he knew that his dead friend wouldn't mind, seeing Demetrios Demetriou's old mother by the grave, he knew that she would mind. She would know something underhand had been afoot and, on the whole, mothers could be safely presumed to be against the digging up of their sons.

And he hadn't liked the idea of Nutty Casper being after the record. But what difference would it make to Demetrios Demetriou if it were Nutty Casper or Spaghetti Weston who disturbed his deathness? If he thought it wrong that someone else should dig up his lost friend, then it would be wrong for him to do the same. Of course, Spaghetti wasn't after the record for his own gain. He hadn't really thought what to do with it, but he was never just going to take it. He would pay the mother for it, or sell it and give her the money. Or it would be owned collectively and kept somewhere, but he didn't know where. (There was no soul equivalent of the British Museum to which such things could be bequeathed or donated.) His motivation was to save the record for posterity, that's all. It could be the only one of its kind. Romance had told him that Diamond Jim had never seen one.

Spaghetti had no reason to think that Nutty Casper's motivation would be anything less, but could Casper be trusted to handle this important and sensitive matter in an appropriate manner? Casper couldn't even handle putting his shoes on in an appropriate manner.

Spaghetti had intended to be quite open on the soul scene about digging up the record, but he had known all along knowledge of the unearthing might upset the mother. She could still be given the money, thinking the money had come from the selling of another record. But the mother would be upset if she saw that the grave had been disturbed. And it was all so pristine.

The mother had picked the record at random. She'd had no idea it was so rare. She had wanted some of the little records to be in the coffin with her son, and Spaghetti would leave the others in there. Another record could even be put in to replace the Romance Watson. If the swap could be made without her knowing, then there would be no possibility of her being upset by it.

Then Spaghetti thought of the dog he'd had when he was

a child. Rufus. He was a lovely, goodlooking dog – until he was run over. (He wasn't so goodlooking after that.) This was Spaghetti's first encounter with death and Mr and Mrs Weston had to act sensitively. They put the bashed Rufus in a cardboard box and then put that inside a bin bag ready for burial. For a couple of days this dead dog package lay in state in the garage and Spaghetti would sneak in and push valuable objects through a little opening at the knot of the bin bag. A marble. A golden key ring with a picture of Tower Bridge on it. Without knowing it, the young Spaghetti was following an age-old human tradition and it was an impulse Mrs Demetriou had been unable to resist too.

Spaghetti smiled at the thought of the Rufus skeleton with the marble and the key ring and whatever else knocking about beside it. That would be a good one for future archaeologists. The Tower Bridge Dog of Birmingham. And then he wondered how he would have felt – how he would feel now – if he found that his mother had removed these symbols of his affection. He would be upset and cross. But what if she had removed them and he was never to find out? There would be no knowledge to be upset about. But it would be a betrayal and it felt wrong. But the old woman could have central heating and be none the wiser. If he had thought of this ethical dilemma earlier in the day, he would have put it to the priest, but he wasn't going back there now. He had to work it out for himself.

# 68

There were times when Romance considered his future when the considering seemed a productive thing to do and some kind of action followed. But there were other times when the considering drove him mad and he was plagued by indecision. And the problem with indecision was that it normally led him to do nothing, which, unfortunately, was itself usually one of the options that he was avoiding choosing.

So when he was standing outside JBP's house, having walked her home after their first meeting on her coming out of St Bartholomew's House, the spectre of nothing loomed large. They had met for a coffee and Romance was in awe of her transformation. She looked wonderful. She was fresh and alive. And she was calm, threw nothing at him and gave no hint that she wanted to. They sat and chatted, nervously lovingly, and then they were standing on her doorstep and it was a moment when something had to be said. When he didn't say anything, she did.

'You don't want me, do you?'

It was more of a statement looking for refutation than a question.

He looked at her and didn't know what to say and was embarrassed by his patheticness. She was a new woman and was now the essence of all that he loved, but he was still a traumatised wreck. She had been told that she had to do it all for herself, but she had actually done it all for him.

He was overwhelmed with the nothing, which rose up and enveloped him, and he was almost choking on it as he walked away through the tear-filled haze.

If he were to write a soul song, it would be all about nothing. He wasn't black and he wasn't poor and he wasn't oppressed and he wasn't living in 1960s Detroit or Chicago or anywhere else in America, so obviously the historical and cultural basis for his writing a soul song wasn't there and so it wouldn't happen – even if he could do it, there wouldn't be any point – but he knew the meaning of heartbreak and that meant he could, at least, fantasise about it.

# 69

*Dear Mr 'Spensely',*

*You may remember me from the letter I sent you regarding a proposed documentary film entitled 'Keeping the Faith', about a northern soul vicar. You replied saying that it didn't fulfil your channel requirements. This I fully understand, as no doubt the subtleties of the idea are somewhat beyond the television audience of today with their narrow attention spans. Also, I can see that the film would not be feature length, and I know that short-form documentaries would normally be placed within a current documentary strand, and the uniqueness and subtlety of 'Keeping the Faith' means that it might not sit easily among other more mainstream, run-of-the-mill films.*

*So I have now enclosed a proposal for another documentary, which I am sure you will agree will have a wider reach due to the many layers upon which it works.*

*The film is to be called 'Looking for Romance (with Steve Davis)' – an interesting title that will catch people's attention – and, unlike 'Keeping the Faith', it has at its core a very well known A-list celebrity: none other than six-time world champion snooker player Steve Davis. Therefore, the film will no doubt have immense popular appeal while also being profound and revelatory.*

*I envisage the finished film to be feature length and therefore suitable as a one-off commission rather than as a part of any established documentary strand and, due to its celebrity appeal, I think it suitable for primetime viewing, ideally on a Saturday evening.*

Despite his disappointment at the rejection of *Keeping the Faith*, Romance was pleased to have struck a conciliatory tone with this letter to Mr Spensely. Romance still thought that *Keeping the Faith* would have been something of a coup for Channel 4 and one up on the BBC, but he thought it best to be diplomatic in his approach, as history is littered with great artists failing to realise their potential due to their intransigent nature. And he had decided that it would be a good idea to approach Mr Spensely directly, maintaining contact, rather than to go above his head. He was a name, at least. And he had read Romance's letter about *Keeping the Faith* and surely would have been impressed by the idea, even if he mistakenly thought that it didn't meet current channel requirements. And it seemed likely that if Romance was to send the *Looking for Romance (with Steve Davis)* proposal to the unknown head of Channel 4, then it would end up on Mr Spensely's desk anyway. (And then no doubt Mr Spensely would be affronted not to have been approached directly and any such affrontedness would further cloud a judgement already shown to be worryingly poor.)

This time, as planned and after much effort, rather than attempting to explain the ideas behind *Looking for Romance (with Steve Davis)* within the body of a letter, Romance enclosed a separate, bound document, incorporating all his thoughts on the film, which included his views on soul, love, religion and the controversial role of snooker in contemporary capitalist society. And on the front of the document Romance had stuck a photocopy of the signed photo that Steve had given him. Adding the photo was an inspired touch and Romance imagined that few fellow film-makers would have reason to use a photo of so famous a celebrity to illustrate their proposals (except, perhaps, those involved in the uni-layered Michael Palin travel documentaries). And he viewed the document as a considerable literary achievement that was full of artistic insights. It was offering a profound critique of a work of art that hadn't yet been made, in the way that art historians on telly talk about the Mona Lisa and suchlike. It couldn't fail to impress. Now all he had to do was wait.

## 70

When he had been alive, Demetrios Demetriou had believed in protecting for posterity mankind's greatest artistic achievements. That's why he had collected soul records. And Spaghetti Weston had no reason to believe that, in death, Demetrios Demetriou would have changed his mind.

Perhaps he was looking down on proceedings. And even if he wasn't, surely his memory should be respected. How would he feel about the separation of the Romance Watson and his corpse? And if he was looking down, there would come a time when Spaghetti would go to him and have to justify his actions. Spaghetti had been confident that the defilement of the grave would mean nothing to his friend, who cared not for symbolic, let alone religious, trappings. And even his corpse would be just a corpse. But the record... what of the record? Surely he would be as keen as Spaghetti that it be rescued and preserved. After all, Demetrios Demetriou had been appalled at the Taliban's destruction of the Bamiyan Buddhas. ('Bloody Taliban,' he had said, as the news came on the car radio in that gap in the music when Spaghetti was struggling with a mangled tape.) But perhaps Demetrios Demetriou was gleaning some perverse enjoyment from knowing that the Romance Watson was there, however fortuitously, to stay round and solid through the centuries like an ancient treasure. In fact, one day, it would most certainly be an ancient treasure. 'What is this curious thing?' some super-advanced archaeologist would muse. And then the carbon dating of Demetrios Demetriou's bones would place the burial a few years after that of the Tower Bridge Dog of Birmingham, and then a weird laser-needle would be directed at the vinyl and the sound of soul would resonate across the centuries. Demetrios Demetriou would like that. Who wouldn't?

And if the laughing Greek boy was looking down and if one day Spaghetti was to be reunited with his lost friend, then Spaghetti reasoned that he could bump into the mother again too. (Eternity would be a long time to avoid her and she might even have Demetrios Demetriou living with her as she had on earth.) She still might not know about him digging up the grave, because she wouldn't have been looking down at the time and Demetrios Demetriou might not have filled her in on compassionate grounds, but then there was the worry that on dying she would suddenly know everything because she would become a part of the common human essence. (This made Spaghetti think how good a name *Soul Essence* would be for a do.) Romance had said something along those lines after Side Door Pete was found dead from a heart attack at the West Wilts Soul reunion. (Who was DJing at the time was still a matter of dispute.) He talked about Pete being a part of the universal consciousness – some kind of life force that was connected to God and such. And if there was such a consciousness and Mrs Demetriou became a part of it, then that would be a bit embarrassing.

There was one thing of which Spaghetti was certain and that was that if Demetrios Demetriou had retained some kind of consciousness of his own and was observing him at that moment then he would be enjoying poor Spaghetti's predicament. In fact, he would probably be pissing himself with heavenly piss. And, however cruel his laughter, Spaghetti supposed that Demetrios Demetriou was due such merriment, and so Spaghetti didn't mind being the butt of it – it would be crueler still of Spaghetti to deprive his friend of it. So Spaghetti decided that he would continue to live with the agony of his knowledge about the record, so that Demetrios Demetriou could continue not to live – due to the cruel joke of nature – but with the possible amusement of the agony. Bastard Demetrios.

Unlike so many others, neither Eddie Campbell nor Ernie Johnson was struck down by some untimely, tragic event while at the peak of his creativity, and no cruel joke of nature awaited either of the young men as it did Demetrios Demetriou. Once The Heavenly Travelers had become Eddie and Ernie, they were the most soulful duo ever to grace the earth, according to Romance, Spaghetti and the rest. But they were never a commercial success, naturally. Eddie developed a drink problem and died a slow, undignified death of cirrhosis of the liver in 1994. Ernie survived his singing partner by over a decade, living as a down and out on the streets of Phoenix. He was killed in 2005 by a hit and run driver.

# 71

When Spaghetti's do at the Rik Tik Bar came round again, Romance was keen to go. At the last one, the music had been wonderful and so had Bettye. Romance was concerned that for the sake of his art – for the sake of his film – he should avoid restrictive entanglements with women. But he decided that avoiding restrictive entanglements with women need not mean avoiding women entirely. Perhaps it depended on the degree of the restrictiveness and nature of the entanglement. A little healthy flirting might even be good practice for his trip to America.

On the soul scene, opportunities to flirt were few. Opportunities to meet new, flirtable women were limited. For Romance, such opportunities mostly arose when soul people DJed in bars or clubs to a more mixed crowd – the sort of places where normal people would go anyway. But this only happened infrequently because, however enthusiastic the soul DJ, they were rarely invited back due to the uncompromising and alienating nature of their music. It might have been the highest artistic achievement of humankind, but it wasn't easily liked by the soulfully uneducated – the woefully uncultured – when blasted at them from close range.

Romance looked for that flicker of interest, that enlightened sparkle in the eye, but a quite-liking of the music was as far it would go and quite liking soul music was not an appealing quality. It wasn't a music to be quite liked. Musically open-minded people quite liked music. Romance would never be so disrespectful as to quite like someone else's music. There should be no quite liking in music. If music was quite liked, it was either rubbish or misunderstood. Romance suspected that all music other than quality soul music was rubbish, but he was prepared to withhold absolute judgement on music he didn't understand – Chinese, Arabic, whale, etc. He was intelligent enough to realise that he was not in a position to appreciate such music, as it belonged to an alien culture. To him, it was horrendous, obviously. All of it. (As was, to Hippy John's father, anything his son had listened to on the radio in his youth. 'It all sounds the same,' he would say, unable to hear past that which most distinguished it from Bach.) But to a sensitive Chinaman, brought up with his music and immersed in its culture, there were no doubt subtleties and sensitivities to it that were inaudible to Romance. And any westerner who quite liked it was an idiot. They could well be quite liking the Chinese equivalent of The Vengaboys in their pathetic attempt to be open-minded. That's *world music* for you. Ridiculous. Ha, and those classical music dimwits who go on *Desert Island Discs* and pick one or two ridiculously trite examples of pop music; in attempting to show the broadness of their minds, the stark shallowness of them shines through.

Sometimes the music reminded the soulfully uneducated and woefully uncultured of other music that they had already been coaxed into quite liking by the moronic mainstream, i.e. poppy tosh like Stevie Wonder or the pop funk of James Brown. They liked it, but not as much as the tosh. They didn't understand it. They couldn't hear it. Better were the women who knew they didn't understand it but were curious and respectful of another's obsession. The trouble with these women, however, was that they were mad.

The quite-likers were fairly easy to dismiss fairly rapidly. The mad ones tended to stick about, because they were obsessives too. Romance wanted a mad one who wasn't too mad. One would come along – Hannah the Tanner from Herne Hill, for instance – who seemed to have just the right level of madness, but then a few weeks would pass and the inner madness would rise up and tip the balance.

Of course, JBP had been a mad one. He had loved her. He still did. And he couldn't live through all that again. (And he hadn't yet met the blond girl.)

So he wanted to go back to the Rik Tik Bar – to hear some good music, to check Bettye's wrists for signs of self-harm and to consider the restrictiveness or unrestrictiveness of any potential relationship – and with Romance in the car were Solomon, Deptford Dave and, via the newfangled CD player, sixties Chicago teenage soulstress, Jo Ann Garrett.

'Who's this?'

'Jo Ann Garrett.'

'Is it?'

'Yeah.'

'On Duo?'

'Yeah.'

'Excellent.'

## 72

The softer, sweeter sound of Chicago soul was no less potent than its Detroit counterpart. In the south, blues and country music reigned and their influence seeped through, and in the big coastal cities, home to the major recording companies, lush popular balladry played its part. But soul, in all its forms, was the result of an explosive mix of gospel and the black, secular music of the day. Gospel, itself, was the result of an explosive mix – of the black spiritual tradition and the European hymn tradition. And they were each a product of their own chemical-like reactions. And so it went back, to the dawn of humankind. That's art for you, and maybe everything else too.

What Romance wasn't really sure of was the (even approximate) date of the dawn of humankind. For him this was an important question, as it signified the point in time from which soul was to evolve. He had seen scientists on telly talk about 100,000 or 200,000 years ago for *Homo sapiens* and millions more for *Homo* other stuff. But it was all rather vague and clearly there was no moment, unless one goes back to the Big Bang and scientists now seemed to be accepting that even that couldn't have exploded out of nowhere.

Could there have been a moment when the first single-celled life form came into being? When the first ape took the first two-legged step? When the first human made the first cave painting? When the first sentence was spoken? When the first song was sung? It was frustrating that there were no definitive answers, but Romance didn't blame the scientists. The soul fraternity couldn't even decide among themselves the date of the first soul record and that was – it must have been – a matter of record.

'Sam Cooke *A Change Is Gonna Come*,' was Deptford Dave's suggestion.

'That was 1964, you idiot.'

'Was it? Well something else by Sam Cooke then.'

'James Brown *Please Please Please*. When was that?'

'1956.'

'Yeah but you know what… who was James Brown's main vocal influence? Little Willie John. *Need Your Love So Bad*. Fucking great record.'

'Oh? James Brown did that later, didn't he?'

'And what about *I Got a Woman* by Ray Charles. That was '54, I think. Sam Cooke was still singing gospel till '57.'

'You know he was part Apache?'

'What?'

'James Brown. He was part Apache. Once you know, I think you can hear it in his voice.'

'You freak.'

'The Orioles, with Sonny Til. They were the most soulful of the doo wop groups.'

'Full of tears and misery, come on baby, see about me!'

'Good old Sonny Til.'

'They were just about the first proper doo wop group too.'

'Yeah but James Brown had been singing *Please Please Please* for two years before the Little Willie John release. He just couldn't get it recorded.'

'Yeah but it came from him singing The Orioles song *Baby Please Don't Go* as part of his act. It evolved out of that song.'

Doo wop. That explosive mix of vocal harmonies and rhythm and blues rhythms. The rhythmic strumming of the original Orioles guitarist, Tommy Gaither, taking the place of swathes of poppy orchestration.

'Careful.'

Solomon was driving. He had started singing *Tears and Misery* too exuberantly for comfort.

In November 1950, Gaither took a bend too fast and managed to crash with considerable irony into a drive-in restaurant. He was killed instantly. Two other members of the group were pulled unconscious from the car.

Romance closed his eyes.

# 73

A flame exists in an instant and then is gone and, as that instant is infinitely short, so Hippy John wondered if it could really be said to exist at all. A moment that is captured on camera exists as an image, but not – and never did – in reality. In reality it only existed as a part of the flow of stuff. Change is constant and the elements of the flame burn and disappear into the air and do whatever they do, but at the same time the flame of the candle in Chichester Cathedral – just like the flame of the candle on the altar of the church in the Birmingham of Hippy John's childhood – stayed alight and was a thing in itself.

Hippy John used to think that he thought too much, and he envied those happy ones who didn't. His thinking always seemed to lead to a confirmation of his uselessness, how pathetic he was and the meaninglessness of his existence. But that didn't happen in the cathedral. The imposing scale of the place could have belittled him but, rather than being depressed by his own smallness, he found that he could take comfort in the greatness of something else. And anyway, there's nothing more intimate than looking into the flame of a candle.

But when he stepped into the cathedral, he didn't see the candle straight away. In fact, he didn't see anything straight away – nothing in particular anyway. The immediate effect of the greatness of the place was too overpowering for him to focus on anything. For a while, all he could see was the space of it, but that was invisible and he was dizzy not even thinking about it. At some moment, the little table with the booklets and postcards, which had been directly in front of him from the moment he walked through the doorway, jumped out at him as if from a bush.

He needed to sit down. And if there's one thing of which churches and cathedrals never seem short, it's places to sit. He took a pew, close to the back (or, from the outside, the front).

The space was awe-inspiring. It wasn't the stone of the cathedral that impressed him so much but the space, which was strange because the space would still have been there even if the cathedral hadn't. In fact, there were a huge number of other such spaces all over the place, which just didn't happen to have a cathedral built around them. Hippy John wondered if the space would still be there even if everything in it were sucked out – all the atoms and particles – everything. Could nothing have dimensions? Could nothing be measured? If space only made sense when there was stuff in it, then did it exist at all?

Without any kind of manmade time-measuring device, the only way of telling how long one has been sitting on an ecclesiastical pew is the degree of achiness of the bum, and there came a time when Hippy John decided that he had been sitting long enough. He stood up. And having stood up, the natural thing to do seemed to be to go somewhere.

He looked about and observed a strange centrifugal force at work that attracted people to the edges, closer to the visible stuff and away from the space, and he felt the draw of it himself. Spending time in the greatness of the space was for the brave-hearted; Hippy John was pleased with himself for having done it, but being there on his feet made him giddy. So he took himself to the whispering coldness of one of the cathedral aisles, and it was there that he was drawn to the candle.

The candle could well have been the candle that he remembered from his confirmation. Hippy John looked closely as it burnt, ever changing, ever the same, and he saw something of himself in the flame. When he thought of himself as a boy, then as a man, then as a helpless man hanging on to the edge of a bridge, then as a man walking into a cathedral for the first time since he was a boy, it was very much as if he were thinking of someone else, and yet the ever changing flame was the same flame too. Perhaps he had a soul after all.

Some German tourists walked by behind him. He heard them talking and one of them was a young boy. It occurred to Hippy John that he could have become an amusing feature – the strange, bearded man by the candle – to be talked about by mothers and children in lieu of high art. He turned and saw the child being held by the hand, and he felt the love his own dead mother.

'It's for Richard, you know,' said a voice from behind him. It was another old woman. 'Are you a fan too?'

Hippy John didn't know what to say. He didn't know anyone called Richard. There had been a young man, Rich – a rough sleeper he had met in the woods – but he hadn't seen him for a long time and, even if this woman knew Rich, how could she know that he had known him and why would Rich have fans anyway? If he had been a pop star or a footballer, surely he wouldn't have been sleeping rough in the woods. And he would have said something. Wouldn't he?

Perhaps she meant Cliff Richard. Hippy John knew about Cliff Richard. And Cliff Richard had lots of fans and lots of them were older women. But she wouldn't have referred to him as 'Richard', would she? He would either be 'Cliff Richard' or 'Cliff'.

'He was an orphan. They buried him here, but we only have a bit of his arm now. His internal organs are in Dover. He made sure the priests wore clean clothes and had their hair cut and prohibited gambling at baptisms. Of course, Henry VIII had it in for him. I come here every day to say a little prayer. Even if I don't feel like it, I make myself. You can write it down, if you want, and put it in the Richard box, but what's the point of that? Do you really think a dead saint would be bothered to unfold and read all those silly bits of paper? The verger does it. I know he does. I've seen him! Much better to light a candle and talk to him straight, even though it says St Crispin.'

And with that the old woman shut her eyes and stood, quiet and motionless. Hippy John waited. He thought it rude to walk away mid-prayer. The woman had talked to him and he hadn't responded and he felt some sort of acknowledgement was appropriate. He hadn't worked out what this would be, but he knew he should wait for her to finish her prayer. And then he kept on waiting. It was a long prayer – at least, it seemed to be. Hippy John didn't know how long prayers lasted these days. He hadn't prayed since he was a child. (Usually, back then, the prayers were orchestrated by adults and were never longer than a few sentences. The Lord's Prayer was quite a long one, but this woman's was much longer than that.) Because he kept expecting the praying to end, Hippy John was finding it difficult to judge how long it was lasting. An infinite number of moments of dashed expectation could add up to anything. And because he was primed for the ending of it, he didn't have the capacity to wonder what she was praying. Then she stopped. She opened her eyes and looked at him.

'Love what you don't like,' she said. 'Learn to love what you don't necessarily like. That's the key. I always feel better for it. It works every time. People used to come from all over to pray here. And there were miracles. Things happened. It was like Thomas the Beckett but without the blood and bits of brain.' Her eyes sharpened. 'And no hanky panky!'

Startled, Hippy John shifted his body weight away from

her. He hadn't touched her.

'He didn't believe in that. Oh yes, he put a stop to all that. Do you pray?'

Now a response was needed.

'Yes,' he said.

It was a lie.

Normally, Hippy John wasn't one to lie and it didn't come easily. But he felt it disrespectful to say no, having seen the woman put so much time into it herself.

The old woman continued looking at him. Suddenly, Hippy John felt that she was waiting expectantly to observe him in action. Not wanting to disappoint, he closed his eyes.

# 74

Sam Cooke didn't see his young son drown in the family swimming pool because he wasn't there. The boy's mother didn't see him drown either, because she wasn't looking. Some say Cooke was racked with guilt for being away from home so much; others say that he blamed his wife.

Ray Charles, however, was a witness to his younger brother drowning in the family laundry tub. He was the only witness and he failed to intervene. He then lost his sight and grew up – haunted by the memory of his screaming, distraught mother carrying little George's lifeless body from the tub – and became a highly talented musician of many questionable habits. He had a foul mouth. He took a multitude of drugs. He impregnated a multitude of women. And he pillaged gospel music. He was Ray Charles 'the bishop', 'the right reverend', 'the high priest of soul'. He would simply substitute profane lyrics for holy ones. *It Must Be Jesus* became *I Got a Woman*. *This Little Light of Mine* became *This Little Girl of Mine*. And he would sing as if he were in church. But it was The Orioles post-

Gaither 1953 classic *Crying in the Chapel* – a pious ballad that caused a storm in the secular music world – that took unsolicited sanctuary in Romance's brain when he was half asleep in the car on the M40.

Romance, Solomon and Deptford Dave's round trip to the Rik Tik Bar didn't unfold according to plan. When Romance opened his eyes, the boys were in Birmingham and he could see that they hadn't crashed, despite Solomon's driving, but he could see too that Solomon had no idea where he was going. By the time they entered the venue and were greeted inside the door by the canine Soul Sam, it was 1.00 a.m. and there was only an hour of music remaining.

J.J. Barnes *Lonely No More* was blaring out. Without having to look, Romance knew that Spaghetti was DJing, as not many had that record and he had heard Spaghetti play it before. A quick scan of the room revealed a hardcore of Birmingham's soul finest and then he turned to the bar and saw Littlehampton Lee, and Lee saw Romance too.

'Fuck me,' Lee said, walking over. 'What the fuck are you doing here? Fuckin' 'ell.'

'We've just come up. We're a bit late. We got lost.'

'You fucking twats. It's been fucking brilliant.'

'No Lainie?'

'No she's here somewhere. Moaning about too much crossover. We were up here last night for the Essential Modern Soul night. That was the fucking business.'

'Oh right. Cool. What about the little 'un?'

'Jimmy wouldn't come to that.'

'I mean Ree, Lee.'

'Oh. We got a kind of a nanny-type person now, so we're out and about mate, givin' it some. I mean I love her to bits and everything, but fuck me it's good to be out.'

'A nanny-type person?'

'Long story mate, long story. But it's all fucking cool.'

'Yeah, I was thinking of getting a nanny,' interjected Deptford Dave.

'What?'

'Well, not a nanny. An au pair. Are they different? Au pairs are just the young ones, aren't they?'

'Dave, you haven't got any kids. You live alone, in a flat above a café on Deptford Broadway. Do you remember?'

'Yeah, but that's why I thought it'd be good for the au pair. No kids. They'd jump at the chance. Normally they cook and clean and stuff and then have kids to look after too, but with me there'd be no kids, so it'll be a doddle compared to going with anyone else. And they're only cheap. I think it's a win-win.'

Romance and Lee were thrown by his logic.

'Isn't what you're talking about called having a Thai bride?'

'No. You two are weird and perverted.'

Perhaps they were. Perhaps they all were. Romance did acknowledge that he gained some perverted pleasure from their display of such shocking dedication in travelling to the Rik Tik Bar, and the fact that, for them, that behaviour wasn't weird was undeniably weird.

The record ended. Silence.

'Spaghetti,' said Lee.

'He's drunk, I suppose.'

'Bladdered.'

'I like it. A bit of peace and quiet at a soul do. I think at five o'clock in the morning at the 100 Club there should be twenty minutes of no music. Everyone just gets a chance to mill about and have a chat.'

'Music is the cup which holds the wine of silence,' said Solomon.

They all looked at him.

Lee spoke first. 'Is that why you're called Solomon? Cos you're so fucking wise?'

'Hail King Solomon!'

Solomon looked surprised. But, thanks to Dave, the question went unanswered.

'He did that record, didn't he?'

'Who?'

'King Solomon. *Separation.* I've got it, somewhere.'

'R&B shite.'

Suddenly the music kicked in. It was J.J. Barnes *Lonely No More.*

'For fuck's sake.'

It was a pleasant surprise to see his old friend Lee, but Romance needed a drink after that journey and he was keen to see his new friend, Bettye. As Lee had been speaking, Romance had been looking over his friend's shoulder but hadn't caught sight of her. At last, he approached the bar, but it was a scrawny, hairy male youth who presented himself.

Romance asked for three pints of Guinness as if they were uppermost in his mind and then, while the youth was pouring, as if to fill the time, he came out with it.

'Is Bettye not working here tonight?'

'Betty?'

'Yeah, Bettye.'

The youth shook its head.

'Oh.'

This was a disappointment. But Romance had devised a plan that he was to put into action in just such an eventuality and that was to leave her a note. And as Deptford Dave had been enthusiastically pointing Solomon in the direction of Solihull, Romance, in his sleepy, dreamy state, had been contemplating what to write:

*Dear Bettye,*

*I met you a couple of months ago at the soul thing. I'm sorry to have missed you this evening. I was looking forward to re-admiring your beauty and charm. I hope that everything is OK with your boyfriend, but if by any chance something awful has happened and the relationship has fallen apart, then perhaps you might consider calling me. Perhaps you have caught him cheating or perhaps you have simply grown apart. These things happen. Being into soul music, I would understand your pain. You could take your troubles to the chapel, and get down on your knees and pray, and then your burdens will be lighter, and you'll surely find the way. But if, like me, and I suspect Ray Charles, you're not chapel-inclined, just remember, wherever the rain falls, green grass grows, and also, as Dorothy Norwood, the great gospel singer, put it in a rare soul outing, 'There's got to be rain in your life (to appreciate the sunshine)'.*

*Perhaps, Bettye, you might allow me to be a ray of that sunshine. (And it need not be a restrictive relationship.)*

And then he would leave his number, just in case she had lost it (easily done). And then a PS about the Dorothy Norwood song:

*It's on the other side of 'Get Aboard the Soul Train' on GRC.*

'There's no Betty. No Betty works here.'

It was when they were half way back to London, somewhere on the M40, that Romance remembered her name was Jane.

'Fuck fuck fuck,' he lambasted himself, as the others wittered on about the place of crossover on the allnighter scene and then, again, about the early influence of James Brown and to what extent a great voice was lost to funk.

# 75

James Brown isn't a popular artist on the northern soul scene. His funky, poppy records of the sixties and seventies have little of the mystical glory of soul. But he was one of the great originators of soul singing in the fifties and putting the funk into rhythm and blues was an achievement that even Romance couldn't deny.

Abandoned by his mother and brought up by his aunt in a brothel, by the age of sixteen James had already been convicted for armed robbery. And yet, when he wanted to sing, it was still to the church he turned.

The Gospel Starlighters. They didn't last long. But because James Brown never recorded as a gospel singer, there was no traumatic switch to rhythm and blues. There was, however, still the problem of procuring a recording contract. His soulful singing was perceived as too raw. But James's live performances were becoming renowned and when King A&R man Ralph Bass heard James singing *Please Please Please* he decided to fly James and his backing singers to Cincinnati to record them. When Syd Nathan, the label boss, heard the record, he fired Bass on the spot.

New styles can be hard to take, Romance reflected, as he began flicking through a box of records. But it's the very newness – being of the moment – that gives something the potential to be moment-free – to last forever. To transcend time.

Humans had been artistic long before *Please Please Please* and Romance knew it. In fact, they became artistic tens of thousands of years before *Please Please Please*. No one really knows why. Language exploded upon us – perhaps that was it. Or perhaps the hand of God gave our species souls. We became self-aware. We became able to anticipate and we became aware of time. Would language have the power to make us self-aware? Was language possible without self-awareness? Perhaps soul was inevitable from that moment: the moment of souls, the moment of self-awareness. Or perhaps soul too, like consciousness, was a miracle.

Romance had had moments in his life that had jumped out at him and grabbed a hold and shaken him. Inevitably, they were a part of the flow, coming from somewhere and going somewhere else, but they shouted out, 'I am a moment! You will never be the same after me! You will remember me forever!' They were evolved but distinct, passing but permanent. Walking away from JBP, filled with the nothingness, leaving her on her doorstep and not knowing why. And lying with her, on the soft grass of the cliff top, awash in the sun and the sounds of the sea, knowing that life could not possibly be any better and so would, inevitably, worsen, as it wouldn't stand still. It would never be as good as that again, and that knowledge and that haunting memory would forever be with him.

His life was punctuated – punctured – by these arbitrary moments. Collective, regular, planned events, such as Christmas and Cleethorpes, gave a comforting pulse and the repetitiveness of them provided solace from the arbitrary nature of life. He would never miss Cleethorpes for this reason alone.

But it was only through music that he was freed from the restraints of time altogether. In the same way that he seemed to be able to hear the forces of pure, placeless space, he seemed too to be able to hear the forces of pure time. Just as the revealed space flowed and was matter-free and immeasurable, so the revealed time flowed and was immeasurable too. It was beyond the time that we commonly perceive – beyond the measurable time that is dependent on the relative motion of objects (from the heavenly bodies all the way down to the inner workings of an atom). This was a true, intangible time that left no material traces. Every instant seemed to hold the past within it and to anticipate the future. It was hearing, having heard and about to hear all at once. It was the past without being remembered and the future without being foreknown. It was pure anticipation. It didn't matter how many times Romance heard a record, an intended surprise in the music always felt like a surprise. He anticipated the surprises in the music and delighted in being surprised by them. The experience was the same, but it was fresh and new. Each listen led to new discoveries. Each listen was the same but different. Time itself was always new and presented itself forcefully through these repeated listens. Time was no more a mere container for successive events than a cathedral was a container for pure space or than the electrical bits and bobs in Romance's brain were the container for his soul or than the grooves in the vinyl of the records he was handling were a container for theirs. It was as if the past and the future co-existed and time was captured. It filled the now and bridged the abyss. The voice was a human's – and it had to be – and yet it pointed to so much more.

So soul music, for Romance, as well as obliterating the boundaries between within and without, blurred the boundaries between space and time too. This soul wave wasn't an event in time and space but was an event of time and space. Every little element existed in time and in space and yet was filled with a timeless, spaceless energy. It was almost too much for him to absorb.

At last he found the record. It was about five in the morning (again). *Please Please Please*. Federal 12258. He didn't know how many times he had listened to it. He didn't know how many times he had listened to any record. But when he took the record out of its paper sleeve and placed it carefully on the deck and pressed start and gently lowered the needle, after two tantalising revolutions the soul took over and all those times were one.

The soul was happening, there and then. It was beyond

the artist. It was with him. Romance watched as the needle trod its delicate path and it was there and then that he was who he was: a part of something bigger, sharing life.

# 76

*Dear Romance,*

*Thank you for your proposal, 'Looking for Romance (with Steve Davis)', which was passed on to me. I read it with great interest.*

*I can see that you are very passionate about this subject and that is a prerequisite for making a film. And you are to be commended for getting Steve Davis on board with this project. There seems to be an interesting side to his character of which most people are unaware.*

*However, while it is interesting to read your views on music – amongst other things – it is unclear how such thoughts will transfer themselves to the screen. In short, I find it difficult to visualise this film and when we commission a film a visual narrative is of primary importance. As well as an idea of the content, a detailed exposition of the form and structure is needed, without which there is little to go on.*

*A film of this nature is very difficult to place on television, even when suggested by a seasoned professional. It is very personal and rather niche. A good idea is to watch television and try to think of ideas that would suit existing documentary strands and direct submissions to those strands, whether current affairs or 'human interest', and to do everything you can to gain some professional experience in whatever capacity.*

*Yours sincerely,*

*Joanna Quick*

*Deputy commissioning editor, documentaries*
*Dear Ms Quick,*

*Thank you very much for your letter concerning my proposal, 'Looking for Romance (with Steve Davis)'.*

*The structure of the film will be based upon the film beginning at the beginning of the journey and ending at the end of it. The other elements will fall neatly into this. As to the form, it will be a combination of highly artistic, static shots and lively cinema verite to suit the subtleties and juxtapositions of the film.*

*I hope that this clears up all outstanding issues.*

*Yours sincerely,*

*Romance*

## 77

If a film were to have been made about the inside of Hippy John's mind, then cinema verite would have been the way to go (although any such film proposal would have no doubt fallen foul of the Joanna Quick visualisation test). But really no cinematic style could ever have come close to doing the subject justice.

His mind was frantic – at least it seemed frantic to him. The old woman had looked so much at peace while she was praying but Hippy John couldn't stop thinking. What should he pray about? How does one do it? Did it matter? Surely, as long as he remained still and kept his eyes closed, it would look as if he were praying. Was that deceitful to the old woman? To God??

He decided to try.

'Dear God.' God? Dear? That sounded odd. Should he pray to God or to Jesus, or to *Lord*, perhaps? Perhaps *Lord* covered both. Perhaps God would spot that. 'Dear God. Please take care of Rich. He seemed like a nice young man. He helped me with the wood and told me about the restaurant and the food they threw out. And please take care of the woman and boy in the village. They were good to me. And please take care of Lee and Lainie. They went out of their way to help me. I didn't appreciate it at the time but now I do. Let me know if I can do anything for them. And please take care of the old lady next to me. I am only talking to you because of her.'

He paused there. There was a lot of asking for people to be taken care of. Perhaps he was overdoing that. Perhaps prayers shouldn't just be about asking for people one had met to be taken care of, but he wasn't sure what else would be appropriate.

'Please give me strength,' he said, 'to do what's right and to live how I should. To go with this life how it was meant to be.'

He had no idea how long he had been praying for. Had he been praying for a good amount of time? Had it been shorter or longer than the woman's praying?

He opened his eyes. The woman was gone. He looked about. He couldn't see her.

# 78

When the boys were on their way back from the Rik Tik Bar – the time when Romance asked about Bettye when he should have asked about Jane – there was some talk of visiting Thelonius Tripp's mural. It wasn't too far out of the way and none of them had seen it.

'Well it's not too far out of the way,' Romance said, as he studied the map.

'Yeah, but it'll be pitch fucking black. We won't see a fucking thing.'

'Good point, well made.'

'We could wait till the morning light and then see it in the splendour of the dawn.'

'Fuck off.'

And those were the final two words on the matter. But it wasn't long before the same three boys found themselves on the M40 again, and this time it was light.

'Oh! It's light!'

'So?'

'So we could go see the Tripp, couldn't we?'

'Yeah. We could.'

They were on their way back from Burnley. It was a sunny summer Sunday morning. None of them had slept.

'We could. We should.'

'We will! We... will!'

It was early afternoon before they found it. Deptford Dave was map-reading but the only map with which he had any familiarity was the London tube map.

'These roads are all the same colour.'

'What?'

'These roads are all the same colour. They should be different colours. Then I could say, "Turn right when you hit the blue road." I don't mean the actual road should be blue but there should be a blue sign or something. Otherwise how are you supposed to know? They're all yellow.'

And he was being constantly distracted by the shapes and colours of the English countryside: the greenness of the greens, the complicated roundness of the trees, the undulations, the lumpiness of everything.

'Fuck me, what's that?'

'It's a sheep, Dave.'

'Well why's it looking at us like that?'

'I think because we've stopped at the entrance to his field because you directed us down this dead-end lane. It's the sheep equivalent of someone standing at your front door, isn't it? Wouldn't you wonder who they were?'

'It'd probably be the postman,' said Solomon. 'He might have a record.'

'Well he looks like he's gonna go for us.'

'Yeah, right. Three London soul boys mauled to death by killer sheep. In their car.'

'It could happen. Look what happened to George Scott.'

'What?'

'George Scott from The Hesitations. He was killed while sitting in his car.'

'By a sheep?'

'Well, they said it was a human, but there's no proof.'

'But he was shot. What animal, other than a human, is capable of firing a gun?'

'A monkey?'

'OK, a monkey. So it could have been a monkey in sheep's clothing. Go up to that sheep and offer him a banana and see what happens.'

'No way. I'm not getting out.'

And it got worse when Dave began hallucinating.

'Wooah!'

'What?'

'The reds all just lit up.'

'What?'

'In the mapbook. All the reds just flashed at me. They must be wired up to something.'

He began turning the pages and looking inside the covers for signs of a connection.

'It must run off batteries somewhere. Wey! The greens just did!'

And so it continued. Different colour flashes induced by

lack of sleep and God knows what.

This is a good reason why the northern soul scene should be subsidised, Romance thought. If it wasn't for the soul scene, crackpots like Spaghetti Weston, Mick the Twitch and Deptford Dave would be loose on the streets. Someone should approach social services about it.

'Why have we got him map-reading?' Romance asked Solomon.

'Because I'm driving and the only other person in the car is you.'

When they did make it to the village it was largely by chance and none of them were aware they had arrived. Deptford Dave was convinced they were somewhere near the flashing blue lake.

'I think we need to turn right soon. On to another yellow road. Look out for a yellow one.'

'A yellow one, right.'

'Ha! Look at that! Another great big bloody mural!'

Romance didn't need to look. The mural leapt out at them. They had turned a corner and then the great big thing jumped out and hit them in the face. The fierce, angular luridness of it was so out of keeping with the general lumpiness of the preceding miles that it momentarily distracted and dazzled Solomon and he swerved on to the grass verge.

'They must really go in for them round here.'

'Bloody hell, it's a bit freaky, init? What the fuck's that all about?'

And then they were past it.

'Could be a village of Satanists. They go in for that sort of stuff in the countryside.'

'It did look a bit like one of Thelonius's, didn't it? What with those weird people dancing or whatever. Quite trippy.'

'Maybe there's like a house-style in Berkshire. And they picked Thelonius because he fitted it so well.'

They had motored on for about another two miles and had begun a meandering discussion about the influence of rural, southern, more blues-oriented sixties soul on the edgier, punchier soul of the northern American cities when Romance and Solomon realised, with startling synchronicity, what had happened.

# 79

Romance was unhappy that *Looking for Romance (with Steve Davis)* had not seemed to have received the attention of Mr Spensely but had been passed to a deputy. Who was this Joanna Quick? She didn't seem very capable. Perhaps Mr Spensely was ill. Of course, it was always possible that he had been forced into early retirement for failing to appreciate standout documentary proposals. Joanna Quick could be filling in until a suitable replacement was found. (She certainly didn't seem to be up to the job herself.)

And then the weeks went by and still Joanna Quick didn't reply to Romance's reply. Her distinct lack of quickness put some doubt into Romance's mind over the capability of Joanna Quick even to perform the role of deputy editor competently. (He could probably do a better job himself, Romance speculated, though he knew in his heart that he was born to create rather than to manage.) Of course, there was always the possibility that Joanna Quick never received the reply to her reply. Things were always getting lost in the system in big organisations like Channel 4. It was also possible that Joanna Quick wasn't slow and inefficient at all and was actually very quick and was busy finalising the budget etc. before replying, or that the idea was tied up in the committee stages and she was doing her very best to push it through. But the delay began to test Romance's commitment to Channel 4, and the time came when he considered that if he was offered money from elsewhere to make the film then he would consider considering taking it, and then Channel 4 would only have themselves to blame.

# 80

Hippy John scoured the cathedral, but the woman was nowhere to be seen. Suddenly, instinctively, he checked his pockets, and then, almost as suddenly, felt ashamed that he had done so. Momentarily, he had been overcome by the familiar feeling of opening his eyes, or lowering his arms, or turning round – whatever it might be – and realising he had been duped. But his pockets were lacking to exactly the same extent as they had been lacking before. It didn't seem as if anything had changed.

'Hello,' said a voice. Another voice, another surprise. 'And welcome.'

The concentration of looking for the old woman had led Hippy John to miss this figure lurking in the foreground. Either that or it had popped out of nowhere.

It was a woman-man. It was a man, in a dress. It was a smiling figure dressed in black come to carry Hippy John away.

Hippy John checked himself. It was a priest.

'He was a twin, you know, St Crispin. Crispin and

Crispinian. What about that? Cobblers. Both of them. Preached in the day, made shoes by night. Stretched on the rack, thrown into the river with millstones round their necks. Survived that, then beheaded. They came into the world together, suffered it together and left it together, but it's mainly the name of Crispin that lives on. Strange that. It doesn't seem fair does it? But then the world isn't a fair place. We all know that.'

He paused and smiled his little but firm smile and his eyes fell over the over-sized sweatshirt.

'Ah, St Augustine. For him, it was time. "What then is time? If no one asks me, I know what it is. If I wish to explain it to him who asks, I do not know." '

The priest's eyes lingered on the sweatshirt. 'What an interesting idea, to transpose time with the human soul.' He stopped, lost in the thought of it. 'Both so real. Both so intangible. He was a clever chap, St Augustine.'

The priest's smile broadened and he opened his arms a little. 'Enjoy our wonderful space. It's a blessing, the cathedral, and it's for everyone. We all need a quiet place to reflect. And there are times when we all need someone to talk to too. Alas, I cannot work miracles, but I am here to listen and to guide as best I can.'

He looked at Hippy John, smile unwavering. Hippy John looked at him with the surprised, wide-eyed look he'd had since the priest's opening words. And as Hippy John's look remained unwavering too, the priest gently edged away and slipped into the cool, stony hollowness of his blessed cathedral.

First the old woman and then the priest. Suddenly everyone wanted to talk to him. Hippy John could feel the goodness of it and so he didn't resent them for it. And it was better than being ignored or, worse, sneered at, which is what he was used to. But he didn't feel the urge to talk back to them. The old woman was potty and the priest, however clever, however wise, however good, seemed divorced from the world as Hippy John knew it. And Hippy John didn't want to talk anyway. He just wanted to be. To feel.

He was pleased that he had ventured into the cathedral. He had been moved by the space of it and he had been moved by the flame, and praying had been interesting, at least. And he had no need to wonder now about the inside of the cathedral or to be intimidated by it. But he was pleased to leave it too. Outside the great entrance, he paused in the even vaster brightness of the day. It was a simple pause for thought; he knew where he was going.

# 81

'Bloody hell, look at it.'

The boys had turned round, gone back and got out of the car. They were standing in front of the Tripp.

'Do you consider it pre- or post-Renaissance in its primary influences?'

'I consider it beyond fucking hope.'

'Do you think it's supposed to be like that?'

'It's a Tripp, init? It's definitely a Tripp.'

'I reckon it was done at Blackburn. That looks like the Empress Ballroom to me.'

'What the fuck are you on about? It was done here, weren't it? It's on the bloody wall!'

'It must be a northern soul thing. You can tell by the pain in their faces.'

'Yeah and that light could be like the light of soul music lighting up the world.'

'There isn't a DJ, is there? Maybe that light is instead of the DJ.'

'Or the DJ could be round the corner.'

'Round what corner?'

'Round the corner of the wall.'

'Yeah but it's even weirder and freakier than his other ones, init? Or maybe it's just seeing it so big.'

'But why the fuck would they want a great big fucking mural about northern soul in their little village?'

'I reckon I was right the first time. It's fucking satanic.'

'Ah, you're admiring my artwork!'

The voice popped out at them like a priest's. But it came from behind them. If it was Satan, he was sounding very much like an old man who had smoked and drunk too much over the years and who had been born somewhere in the southern English countryside at some time in the first half of the twentieth century. If it was Thelonius Tripp, he must have aged before his time and forgotten that he came from Brockley.

The boys turned together to see a grinning Gerald. None of them said anything.

'It's good, ain't it?' grinning man continued.

'You're not Thelonius Tripp,' said Solomon, wisely.

'You're not even anything like him,' said Deptford Dave.

'Actually the eyes are quite similar,' offered Romance. 'He's got that wide-eyed Thelonius look.'

'Eyes bollocks,' said Deptford Dave, ambiguously, his own eyes outdoing those of Gerald and the absent Thelonius combined.

Gerald now lost his grin and looked worried. He was taken aback at how the conversation had turned.

'What have you done with Thelonius?' demanded Deptford Dave.

'Dave, just because this man is not Thelonius, doesn't mean he's done anything with Thelonius. Thelonius is in London. I spoke to him yesterday.'

Dave was quiet while he thought on this. He wanted to unmask the man, as if they were in the final scene of an episode of *Scooby Doo*. The others wanted to know who he was too, but they were happy to presume that they were seeing an accurate representation of the man inside.

Gerald was used to being blamed for things. He was now worried that something had happened to his friend Thelonius. He didn't have many friends and he couldn't afford to lose any.

'Thelonius is a good man,' he said. 'And I'm a good friend of Thelonius. We both see the world through artists' eyes.'

He looked at Deptford Dave then quickly looked away from Deptford Dave.

'But Thelonius did this, didn't he?'

'Well, he helped, yes. It was a joint effort. It was an artistic collaboration, if you like. We shared a vision.'

'What's it about then?'

'Well, you know, that's not an easy question you know. It's very deep and symbolic. Really you should look into it and see where it leads you. People take away different things from it. It's supposed to make you think. To make you feel.'

'So you don't know then?'

Gerald wasn't used to such truculence. The villagers hated

the mural but were too polite to interrogate him about it. And they knew that he had been working under instruction. And Thelonius had done nothing but praise him for his assistance and his enthusiasm. He was left feeling that he'd had a big creative input, and he had heard the others saying it was deep and could mean different things to different people.

'It's had a lot of local interest, this has. The news people from Reading were up here.'

'Yeah, I'm not bloody surprised.'

'So what record's being played then?' Dave asked, as a further test. 'There's no DJ and you can't see the record.' Gerald looked confused, but the other two boys rescued him.

'Sometimes it's difficult to tell anyway, when they're going round.'

'Yeah but it won't be going round, will it? Because it's a painting.'

'If it's an accurate painting, maybe they don't really go round then.'

'What?'

'Well, if the record's not going round at that precise, fixed moment, then how could it be going round at any other moment? At every single moment that you can think of, it must be still. So it's always still.'

'Where does the music come from then?'

'I dunno.'

'Well that doesn't make sense then.'

'Time's a relative thing, and it's all down to the relationship between the observer and the universe. That's basic Einstein.'

'So if the observer's Dave and he's an idiot, then time stops.'

'Yeah. It's a black hole.'

'Fuck.'

'So how come you got roped into helping out with this then?' Romance asked the bewildered Gerald. 'Do you know the soul vicar?'

'The soul vicar?'

'The vicar.'

'The vicar's a good man.'

'I should bloody think so. Is he about? We should say hello.'

'It's Sunday.'

'Yeah.'

'So he'll be vicaring. Probably up at the church. He'll be telling people about God and what-have-you.'

At the mention of God, there was a screeching of brakes. Then the screeching of brakes was followed by the smashing, cracking of wood and that was followed by silence.

'Oh no, not again,' Gerald said, and they all looked down to the road. A blue Mini was now parked in the middle of a well-kept lawn like some pop art garden feature.

'The Moore-Hacketts aren't going to be happy about that. Not at all.'

# 82

No one knew the age of Gerald, including Gerald, and years of drink made guessing impossible. But he had certainly been in the village for a long time and it was a good home to him. Hippy John had never had as serious a drink problem but he had nowhere to call home, and the argumentative, baby screaming, record-filled building site of a home that was Lee and Lainie's had seemed to him an English Shangri-la.

When he stood in the doorway of the cathedral, the brightness of the world all around him, he knew the moment to be the beginning of a journey back to Lee and Lainie and, when he reflected on that moment, it felt as if walking to Littlehampton was the next thing he did. In fact, there were many (possibly an infinite number) of little things that he did in between and some bigger ones too (most notably his visit to the Richard of Chichester Association drop-in centre). It's just that to him, it felt as if it were the next thing.

But he didn't retrace his steps; he walked along the main

road. He walked steadily, rhythmically, and the rhythm of the walk was complemented by the irregular sounds of passing cars and, in the gaps between, by birds, a distant tractor and a small, creaking bicycle with an oversized human load, and the sweet melody of it all was a framework within which his mind could wander, and he thought about where he was going and where he had come from and the journey of his life. It seemed so random, his moment of being – each moment of being – and the regularity of his steps was matched by the thrilling, instinctive rapidity of his thought.

The RCA people were good people. He had liked the man in there. He had long known about the drop-in centre, but in the misery of his previous existence he had felt fearful about dropping in. That seemed strange to him now. The man had been warm and welcoming and they had sat down and discussed the hippy's situation. Hippy John talked about Littlehampton and the man talked about the bedsits they had there and the day centre they had in Bognor Regis and none of it was a foregone conclusion but Hippy John seemed to tick the boxes both in terms of his situation and his mindset and there was no time like the present to fill in the form and the man had a feeling that one of the bedsits might be becoming available and, if so, even though there was something of a waiting list, he could see that Hippy John's case was a good one. And Hippy John didn't mind being a good case. He wasn't ashamed of it. It wasn't a bad thing, being a good case.

And in the bedsit Hippy John was going to drink tea that he was going to brew himself. He was going to eat food that he was going to prepare himself. He was going to walk round the block, walk to the seafront, look at the sea, think about it, visit the job centre and present himself as a man able to work and with fixed abode. He was going to drop into the drop-in centre, thank everyone there and lose himself in the soft, warm dryness of his bed. And when he felt that he had an air of reasonableness about himself, he was going to go round to Lee and Lainie's.

He still wasn't sure if he deserved all the help he had been given – and, since Lee and Lainie, it was the RCA who had taken the lead – but he was definitely grateful for it.

# 83

The Moore-Hacketts were very rarely happy. They weren't really happy types. When they met, and when they first kissed, and when they married, the feeling they shared was relief that things were happening in their lives that were supposed to happen. Happiness wasn't a part of it. And when they were in the pub on the Sunday lunchtime that the blue Mini made its surprise visit to their lawn (and when Gerald made his comment to the soul boys that the Moore-Hacketts weren't going to be happy) they weren't happy either. Mr Moore-Hackett had ordered boiled potatoes but had been given sautéed. This, in itself, didn't make him unhappy – he liked sautéed potatoes and possibly even preferred them to boiled (he hadn't noticed sautéed on the menu) – but he was never going to be happy when things weren't happening as they should happen.

So when they arrived home from the pub and they saw that their fence was smashed and that the lawn that had been and should have been lovely was lovely no more, they were never going to be happy about it. Gerald had known that. The Moore-Hacketts weren't happy. They weren't happy at all.

It was the second time in a month that a car had driven through their fence on to their lawn. They had only just had the fence repaired and the lawn had barely recovered from its last onslaught.

'Oh no. It's happened again,' was Mrs Moore-Hackett's response. 'That bloody thing,' was Mr Moore-Hackett's.

He was referring to the mural. They were both convinced that the mural was the reason that their little corner of the road had suddenly become an accident black spot.

'We should have said something to the news when they were here. They only came because of all the accidents there'd been, but all they got was the blasted vicar saying how lovely it was.'

The Moore-Hacketts hadn't wanted to make a fuss. They weren't the kind that made a fuss.

When they opened their front door there was a piece of paper on the floor of the hallway and on it was written a message:

'I momentarily lost concentration because of the horror painting,' followed by the contact details of the driver.

If they needed evidence, they now seemed to have it.

'Do you think we should show it to the vicar? How do you think Gerald would take it?'

Mrs Moore-Hackett decided that the first thing to do was to have a cup of tea.

## 84

Romance had a job to do and he put aside an hour a day, excluding travel: half an hour each side of the time that he had seen the blond girl on the escalator. So on the subsequent afternoons he stood at the entrance to the tube station, and he was beginning to wonder for how many days, weeks or months this would go on when she marched into view. And it was a march. This girl was in a hurry. She meant business. But Romance had no choice but to seize the moment and he stepped in front of her.

'Excuse me...'

She looked at him, irritatedly.

'You have lovely hair.'

She stopped. Her demeanor changed. Her face lit up. Her eyes glowed. She smiled a broad, friendly, beautiful smile.

'Oh thank you!' she said, accentuating the *thank* and tilting her head to accentuate the friendliness of it.

She looked at Romance, waiting for whatever was to happen next to happen. She was in no hurry at all.

This was quite unusual. Romance hadn't been expecting

her to stop. He hadn't anticipated it. Instead of all this friendly, wide-eyed, patient smiling he had been expecting at best a cursory, on-the-move 'Thank you', and he wouldn't have been surprised to find himself on the end of one of those get-away-you-crazed-pervert-before-I-call-the-police big city stares.

'I haven't really thought what to say next,' was all Romance could think of to say next.

'Oh never mind, I'm in no hurry. I'll just wait here until something pops into your head. Whatever it is, I'm sure it will be tip top and well worth the wait.'

She had an exaggerated, ditsy way of talking. It suited the brightness of her lipstick.

'You have nice eyes too.'

'Ooh, that's nice. Yes, that was a lovely thing to say. You're not doing badly. Not doing badly at all. So tell me, do you come here often?'

Romance had been going there often, at least that week, but this was dangerous territory. If he admitted his stalky behaviour he might scare off his pretty prey. On the other hand, she might delight in his irrational devotion.

'How are you when it comes to irrational devotion?' he asked.

'Oh, pro,' she answered, without hesitation. 'Yes, definitely pro. You can't beat a bit of irrational devotion.'

And then she paused, her eyes dropping momentarily.

'But really, when you think about it, don't you think that any kind of devotion would have some underlying reason for it? Or maybe all devotion is irrational. And if you're going to be devoted, you should be devoted to something good and lovely, like squirrels. Not Hitler, for example.'

'Squirrels can be quite mean. When I was a child, there was a squirrel who lived in the tree in our garden. Whenever anyone went under that tree, he'd throw things at them – try to drop nuts or whatever on our heads to get us away.'

She laughed. 'Well good for him. Too right too. Aren't you going to get that?'

'Get what?'

'Get that.' She nodded down to his side somewhere. 'Your phone's going.'

'Oh,' he said. 'No. I'm talking to you.'

'Oh but what if it's important? It could be the object of your irrational devotion. Or it could be your wife.'

Romance smiled, but still ignored the unrelenting ringing.

'It's not my wife. She never phones. And anyway, she'll be busy getting the kids their dinner at the moment.'

'Oh will she now? Well perhaps it's that girl down the road who you're having an affair with – you know, the one with the lovely eyes and the good hair.'

'Oh no, it can't be her. It's her Pilates class this evening.'

'Oh, is that what she says?'

Romance took his phone from his pocket and looked at it. 'It's my friend Lee.'

'Oh is it? Let me talk to him.'

To head her off, Romance answered.

'Lee. How you doing?'

'Yeah, good. Lainie's doin' me fuckin' 'ead in, but that's just normal I s'pose.'

'Hello Lee!' the blond girl shouted.

'Who's that?'

'To be honest Lee, I'm not entirely sure. I've only just met her. We're standing outside Baker Street tube station.'

'Oh.'

'Anyway, what's up?'

'Fuckin' Spaghetti twatface Weston. He can't do Saturday, can he? He's gone and got himself fuckin' arrested. I was hoping that you might be able to step in.'

'Arrested?'

'Yeah, the fuckin' twat. He was climbing up Birmingham City Hall or something. Dressed as the Duke of fuckin' Wellington.'

'The Duke of Wellington?'

'Yeah, that's what he said. Don't ask me. He was allowed one phone call so he called me to say he couldn't make Saturday. Then I had to phone Annie and tell her she had to feed the bloomin' dog. He's fuckin' lost the plot mate. Do you reckon you can do it? You play the same kind of crap, don't you?'

'The Duke of Wellington's been arrested?' blond girl asked.

'Hm? No, it was someone we know dressed up as the Duke of Wellington.'

'Is that illegal?'

'No.'

'Like impersonating a police officer?'

'Lee, I'll call you back mate. But yes, of course. I'll do it. I was gonna come down anyway. I'd love to do it.'

It was then the blond girl took the phone. Romance didn't resist. He knew that relationships were a matter of give and take.

'Listen Lee, I hope you're not leading my friend astray. I don't want the two of you getting involved in any criminal activity and that includes illegal impersonation.'

Lee didn't reply. Romance took the phone back.

'Lee, yeah I'll do it. I'll call you in a bit.'

Lee was still silent and Romance hung up.

'Well I don't,' blond girl insisted. 'We've only just met. I don't want to be one of those prison wives or those women who are engaged to men on death row with Channel 4 knocking at my door. What would my mother say if I popped up on one of those programmes?'

'He just wants me to DJ at this little soul do he's organising.'

'DJ? Ooh, how exciting. Soul, you say? But who do you have to go as? Who do you think I should go as? I've always wanted to go somewhere as Nell Gwynn. What do you reckon?'

The blond girl thrust out her breasts and pouted comically.

'Yes, I think you should,' Romance replied. 'I think that would be absolutely fine.' And he looked into her eyes, smiling, and he continued looking for a little longer than was socially acceptable.

# 85

*Dear Sir/Madam,*
 *Soul music was born from struggle. It is a music of the disadvantaged and its message is one of pain and heartbreak. And yet it gives hope. Its effect is a joyous uplifting of the spirit.*

And there, Romance paused. He was happy with that. He knew the letter had to be longer – much longer – but he was happy with the sentiment so far. Soul music wasn't an artistic diversion for the privileged and it wasn't a facile expression of youthful rebellion. It was profound. As music, it was intangible and ephemeral, and yet it spoke to the soul and was the key to living. It didn't explain our place in the cosmos, but it delighted in the mystery. And it was because of its complete and utter intangible profundity that Romance considered it to be the ultimate artistic achievement of man. And the way that Romance could best propagate the ultimate artistic achievement of man was through his own art. And if television executives were too blinkered to appreciate the artistic quality of *Looking for Romance (with Steve Davis)*, then he would seek funding from those who were expert in appreciating quality artistic ideas. Arts bodies. He didn't know anything about arts bodies, but he knew they gave grants, and he couldn't think of anything more deserving for such a grant than his film. After all, they gave grants to opera, didn't they? And opera wasn't nearly as deserving.

He had watched an opera on telly once, in an effort to be open-minded, because he did consider himself a creative type. And he was genuinely curious. Obviously soul was a superior art form to any other kind of modern music, but he was aware that opera excited the passions of its adherents to a seemingly unreasonable degree and he was curious to find out why. So he sat and watched one on BBC2. It was by Mozart.

He sat and watched one, for as long as he could bear it. He couldn't sit through it continuously. That was impossible. It was too painful. When he felt driven to, he would turn down the sound and put on a record.

But there were some good tracks in it. In fact, there were times when he thought the music was beautiful. The problem was that even at those, the best of times, the subtitles would reveal the lyrics to be ridiculous. They were farcical. What sounded like a beautiful love song turned out to be about a man hiding behind a bush who wasn't able to recognise the woman he loved, even when he heard her voice, just because she was wearing someone else's hat. Or something.

Did none of these opera buffs bother following the lyrics? Did they not care? For Romance, any semblance of beauty was lost because the message was so trite. Of course, the lyrical message of a song can be ignored, but then it loses much of its emotive potential. It's the difference between a great soul record and a northern instrumental.

And the bits between the tracks were tedious. The music was being dragged out unnecessarily. There is nothing like the discipline of the 45, Romance was propelled to think, again.

Romance didn't blame Mozart, entirely. Like Beethoven, he was just unlucky to be born Before Soul. Lyrics before soul music were just silly, because no one had yet thought to sing about how they really felt. This only happened when gospel-style singing was brought into secular music, because the only subject that merited such an emotional outcry, if not God, was the pain and heartbreak of love. No one decided it; it just had to be. And like all great, miraculous, unplanned leaps forward in human evolution, once done it all seemed so blindingly natural and obvious.

And Mozart wouldn't have been introduced to gospel singing, as it didn't exist then, and even if it did there was no recorded music, and so he wouldn't have heard it in Vienna or wherever he happened to be. And because there was no recorded music, Mozart couldn't really be blamed for having live performance as the only outlet for his music. That's just how it was in the days before records. He had to put on a show and to entertain people for a whole evening.

The worst thing about opera wasn't that it existed (in the age before records someone like Mozart had to do something) or that there were strange, annoying people who were fanatical about it. The worse thing about it was that it was subsidised by the government and kept on receiving grants year after year. How on earth did opera wangle that one? There wasn't even a strong British operatic tradition to protect and, in pandering to the privileged, it certainly didn't perform anything like the valuable social service of the northern soul scene. Even though Romance wasn't a fan of pop and rock music, he saw more of an argument for subsidising the pop and rock industries, because, since the sixties, British acts had been very much at the forefront. Britain had a proud cultural tradition in these disciplines. Britain gained esteem across the globe for producing original and pioneering pop and rock music. And it mattered to many more people. Subsidise that. Protect that. Play to one's strengths.

In fact, the more he thought about it – and when he remembered the silly man popping out from behind the bush, he thought about it some more – the more Romance could see the case for subsidising the northern soul scene. Obviously, the music was all black American, but appreciation for the music was a peculiarly British affair. Much of the music would have been lost to the world if it hadn't been for British enthusiasts keeping the soul fires burning. And the northern soul scene itself – the clubs, the dancing, the record collecting – was a British cultural phenomenon.

And like other British music cultures, the northern soul scene had become a British cultural export. At the time Romance was thinking these thoughts, the northern soul scene was growing in Europe and it was to Britain that the continental soul folk looked. And even in America it had become a British import and the music was called *northern soul* after the north of England, even though it had all been made in their own country. Protect that. Subsidise that. Britain should be proud of it. Opera would continue elsewhere, without the help of the British taxpayer. Soul music was more needing and deserving.

All this thinking could have been enough to depress Romance (obviously not to the extent that JBP was depressed, but enough to be annoying). And it probably would have depressed him, if it wasn't for the fact that this potentially depressing thinking was informing his next great idea, which was to write to arts bodies for funding for his film.

And then *Looking for Romance (with Steve Davis)* would be shown at arts festivals and the like. There were probably film festivals for artistic films. And not only would his film be an artistic film, but it would be about something artistic too, so it would be doubly artistic. No doubt there were arts cinemas all over the country crying out for a film like his. And then, the film having achieved success in this artistic realm, Channel 4 would come knocking. And because – of course – the film would have been made by then, the television executives would be in no position to make demands that would compromise its artistic integrity.

Obviously, the letter needed much work and, obviously, Romance needed to find out where to send it. But he was pleased with the start. And he decided to ask his artistic friend, the northern soul painter Thelonius Tripp, for information about arts bodies and for top tips on targetting them.

# 86

'Bloody hell, look at it.'

The words may have varied slightly, but the sentiment of the driver of the crashed Mini was the same as that of the boys when they had stood in front of the Tripp and the same too as Mr Moore-Hackett's would be when he was to look at the mural through his living room window, across his damaged lawn and over his damaged fence, tea in hand.

Neither Romance, Deptford Dave, Solomon nor Gerald witnessed the Moore-Hacketts' return from the pub, because by that time they were all in the pub themselves. Romance had thought it appropriate to ask the shaken driver for a drink.

After hearing the smashing of the fence and seeing the irreverently parked Mini, the soul friends and Gerald had gone to inspect the damage and to assess the eccentricity of the driver. They had found Dave (another Dave – the driver) to be surprisingly uneccentric, given the nature of his parking. And his high state of concern – for the fence, the lawn and the car – seemed quite fitting for the circumstances.

'Why did you park there again?' Deptford Dave asked, wrongly presuming that a motive must already have been established.

'I was disturbed by that mad painting. The wall!'

'Oh yeah. The Tripp. It's an original, you know.'

'It's certainly bloody original!'

'It's about northern soul.'

Dave (the driver) seemed like a nice guy. The boys were happy to do whatever they thought necessary to calm his nerves. Deptford Dave thought this best done by interrogating him about his taste in music.

'Are you into that?' he asked, pointing at a CD case on the passenger seat. 'Were you listening to that bollocks? No wonder you bloody crashed.'

'No, I crashed because of the painting.'

'Oh yeah.'

'It's official. Soul music is dangerous!'

'Well maybe it's just wrong to try to represent visually something that is a wholly aural experience.' The boys looked at Solomon. 'Music's beyond art, and all art aspires towards the condition of music. Something like that.'

'It could just be a bit of a crap painting,' retorted Dave (the driver). He looked up at it. 'The trip?'

'Do you know Thelonius?'

Dave (the driver) thought this an odd question, couldn't understand its intent and ignored it.

'What's northern soul got to do with this village? I

thought when I saw it that it was something religious. I thought it was about God and the last judgement, or something like Jehovah's Witnesses or something.'

There was a pause in the conversation. Gerald almost stepped in to affirm the meaning of the mural but, because he didn't know, the words didn't come. The boys had all forgotten that the painting was about something religious. That was the whole point of it. It was nothing to do with soul music at all.

Romance was the first to speak.

'Northern soul. Religion. Whatever.'

'I've got to go,' said Dave (the driver), having finished inspecting his car.

'Come to the pub. You could probably do with a drink.'

'No. Thanks. I'm late as it is.'

Dave (the driver) then wrote the note that he was to push through the Moore-Hacketts' door, then he pushed it through the door and then, with the help of the soul boys and Gerald, he reversed his Mini off the lawn, damaging the lawn more in the process, and through the smashed fence, smashing it a little more in the process, and then drove off studiously avoiding so much as a glance at the conspicuous cause of his accident.

'He was a nice guy,' said Deptford Dave. 'I liked him.'

And then the boys and Gerald set off for the pub. Gerald led the way. Already, the boys had forgotten that the pub idea had been for the benefit of Dave (the driver). Gerald hadn't forgotten but wasn't going to say anything.

## 87

Hippy John had returned to Lee and Lainie's with a purpose. Now that he was a man of worth, he considered himself to be of use, and he intended to offer his services. With his experience of labouring on the site of the building of the bridge over the Itchen – albeit as a younger man – combined with a renewed mental stability, he felt sure that he was in a position to help Lee in his work.

'Fucking hell,' Lainie said on opening the door. (Usually, she didn't pronounce the *g* in *fucking*, but this was a drawn out *fucking* that warranted it.) 'The fuckin' 'ippy's back!' And their acquaintance was renewed.

'Bloody hell. You what?' asked Lee, when the hippy was inside, sipping tea, offering his free labour, disappearance and reappearance explained to the best of his ability.

'Well, yes,' said the hippy.

'You fucking nutcase. It's a pile of fucking crap! It's dangerous, filthy, knackering and shit. You're fucking mental.'

For once, Hippy John didn't think that he was and at six

o'clock the next morning he was ready and waiting on their doorstep.

'Oh, fuck,' said Lee. 'Get in then, you twat.'

Hippy John was a liability. Lee and his mate, Trevor, were working on a ground floor flat renovation in East Preston. The living room needed a new ceiling, the hallway needed replastering and the kitchen and hallway needed to be fitted with slate floor tiles. The old ceiling, the old hallway plaster, the old carpet and lino all had to come out and, whenever any of it was on its way out, Hippy John was in the way.

Hippy John wasn't used to working and he wasn't used to being in a confined space, and so working in a confined space didn't come naturally to him. Because he didn't know what to do, he kept asking questions, but Lee and Trevor quickly found that it was substantially quicker to do everything themselves than it was to stop to explain and answer hippy questions. And the result was that he was in the way.

It wasn't like working on the bridge. That was outside, in plenty of space and there was little damage to be done or work to hinder wheeling sand from one place to another. And there were scores of other people on the site, so any uselessness was less obvious. The confines of the flat concentrated his uselessness. As well as being in the way, he trod on things that weren't meant to be trodden on, and his attempts to keep out of the way were a distraction, as Lee wondered where he was, what he was doing and what damage he might be wreaking.

He was positioned outside, to manage the rubbish that didn't need managing. Then he fell over, cut his head open on a piece of ceiling rubble and Trevor had to take him to hospital.

## 88

'Arts bodies? What arts bodies?'

'I don't know. That's what I'm wondering.'

'Bodies? Arts bodies.'

'Yeah. You know... bodies.'

'And they give you money to do your art?'

The boys were in McDonald's again, having been up all night dancing again. The northern soul artist Thelonius Tripp was supposed to be the one informing Romance.

'I suppose so. But I don't know anything about them. Apart from the

fact that there's something called the Arts Council.'

'Council? An arts council? Do they cover Peckham?'

Romance could see that he wasn't going to get very far. Thelonius Tripp was an unusual artist, not only because it had never occurred to him to paint anything other than northern soul dancers but also because he had no concept of the arts world beyond the painting of northern soul dancers. Romance knew there were other kinds of artists, but he didn't know any of them because all his friends were soul people and if you were a soul person who was an artist you were, in fact, Thelonius Tripp.

But Romance had heard of the Arts Council because he wasn't an idiot, so, with no other ideas emanating from the northern soul arts scene, he decided to phone the operator to find out their number, and then he would phone the Arts Council to find out their address. He would then edit his *Looking for Romance (with Steve Davis)* document to make it sound more of an art film and less of a primetime television documentary (as Romance already considered the film to fulfil both of these roles, this was largely a matter of vocabulary), print it, finish his arts body letter, print it and then post. His plan worked to the letter, and then the letter came.

# 89

*Dear Romance,*

*Thank you for your letter concerning your arts project, 'Looking for Romance'.*

*We receive hundreds of applications for funding each year, so apologies for this standard letter.*

*All applications are carefully considered, but we regret that we cannot enter into personal correspondence about the merit of each project. If we consider your project suitable for further consideration, we shall be in touch with you in due course.*

*Yours sincerely,*

*Jeremy Sedgwick*
*Specialist advisor, Visual Arts*
*Arts Council England*

Romance wasn't hugely disappointed by the letter. He felt sorry for Jeremy Sedgwick and his colleagues at the Arts

Council. He imagined that they would have to process so many requests for funding, the vast majority of which were probably ridiculous. The number of crazed people with hare-brained ideas was no doubt limitless. He would just have to be patient for them to come to his letter. An idea as original and creative as his was bound to leap out at them. And as well as being an original and creative idea worthy of funding, it would be good PR for them because their name would appear on the end credits. So they would be in touch, in their own time. Until then, Romance would concentrate on choosing which other records, in addition to Romance Watson's *Where Does That Leave Me* would be in the soundtrack. And, for the sake of his art, he had to be wary of restrictive female entanglements.

# 90

Like Sam Cooke, Marvin Gaye was a womaniser, but as a recording artist he was wary of female entanglements. However, for purely commercial reasons, he was pressurised by Motown boss Berry Gordy into recording duets with female Motown singers. The results were mundane. (And it was exactly that kind of compromise Romance wanted to avoid.) Thelonius and the vicar, however, saw eye to eye on the mural. They were kindred spirits. They were joined by an unholy appreciation of artistic mediocrity.

Mr Moore-Hackett had less soul but more sense.

His wife had hoped that after he had drunk his cup of tea his anxiety would wane. In fact, it worsened. (She was sensible enough to know that this wasn't because of the tea, and that, in fact, there was no telling how much worse his anxiety might have been had it not been for the tea.) His nervousness was palpable and every time he looked out of the window its physical manifestations intensified.

'Right,' he said, as some kind of a culmination. 'I've had enough of that bloody thing.'

Mrs Moore-Hackett didn't know what was coming, so she rushed to re-boil the kettle. She didn't know what was coming but she knew that something was and the anticipation scared her. Her husband was overcome by a wave of indignation and she had seen it happen before (eg. 1987 Leydene Green Arts and Craft Fair landscape photography competition/trophy contestation). Nothing good ever came of it – at least, the results were unpredictable – and her job was to calm things down. On the whole, things were best left. These excited moments couldn't be trusted.

Mr Moore-Hackett knew that he had half a tub of magnolia paint in the cupboard under the stairs (thanks to some very economical decorating) and he was out of the house with it before his wife had finished pouring. A minute later he returned for a bigger paintbrush, then he went out again and then he set to work.

# 91

Neither Lee nor Trevor saw Hippy John fall over and cut his head on the ceiling. They were inside, tearing at other bits of ceiling. (Hippy John didn't cry out but, if he had, they probably wouldn't have heard him.) So when Lee walked out of the house to go to the van and saw Hippy John sitting with blood pouring down his face, he didn't know how long he had been like that. And Hippy John didn't have much of an idea either. He was dazed and breathless.

'Fuck me,' Lee commented, and he then shouted for Trevor. They ripped a fresh dust sheet and wrapped some of it around Hippy John's bloody head, and then Trevor took him away.

Hippy John didn't know why he had fallen over. He didn't think he had tripped over anything. He had been using a shovel to gather the rubble and had lost his balance.

'You're a fucking liability, mate!' said Trevor, firmly, when they were in the van. Hippy John saw that he was smiling.

And Trevor was right. He was a fucking liability. He could see that. He was still a little dazed, but he could see that.

And when the nurse was leaning over him, carefully peeling away the cloth, squirting disinfectant into the wound and picking at it with her tweezers, he could see it then too.

'Sorry,' he said. 'I'm an idiot.'

He looked at her. Her gaze remained fixed on the wound. She was picking and concentrating.

'Oh,' she said, 'these things happen.'

'In fact, you know what, I'm a fucking liability.'

She stopped and looked at him and he smiled, and then she smiled too. She continued picking.

'Yes, you are,' she said. 'A fucking liability. A fucking, tossing, twatting, pratting, bastard liability.'

She looked, hard, into his eyes. Hippy John smiled, and then, when she looked away again, he smiled so broadly he felt it in his wound.

## 92

'Music is a moral law. It gives a soul to the universe, wings to the mind, flight to the imagination, a charm to sadness and life to everything.'

Deptford Dave looked at Solomon.

'Who said that?' asked Romance.

'It was Solomon!' said Dave. 'He's lost it.'

'No, I mean, originally.'

'Plato,' said Solomon. 'He was a clever dude.'

'Yeah but where is he now?'

'I still think there's something fucking satanic about it.'

'But it's by Thelonius. You think Thelonius is in league with the devil?'

'Maybe just hoodwinked a bit.'

'And it's about northern soul. Do you think that's satanic?'

'Yeah but it's about northern soul. It isn't northern soul. It's a painting. It isn't music.'

'I think that's what soul music does, but he said music. But then he was before soul music, wasn't he, Plato? They didn't even have records back then.'

'There is a record label called Plato. The Kickin' Mustangs. Lovely group ballad thing.'

'It's about religion. The mural, I mean.'

'Oh yeah.'

'Soul might be satanic. The gospel people thought so, didn't they? The devil's music – that's where it all began.'

'Oh, so now we're all in league with the devil.'

'The Taliban think it's satanic.'

'The Taliban think everything's satanic.'

'The Taliban don't like northern soul?'

'They hate it. That's why they are like they are. It makes them livid.'

'They think all music's satanic. It stirs up the emotions so much that it interferes with your relationship with God, because only religion should create such states of emotion and take you out of yourself like that.'

'Yeah. Soul is dangerous! Surrender to the dark power! It's like the Isle of Sirens.'

'Oh yeah, they were Greek too.'

'Keep close, cried the captain! Ignore them, let them be!'

'Love is blind and desires have no fear.'

'Desires are heaven to me.'

'And off he leaps into the sea!'

'Jerry Butler wasn't Greek. He was from Chicago.'

'I thought Curtis wrote it and he definitely wasn't Greek.'

'Yeah but how can he be singing a song himself about the danger of beautiful singing?'

'Yeah, we've been lured in and now look at us.'

'Fuck it. It's Jerry Butler and Curtis Mayfield. They can do what they want.'

'On the other hand, you could say that without music the emotional part of our nature would be enfeebled.'

'Would be what?'

'Enfeebled. And so it strengthens the intellect and our moral fibre.'

'Bollocks, I'm fucked.'

'Or maybe it doesn't.'

'And what about bollocks music? What's that like? Bollocks religion?'

'Could be, Dave. Like Scientology, maybe.'

'Anyway, all religion's bollocks. Apart from proper gospel music.'

'That's not a religion. That's the music of a religion. Like hymns.'

'Hymns bollocks.'

Gerald was a sociable chap, but he was struggling to feel a part of the conversation and, when one of the regulars offered to buy him a pint, he gladly accepted. The boys drank up and left him and walked back towards their car. As they turned the corner round the village hall they all looked up to see half a mural, half a magnolia-coloured wall and one whole man splattered with paint.

'Some of the Tripp has disappeared,' ascertained Deptford Dave.

'It's all right, Dave. It's still there. It's just underneath.'

They walked up to Mr Moore-Hackett.

'So you're a painter too. This village is full of them!'

He couldn't deny it. All he could do was look at the young men.

'You're more of the minimalist school, I see. Well, there's an argument for it. There certainly is.'

'Where's Thelonius?' demanded Deptford Dave.

'You've run out of paint!'

'Or it could be an artistic statement. It could be a performance.'

'In a way, I think his half better represents soul anyway. It's pure. It's like a shade. A light without a source. Of this world but not of this world. Some intangible dimension.'

'Tell you what, that painting was fucking rough though, wasn't it? Imagine waking up to that every day. Imagine the poor buggers who live over there.'

'I hope it's not emulsion paint,' Solomon added.

It was.

'What you need is masonry paint.'

The boys left Mr Moore-Hackett standing before his miscreation. He watched them leave, took a look at his failed act of rebellion and went home for some tea.

# 93

There were some in the gospel community who saw Sam Cooke's death as divine retribution. And for others, if the killing itself wasn't the work of God, their sympathy was tempered by a feeling that it was deserved. In this they had something in common with the southern racists, who viewed Cooke as an upstart negro and felt their way of life threatened by his success. The rich, smooth, suave black man in his dapper suits, appearing on their televisions, singing to their women. It felt natural that he should be taken away. Of course, music allows something of the essence of a person to continue being a part of the earthly world and there's not much anyone can do about that.

When Romance sat and watched his *Please Please Please*, in the middle of the night having returned from God knows where, he sat and watched it intently from the beginning to the end. There was something about the very physicality of a record. He didn't understand the science of how a slab of vinyl could hold sound and how that could be released through a needle but, however it worked, it was clearly a physical process and there was someone, somewhere who understood it. The magic lay not in the fact that vinyl held sound but in that it held such beauty and soul, and as the groove passed under the needle, round and round, James sang and the music was so alive that Romance felt as if his own experience of life was something magical caught in the physical world as soul is caught by a record, and that perhaps there was a greater reality beyond it, overlooking his life-experience as it followed its defined, physical course. And as he watched the record go round and round, the needle caught in its single groove, he was awash in the music, which came to him with such audible momentum that it was pure motion itself, above and beyond the motion of the record. Perhaps he was sensing the pure motion that lay at the heart of the universe and transcended its physical being, existing beyond physical space. Maybe this transcendental motion lay behind the motion of all physical things, from vibrating strings to the motion of the cosmos and, if so, it was beautifully represented by the revolving motion of the record. But if the universe and the relative speed of all things in it was put on 33 instead of 45, who would know? There would be no pitch change. Time is judged by the relative movement of things. Perhaps there's an underlying speed that's changing all the time. What if things stopped moving? What if strings stopped vibrating and electrons stopped circulating and the heavens stopped revolving? Time would not be measurable. Would time then cease to exist? Would the concept of time make any sense? Would the universe then be dead and, if so, did that mean that it was now alive? If he stopped thinking, he would be dead, wouldn't he? How could his consciousness survive outside his body? *Please please please.* His own life-song would have finished playing. *Don't go, baby don't go.* The motion of it was beyond the record and beyond its constituent parts and beyond James Brown. Romance could feel the motion in the music and it was like the motion of his thoughts, he thought. But then it was five o'clock in the morning, again, and he was fucked, again.

## 94

When Romance played at Lee's do, shortly after having met the blond girl, it went wonderfully. There were fewer complaints than they had expected. It was only a small do – in a bar on the front in Worthing – but there were enough soul types to carry the evening and they were up for hearing records beyond the obvious.

The blond girl wasn't with Romance in Worthing because it was her evening to mind the phone at The Samaritans (she could throw herself lovingly into the wildest chat and had a remarkable success rate), but she went to the subsequent London dos with him and she ventured out with him to the Bracknell Soul Extravaganza ('for mad cows and Englishmen') where the vicar was DJing.

'I thought you said this was an extravaganza?' she had said, as they walked into the Bracknell Ex-Servicemen's Club.

'Yes. It's a soul extravaganza.'

'And what exactly is extravagant about it?' she asked, looking about.

It was a good question.

'The music is extravagantly good and the beer is extravagantly cheap.'

'That is a misuse of the word extravagant and I think you know it.'

And then she danced.

And Romance loved watching her dance. She had taken to it like a priest to holy water. She hadn't been intimidated by the distinct style of it. She didn't attempt anything fancy and was restrained and unostentatious, but she was confident and assured and danced with grace and with a tightness that was true to the music, and it was a pleasure for Romance to watch her become increasingly at ease and to see the soul in her coming to the fore. She was happy to launch herself into the soul scene and she was happy to launch herself into a relationship, and Romance envied her willingness – her ability – to embrace the moment.

He was hesitant. He was hesitant about committing himself, and not just because of his art. Something of his own moment-embracing had been knocked out of him by the flailing arms of a loved one and he cowered more than he wanted to before the heaviness of those time-forces. The blond girl was fun to be with but she wasn't the dark, sultry, introspective type he had always imagined his partner-to-be to be. JBP hadn't been that either, but he was young then and emotionally reckless and wanted to live his life. When she lay on the bed and told him that she was scared of how much she liked him and didn't want to be with him because he would leave her after a couple of years, he thought she might well be right. (And if she was right, her powers of perception were to be greatly admired.) 'But life is for living and what a memorable couple of years those could be,' his young mind told him. 'Who knows what the future holds? All we know is that we love each other,' is what he told her. He might have considered her lacking in introspection as well as sultriness, but she was wiser than him. 'I think I have her,' he told the dog, on his way out.

And now here he was again. A lovely girl was in his life. And this one was happy and funny and bounding about the place. And she went to soul dos with him and loved the music and laughed at the people. But even though she was happy and funny and bounding, she was sad too, because she knew what heartbreak was and she had soul.

'Aren't you into any other kind of music?' she asked Mick the Twitch, as he was twitching his way through a sales box.

'Well, mainly northern,' he twitched. 'But I do like some seventies stuff, you know. I'm pretty big into crossover.'

'Listen, we're talking about music here, not dressing up in women's clothes. But each to their own. You're among friends here. Now, is it only soul music you like? Just soul? I mean, what about other music? There's a whole world out there.'

Mick had never been asked this at a soul do before and soul dos were the only type of do he ever went to. These places were his sanctuary from the awkward otherness of that whole world out there.

'I've always collected deep soul too,' was his panicked response. 'But mainly sixties.'

She was a tease. She loved the awkward otherness of these people.

'Right,' she would say, ever so seriously, 'have you ever heard of The Rolling Stones?'

But she wasn't dark and sultry, and the trauma Romance had experienced at the implosion of the JBP relationship haunted him still. He wanted to be wise, as JBP had tried to be and as King Solomon had asked to be.

'He had 700 wives, you know,' the vicar said, when Romance asked him about the wisdom of Solomon, 'and another 300 concubines. How wise is that? Asking for trouble, if you ask me. I've been waiting to intervene in a dispute over the ownership of a record. I'll take it and threaten to break it in two and then the true owner will jump forward and say, "No! Don't do it! Let him have it! Just don't break it!" Hasn't happened yet though. I wonder if it ever will.'

Romance doubted that this particular vicar was an imparter of great wisdom, but he did have some blinding records.

'I'm going to organise a memorial do for Demetrios Demetriou,' Romance said to the vicar.

'Oh, splendid.'

'We'll try and raise some money for that weird type of cancer he died of, whatever it was.'

'Yes. Good idea.'

'Will you DJ?'

'Of course! I'd love to!'

The vicar hadn't really known Demetrios Demetriou. In fact, he couldn't remember him at all. In fact, he'd never even heard of him (even though Demetrios Demetriou had been in his house and had danced to a fair few of his records). But he wasn't going to pass up another opportunity to perform.

'Arse!' said the blond girl, when Romance told her the news.

Romance looked quizzical.

'Arse!' she said again. 'That would have been a better name for the night. A Rare Soul Evening. Maybe you could put one on. Put on an arse. You have the best records, anyway.'

Romance knew that his collection was pitiful compared to some, but he loved the fact that the blond girl liked his records. Either her view was coloured by how much she liked him or she simply had impeccable taste. Either way, it was good news. A win-win. And he determined there and then to introduce her to his dead friend, Demetrios Demetriou.

But it was after that, on Romance's follow-up visit to the coast, without the blond girl by his side and with hippiness in the air, that his battle with the heavy forces took a distinctly positive turn.

# 95

Mr Moore-Hackett took off his paint-splattered clothes and wondered why he hadn't changed out of his best pub casual wear. He felt silly. But he also felt mildly courageous and, however mild the feeling, it was something quite new to him. He had seen those boys in the pub with Gerald, and the fact that they – friends of Gerald – shared his feelings about the Tripp was the source of this new (if mild) feeling.

'Vicar, I want that mural painted over,' he said, standing on the doorstep of the vicarage that evening, clasping the letter from Dave (the driver). 'It's an eyesore and it's caused an accident black spot and sooner or later someone's going to get seriously hurt and it'll probably happen on my lawn.'

Then the door opened.

'Oh hello. Mr Moore-Hackett,' observed the vicar, correctly.

'Hello,' said Mr Moore-Hackett.

'What can I do for you?' said the vicar.

'Well,' Mr Moore-Hackett began, nervously, 'I have a slight issue with the mural on the church hall.'

The vicar knew that Mr Moore-Hackett had an issue with the mural. Gerald had already been round, accusing Mr Moore-Hackett of vandalism, Papism, atheism and Masonic witchcraft. The mural had been defaced and he had it on very good authority (Mrs Toliver from the Post Office) that Mr Moore-Hackett was the culprit.

Mr Moore-Hackett was presuming that news of the magnolia embellishment hadn't reached the vicarage. He was hoping that it would be legitimised retrospectively in light of his visit but, if not, he would plant the thought that there were others who shared his artistic perspective.

'Oh?' said the vicar, both to Gerald and then, later, to Mr Moore-Hackett.

'Vicar, that man has no respect for artistic endeavours and the creativity of man,' Gerald had said.

'It's just that it's a bit… fierce, isn't it? One or two drivers seem to have been distracted by it,' Mr Moore-Hackett contended a little later.

'Oh,' said the vicar, to Gerald and then, later, to Mr Moore-Hackett.

'Yes. Well,' said Gerald.

'Well, that's it really,' said Mr Moore-Hackett.

'And what do you suggest?' said the vicar to each, in turn.

'Well, the damage has been done vicar.'

'I'd rather see the thing painted over actually. I don't think I'm the only one.'

'Oh, I see. Right. Well, OK. Very well. Things come and go. Everything is transient. Shall we get the parish council involved? I don't think so. They'll only drag the matter on.'

It seemed to Gerald, and then later to Mr Moore-Hackett, that the vicar was somewhat distracted. It seemed to the vicar that there was no point going to the bother of thinking of different responses when the same would suffice. And he had more important matters on his mind.

'If I were you I'd just go ahead and do what you like with it and no one will probably notice. I'd certainly be none the wiser.'

The vicar winked at Gerald and then, later, at Mr Moore-Hackett, which did little for the ease of either.

'Right. Very well. Yes, thank you.'

'Right. Oh. Very well.'

The vicar smiled (at Gerald and then, later, at Mr Moore-Hackett). 'Sorry, I've got some fish fingers on.'

'Oh, righto. Well, OK then.'

'Oh! Right! Oh. Very well. Well, thank you. And we'll be seeing you.'

'Yes. Bye.'

'Goodbye.'

'Bye.'

Gerald and then, later, Mr Moore-Hackett, walked away.

What did he mean, 'Just go ahead'? Go ahead with what? Repainting the mural? But what about Thelonius? Gerald was confused, but at least he had said what he had intended to say.

And Mr Moore-Hackett was confused at the vicar's response as well. How could anyone fail to notice? How could the vicar be none-the-wiser when he had just been forewarned?

Still, despite the confusion, Mr Moore-Hackett felt something bordering on happiness. He was proud of himself. And he determined to go to B&Q to buy the appropriate amount of masonry paint and get to it. He would put aside the whole of the next day for the job. He would do it all himself. He was already looking forward to it.

# 96

Taking blond girl to see Demetrios Demetriou was easy. All Romance had to do was ask her. He was keen to take her – to introduce them to each other and to see if it felt right.

'He was a top guy. I'd like to introduce you.'

Blond girl liked Romance's live friends and she had no reason to think she wouldn't like his dead ones too.

'That would be lovely. I'd like to meet him.'

But it wasn't easy finding Demetrios Demetriou's grave. Unlike Spaghetti Weston and Soul Sam, Romance and the blond girl found the cemetery without any problem, but finding the grave was proving more difficult. Since the funeral, Romance had visited a few times by himself and after the first time, knowing what the grave looked like, he had always found it quite easily, despite the rows and lines looking much the same. When he knew that he was in the vicinity, Romance looked for the dark wooden cross and then he was sure he would see the gravel, the potted plants and the windmill.

'Are you sure we're in the right cemetery?' teased the

blond girl.

'Yes.'

'And are you sure he wasn't cremated?'

'Yes! I saw them put him in the ground.'

'Maybe you dreamt the whole thing. You could have. It could have been precipitated by the trauma of not being invited to the funeral. Or the cremation.'

'It's gotta be here somewhere.'

'I like that one.'

'What one?'

'That one.' She pointed to a strange stone contrivance.

At the base of the headstone was a stone box that to Romance's record-obsessed mind looked very much like a 45s carrying case. The proportions seemed right and there was even a stone nodule where the fastener would be. He was curious enough to move closer and, when he was in front of the grave, he was surprised to find the carved shapes of records leaning against the side of the box. They had to be records. They couldn't be anything else. He was impressed.

And then he wasn't impressed. He realised the grave couldn't be that of a dead soul person – it couldn't because, if it had been, then Romance would have known him (or her) or at least known of him (or her). And that meant some other kind of deceased person who had been into some other kind of music was being honoured by this stony homage to vinyl. This annoyed Romance and was particularly unimpressive, because no one is into music as soul people are – a fact that wouldn't matter if it wasn't for the other very pertinent fact that so many non-soul people prided themselves on being *into music* – and going to the extent of being honoured by this monumental homage was, in Romance's eyes, a grave and monumental insult to those who really were into music and those were soul people. Romance couldn't be sure if this idea for a memorial had been the deceased's (prior to deceasing) or if a friend or relative had thought it appropriate post-decease. He hoped it had been a friend or relative's idea; it would be as delusional, but there would be less temerity to it. He checked the name on the grave: Demetrios Demetriou.

Romance wondered what the chances were of another Demetrios Demetriou being buried in close proximity. Slim, no doubt. And he would have to be another Demetrios Demetriou perceived, by himself or his family, as passionate about music – on vinyl, at that. Romance had no idea how common a name Demetrios Demetriou was within the Greek community. He thought it translated as James of James, or James Jameson, of which James Jamerson – name of the renowned Motown bassist – would be a derivative. And then there was also the soul singer Jimmy James (two of them, in fact), and he was reminded of James Barnes and Jimmy Barnes and J.J.Barnes and suddenly music people with the same name were looking far from unusual and that was just within the world of sixties soul. There were at least three George Jacksons. There were four groups called The Magnetics, from different cities in the States, five or six called The Topics, The Prophets, The Admirations,

The Satisfactions, The Precisions or The Inspirations and a whole bunch of Ambassadors, Creations, Dynamics, Enchanters, Sequins and Echoes. (Which group was the original Originals? Who were maddest Mad Lads?) The number of Jades goes into double figures, all singing at the same time and unknown to each other. But what were the chances of one Jades group being buried together next to another?

'I think this might be it,' Romance said. 'This must be his grave. They've changed it.'

'Oh, I like it. It's very clever, isn't it? I mean, someone's managed to do all that. If he liked his music, he'd be happy with that. Oh yes.'

'He liked his music.'

Romance was disturbed by the new grave. The new design didn't offend him, as long as it really was the grave of his friend, but if it really was the grave of his friend then it meant that someone had dug up the old grave.

'Well nice to meet you, Demetrios Demetriou. Romance has told me a lot about you.'

'You OK mate? She's a bit of a nutter, but she's lovely.'

There was much he wanted to ask his friend.

'Oh don't listen to him, Demetrios.' The blond girl rummaged in her bag. 'I've brought you a present to remind you of the world.'

'To remind him of the world?'

'Yes.'

'Do you think he needs reminding?'

'I don't know. How good was his memory?'

Romance didn't answer. (He couldn't remember.) He was intrigued at what the present might be.

Out of her bag she took another bag – a plastic one – and then crouching down at the graveside she took a fist-sized object from the plastic bag and placed it on the grave. It looked like a scone. Romance continued looking at it.

'What's that?'

'A scone.'

The blond girl then reached into the bag and in turn took out three more large scones and placed them neatly on the grave as four corners of a square.

'There you go, Demetrios. I made them myself.'

'Scones?'

'Yes, scones. I'm good at making scones. Everyone likes my scones.'

They did look well made and they would have blended quite organically into the surreal garden grave of before – scone hills ready to be eroded and integrated into the dreamy landscape – but on this new grave they were an organic abstraction. The blond girl was beyond such considerations and Romance loved her for that. The scones made as much sense as anything.

'Oh! Oh!'

The two of them turned round. The blond girl didn't know the small old woman in black, but she smiled anyway because she was a smiley person.

'Oh, you come! You come!'

'Hello. Are you OK?' asked a slightly panicked Romance, wondering if Mrs Demetriou had just arrived for a visit or had been hiding behind another grave all along, keeping watch on the grave of her son, waiting to catch grave desecrators in the act. Perhaps the scones had lured her out. Perhaps scones were the Greek Orthodox equivalent to haram and the grave was now hideously defiled.

'You come visit my son! Thank you! Thank you! You good friend. Oh thank you. You very good friend.'

'Hello,' beamed the blond girl. 'Now you must be the mother. It's lovely to meet you. I didn't know your son but I have to say it sounds like he was a wonderful person and a lovely man.'

'Yes! Yes!'

'And I have made some scones for him. I do hope he liked scones. It would be such a shame if he didn't like them.'

'He like! He like! Scon-es. Yes, scon-es. He like scon-es very much. Oh you make? Oh! Thank you! Thank you! Oh he like! Thank you!'

'It's a very good grave, Mrs D. The stone is beautiful and Demetrios would love the record box.'

'Yes, yes! The box! I think he like. He like the records, Demetrios. He like the little ones very much.'

'Oh, we all like the little ones,' added blond girl.

'It's a very solid grave, this one,' added Romance. 'It's built to last, isn't it? It would be a job to move it.'

'Ooh, it's lovely,' said blond girl.

'I didn't realise you were going to change the grave.'

'Yes, yes. We change. The other, just for a little. We change.'

'It must have been quite a job to change it – digging up the other one and putting this one in.'

'We change. Now this one, very nice. Very good.'

'Someone's done a very good job. It looks very good. And very solid. Did you see it happen? Were you here?'

'I come. The men they do it. They make the grave, and I say like this, with this one, and with this like this, and then they come and do it. The old one, it OK, but just for little. Just for little, until this one it come.'

'So there wasn't anything wrong with the other one? I mean, it hadn't been disturbed or anything? It wasn't damaged in any way?'

'Damage? No, no! But this better! This one, real, forever.'

'Yes, it's very good. Very good.'

It was very good. There was no denying it.

'But the other one, when they changed it, you were here? It must have taken a few men to dig it up and change it.'

'The men, they come and do it. They do it good. They do good job. I very happy.'

'And it was just the men from the grave company? The proper men? I mean, no one else was involved, were they?'

'No one else?'

'I mean, no one was digging about or working on the grave who shouldn't have been here. I mean, that wouldn't be proper.'

'They the men. The grave men. They very good. Look,

it very good now. My son, he have good grave. Very nice one. I think he like. And now, the scon-es! Oh, thank you! Thank you! He like scon-es very much! Ohh!'

'Oh it's my pleasure! Really! And when I come next, I shall bring some more. It is nice to have one's scones appreciated.' She threw Romance a mocking, quick, sarcastic smile. 'I shall make sure that whenever possible Demetrios has a good scone or two. He deserves it.'

'Yes! Yes! Thank you! Thank you!'

Romance wasn't following the scone talk. His concentration was elsewhere. He was trying to ask his friend if the record they both cared about was still with him. And he was sharing with his friend something of the feeling of the weight of the new, heavier, less time restricted grave. And then, somehow at the same time, he was wondering how the group And The Echoes arrived at their strange name, being distinct from any of the other Echoes groups and from E.J. & The Echoes too.

# 97

When Gerald, and then Mr Moore-Hackett, visited the vicarage to discuss the mural, they were both right in suspecting that the vicar's mind was elsewhere. He was in the middle of making a compilation tape of sixties soul singers all with the Christian name Bobby. There were plenty of them. He had been surprised at the number of Bobby records in his collection. (And he didn't collect Bobbys in particular. Why would he?) He had been cueing up a Bobby Patterson record when the doorbell had rung the first time and a rare 45 by Bobby Williams when it had rung again. The importance and the pressing need of the Bobby tape wasn't the kind of important and pressing need that either Gerald or Mr Moore-Hackett would understand or appreciate, and so, to cut short the conversations, the vicar decided that fish fingers could serve as a tasty pretext. He didn't feel bad about it. It was a lie, but no one had been hurt. (And he did genuinely like fish fingers, so it could have been true.) He was half aware of what he was saying about the mural and transience etc.; he was saying whatever he felt he needed to say to end the conversations as quickly as possible. He did like the mural and he did care about it, but it wasn't the most important thing in God's universe or even the village. There were undoubtedly more important things and the Bobby Patterson and Bobby Williams records were two of them. And the tapes he was making were at least of equal importance.

It had been as the vicar was looking at the mural one bright sunny morning, wondering how he might develop his soul outreach, that he had been overcome by an evangelical desire to make tapes of his records and then to make copies of the tapes and distribute them to anyone he felt might have the sensibility to fall under their influence, and by giving them clever themes he supposed that he would be giving them more popular appeal. The soul scene was rife with collectors swapping tapes but, like the best of missionaries, he wasn't going to neglect his own community. Oli. Caitlin. Mrs Woo.

He listened to Bobby Williams and heard afresh how Bobby had lost his girl and how he couldn't cry enough tears to wash away the pain, and he watched the tape spools go round, capturing the rapture, and he thought of what he had said to Gerald and to Mr Moore-Hackett about transience and decided that it would be an excellent topic for a sermon. Nothing in or of this world lasts forever, but it's the journey that matters and it's a wonderful journey, and spiritual fulfilment and inner peace are only achieved with comfortable recognition of that. Then the tape ended before the record. The spools stopped turning and the motor whirred.

'Fuck! Fuck! Fuck!' said the vicar.

## 98

'Fuck,' said Lainie.

'What?'

'Fuck, fuck, fuck.'

'What?'

'We shouldn't have left him alone.'

'What?'

'We shouldn't have left him alone,' Lainie repeated. 'How could we leave him alone for so long with Ree? Anything could have happened.'

'No it couldn't,' Lee replied. 'It'll be fine.'

'The man's a nutter. I don't know what we were thinking.'

'He's fine. He's all sorted now.'

'Sorted? Yesterday he asked me if I thought his carrots would mind being eaten! He's not fine. He's a headcase. Put your foot down.'

'Why the mad panic now? We talked about it all before.'

'Yeah, you talked me into it and I was a fucking idiot for listening. Just get a fucking move on.'

It was true. Lee had talked her into it. Lainie's mother

was away and allowing Hippy John to babysit was the only way Lainie could accompany Lee to the Worthing do. And Hippy John was keen to do it.

On his return from hospital having fallen over and hit his head on the ceiling, it had been mutually agreed that Hippy John's services on the building site were surplus to requirements.

'Listen, mate, you're a fucking liability.'

'I am.'

'You helping out on site is a crap idea.'

'It is.'

'So. Bugger off, you twit. Enjoy your flat. You know what, if you want to do something maybe you can babysit for us. That'd be quite good. I might ask Lainie about it. But only if you want to.'

'OK.'

And clearly Hippy John was much better. Any concern with carrots didn't mean he was a danger to himself or to anyone else. He had grown to be good with Ree and she was evidently comfortable in his presence. But this was the first time that he had been left in sole charge of her for anything more than a matter of minutes.

'I'm sure you'd have heard from him if there was a problem,' chipped in Romance from the back of the van. They had both forgotten he was there.

'What you've got to bear in mind,' answered Lainie, without turning her head, 'is that he's a stupid fucking hippy twat.'

'I quite like him,' said Jimmy, from his squeezed position between Lee and Lainie.

It was a rare contribution from their little friend and doubly so for being an opinion. It was enough to freeze the conversation. For a minute. Naturally, Lainie unfroze it.

'Jesus Christ,' she said, shaking her head. And then, 'What if he's been playing with the electrics again?'

'Why would he do that?'

'Because of you saying he could help you about the house! It's bad enough living in a fucking building site, but at least that's better than living in a house made fucking deadly by some dozy twat where you're liable to fucking die every time you turn the light on. You won't have him work with you, but it's all right for him to do what he fucking likes to our place. You're all safety this and that at work but when it comes to your own family, I mean who gives a flying toss?'

It was true. Lee had told Hippy John that he could help him about the house. After he had been such a disaster on site, Lee had felt sorry for him. The hippy had been so keen to help. So on a subsequent visit to their house-in-progress Lee had told Hippy John that there were always jobs that needed doing in there and that he could help whenever he was working on the house himself. Hippy John had thrown himself into helping with the electrics; he had it in mind that this was work that depended more on intellect than physical strength and so one to which he was more suited. But after Lainie received an (albeit minor) electric shock turning on the light on the landing, it had been agreed that he be kept away from such work.

'That's what's probably happened,' continued Lainie. 'This is his opportunity to prove himself, init? He's so desperate to please you Lee cos he's so fucking in love with you.'

It had been a good evening. The music had been excellent and two non-soul types requesting Stevie Wonder was an (all-be-it slight) improvement on the previous month's 'anything but this'. (Lainie had had a moan, but that was to be expected.) Romance had played again as Spaghetti hadn't been able to make it, again. As the Duke of Wellington – sole representative of RUFUS (Rights Unalienable For Us Stepdogfathers) – Spaghetti had only been held in the cells for a couple of hours and so was free and at large (although barred from all fancy dress shops within a thirty mile radius of Smethwick), but he had told Lee his dog was feeling poorly and wasn't up for travelling. And Romance had had a lot to drink. He couldn't DJ otherwise; it didn't seem to work. He needed the drink to calm him and to give him the confidence to talk on the mic. He had tried it sober and it felt disjointed and stumbling. And because he'd had a lot to drink, he was staying the night on Lee and Lainie's sofa.

Lee looked at the road ahead and out of the night came the signposts and roadside buildings that he knew so well, but it seemed an age between them now. He pictured their little house in Littlehampton, and inside Ree was asleep in her cot and Hippy John was leaping at the opportunity to do a favour for his absent friend. The sockets had to be fitted in the record room. Lee had told Hippy John not to touch them, but now he could imagine the hippy giving the job a go in order to prove him wrong and to demonstrate his competence, and even Lainie would then be happy that progress was being made. Lee had watched the hippy attempt to wire a socket before, and he'd had to stop him because the hippy didn't know what he was doing. It was undeniably dangerous. Being confident that Hippy John would be OK with the baby was one thing, but Lee hadn't considered that he might tackle the building work in some way. What if he gave himself an electric shock? He could be rendered unconscious or thrown across the room and knocked out that way. And then what if Ree managed to climb out of her cot? She had come close to doing so on several occasions now. And then what if the socket caught fire? Even if he hadn't had an electric shock and been rendered or knocked unconscious, what would the hippy do then? Lee doubted that Hippy John would have the presence of mind to call the fire brigade. He would be ashamed and would try to tackle the problem himself, and now Lee could see the fire growing and Hippy John was there, panicking, desperate and useless.

How long does a fire take to melt adjacent vinyl? That was a fact worth knowing, but Lee came to the startling realisation that he didn't know it. Hippy John probably wouldn't even realise the vinyl was melting until it was too late and carrying all the records out of the record room would be a lengthy and laborious task, even for someone of sound body and mind, let alone a frail, dippy hippy.

Now the house was ablaze and the records were lost, and Lee was picturing the glow in the sky and then turning into their street and a crowd of neighbours being kept away from the house by the West Sussex Fire Brigade. There's a moment of silence as the scene sinks in, and then Lainie becomes hysterical. A policeman tells them they can't drive any closer. It's only when a neighbour runs to tell her that Ree is OK that Lainie quietens and then collapses in a heap of tears. Lee looks at the house and imagines a pool of melted vinyl inside and then sees that it's beginning to flow out from under the door and then, as the crowd gasps, the door opens and there's a figure in the doorway clutching something to his breast. Hippy John pulls his feet forward through the sticky morass, teeters and collapses in the street, still clasping the small 7" carrying case containing Lee's most prized and valuable records. Lee rushes to him and Hippy John catches a glimpse of him through the haze and smiles and tries to say something and then pushes the record box to his friend before fading away.

But when Lee turned the corner of Abner Road, there was no tape across it and there were no fire engines or people on the street. And when he pulled up outside No. 34, he could see there were no outward signs of any damage.

Without speaking, Lainie was out of the van and into the house and, by the time Lee and Jimmy were on the pavement with Lee's play boxes and Lee had locked the van, Lainie had been up the stairs, checked on a happily sleeping baby, gone down again, looked at a quietly sitting hippy, gone up again and was almost in bed.

'Nice one Lee. Yeah. See ya.' Jimmy walked away.

'See ya, mate.'

Lee walked into the house, carrying his records. He shut the door behind him and went into the living room, where Hippy John was sitting on the sofa.

'You all right?'

'Yes.'

'Everything been all right?'

'Yes.'

Lee paused, looking at Hippy John, and his face contorted with concentration.

'Oh... fuck.'

He walked out and Hippy John wondered where the conversation had gone wrong. To him, it had seemed quite a good one.

But Lee had forgotten about Romance and had to go back to the van to wake him up and wheedle him out. And by the time he had done that, he was ready for bed himself. He left Romance to make himself at home on the sofa and Hippy John to make his way out.

'Hello,' Romance said.

'Hello,' Hippy John said.

For a drunken Romance and a dippy hippy, that wasn't a bad start.

# 99

Spaghetti reflected on the conversation he'd had with Romance. He felt bad about letting Romance down. It was good of Romance to be organising Demetrios Demetriou's memorial do and it was a privilege to be asked to DJ. But, on further reflection, he felt worse about letting down Demetrios Demetriou. After all, the event was in his honour. Demetrios Demetriou was dead and, as far as Spaghetti was concerned, Demetrios Demetriou was going to stay dead, but he might still have been keeping a keen heavenly eye on things. If, as a heavenly being, Demetrios Demetriou was as nice as he was as an earthly being – and Spaghetti could think of no earthly reason why he wouldn't be – then he wouldn't be cross with Spaghetti for cancelling. He wasn't the type. And by the time Spaghetti was ruminating on this matter (which was for much of the day after Soul Sam's funeral), he realised that the heavenly Demetrios Demetriou might even have met the heavenly Soul Sam, in which case he would be in an excellent position to appreciate Spaghetti's loss (presuming that Soul Sam had gone to heaven, that it was the same heaven and that Soul Sam was as impressive a heavenly dog as he was an earthly one). Spaghetti wondered at the chances of the two of them bumping into each other: slim, probably, considering the numbers involved. But perhaps these things were arranged and happened automatically, depending on the earthly relationships.

If the soul of Demetrios Demetriou had been reincarnated and had come back as something else then, whatever that something else was, it wasn't Demetrios Demetriou and probably it wouldn't even be able to remember being Demetrios Demetriou (if it even had a functioning memory), and so Demetrios Demetriou, if the name had any real meaning, would still be considered dead, and even if that something else was, in some weird way, still Demetrius Demetriou, then it could only possibly witness the memorial do as an insect – maybe literally a fly on the wall – or an even tinier being, as every other living thing there would have been born long before, and what were the chances of that particular insect or tiny being being there then? It would far more likely be in Africa or the Amazon or, if in England, in a less reputable bar – in West Bromwich maybe. But then Spaghetti couldn't escape the feeling that he should be respectful to the memory of Demetrios Demetriou, even if he didn't believe Demetrios Demetriou was observing in any way. After all, he would expect his and Soul Sam's joint acquaintances to be respectful of Soul Sam's memory, whether they believed in an after dog-life or not.

However, the irrefutable fact was that the measure to which he was keen to show his respect to the memory of Demetrios Demetriou was outweighed by the burden of his grief for the death of his dog. Soul Sam's death meant that he wasn't in the mood to celebrate the life of another. Therefore, as he had told Romance, he couldn't DJ at the do. And to DJ would be a disrespectful act in itself. Such ostentatious behaviour was not appropriate when still in mourning, and it would also be disrespectful to the people who would be there and to Demetrios Demetriou himself because Spaghetti wouldn't be able to give it his all.

Spaghetti considered his arguments again and decided that he was right. But, for some reason, he was still concerned. He would phone Lee. He felt sure that Lee would put his mind at rest about his non-attendance (partly because he knew that Lee would be keen to get a longer spot anyway).

## 100

For a while, the two *hellos* were as far as the conversation went between Romance and Hippy John. Romance was too drunk to think of any sensible questions and Hippy John didn't talk much anyway. (He was, however, concerned that having only just met this friend of his friends' a premature departure might be construed as impolite and, even though he was the one to be leaving and Romance was the one to be staying, he felt that it was he who was more the host.) When Romance flopped on to the sofa, Hippy John sat down on a record box and tried to think of the customary follow up to 'Hello'.

'Did you have a good night?'

Hippy John was pleased with that. It sounded like the kind of question other people would ask.

'Yeah, it was excellent. Went quick though. It would have been good to have got another hour or two.'

'Our time is but a shadow that passeth away.'

Romance eyed the hippy.

'You're not wrong there mate.'

Hippy John smiled. He was communicating.

'What's that from then? It sounds gospelly.'

'It's from a church.'

'Oh. I don't know it. But I'm not too well up on the early gospel stuff. I like the Soul Stirrers. Alex Bradford. A bit of doo wop too, but we're soul people, aren't we?'

'Yes,' Hippy John agreed.

There was a pause as they both reflected upon this.

'Is Romance your real name?'

'No. It's a nickname. It's just what people call me. It's after Romance Watson. My mate started it cos I wanted his record. He's dead now. It's a good name, though, init? I want to find him before he pops his clogs.'

'The breath in our nostrils is as smoke.'

'He was a gospel singer, you know. Back in the day. He only made one soul record. *In your eyes, where the glow of our love used to shine, another love is hiding where my hiding place used to be. So where does that leave me?* Pain and misery, hippy. It's what it's all about!'

'Our life shall pass away as the trace of a cloud and shall be dispersed as a mist.'

'Bloody hell, and I thought deep soul was mournful.'

'It's in the Bible. I looked it up. And sometimes what appears like a negative thing is, in fact, a positive thing.'

'Yeah well that's one of the things I love about soul music. If you listen to the lyrics it's bloody miserable, init? But the music is uplifting. It's something about the wonder of just being alive. And being sad is a part of that. It's more than just music, isn't it?'

Hippy John was proud to have elicited such a response (even though he didn't know what Romance was talking about).

'What appears like a negative thing is, in fact, a positive thing,' Hippy John repeated. 'Love what you don't like, and then you'll be happy.'

The effect of this statement wasn't immediate on Romance. Love what you don't like and then you'll be happy. It crept up on him. It crept up on him, found its way into his brain, ran round in there, found his package of thoughts and feelings about the blond girl and the resulting reaction sent ripples through his body. It was as if, in slow motion, he had pushed open the door of a phone box, taken a tentative step out and had then been struck by lightning.

He then dribbled a bit and fell asleep. Hippy John crept out.

# 101

When Terry Gibbs stepped out of the phone box opposite the Cutty Sark, having successfully made his call to Greenwich Clean Time, he wasn't struck by lightning. He was struck, hard, on his head, by what had been the wooden leg of a bar stool. The youths responsible had been intending to mug him but had run away in panic at the sight of the unexpected unconsciousness of their victim.

In Romance's life, the lightning moments tended to be more sheet lightning than forked lightning: walking away from JBP, the death of Demetrios Demetriou, hearing about the unpopped clogs of Romance Watson from Hemel Hector. These were all pivotal and precise moments, but none were a bolt from the blue. Each had a grounding in the past and seemed to be the cumulative result of successive events: a shocking, diffuse brightening caused by cloud-to-cloud electrical activity, as when Al Green was doused with a saucepan of boiling grits by his girlfriend. (The police found a note in her purse explaining her reasons: 'The more I trust you, the more you let me down.' She committed suicide; Al found God.)

Romance's moment with Hippy John, when his attitude to his relationship with the blond girl took a sudden turn, was something in between. The spark must have come from within as well as without and yet it was totally unexpected.

'Perhaps like ground-to-cloud lightning,' suggested Spaghetti, when they were discussing the matter in the pub before the 100 Club. 'It goes from the ground up to the cloud and then rebounds back to the ground when it could hit you on the head.'

'How do you know so much about lightning?' asked Solomon.

'I looked into when I got Sammy. I was worried about taking him out in the rain.'

'You daft twat.'

'It's like Sugarpuffs, init?' said Deptford Dave.

The others looked at him.

'You know, when they go up and down off a record.'

'What?'

'Have you never done that with your Sugarpuffs?'

'Done what?'

'Made them go up and down off a record.' They looked at him some more. 'You get a record, right, and then you rub it with a woollen scarf or something, and then you hold the record over your Sugarpuffs and they jump up to it and cling to the vinyl and then they fall off back to the other Sugarpuffs and then some more jump up. It's cool. It's electricity, init, or something.'

'Does it matter what the record is?'

'I dunno. I don't think so.'

'Does it work with Puffed Wheat or does it have to be Sugarpuffs? What about other wheat-based cereal products?'

'I dunno. I only eat Sugarpuffs.'

'It sounds like it could be a good way of telling how good a record is. Maybe the more soulful the record, the more electric it is. Then when you go round record fairs you won't need a little player or anything, just a bowl of Sugarpuffs.'

'Does it work with socks or does it have to be a scarf? I don't think I've got a woollen scarf.'

'Yeah but that can't be right because if it works with Dave's records it can't be anything to do with them being any good.'

'You could just use a sheep.'

'What else do you know about lightning then?' someone asked Spaghetti.

'That in America they spell it without an *e*.'

'Fucking bollock heads.'

'It doesn't have an *e* anyway.'

'What about Lightnin' Slim?'

'No *e*.'

'No *g*.'

'For fuck's sake.'

'Who gives a toss. Fuckin' R&B shite.'

The conversation before the 100 Club invariably reverted to 'fuckin' R&B shite'. Romance liked the assuredness of it. And he liked the soulful combination of bullishness,

nonsense and emotional openness.
 'Anyway, you should fuckin' go for it mate.'

# 102

If Romance, when he met JBP after she came out of St Bartholomew's House, had been as he was that time in the pub before the 100 Club when they talked about Sugarpuffs, then he would have acted differently. But he wasn't. He was younger then and every cell of his body was older and if his life was a flame then it was to be blown about a lot afterwards and quiver in shock too.

'I want us to be a couple again. It just doesn't feel right not being with you. I feel like we were just made to be together,' he might have said. 'My life has been empty without you and after everything you've gone through you look so wonderful.' And then they would have held each other.

And if he had been as he was that time in the pub a couple of years after JBP came out of St Bartholomew's House, he would have gone back to her and said pretty much the same thing, although this time probably sitting at the little table on the little terrace in her garden, and she would have listened, patiently, as he continued:

'I know it's taken me a long time, but after everything that's happened I just haven't been clear in my head. I haven't known the right thing to do. I've been terrified of making any kind of decision. But I know that it's the right thing now. I suddenly realise it. I really feel like I've changed. All the things that made me doubt if it was the right thing just aren't there anymore. I was worried about you being depressed, but now I love the fact that you suffer from depression, because it's you and it's who you are and without that you'd be someone else. And I love the fact that you're an alcoholic and now you can't drink, because it's probably just the other side of the coin of all the wonderful things about you and you wouldn't be who you are if it wasn't for all the bits that make up you. I look into your eyes and see a soul so deep. With you, I am me and without you I'm not. That's just how it is. The sadness about you makes the joy all the more. The bad things about you don't exist anymore. Any part of you is a part to be loved, and I've grown to love all of you as I have grown myself. And I know I'll never meet anyone else like you. I've never been surer about anything.'

It might have been something like that or, if Romance's wits were less about him, he might have inadvertently broken out into poor soul lyrics.

JBP would have looked at him, hard. She had spent a long time wanting to hear such words – almost dying to hear them. She had loved him more than she had ever loved anyone and more than she thought it possible for anyone to love anyone, and she would go on loving him too. She knew that.

'No,' she would have said. 'It's too late.'

When Romance was speaking he would have been mostly looking down, at the table, and across, at the garden, or at JBP's hand, her knee or the fold of her jacket at her elbow. He would have been embarrassed to look her in the eye. Ashamed, perhaps. But now he would have looked up at her. And he would have seen the loving harshness in her eye. A thin layer of water held tight as ice across the gaping deepness of her soul. And he would have felt his insides being pummelled as if by a gang of drunken, angry young men.

# 103

*In your eyes, where the glow of your love used to shine*
*In your eyes, where my lovelight used to be*
*Another love has erased and replaced the love I used to see*
*So where does that leave me?* [11]

When he first heard Romance Watson – when he was sitting on the edge of the bed in the bedroom of Demetrios Demetriou – Romance was a young man. The boys were surrounded by boxes of records and Demetrios Demetriou was playing whatever caught his fancy, and Romance was captivated instantly by the tight, lolloping introduction of gyrating latin percussion and the gentle, teasing organ and then, when the deep, loving, pained voice kicked in, it resonated through him and he felt it in his stomach.

*To your arms, where I used to run from all the world*
*To your arms, where my secret shelter was*
*Another face is hiding where my hiding place once used to be*

*So where does that leave me?*

'Fuck me,' Romance had said.

Then the trumpets blasted in, taking over, sweet and brutal, piercing and caressing, pleading with the disdainful percussion. The agony and the ecstasy of it. Stop, tease, percussion, stop, voice.

When it was over the boys laughed together; Romance laughed in delight and amazement at the record and Demetrios Demetriou in delight and amazement at the sharing of the experience of it. Neither of them had lost love like that. But Romance felt emotionally drained.

'Fuck me,' had seemed an appropriate response.

Demetrios Demetriou took the record from the turntable and passed it to Romance. Romance looked at it, held it and felt the weight of it and the pressure of it as he gently squeezed it, holding it with his right hand, middle finger through the central hole and the rim of the vinyl pressing into his palm.

'Romance Watson.'

Romance quivered a little. It could have been a post-orgasmic quiver or one that comes from having just been hit by something.

## 104

There was no divine revelation for Hippy John when he was beaten up that time before the bridge. In fact, he found it very difficult to put a positive spin on the experience.

He was set upon on the little green by the walls in the historic city of Chichester. The young men were drunk and the attack was motiveless – at least, Hippy John had done nothing to antagonise them. He heard them first and then, as they drew close to him, there was the acceleration of panic as he stumbled and failed to find an innocent reason for their approach. Even though he could sense what was coming, the first blow shocked him to the core. It was as shocking for its shock as its pain. And then each blow and each kick was like the shattering of another brittle body inside him. The pieces flew about and pierced him from the inside out. However long it lasted, it seemed both to be over in a flash and to take an age. And then he lay, quite still, not daring to disturb whatever remained of his delicate structure, his cheeks and lips being caressed by a drying stream of blood, desperate to cling on to him.

The shattering shock of it and the lingering smell of them. Their spittle a stinging, staying, vomiting rebuke upon him. And the warmth of their hands. The blows weren't from any cold, inanimate weapon. They were warm-blooded, filled with life. Human intimacy had come to him at last and this was it and he remembered the warmth of his father's cheek as his open hand landed on it, swung hard and deliberate. The horrible warmth that he had never known. The cry of his battered mother and the red fury of his father, which was Hippy John's house-leaving present to her.

When it was light, he lay there still and no one came to help him, and his own, dead blood clung to him still in some feeble, petrified embrace. And there were horrible bits of it sticking to him still as he gasped the stinking, alcoholic breath of his long gone attackers and clambered over the side of the bridge.

## 105

And when Romance held the Romance Watson in his open hand, he tightened his grip so the edge of it pressed harder into his palm and he delighted in the acute pressure of it. He had heard it and now he wanted to look at it and feel it.

It was a very plain label. Paper bag brown with a white horizontal line through the middle. 'Coral' at the top in black. '62442' typed on the left side and then 'Romance Watson' and 'Where Does That Leave Me' typed underneath the centre hole. And below that, handwritten in biro, 'Van McCoy, 2'49.' It wasn't printed. Someone who worked at the record label had typed and written the information straight on to the label.

'I wonder why they thought it necessary to make a test pressing. It's so obviously such a brilliant record.'

'No, it's a test pressing. To test the quality of the press – before they press loads of them.'

'Well it's fucking quality.'

'No, to test the audio whatever. Then they did the demo, I suppose, for the DJs. Yeah, a quality record, but no one bought it though, did they?'

Two minutes and forty-nine seconds. Such an ordinary number, on the face of it.

'The one that came out's a bit different. This one has the organ a bit more pronounced. It's just going for it a bit more.'

'I do like a pronounced organ.'

'It's not mint, is it?' Demetrios Demetriou had said. 'vg++ probably.'

Romance wanted records as he wanted nothing else and this one was special. A special record and a very special special press too. Spending spare income on anything other than records seemed such a waste to Romance, because for him only records transcended the material and therefore the act of spending itself. He viewed the extravagant waste of non-record spending with disdain and nowhere more so than at the marina in Southampton where expensive yachts soaked up the record money of the soulfully illiterate. Ironically, it was at the Southampton marina where Romance had a conversation with Hemel Hector that was to lead to a new chapter being added to the story that had begun in his friend's bedroom all those years before.

It was outside a bar, inside the marina, not too far from the Southampton end of the Itchen Bridge, one sunny Sunday, that Romance found himself sitting next to Hemel Hector. From where they were sitting the bridge was just out of sight, but they wouldn't have seen Hippy John, Lee or Lainie or the irate motorists anyway. A small seaful of water had passed under the bridge since then.

Romance and Hemel Hector were part of a little soulful group enjoying an al fresco drink. Juggy from Pompey was DJing inside and none of them much cared for the records he played. They were there for the afternoon and evening and had plenty of music ahead of them. At that moment, Hemel Hector's table-mates were more interested in hearing about the time he spent in a tape vault in Nashville listening to unreleased Scepter/Wand and Musicor material and what it was like to hear, for the first time, *It's Torture* by Maxine Brown and Melba Moore's *The Magic Touch*. He enjoyed telling the story to the wide-eyed youngsters. He had always thought this south coast lot a good bunch.

'So why are you called Romance?' he said, to Romance.

Romance hesitated. Obviously, it wasn't his real name. (It didn't occur to him to ask Hemel Hector why he was called Hemel Hector. He presumed that he was from Hemel Hempstead, but it seemed just as unlikely for someone to be called Hector as Romance.)

'It was Demetrios, I think. He knew I had this thing about Romance Watson. He knew that I really liked it so would tease me about not having one. Cos he had this super rare test pressing.'

'Of Romance Watson?'

'Yep.' Romance nodded. 'And he's still got it too, the jammy bastard,' he reflected.

'I didn't know there was one. A Coral test pressing?'

'Yeah. It's a bit different. It has a slightly more pronounced organ.'

'I'd like to hear that. Good old Demetrios.'

Hemel Hector was lost in thought.

'He's still around, you know. The name lives on.'

Romance had never heard Hemel Hector say anything so deep and spiritual before. And he was touched at the thought that his deceased friend had made such an impression on this icon of the northern soul scene.

'Yeah, last I heard, he was singing in some church in Philly.'

Now this seemed unlikely. Romance was willing to believe that somehow the spirit of Demetrios Demetriou lived on, whether in the hearts of those who knew him or as a part of the universal consciousness, but why would it choose to present itself in a church in Philadelphia? And even if it wanted to sing, how could it be heard? And even if it could be heard, how could those listening know they were listening to the spirit of a certain Demetrios Demetriou of East Acton, west London, England, never having been introduced? Plus, he couldn't sing for toffee.

'Is it Greek Orthodox?' asked Skipper Lee (a different Lee).

'What?'

'Is it a Greek Orthodox church? I didn't know they had them out there.'

'They have them all over,' said Leeds Dave. 'You just don't notice them. It's like the masons, or scientists. Spaghetti Weston told me he was gonna be one. They said he could be one but not Soul Sam.'

'Soul Sam told me he was an atheist,' said Hemel Hector.

Dave looked at him, but didn't say anything. He reckoned if someone thought dogs could talk, there was little point entering into a debate about it with them. Anyway, why would Soul Sam be an atheist? It was a question that was best left, and the question of the soul of Demetrios Demetriou singing in a church in Philadelphia, whether Greek Orthodox or not – which was the one vexing Romance – was best left too, at least for the moment.

'Imagine spending all that money on a stupid yacht,' said Solomon. 'Think of the records you could get for that.'

And with that there was silence, as each of them thought deeply upon it.

## 106

The next time Romance visited the cemetery he was alone. The rebuilt grave/blond girl/scones/mother combination had been quite overpowering and he wanted some quiet time to reflect with his friend. It was a bright, chilly morning and the cemetery appeared empty of other living people.

It was still a struggle to find the grave, even with the little stone record box to look out for. There were so many graves – so many people who had lived and then died. Who were all these people? Romance had known a few people who had lived and then gone on to die, but nothing compared to the number who hadn't. He walked along the rows of graves and they teased him with their non-Greek names. Richard T. Riccall. Florence Georgina Kerr. Tamala Bellamy. Michael Terrence Keyes. When he came across the grave of his friend it was quite sudden and he stopped with a jolt. Demetrios Demetriou. Always remembered. Soul eternal.

Romance paused and then edged in front of the grave

and stood facing it. He stood straight and still.

The grave seemed more squeezed in than before. Strangely, a woman on either side, young and old, had given the impression of more space.

He found himself rooted to the ground. The weight of his body was channelled into the earth. He liked the thought that this was out of respect for his friend, but then he realised that for some reason, there and then, it felt natural to him to be so rooted and to feel a part of the place. Any movement seemed unnatural and, when he caught a glimpse of another living figure moving between the graves, he was annoyed by the foreignness of it. He tried not to look and concentrated on the fixed things in front of him.

Alfred 'Bertie' Tolbert. Devoted husband, father and grandad. And neighbour of Demetrios Demetriou unto eternity. It's a bit hit and miss, isn't it? You don't know who you're going to end up with! What if Alfred Tolbert was a miserable old sod?

And looking above the grave of Bertie, lines of graves fell away and then a tree rose from them and opened itself to the world. There were quite a few trees in the graveyard, but Romance was drawn to this one. He didn't know about types of trees, but this one was the most quintessentially tree-like. It was well proportioned, nicely symmetrical and a good, average tree-size. Like Romance, it was rooted and unmoving, and it reached out to him as it reached out to the world, and in it he felt the presence of his friend, arms spread wide, Christ-like. It must be feeding off the dead bodies, Romance thought. Maybe that's why it's so healthy looking.

Romance felt the presence of Demetrios Demetriou in the tree more than the grave. There was nothing wrong with the grave – it was a good grave and the record box made him smile – but Romance had been there at the burial and he remembered seeing the coffin in the grave and how deep it was. Whenever he had been in a cemetery before, he had seen the graves as covers for the dead, but the truth was that the dead were far below, and presuming they were all buried at the same depth (which, according to Spaghetti, they were, because of the plague) then there would be a deep stratum of dead, quite apart from the gravestones. There was a parallel plane of the dead and Demetrios Demetriou was in that one, not this stony one, taken well away from this surface world of individual graves with their names and ages and living visitors. He was a part of the earthy mush, whether he liked it or not. Any new body would slowly just become part of the mush and the tree fed off the whole lot, not just Demetrios Demetriou, and as Romance looked at it now he saw the essence of life opening its arms, reaching to the sky from deep below and offering itself to him and the surface world and to anyone with the wit to give it any attention. The tree was life and love, so it was the living love of JBP, among all others, and it embraced him as he stood rooted to the spot where he had stood before with the blond girl at his side. It was an accepting love. Encouraging, even.

Romance had been, and was, surprised at the extent to which he had been affected by the death of his friend. Still, he thought, it was nothing to how it must have affected Demetrios.

# 107

Later in the evening of the day of the Southampton alldayer, after Hemel Hector had DJed and played a couple of his renowned RCA discoveries (unreleased tracks from the RCA record label, not long lost recordings of down and outs from Chichester) and when he was at the bar being lauded, Romance sidled up to him to ask him about Demetrios Demetriou.

'What's all this about Demetrios Demetriou in Philadelphia?'

'What?'

'You said something about Demetrios Demetriou singing in Philadelphia.'

'He's six foot under, you twat. I saw you at the funeral.'

'Yeah, I know he is. With that Romance Watson too.'

'Eh?'

'That test pressing of Romance Watson is down there with him. The slightly different mix one. His mum put it in.'

'Did she? Ha, and no one's dug it up yet?'

'No,' Romance answered, somewhat ashamedly.

'And why did she do that then? And why that one?'

'I think she just picked it randomly, with a few others. Maybe she knew it was a special one.'

'Blimey. Anyway, that's who I was talking about, in Philadelphia. Not Demetrios.'

'But I saw her the other day, at the cemetery.'

'No, Romance Watson, you idiot.'

'Oh.'

Oh!

# 108

*Come on children let's sing!*
*About the goodness of the Lord!* [20]

So, Romance Watson was alive. Alleluia! This was good news, especially for Romance Watson. And it was good news for Romance too, because meeting a living Romance Watson was to be the climax of his film. And Romance Watson was still singing too. Alleluia! He was singing gospel music in a church in Philly. Perhaps, then, he was still capable of singing a decent rendition of *Where Does That Leave Me*. However, for Romance, hearing that Romance was alive and that he was singing in Philadelphia wasn't a wholly pleasing experience. In the film, Romance was supposed to find out for himself what had become of Romance Watson and to track him down and surprise everyone watching, and himself too, by finding Romance and by having an emotional encounter. (Romance imagined filming Romance singing *Where Does That Leave Me* for the first time since 1965, perhaps as Romance stood in his kitchen or sat on the bus, thereby creating a wonderful and highly artistic juxtaposition of the most ordinary of locations and the most extraordinary of events.) Now where did this leave Romance?

It was funny, Romance mused. Until he heard that Romance Watson was alive, he had never considered that he might not be. This was particularly odd considering the number of soul singers who had taken the last train to glory (to join the choir invisible) – snuffed it – when they were still in their prime. He had simply taken it for granted both that Romance was alive and that he would find Romance. Romance had not only had an unswerving faith in his film idea but had also had an unswerving faith in Romance Watson himself. Now his faith in Romance Watson had been shown as justified. But the showing of it seemed to compromise his film idea. This was confusing to Romance, because until then his faith in his idea and his faith in Romance Watson were very much bound together. And he was feeling guilty, too, for feeling confused, because the decent feeling to feel would be pure delight that another human being was alive and well enough to be singing. He couldn't help but think of his art first. He would reflect upon the matter, he decided, and try not to panic. (Perhaps this was the sorry plight – the sorry, squalid morality – of all great artists.) Romance Watson was alive and singing. It was wonderful news that Romance was very sorry to hear.

Hemel Hector was very much in the business of tracking

down aged soul singers. They were dispersing as a mist at an alarming rate. He visited America often, acquiring the rights to old recordings, searching the vaults of obscure record labels for unissued material and, whenever he could, interviewing the original artists about their less than successful careers. Sometimes he would even tempt them over to perform at the Cleethorpes weekender. They were always surprised and delighted that their creative efforts, hardly recognised and long since forgotten in their homeland, were being so appreciated in the land of Princess Diana.

And now he had news of Romance Watson and was happy to share it. (But Romance wasn't going to tell Hemel Hector about his film idea. He was determined to be very careful that such an inspired idea didn't leak out.)

'Yeah, I mentioned his name to some studio guys who were involved in gospel. And that's what they said. He's still knocking about. They thought he'd been involved in some new gospel recordings from this church. I looked the thing up and have the address somewhere but never got round to doing anything about it. I mean, it's only the one track really, isn't it? Unless there's some unissued stuff, but I doubt it. There wasn't much good stuff on Coral. Not soul, anyway. He did that other thing, but it's not of any interest to us. But if he's still singing then his voice must still be good.'

'What was the church, do you remember?'

'No. But I'll find it and let you know, if you want. Are

you gonna go out there? Go meet your namesake?'

'I don't think so. I might write to him though.'

Romance wasn't the jealous type, but he was now more jealous than he ever had been and he was jealous of Hemel Hector for knowing that Romance Watson was alive and singing in a church in Philadelphia. He knew he had no reason to be cross with Hemel Hector, who had known nothing of Romance's idea, and it was silly to feel betrayed by Romance Watson himself. But he couldn't help but feel resentful. It was his own faith in his idea that had somehow rebounded on him, just as his faith in the power of his love for JBP had done years before. And there was no one he could talk to about it, except, perhaps, JBP herself. So he talked to JBP about it.

'Stop being such a prat,' was her considered response.

And she was right. He was a prat and he should stop being one. His feelings of resentment were silly and self-indulgent, because Romance Watson would no doubt be delighted to be immortalised in a classic documentary and that delight could only be realised by Romance's total commitment. And *Looking for Romance (with Steve Davis)* was a sound idea. In fact, it could work all the better for Romance's newfound knowledge. He would know where the journey had to end and he could manipulate the narrative. The television executives would never know and the viewers would never know either. Even Steve Davis need never know.

Romance was aware that there might be ethical

considerations in deceiving the viewer, but surely the art came first. Television was undoubtedly full of such manipulations of the truth. It was the nature of the medium. Perhaps it was the very nature of art itself. Romance surmised that the reality of the journey to find Romance Watson didn't matter. What mattered was the message – the communication of the feeling, not of the experience. The implication would be that the journey was real, in every sense, and no one would know otherwise, except, when the film was shown on Channel 4, Hemel Hector. He would be bound to watch it, as there is never anything decent about soul music on telly. Somehow, for the good of the music, Romance would have to ensure that Hemel Hector didn't snitch on him to Ofcom or *Right to Reply*.

# 109

'All right? It's Spaghetti!'

What was spaghetti? Hippy John knew what spaghetti was, but he didn't know to what spaghetti the man on the phone was referring. He tried to think if he had asked anyone a question of late to which the answer might have been spaghetti.

'What you up to mate? All OK down there? Still thumping out yer choons?'

Hippy John recognised the accent. It was the accent of his childhood and youth. But he couldn't think of anyone from Birmingham who would be interested in renewing contact with him. He hadn't really had any friends there and it certainly wasn't his Aunty Edith. Thumping out yer choons. Spaghetti. Then he remembered that he didn't have a phone and that he was babysitting at Lee and Lainie's.

'Is it Lee you want?'

'Yeah mate. Who's this?'

'I'm their friend and part-time childminder. I'm John.'

'John? Oh. Right.'

There was a pause while they each thought where to go from there.

'Childminder?'

'Yes.'

'Do they have a child?'

'Yes.'

'Lee and Lainie?'

'Yes.'

'I had a dog, you know, but he's recently passed away. The funeral was yesterday.'

'Oh, I'm sorry,' said Hippy John, for want of anything else to say. And, having said it, he was surprised to feel a slightly smug sense of satisfaction at saying sorry when, for once, there was no self-loathing involved. And, more than that, he didn't even mean it. (He wasn't happy to hear of Spaghetti's loss, but he refused to equate the beautiful, adorable, lovely and loving little girl who was curled up with him on the sofa with a dog.)

'Actually, that's why I was phoning,' continued Spaghetti. 'Maybe you could let Lee know. Soul Sam has passed away, and so I can't make Saturday.'

'Soul Sam has passed away. So you can't make Saturday. OK. Should I say to whom is calling?'

'Spaghetti.'

'I'm sorry?'

'Spaghetti.'

'I mean, should I say who the message is from? Should I take a note of your name?'

'Yes, Spaghetti.'
'Spaghetti? As in *spaghetti*?'
'Yes.'
'Are you sure?'
There was a pause.
'Yes.'
'Soul Sam passed away. Spaghetti can't make Saturday.'
'That's it.'

Hippy John was confused. He was used to being confused and he was used to resigning himself to it, but he wanted to pass on this passing away message accurately. It sounded as if it was important. And so many times his father had berated him for not taking a message properly, and even when the person on the phone had said they didn't want to leave a message, Hippy John's father would still shout, 'But who was it? You should have taken a message!' And Hippy John had to remember this one too, because he didn't have a pen.

Of course, Hippy John knew there was no such thing as talking pasta, and he doubted there would be even in a parallel universe, so he surmised that the person on the other end of the phone was a male human being claiming either to be spaghetti or to be called Spaghetti. The latter seemed more feasible. Perhaps spaghetti the pasta was named after a Mr Spaghetti who invented it. And if a man could be called Spaghetti, a dog could certainly be called Soul Sam. But Saturday. Saturday was when Lee and Lainie were going to London for the memorial do of their friend.

Hippy John knew this because they had already asked him to babysit. So he knew that Lee couldn't be due at any dog-related events. And they didn't have a dog.

'They don't have a dog,' Hippy John said.

'Who doesn't?'

'Lee and Lainie.'

'No, I know that. I'd know if they had.'

There was an uneasy pause. Hippy John knew that it was his turn to say something, but he was thinking. Spaghetti had been about for a long time, and it came from Italy, not Birmingham, so this man wouldn't be the one who had invented it. But Spaghetti was an unusual name, so it was likely that he was a descendent of the spaghetti inventor. The inventor himself must be long since dead. He probably had a wild, Italian, pasta-fuelled send-off. But a dog funeral? Hippy John had never heard of a dog funeral.

'The breath in our nostrils is as smoke. Our body shall be turned to ashes, and our spirit shall vanish as the soft air.'

If Spaghetti had been an English-understanding dog, his ears would have pricked up.

'Who's that by?'

Hippy John wasn't sure. It was the Book of Wisdom.

'It's from the Bible.'

'What is it again?'

'The breath in our nostrils is as smoke. Our body shall be turned to ashes, and our spirit shall vanish as the soft air. For our time is a very shadow that passeth away.'

'That's good, init? There's some quality lyrics in the Bible.

Was that like, a miracle dog?'

Hippy John didn't know anything about miracle dogs, in the Bible or elsewhere, but he did know – at least he had good reason to believe – that the gravestone in the little church near Littlehampton had a dead human beneath it. (Who would call their dog *Sir William Hightower*?)

'I think it's about people, actually,' said Hippy John, some fresh smugness returning.

'Is it? Still, it might be a good thing for a headstone. The bit about the nostrils. I might look into that.'

'Lee's going to a memorial event for his friend on Saturday,' said Hippy John.

'Yeah, that's it. That's what I was phoning about. That's what I can't go to. Because of Soul Sam.'

'And Soul Sam is a dog?'

'Yeah, but now he's passed away and I'm cut up about it.'

'But the memorial do is for a human, isn't it? How can you miss that because of a dog?'

Hippy John hardly knew what had come over him. As well as smugness, he was now experiencing indignation, and not only experiencing it but showing it. In fact, he was being brazen.

'He was my dog.'

'And wasn't he your friend?'

'Well, yes.'

When Hippy John had wanted to die, he hadn't even wanted to be remembered. There would have been no memorial event for him. He hadn't even imagined there would be a funeral. He didn't think he would be missed and he had wanted his body to remain at the bottom of the river or, even better, the sea. But now he was concerned that a deceased young man he had never met be shown all appropriate manner of respect.

'I was planning on being there in spirit,' continued Spaghetti.

'But if it's in spirit, do you think he'll know you're there?'

This was a good question and Spaghetti didn't have an answer to hand. If Demetrios Demetriou's spirit was there, presumably it would notice the living humans who were present, and presumably it would notice the spirits of any deceased people that had come along too, but whether or not it would notice the spirit of a living, bodily person was another matter. And how could Spaghetti's spirit be there when the rest of him was alive and in Birmingham? It couldn't, really.

'Soul Sam's spirit might be there. He got along quite well with Demetrios Demetriou. The two of them saw eye to eye on quite a lot of things.'

'Our life shall be dispersed as a mist.'

Hippy John had been thinking that dead people might end up all in the mist together or possibly even merging with the mist. But he didn't know about dogs and he couldn't think of anything to say on the matter and he wasn't inclined to anyway.

And then baby Ree started crying.

'I've got to go.'

'OK. Bye.'
'Bye,' replied Hippy John. (That bit was relatively easy.)

# 110

*Christ Community Baptist Church*
*136 - 138 Harthon Ave.*
*Philadelphia*
*Pennsylvania*

Romance wasn't at all sure if he should write to Romance. He looked at the address again. What should he say? And how would any prior exchange of letters impact on that moment in the film when Romance supposedly discovers Romance? If they had already been in touch, it could ruin everything. What if when they met Romance said, 'Hello Romance, good to meet you at last,' or something like that. Romance could prime Romance and persuade him to be in on the act (for the good of the film and, therefore, the music), but then some authenticity would be lost. But it would be useful to know where he was going to be at a particular time and to have an idea of how friendly and receptive he might be. Perhaps if Romance popped up completely unexpectedly, Romance would be so taken aback he wouldn't be able to speak. He might even have a heart attack; he had probably never been on telly before. And what if it was the wrong Romance Watson? It's an unusual name, and so Romance doubted there would be more than one, especially among gospel singers, but America was a strange place and the name might not be so unusual there. And Romance knew that in America there were people with all kinds of weird names. He thought of Pigmeat Markham, Mongo Santamaria, Herman H. Harper II and Prince La La. And he then recalled the number of soul singers and groups with the same names. It would look bad in the film if after a long search eventually Romance found Romance and it was the wrong Romance. (*Where Does That Leave Me*? Never heard of it! It sounds like the devil's music!) Embarrassing, in fact.

So Romance decided to write to him.

# 111

*Aretha Loleatta Towanda Rozetta* were her given names. *Ree*, she had become. And Hippy John had been babysitting her often for Lee and Lainie. Lainie was resistant at first, but seeing how affectionate he was with Ree, and how Ree took to him, the argument for a petulant youth became a difficult one. Lainie's mother was always willing, but they didn't like to overburden her. So since Hippy John was in Littlehampton, it seemed to make sense to use him and he loved it. Lee and Lainie paid him – not much, but something – and this was a welcome boost to his benefits, but he would have sat with Ree for nothing. He took pride in being useful to Lee and Lainie and he took pride in being amusing to Ree. He didn't take pride in receiving money and housing benefit from the state, but he took pride in being recognised by the state as a member of society worthy of support. And he took pride in helping at the homeless drop-in centre in Bognor Regis, to where he would bus and walk three mornings a week. It felt good to be wanted and to be useful. And he loved the baby. She made him smile and he made her laugh. He could spend hours looking at her, making faces, and she would watch him, wide-eyed, and suddenly she would break out into a spasm of snorting giggles and the simple warmth of it would make him chuckle. He was diligent, attentive and happy to change her and to clean her, and when he heard a car pull up he always hoped that it wasn't Lee and Lainie returning so soon. Back in his bedsit he missed that innocent, dribbly little face and the fresh smell of new life, but he would settle into his bed warmed by his evening and grateful for the comfort of his sheets.

He had given Lee the message from the man who said his name was Spaghetti.

'What? Soul Sam has died?' exclaimed Lee.

'Yes, that's what he said.'

'Fuck me,' Lee said, sitting down from what seemed the sheer weight of the news. 'Soul Sam.'

So it seemed this must have been one very special dog after all.

'Lainie, Soul Sam has died,' he said as she came into the room. 'Spaghetti phoned when we were out.'

'Well he was getting on a bit. Hector probably asked him to DJ at Cleethorpes and he had a heart attack.'

'Soul Sam,' said Lee again, to himself.

And when Hippy John was comfortable in bed later that evening, he wondered at the high regard these soul folk had for this departed dog and whether it was all dogs they held in such esteem or whether Soul Sam was, indeed, some kind of miracle dog.

Hippy John liked dogs. He really did. And he could even understand why some people preferred their company to that of beings of their own species. Cruelty from one's own species is always harder to bear. And many a time he was on his bench in Chichester and a dog would bound over with baby-like enthusiasm in its eyes, only to be called coldly away by its owner. But it was strange to him to hear this dog being talked about in this reverential way. Perhaps these soul folk knew something he didn't. Perhaps they knew that dogs were the incarnation of loyalty and faith and that in watching how we treated them God was judging us. Or perhaps they had discovered that dogs were God's way of watching us – he was actually watching us through them. The truth was that all of the soul folk did know something that Hippy John didn't know, and that was that Spaghetti Weston was an idiot.

# 112

*Dear Romance,*

*I am very pleased to hear that you are still singing. I am a great fan of your wonderful record, 'Where Does That Leave Me'. You might be surprised to hear it, but there are many people in Britain who love that record and it has been played regularly on the northern soul scene for many years now. (Firstly at Stafford, I believe.)*

*I used to be very jealous of my friend Demetrios Demetriou because he owned a copy of the record (vg++). It was actually a test pressing. (Did you know there was a test pressing? The organ is slightly more pronounced. Maybe you're aware of others? Did you record anything else back then that wasn't released?) I am not so jealous of him now because he is dead, but you might be pleased to hear that his rare copy of your record is with him still, in his coffin, and will remain united with his corpse/skeleton forever, unless his coffin is broken into by graverobbers or archaeologists. (There are some other records in there too, but I'm not sure what they are as his mother picked them, but, whatever they are, I'm sure that yours is the best.)*

*Soulfully yours,*

*Romance*

*PS*
*It would be interesting to hear from you details of your movements over the next year or so. Are you always at this church? I wonder if you have some kind of itinerary.*

Romance couldn't think of much else to say, but he decided it was probably best to keep the letter brief and to the point. He was pleased to have thought to mention Demetrios Demetriou. That was a nice touch. At least, if he was to hear back, he would ascertain whether or not this was the right Romance Watson, as he could think of no reason why any other Romance Watson wouldn't admit to not being the singer of *Where Does That Leave Me*. (And if they didn't, they would surely be found out by Romance's incisive follow-up questions.)

He folded it, put it in an envelope, wrote the address of the church on it, went to the post office, bought a stamp for the USA, stuck on the stamp, admired his handiwork and posted it.

# 113

The soul vicar's church was quite different from the Christ Community Baptist Church, but then rural Berkshire didn't have much in common with downtown Philadelphia (despite the fact that the founder of Philadelphia, William Penn, kicked his blessed bucket in Berkshire). Philadelphia, the city of brotherly love, spawned some talented soul acts in the 1960s. Only the black record labels of Detroit and Chicago are revered more on the northern soul scene. And in the 1970s the soul music of the city exploded into the mainstream with Philadelphia International Records and *The Sound of Philadelphia*.

Even though the village had its very own soul vicar, the music scene of Upper Larksdell could never be considered explosive. One of the Pritchett children was doing very well on the flute and Mrs Dearborn, the church organist, wasn't as bad as people said (it's a very difficult instrument to master), but there wasn't the cultural vibrancy of 1960s inner city Philly. The cultural highlight of the week was Chinese dancing in the church hall every Tuesday afternoon with Mrs Woo.

Mrs Woo needed to be congratulated and encouraged. She was ever threatening to withdraw her services due to the depressing lack of progress in her enthusiastic but hapless pool of ageing female village talent. If this was to happen the vicar knew that he would be blamed, by both ageing men (who had become accustomed to their two hours in The Three Bells on a Tuesday afternoon) and ageing women alike, and it was his attempt to catch Mrs Woo on the Tuesday afternoon that drew the vicar to the church hall and to the gleaming new whiteness of the church hall wall.

'What do you think, Gerald?'

Gerald was sitting, looking at it, and looking uncomfortable.

'It's all gone.'

'What has?'

'The painting.'

'Yes, but look what we have! A white wall! I think it's quite beautiful. The painting of the spirit. Anyway, everything's transient. Just think of it as a blank canvass. It's the journey that matters, Gerald – the act of creation. Nothing lasts. The act itself is what matters.'

Mr Moore-Hackett hadn't been entirely sure if his anti-painting painting of the wall was an act of creation or of destruction. But whichever it was, the act itself had certainly been more satisfying than the end. To him, once the thrill of the act had waned, the white wall looked pitiful and aggressive, like a wounded beast. (It was reflective of him in a way that the mural hadn't been.)

Gerald smiled. He had enjoyed the act of creation. In fact, he had only really enjoyed looking at the horrible painting because it reminded him of the act. And he enjoyed hearing the vicar's next remark too:

'I might get in touch with Thelonius. See if he has any ideas.'

# 114

Unlike Romance, Terry Gibbs the soul vicar was used to sending letters to America. And, also unlike Romance, he was used to receiving letters from America too. And he was used to receiving records from America and bulky record lists.

The records came in brown card sleeves or packed tight in small card boxes. They would come from specialist soul record dealers who had advertised in American record collectors' magazines, one of which had been passed on to the vicar and to which he had then subscribed. The dealers would list their rare records in the magazine and then, once they had the addresses of purchasers, they might send lists directly. The vicar would spend hours painstakingly examining these lists of records. There were records that other DJs played and that he had grown to know, but there were always many he didn't know. Sometimes, on recognising a label or an artist, he would take an enlightened punt, but even the number of labels and artists seemed limitless. Usually, they required bids to be submitted, and so more thought, more careful consideration, and a written list of bids to be posted to America days before the deadline: $5, $10, $100. Sometimes $500. Occasionally more. He addressed his envelopes to strange sounding places: Harrisburg, Pennsylvania; Kalamazoo, Michigan; Walnut Creek, California. And they would write back, listing his successful bids, and he would drive to Queensbridge or to Breney Green and go to the bank, buy dollars, wrap the dollars in paper and post them, and then the records would arrive, and in this way he was in touch with the home of soul.

Romance had never heard of Harrisburg, Kalamazoo or Walnut Creek, but he knew that America beyond the big cities had played its part in the story of soul, and he imagined leaving Steve Davis in a record shop and walking along the pavements of places that could have been Harrisburg, Kalamazoo or Walnut Creek and filming himself asking for needless directions from pretty American girls who would then marvel at his accent and his foreignness. And he would act coy but then ask them to join him for a tea, at which they would laugh, and then they would go with him for a coffee, and they wouldn't mind being filmed because they all wanted to be on telly.

But this was in his imagination and he had no direct contact with such places. So when his letter came and it had an American stamp and his name and address were written in that strange American way of mixing upper and lower case letters, it stirred him inside. It could only be from

Romance. It couldn't be from anyone else. It just couldn't.

*Dear Romance,*

*Thank you for your letter! All the way from the land of Princess Diana!*

*Yes, I recorded 'Where Does That Leave Me'. That takes me back! It's incredible that you know the record over there in the north of England. That record never really done anything. How did you come across it? That would be interesting to hear. I am honored that you know it, my friend, and thank you for your kind words.*

*By the grace of God, I am still singing, and every day I give thanks to the Lord for being so blessed. As in my youth, I now dedicate my voice to Him.*

*I don't know of any test pressings. It's strange that such a thing came to be in England. I don't remember recording anything for Coral that they didn't put out, but it was a long time ago and every day I was singing in some place or other.*

*I am so sorry to hear of the passing of your friend, Demetrios Demetriou. By the grace of God, he is in a better place and I pray that he may rest in peace. May the Lord give you strength.*

*'Tis the old ship of Zion. Get on board! Get on board!*

*In His name,*

*Romance Watson*

*PS*

*This year I plan to mostly be in the Philadelphia area. I do not get about as much as I used to. And you are called Romance too! That's great! It's not such a common name over here. It's interesting to know it has its roots in Europe.*

A letter from a soul man, from soulland. And not just any soulman. If another pair of eyes had been there, they would have seen Romance tremble. He wanted to tell someone. He wanted to show someone. He wanted to tell Demetrios Demetriou. He stared at the letter. Romance Watson. He touched the letter and the letter touched him back. Ha! Touched by the hand of soul!

# 115

'Ooh, that's nice,' said the blond girl.

Romance smiled.

'He likes God quite a lot, doesn't he?'

Romance smiled.

'Does he think you live in the north? Why's that?'

'I don't know.'

'The old ship of Zion. That sounds fun.'

Romance smiled.

'And are you going to get on board, Romance dear?'

Romance smiled. ''Tis the old ship of Zion. Get on board, get on board.'

'Well I will if you will.'

Romance knew about the old ship of Zion. At least, he was familiar with the phrase.

> *'Tis the old ship of Zion, get on board, get on board.*
> *It has landed many a thousand, get on board, get on board.*
> *Ain't no danger in the water, get on board, get on board.*
> *It will take us all to heaven, get on board, get on board.*

It was a traditional gospel song, from a traditional nineteenth century spiritual. And like many old spirituals, and like Romance's film idea *Looking for Romance (with Steve Davis)*, it had a double meaning.

'It's a song about going to heaven. But it's also about the Underground Railroad. Slaves escaping to Canada.'

'And what does Romance mean by it? I think he just means you should embrace life. He seems like a happy man. I think you should do what he says.'

Perhaps the blond girl was right. But there was a problem and it was sitting beside him. And it was her.

She was beautiful. She was an angel. But as well as being terrified of committing himself because of the whole JBP experience, Romance was determined to put his art first, for the good of the music. *Looking for Romance (with Steve Davis)* had been on hold while he was with JBP but it couldn't be on hold forever. Romance owed it to hamanity to make the film and the time felt right. Now blond girl was there for him, which, admittedly, was lovely and wonderful, but how could he go looking for romance if romance had already come to him? The authenticity of the film was already compromised by his having found Romance – or Romance having come to him – and now here was the prospect of a romantic relationship too. Her big eyes could swallow him up. Look at them.

Perhaps if the Arts Council read his letter soon, he could make the film and then come back and be with blond girl. But he would still have to pretend that he had no romantic interest in his life. And what would she think of the finished film? He would then be famous for being a man in search of romance (as well as for being an innovative film-maker) and that might not be the kind of man she wanted to be with, even if the thing that he was famous for (other than for being an innovative film-maker) wasn't actually true.

Maybe blond girl wouldn't be about that long anyway. Romance knew that the editing process would be a long one (the general public are always surprised at how long that part of the filmmaking process takes) and the relationship could be over before the film is ready to be shown. Romance was unaware of the statistics, but he knew that most relationships didn't last. His art, however, would speak to mankind through the ages. Surely that was more important than his personal life.

'What would you do,' he asked JBP, 'if you were in this position?'

'Jesus Christ,' she replied, ambiguously. 'Don't be a prat all your life.'

He needed to ask someone else, but who? And then it came to him.

# 116

Romance knew that the Underground Railroad wasn't a railroad (railway). And it wasn't literally underground. (So it certainly wasn't the tube, or anything like that.) It was a clandestine system, and it was the system that was used by slaves to escape north. It consisted of a series of safe houses (stations) and local guides (conductors). The lyrics of some spirituals, many of which then made their way into gospel music, are said to give instruction on escape routes to escaping slaves and they were passed through song among the slaves. The clearest example of which Romance was familiar (he had seen a documentary on the subject) was *Follow the Drinking Gourd* – the drinking gourd being the constellation of the big dipper, which pointed the way north.

> *When the sun comes back and the first quail calls*
> *Follow the drinking gourd*
> *For the old man is a-waiting for to carry you to freedom*
> *If you follow the drinking gourd.*

*The riverbank makes a very good road*
*The dead trees will show you the way.*
*Left foot, peg foot, traveling on*
*Follow the drinking gourd.*

*The river ends between two hills*
*Follow the drinking gourd.*
*There's another river on the other side*
*Follow the drinking gourd.*

The traditional song *Wade in the Water* is clearly about crossing the River Jordan to enter paradise, but it has also been interpreted as encouraging escaping slaves to take to the water in order to throw off the scent pursuing bloodhounds:

*If you don't believe I've been redeemed*
*God's gonna trouble the water.*
*I want you to follow him down to Jordan's stream*
*My God's gonna trouble the water.*

But most spirituals are less specific and were designed to give hope and encouragement rather than instruction. They are Christian songs, in which Jordan, Heaven, Zion or The Promised Land may be given the supplementary, rather than alternative, meaning as the free north or Canada.

*Swing low, sweet chariot, coming for to carry me home* could be interpreted as an encouragement to use the Underground Railroad, as could *Steal away, steal away, steal away to Jesus*, and one of the most popular spirituals, *The Gospel Train*:

*The Gospel Train's a-comin'*
*I hear it just at hand.*
*I hear the car wheels rumblin'*
*And rollin' thro' the land.*
*Git on board children, git on board children, git on board children*
*For there's room for many a more.*

The gospel train – or the freedom train – became an enduring metaphor and is common in twentieth century gospel music and, when a host of sixties and seventies soul singers were pleading with their audience to get on board the soul train, the metaphor rattled on across fresh terrain.

But it was the 1966 gospel-soul version of *Wade in the Water* by The Salem Travelers that was the first record Terry Gibbs the soul vicar played at Demetrios Demetriou's memorial do and Romance was there to hear it with the blond girl at his side.

*I stepped in the water and the water was cold!*
*He's gonna trouble the water!*
*It chilled my body but not my soul.*
*He's gonna trouble the water!*

# 117

*Dear Romance,*

*Thank you so much for the letter. It was wonderful to hear from you. 'Where Does That Leave Me' has always been such a favourite of mine (and my friend Demetrios Demetriou really liked it as well). I wonder how you came to record the record?*

*I wonder, also, at the sacrifices a great artist such as yourself has had to make for his art. You sing with such soul. There is much pain and heartbreak in your voice. And decades later the record still has such power. It sounds as if you suffered greatly, but through this suffering has come a great work of art. I wonder how you feel about it now. However painful it was for you as an individual, surely it was good that you suffered in this way, because the rest of the world has been enriched by your art.*

*I find myself in a similar position. There is the possibility that I am on the verge of creating a great work of art, and my art, too, will be about the forlorn quest for love. The problem is that I have met a wonderful woman. I would like very much to be with her, but I feel I should put my art first, for the benefit and enrichment of future generations, as, perhaps, you once did yourself. (I am also finding it difficult to commit anyway, because I have been hurt in the past, although not in the same way as you.)*

*Being an artist seems to be a lonely profession. It is painful to listen to your heartfelt disappointment of losing your woman to another man. But you should know that over here people are listening to your record and finding solace in it. Hearing your experience, expressed so powerfully and emotionally, makes any personal problems of one's own more bearable.*

*Problems of the heart can leave one feeling very alone. It seems to me that the sharing of one's feelings through art somewhat lifts the burden for others who are suffering alone. For me, this is one of the great things about soul music.*

*Soulfully yours,*

*Romance*

# 118

*When the great river meets the little river*
*Follow the drinking gourd*
*For the old man is a-waiting for to carry you to freedom*
*If you follow the drinking gourd.*

Lee was shaken by the news of Soul Sam's crossing of the River Jordan. He had grown up with Soul Sam – at least, he had grown up on the soul scene with Soul Sam at the fore. He had travelled the length (if not the breath) of the country to hear Soul Sam DJ, driven by the thirst to hear new records and to hear the boundaries to which serious soul music could be pushed. Soul Sam had always been there. He had been relatively old at Wigan and had been a soul father figure to so many ever since. This was awful news. The soul scene wouldn't be the same without him.

And how did Spaghetti Weston hear the news before him? Neither of them was particularly close to Soul Sam, but Lee liked to think he had a closer musical connection. (Spaghetti wasn't as into the seventies stuff.) And why would it mean that Spaghetti couldn't make Saturday? If he couldn't make it because he was so upset, then how could he presume that Lee wouldn't be as upset? Maybe there was a funeral to go to, but why would Spaghetti be invited and not Lee? And what about all the others who were going to Demetrios Demetriou's memorial do?

'What's the big deal?' said Lainie. 'What you play's as good as what Sam played anyway.' Lee took the compliment, but he knew it wasn't true. 'And fuck it, Demetrios was a mate. If Spaghetti isn't going cos of Soul Sam then fuck him.'

Demetrios was a mate, and a good one too. He was a top bloke. Lee couldn't think of anything that would keep him away from the do on Saturday, other than something dreadful happening to Lainie or Ree but he wasn't going to mention that.

He wondered what would become of Soul Sam's records. And he hoped Soul Sam had left a will.

'I hope he's left a will,' he said, out loud.

'Jesus Christ, is that all you can bloody think about? The poor man's records?'

Lee was thinking about the poor man's records, but he didn't consider it disrespectful. He knew that Soul Sam would have wanted to be remembered for his records. And he knew that Soul Sam would have been happy to be defined more by his records than anything else. He lived simply and had no family and pursued no other creative pursuit. His records were everything to him. His collection was the embodiment of his spirit.

'I should make a will,' said Lee. 'I keep thinking it but never getting round to it.'

'What, for that pile of shite?' Lainie said, with a nod up towards the record room. 'Yeah, right, put it at the top of your to do list marked *urgent*. I mean, obviously, finishing building a home for your family can wait.'

'You just said what I played was as good as what Sam played!'

'Yeah, and what he played was a load of fucking northern shite.'

Lee knew he couldn't win. Lainie was formidable. And that's why he loved her so much. He would be lost without her and he knew it.

# 119

*A Change Is Gonna Come*

A tradition of hidden meaning became pervasive in secular black music too. In order to fool the censor, many of the lyrics in twentieth century blues and rhythm and blues appear to be about dancing, but they have a strong sexual subtext. *Roll with Me Henry, Hand Jive, Wang Dang Doodle...* the list goes on and on. And on.

The soul explosion of the 1960s was concurrent with the increasing politicisation of black youth and the rise of the civil rights movement, but record companies were nervous and hesitant about releasing overtly political songs. The resulting generalities and vagaries were a credit to the spiritual tradition. An unpublicised album track, Sam Cooke's *A Change Is Gonna Come,* became a seminal soul classic, and Curtis Mayfield's *People Get Ready* was a song straight from the cotton fields:

> *People get ready, there's a train a-comin'*
> *You don't need no baggage, just get on board.*

*All you need is faith to hear the diesels hummin'*
*You don't need no ticket, just thank the Lord.* [21]

Curtis's train was the train to the Promised Land, the train to freedom and also, in the spirit of soul, the train to love. Love was at the fore, whether love for one's fellow man or the love between a man and a woman. All aboard, the love train. Rhythm and blues artists, who had been singing about sex, could get on board the love train. Gospel artists, who had been singing about Jesus, could get on board the love train. In the fifties the two camps were in opposition, but there was a third way and the way was love. The way was soul.

Romance, Spaghetti, Nutty Casper and all the others all worshipped love. For them, love was the human quality that transcended being human. It is rooted deep inside us but is not of this world. It is spiritual but there is no denying it. And for Romance, Spaghetti, Nutty Casper and all the others soul was its music, because soul seemed to be made of the same stuff. Soul music spoke to these boys and it spoke of love. The lyrics were of love and the driving force of the music was something to do with love too. They felt the pain and the heartbreak. The love crashed through them. The singers sang as if they had lived this love and it had ripped them apart, but they were true to it still because it came from without as well as within. And hearing the pain eased the pain of living. It made each of the boys less alone and it bound them.

Of course, not everyone got it, but that just made the relationship more powerful. There was an intimate relationship between the singer and the listener that was beyond any particular place and time of listening. It was a creative relationship and the profoundness of the art depended on it.

And when little Annie told Spaghetti not to be so stupid and that the man was just singing a song that someone else had written and he had never loved that woman because it was just his job to sing it and it was ridiculous to regard this as any kind of sacrifice, Spaghetti knew that she was right, but he knew that she was wrong too. As with religion, taking it literally was missing the point. It was deeper than that.

# 120

One of Sam Cooke's last television appearances was on *The Tonight Show*. The producers of the show wanted Sam to sing one of his hits. He refused. He refused to sing anything other than *A Change Is Gonna Come*. The producers were furious. But they had to let him sing it.

And it has been reported that record company executives were furious at Cooke too, because he was looking to sing more overtly political songs and to deepen his association with the civil rights movement. And a furious white establishment has led idolisers of Cooke down a conspiratorial road. The west coast mafia was hired to kill Cooke. There was a cover up by the LAPD. 'My brother was first class all the way. He would not check into a $3 motel. That wasn't his style,' said his sister Agnes. And yet there he was. ('He would walk past a good girl to get to a whore,' said his candid manager, Bumps Blackwell, and throughout his career Sam was dogged by paternity suits.)

But Spaghetti and Romance had never known Sam Cooke and they didn't know anyone who had. For them, the message was in the music, not the man. They worshipped music, not people. The details – good or bad – of the lives of the singers were not irrelevant from an individual, moral perspective, but they were irrelevant to the music. The motto of Gordy Records applied: *It's what's in the grooves that counts.*

But they had known Demetrios Demetriou and, even though they didn't idolise him (why should they?), they loved him.

'We may not be remembered when we're gone, but we have love,' remembered Romance, as he pondered on the endurance of love beyond anything else (even though he did remember Demetrios Demetriou and even though he helped to maintain a knowledge of Johnny Davis – the falling rubbish cart man – too).

Romance received another letter, but this one had the queen on it. And he recognised the handwriting immediately – he had always thought there was such tenderness and innocence about it – and just seeing his name written in that warm, upright, delicate hand was enough to induce a wave of remembered love.

*Dear R,*
*Good luck with Saturday. Demetrios was a lovely man and I know he was a good friend to you, as you were to him. It's wonderful that you are organising this night for him and for the charity. He would want you all to enjoy*

*yourselves and I'm sure you will!*

*And I want to wish you all the best for your new relationship too. You deserve to be happy.*

*All my love,*

*JBP*

A tear fell and stained the paper and smudged some of the ink, and he pushed the letter away before he damaged it more.

He wasn't surprised that she knew about the memorial do; after all, he had been trying to publicise the event. But he did wonder how she knew about the blond girl. He had never been able to hide anything from her, he reflected. She was one of those wonderful women who simply know everything, all of the time.

# 121

*Dear Romance,*

*Thank you for your very interesting letter. It is quite something to hear that my record is having an impact after all these years. When Coral put it out, they didn't really push it. It got a few plays in the Chicago area but that's about it.*

*But you should know that I have lived a blessed life, and I thank the Lord for that. In the 50's I was with the great Roberta Martin and I learned much from singing with her, and I was fortunate to meet my lovely wife when I was still a young man. When I left Roberta Martin, my recording career didn't really take off like I had hoped, but I was so lucky to have my beautiful wife and I always had my faith too. I was doing the clubs around Chicago and we got by fine.*

*So you should know that when I did 'Where Does That Leave Me' it wasn't about my own life. It was a Van McCoy song and it was Nancy Wilson who got it out first. In fact, I think there was another singer who did it before her. But*

*I liked it and was lucky to be given the chance to record it. The only way to sing is to sing it like it's about you and a great songwriter like Van McCoy can write them so it makes it easier to do that.*

*When I sing, I sing from the heart and it's the only way. It's wonderful to hear that you are involved in a project of your own, and the only way to do it is to do it from the heart. But you must never turn your back on love. Love is everything and God is love and it is the love of God and the love that I shared with my lovely wife that gave me the strength to sing. If you can touch others through your art then that is a wonderful thing, but love guides and strengthens. God doesn't like suffering and to bring it on yourself is an unGodly thing. Love will give you the strength to put yourself in the place of others who are less fortunate and if you can do your art for them, then that makes it a noble project. If you have found love, then that is a rare thing and you should embrace it with all your heart.*

*I wonder about this project of yours. I feel it is a wonderful thing.*

*God bless you,*

*Romance*

Romance knew a little about Van McCoy. He was most famous for a tacky disco thing in the seventies, which even made it on to *Top of the Pops*. But in the sixties he was a prolific songwriter, arranger and producer, working with numerous soul artists, and he was responsible for many of the soulful beat ballads of which Romance was so enamoured.

And so he wrote *Where Does That Leave Me*. That shouldn't have surprised Romance. In fact, he had seen Van McCoy's name on the record when he had looked at it in Demetrios Demetriou's bedroom. But it was still a shock to hear that Romance was a happily married man at the time. Romance had heard the Nancy Wilson version, and it was good too, but he had always presumed Romance's was the original.

Putting love first seemed sensible and right, and receiving advice from Romance Watson was an honour indeed. But Romance hadn't informed Romance that looking for romance – and Romance – was the subject of his artistic endeavour. How could he continue with such a project having already found romance (as well as Romance)?

But when Romance Watson sang *Where Does That Leave Me* was he deceiving the listener because it wasn't true to his own life? No. It was art. It was above such mundane considerations. It was indicative of a deeper, more profound truth. Romance Watson was an artist; he felt it as he sang it and it was the communication of the feeling that mattered. It is the power of the imagination that ennobles the artist. If it was OK for Romance to sing *Where Does That Leave Me* as if the song were about him when it wasn't, then perhaps it was OK for Romance to make *Looking for Romance (with*

*Steve Davis)* having already, in real life, found romance (as well as Romance).

But Romance knew that the viewers of documentaries expected truth (by definition, documentaries were not fiction) in a way that listeners to a record did not. Records were written, like drama on telly. Romance had been surprised that *Where Does That Leave Me* had not been about Romance's own life, but he knew he had no right to be cross about it.

And now, with blond girl in his life, Romance was adding deceit upon deceit.

> *Can't you know lies can be seen in your eyes*
> *And from wrong you'll never be free.*
> *While you sit cryin', you've been lyin'*
> *You've been cheatin', cheatin' on me.* [22]

Romance imagined the reaction of Curtis Mayfield if he was ever to see the film and then discover the truth, and it didn't feel good.

## 122

'It's just a temporary thing, but it'll do, won't it?'

Spaghetti Weston was pushing a record into the earth at the head of Soul Sam's grave.

'We'll get something permanent sorted, but this ain't bad, is it?'

He was worried that the allbeit temporary grave wasn't of the highest calibre. But Spaghetti had been pleased with his moment of inspiration. There was a seventies record label called *Sam*, and he had a few things on it that he didn't really rate and weren't expensive, so he had dug one out and was now digging it in, adjusting it in the earth. When it was half buried, it made a semi-circular gravestone and the word *Sam*, on the top half of the label, was free of the earth.

'Actually, it ain't really a gravestone, is it? It's more like a graverecord. But you liked records, didn't you, Sammy boy? We'll see how we get along with this. I was imagining something a bit bigger, but then it's quality not quantity, that's what I always say when someone's boasting about the number of crappy records they got, although I s'pose a lot of quality is better than a little quality, but you can only have one gravestone, Sammy. Or recordstone. I mean, graverecord.

'I quite liked that thing about the nostrils and it did make me think of you. *The breath in our nostrils is as smoke*. Do you think it's a bit queer for a graverecord? I mean, a gravestone? Maybe *In Dog We Trust* is snappier. Snappier! Ha! And I know you didn't smoke. You didn't approve of smoking, did you Sammy? But it's not about smoking though. They didn't smoke in the Bible, did they? I checked with Annie.'

Spaghetti had checked with Annie. 'Of course they didn't bloody smoke in the Bible,' she had said. 'And Abraham said unto Isaac, "Give us a bloody fag mate, I'm gasping." It's the Bible, not bloody…' she struggled for an analogy, '*Eastenders*.'

'I know it's not *Eastenders*. But they could have just left that bit out, couldn't they? For PR reasons.'

'No! There was no such thing as smoking then! It was Francis Drake or Walter Raleigh or whatever. The one with the potatoes. Why are you on about this anyway?'

'*The breath in our nostrils is as smoke*. It's from the Bible. I thought it might be good for the gravestone. Because of Soul Sam's nostrils.'

Little Annie looked at her man and, as was so often the case, didn't know whether to laugh or cry and the not knowing led to just more looking.

'What do you think it means then?' Spaghetti asked.

'I don't know,' Annie replied, with a distinct air of

resignation. 'Is that it? What's the rest of it?'

'Something about life being a shadow that passieth away.'

'Well it's about the transience of life then. Here today, gone tomorrow. That kind of thing.'

'Is that too depressing for a gravestone?'

'Could be. But it could be about how important it is to value life when you've got it, or when someone else has got it, because of how precious it is. Or about how when it goes, it does go, but it goes to being in the air or wherever. That could be a positive thing.'

Spaghetti looked at his woman, wanting more.

'And if it's a shadow it must be a shadow of something – something that was there before and will be there after maybe. But I don't bloomin' know. Can't you go and ask a priest or something?'

Spaghetti thought that was quite a good idea. Next time he was in London, he could go to ask his Greek priest friend. Or there was always the soul vicar.

'What do you think, Sammy boy? Maybe you'd like to stick with the record. Let's see how much Annie moans about it. I quite like the thought of your spirit being mixed in with the air.'

Mixed in with the spirits of all who had lived, he thought. So that included Demetrios Demetriou. Spaghetti had been proud of Soul Sam when he had been alive and he wanted to be proud of him still. And as he stood, respectfully, in front of the dog-grave, he felt the freshness of the air around him – he felt it pressing against him – and as he breathed, deep and slowly, he felt it fill his body, in and out, through his human nostrils.

'They don't smoke on *Eastenders*, anyway,' he thought suddenly. 'The BBC don't allow it.'

# 123

Romance was very happy, proud even, to show the blond girl the first letter that he had received from Romance. But he wasn't going to show her the second. And when he showed her the first one and she read the part where Romance said that he was sorry to hear about Demetrios Demetriou, the blond girl said, 'Ahh, that's sweet of him,' and her sincerity moved Romance. Her appreciation of Romance Watson was very recent compared to his, and she had never known Demetrios Demetriou. Yet Romance saw that she was genuinely moved, and now he was moved by her being moved (as well as by the letter). She was filled with humanity and she was filled with love.

'Would you help me sort through Demetrios's records?' was Romance's response to the angel he saw before him.

'Yes, of course!' she said. 'I'd love to!'

She could sense what an honour this was.

*I looked over Jordan and what did I see*
*Comin' for to carry me home*

*A cheeky blond angel comin' after me*
*Comin' for to carry me home.*

Romance did ask Spaghetti if he wanted to return with him to Demetrios Demetriou's old house, to meet his old mother again and to look through the records again. Their first visit had achieved little, other than to instil a state of despair in the boys at the thought of a six foot under vg++ Romance Watson test pressing. But Spaghetti couldn't make it. Poor Sammy boy was looking a bit down again and really didn't feel like travelling, again. And, even though he didn't mention it to Romance, Spaghetti didn't feel much like travelling either because he was feeling a bit down as well. Annie had told him that it should be *in*alienable rather than *un*alienable (making RIFUS, which was blatantly nonsense) and even when Spaghetti assured her that he had checked and that *un*alienable was a legitimate alternative spelling, Annie had said that it still sounded silly and if it had to be a *u* then surely *unconditional* would have been better. Spaghetti didn't want to give her the satisfaction of knowing she was right, so when he thought that she was right he kept the thought to himself. And anyway he had already given the meaning of RUFUS to the Birmingham Mail and at the time they had seemed quite impressed by it (once Spaghetti had explained that stepdogfathers were not fathers to stepdogs because they, by definition, would be stepfathers, and that a dogstepfather could be mistaken for a dog with a dogstepson).

So, when Romance returned to Demetrios Demetriou's old house to meet Demetrios Demetriou's old mother again and to look through the records again, it was just with blond girl. And she had brought some cake.

'It's cake!' said the blond girl to Mrs Demetriou.

'Oh! Cake!'

'I thought you might like some cake. You can't beat cake, can you?'

'Cake? For me? Ohhhh.'

'Yes. I made it myself. So be careful.'

'Oh, you very kind. Thank you, thank you. Please, please.'

They sat down.

'Oh, cake. Thank you, yes, thank you.'

Romance hadn't wanted to sit down. He was keen to get to work. He wanted this visit to be a constructive one.

'We've come to look at the records again,' he said, unnecessarily loudly. 'We're going to make a list of them.'

'Oh yes. The records.' She looked at the blond girl. 'He like the records very much. He like the little ones!'

'Did he? Well, from what I hear, he had very good taste.'

'Yes, he like the little ones. My son!' She began to cry. 'My son! He gone!'

The blond girl went to her, leaned over her chair and put her arm round her.

'It must be very difficult. He was a wonderful person, wasn't he?'

'Yes! Yes!'

It was twenty minutes before they were upstairs.

'She's a nice woman,' said the blond girl, sadly.

Mrs Demetriou was a nice woman. And Demetrios Demetriou had been a nice guy. And he had left behind all these records.

'We need to put them into some kind of order and to make a list of them. And we need to grade them. It's gonna take ages. Are you sure you're up for it?'

'Yes, of course!'

'What would probably be best is if I picked them out and played them and graded them and then read out what they are and what grade they are and then you write it down? And I put them in order as I go.'

'Oh,' said the blond girl, disappointedly.

'What?'

'Can't I play them?'

'Yeah, if you like. You've got to be careful with them.'

'Of course!'

She was careful with them. She handled them very delicately. Romance had been nervous about her touching them, but as he watched her take each record out of its card sleeve, carefully not touching the grooves of the vinyl, he wondered at her wonder and delighted in it. When she put a record on the turntable, she held it by its edge with the middle finger and thumb of both hands and placed it slowly and gently over the plastic middle. And when she put the needle on the record, it was with a slow, feminine love, and she waited for the music to start with a paused, still, excited expectation. Romance and the blond girl both listened intently to the noise of the vinyl during those two or three music-free revolutions and Romance made quick judgements of the condition – vg+, vg++, excellent, mint minus. These judgements were then confirmed or adjusted as they listened to the music and, once the blond girl had become familiar with them, they became a matter of playful negotiation.

Romance knew nearly all of the records; the blond girl knew hardly any. He scribbled his list, rarely having to ask for artist, title or record label. When he was done with each one, he would say 'OK', but the blond girl wouldn't be hurried. She would only lift the needle from the vinyl when she was ready. She wanted to listen to these records – at least, she wanted to listen to the ones she wanted to listen to. For some, she was amusingly disparaging; for others, she sat in awe and had to listen to the end.

'This one's rubbish,' she would say. 'Put it down for a fiver.'

'Oh, I like this one. Who's this? Oh I like Walter. £20 I reckon.'

'A bit nonny nonny. Sounds like a bloody cowboy record.'

'Oh yes, this is more like it. Now this has got soul. The Hesitations. £50!'

She had no idea about rarity or value and plucked figures from the air. It was a novel approach to pricing, which Romance loved and ignored.

'Right, this one looks different. I'm confident about this one,' she said as she put another record on. A little bit of surface noise, but nothing too bad. And then…

That percussion. That organ. For an instant, Romance didn't know where he was.

'Oh I like this.'

And then the voice.

'Oh yes. I like this. I might even buy this one myself. Who's this then?'

'Romance Watson,' said a recovering Romance.

# 124

George 'King' Scott, the lead singer of The Hesitations, spent his last moments in this world sitting in a parked car. Deptford Dave had been right about that. With George in the car were his wife and two other members of the group: his younger brother Charles and Leonard Veal. It was a winter's night in Cleveland and they had all been to a wedding reception. Leonard Veal – former singer with the doo wop group The Metrotones, aka The Five Jades, aka The Five Gents – was handling a gun, and his story, which was supported by the wife and brother, was that it went off accidentally as he was putting it into the glove compartment. George Scott was shot in the head and killed. Leonard Veal was charged with second degree murder, but the charge was dropped before the case went to trial.

George Scott died just a few weeks before The Hesitations' version of the song *Born Free* became a chart success. It would have been the breakthrough for which the group had been waiting, and the song, written for the film about an orphaned lion club, became a civil rights anthem.

But the cheesy *Born Free* wasn't popular on the British soul scene. It didn't compare well to their more sublime, chart-failing soul offerings. The group deserved to be remembered for other things.

Hippy John didn't have a wife or a brother, but he had a mother and it was she who died. He wasn't with her at the time. And he wasn't at the funeral. He didn't know about it. It was weeks after the funeral before he even found out that she was dead. He phoned home, prepared to hang up if his father answered, and was greeted by an unfamiliar female voice, which became familiar when the speaker introduced herself as Aunty Edith. And then he heard all about it and the effect it had on him was as if he had pulled the trigger himself, accidentally or not.

He missed the funeral because he had left her and he hadn't stayed in touch, and now there was nothing he could do about it. She was gone. She had died of an unremarkable illness, much as this Demetrios Demetriou fellow had done, and when Hippy John clambered over the side of the Itchen Bridge he was wishing that he had died in his mother's place. And now this pasta man wasn't going to go to the memorial do of Lee's dead friend and Hippy John wasn't happy about it. He didn't know what was going to happen at this memorial do and he didn't know how many people had been due to attend, but he was unhappy that it would now be one short. Any friend of Lee's must have been a decent person.

And what if he hadn't been a decent person? He had still been a human being. A human life had been cut short and this was a tragedy, for all humanity.

Clambering over the side of the bridge, Hippy John had not valued his own life and he was now chronically ashamed of that. He was only breathing and able to think these thoughts because a couple of passing strangers had valued his life for him. They had known nothing about him. He had been a pitiful example of a human being, but to them he had still been a valuable human life.

Lee's friend had died and, by the sounds of it, he hadn't even wanted to. It was probably the last thing he had wanted to happen. Hippy John had wanted to die and had been saved and was now thankful that he had been saved. It didn't seem fair. It wasn't fair. Hippy John was a lucky sod and the least he could do was appreciate it. He now felt he owed much to the dead Demetrios Demetriou. He didn't feel that Demetrios Demetriou had died for him in some Christ-like gesture, but death had taken the one who had been full of life as it had taken the selfless, loving parent, and it wasn't fair, and so Hippy John now owed it to the dead Demetrios Demetriou to respect his memory.

He decided to ask Lee if he could accompany him and Lainie to the memorial do. This might compensate for the loss of the pasta man. Ree would have to stay with Lainie's mother but that wouldn't be so bad, and Hippy John would happily repay them by babysitting any number of other times. He had never met Demetrios Demetriou and he wasn't a soul man. He had never even heard of The Hesitations. But going to the memorial do just felt like the thing to do.

# 125

Van McCoy lived to see his name at the top of the charts. A decade after writing *Where Does That Leave Me*, Van was the disco king. *The Hustle* was number one in America and, as well as being master of the hustle, Van was writing and producing numerous other disco hits. To Romance and the others, it was all nonsense. It was soul music that spoke to them and it was soul music that would continue to have a voice through the ages.

Naturally, Van began his musical journey as a child singing in his local church. Then came doo wop and a handful of doo wop releases with The Starlighters before Van was snapped up by an established record label in New York as a producer, arranger and songwriter. Soul music was simmering, threatening, and Van was there.

In the sixties he wrote hundreds of songs, many of which were recorded by artists whose names are etched into the hearts of many a northern soul fan: Chuck Jackson, Jackie Wilson, Sandi Sheldon, Barbara Lewis, Esther Phillips. (Just hearing the name Jackie Wilson was enough to provoke enough electrical activity in the mind of Mick the Twitch to subdue any oncoming twitch to the extent that it was barely perceptible.) He wrote for and produced the youthful and ever so soulful Gladys Knight and the Pips before their move to Motown, as well as Bettye Everett, Erma Franklin, Irma Thomas and The Presidents.

He left behind such a rich and soulful legacy that Romance viewed it as criminally perverse that it was *The Hustle* for which Van was remembered.

Having written hundreds of songs about heartache, and having arranged and produced hundreds more so as to squeeze that last globule of heartache from them, Van McCoy died, aged 39, of a broken heart. Success got the better of him. He wasn't comfortable being a disco superstar. He hadn't anticipated it. And fame was no substitute for love. Never having married, the women in his life were his mother and his grandmother and it was when they both died on him that he had the heart attack.

# 126

'Where did this come from?'

'Where? It was in that box. So he's called Romance, like you?'

In what box? In that box. Romance and Spaghetti had searched through every box. He was sure they had. They had flicked through all the records of all the boxes. How could they have missed it? They must have. They must have missed it. Maybe one of their record flicking fingers had passed over two records instead of one, but that was very unlike either of them. Maybe it was there, staring up at one of them – Romance Watson *Where Does That Leave Me,* brown-paper-brown label – just at the moment when the mind of the body of those fingers had been distracted by words from across the room or by some faraway thought. And blond girl picks it out so easily, one record among many. It seemed so unlikely.

It was unlikely, Romance thought. But then it was more likely than the record having been dug up and returned surreptitiously. Romance had studied the grave himself and observed how difficult a task digging up the record would be. (In fact, on observing the depth of the grave at Demetrios Demetriou's funeral, and with no sign of any industrial diggers on site, Romance's estimation of gravediggers had risen significantly.) When the earth was bare, one man and a spade were presented with a heavy task. But with a stone grave on top, he couldn't see how it could be done without a team of men and some powerful equipment. Even if Spaghetti Weston and Nutty Casper had joined forces, only the most liberal-minded could consider that a team in any meaningful sense. And to put the grave back without any sign of disturbance would have been surely impossible.

'If someone was to dig up a grave in order to get a record that was buried in it, can you think of any reason why they would then break into the house that used to house it and sneak it back into the record collection without anyone knowing?'

'No,' said the blond girl. 'I can't.' And she didn't want to think about it. She was listening to the record. Romance saw her listening and now his confusion about the sudden appearance of the record was matched by the thrill of seeing her listening so intently, and the combination of that confusion and thrill was itself confusing.

The record finished and the blond girl let it continue revolving. Listening to the repetitive clicks of that final groove seemed a necessary antidote to the overwhelming aural experience that had just been.

'I love that one,' she said, watching it go round.
And Romance loved her.

## 127

'The hippy came round when you were out,' Lee said to Lainie when she was back from her mother's. 'He wants to come on Saturday.'

'What?'

'On Saturday. To London.'

'Why?'

'I dunno.'

'He wants to come to the memorial do?'

'Yeah.'

'He never even met Demetrios Demetriou!' She looked at Lee, quizzically and accusingly. 'And you didn't even ask him why he wants to come?'

'Well, no, not really.'

'Not really? Either you did or you didn't.'

'Well, no then.'

'And what did you say?'

'I said he could.'

'Oh right. So really you're just telling me that we're taking the hippy on Saturday. You're not, like, asking me if it's OK or anything?'

Lee shrugged.

'What about Ree? He was gonna babysit Ree.'

'She can go to your mum's, can't she? If it's a problem, I'll just tell him and change things back.'

'No, Lee, it's not a problem – it's never a problem. We have a hippy in our lives and now he wants to be our best mate and to meet our friends and to make out he knows our dead ones. Maybe we should just invite him on holiday with us too. Oh no, I forgot… we never go on holiday. Unless you count a rainy weekend in Cleethorpes with a bunch of fuckin' lunatics. Actually, you know what? I should just fuckin' marry him. That would solve a thing or two.' She handed Ree to Lee. 'There you are. It's your daughter.' And she went into the kitchen.

Lee cradled Ree and smiled. 'You're gonna be a nightmare too, ain't ya? Men of Sussex, watch out!' He held her up to him and kissed her forehead. 'I love you!'

# 128

On the afternoon of the memorial do, Spaghetti Weston was at home in Birmingham. He was sitting down to watch a video of *The Antiques Roadshow* that he had recorded the previous Sunday. He liked *The Antiques Roadshow*. He wasn't interested in antiques, but the dashed expectations and delighted surprises reminded him of record collecting. And he had heard their ceramics man, Eric Knowles, on the radio once playing northern soul. He was from up north somewhere and used to go to the clubs back in the day and that gave Spaghetti a loyalty to the programme and a knowing thrill whenever the foppish, mustachioed man popped up. He hadn't been able to watch this episode when it was broadcast because Annie was with him and she wasn't so keen, and then the trauma of Soul Sam's death had pushed it from his mind. He was pleased now to remember it and he was looking forward to its consoling properties.

Spaghetti had been along to the show once, when it was at Wightwick Manor near Wolverhampton. He had taken his copy of Shirley Edwards on Shrine. He didn't have a good day. Having queued to reach the reception, the woman there told him that they didn't feature vinyl on the show.

'Are you sure?' queried Spaghetti. 'It's rare and valuable. And I think Eric Knowles might be interested. He has an interest in this kind of thing.'

'No musical instruments either. It's just not what we do. Eric only does ceramics on the show. And he's not with us today.'

'I don't have any ceramics. I only have records.'

A dejected Spaghetti spent a couple of hours wandering about, watching the proceedings, holding his copy of Shirley Edwards. There was a woman with a watch that had been her grandfather's. He had taken it to war with him and it was inscribed on the back, although Spaghetti didn't hear with what. She seemed pleased to hear that it was worth £150. Spaghetti suspected she was feigning her delight for the camera.

'Shirley Edwards is worth loads more than that,' he said to himself, although, like the watch woman, he had no intention of selling. He just wanted to be on telly and he had wanted the Shirley Edwards to be on telly too. They might even have played it.

Ceramics. What was the point of ceramics? He could understand the use of having things to eat off and of having things to put other things in that needed to be in something. But the fuss that society made over them seemed out of all proportion. They couldn't be listened to. They didn't mean anything. Still, Eric had to make a living and he couldn't be begrudged that. He might even have had an expensive record collecting habit that needed funding.

The episode Spaghetti had recorded was from Yorkshire somewhere. A big castle, by the looks of it. An old woman had a painting of a horse. It was rubbish. Who would want a great big horse staring at them as they ate their Cornflakes? A jockey, maybe? Even ceramics were better than that. At least they had some kind of use. Then the TV people showed a close up of the horse painting and its gleaming nostrils, and Spaghetti saw that it was the impression of a specific horse that had once been alive and had run and filled its lungs with air, as Soul Sam had filled his as he climbed the stairs to the record room and as Demetrios Demetriou had filled his as he took to the floor of the 100 Club. 'Life is a sort of shadow that passieth away,' he said to himself as he stood up, and before Eric Knowles had a chance to show himself Spaghetti was blasting out Jimmy Gresham *This Feelin' I Have*. One record then followed another in a creative whirl of soul and, when the best set he had ever heard came to an end, he put on his dancing shoes and was out of his Brummie door.

# 129

Romance and the blond girl arrived together at the venue over an hour before the start time. Romance wanted to check that all was ready for the soulful onslaught and he had arranged to meet Solomon there too. And he was expecting Nutty Casper to whirl up. Nutty Casper had been very keen to help with the organisation. In fact, he had wanted it to be a joint endeavour. Looking into Nutty Casper's wide, nutty, longing eyes, Romance hadn't been able to think of anyone less equipped to help in any way at all. But he hadn't been able to say no. In the days leading up to the do, Romance was relieved not to have heard from him. Perhaps he had forgotten all about it. Perhaps he had gone to the wrong venue and at that moment was haranguing its bewildered staff for forgetting about the event and deriding their irresponsibility and their lack of respect for the deceased and for cancer sufferers in general. (So what if it was Natasha's birthday and Rupert had organised a party for her? The soul folk were on their way!)

'It's a nice place,' said the blond girl when they were

let in. 'Yes, this is going to be top notch.' She wasn't only complimenting Romance on his venue-finding prowess; she was pleased for Demetrios Demetriou too. 'Quick, get some records out before anyone else gets here. I want to DJ. This could be the start of something big.'

Romance was happy to get some records out. He wanted to check the sound system. That was the main reason he had wanted to arrive so early. And it was a joy to watch the blond girl line up the records and play them. She was careful with them and revelled in the act and showed all due respect. And, with a bit of tweaking, the sound was good. Hearing wonderful music played loud to an empty room over a decent system was a rare treat and the thrill of it mixed with and added to the anticipation of the evening ahead.

'Oh, I want to play this one,' the blond girl said, coming across Romance Watson in the box.

Romance had felt uneasy about bringing his friend's record. He had committed himself to buying it and had agreed with Demetrios Demetriou's mother that he would pay for it, with any others he wanted. (He was going to ask Diamond Jim for an estimated price and would pay in instalments if necessary.) But he still felt that it was Demetrios Demetriou's record, and perhaps he always would, and he wasn't sure about playing it in public as his own.

The blond girl could see he looked anxious. 'It should be played. He'd want it played, and you should play it later too,' she said. And she was right. Records were for playing. And anyway, there wasn't anyone else there then to hear it and to think it was Romance's record, apart from the Chinese guy who had let them in and he was busy preparing the bar. And Romance had brought it with him, after all.

It was fitting that it should be played and Romance decided that he would play it towards the end of the evening, with an appropriate introduction about Demetrios. And, as he was thinking carefully what that introduction might be, he watched the blond girl carefully place the record on the deck and delicately lower the needle. She cradled the headphones with the tender affection of a mother or a lover, as if she were concerned at their readiness for the soulful onslaught to come. She then concentrated hard on cuing the record and waited, watching the lesser record run its course, and as the lesser record faded away she pressed play on the Romance and the teasing percussion filled the room.

Romance looked at the blond girl and, as the richness of Romance's voice washed through him, he was overcome with love for her. The voice, and the woman. The voice and the spirit of Demetrios Demetriou too, not just enabling him to see the beauty in the woman but demanding it. And when the trumpets blasted they were berating his hesitation. They were the exasperated cries of lost souls.

*In your heart, where I used to live and share your love*
*In your heart, where I thought I'd found a home…*

And the voice was a warning that for the first time filled Romance with terror.

*I found myself, locked out cos now someone else*
*Has got the key…*
*So where does that leave me?*

Romance couldn't bear the thought of losing her. He couldn't bear the thought of her being with anyone else. And as he listened to Romance and as he watched the blond girl listening too – truly listening – he wanted her just as she was. Dark and sultry could take a running jump. He didn't want to change a ditsybitsyglitzything about her. The slightest change might have unforeseen consequences. The hippy was right. In loving everything about her, whether he liked it or not, he could love her. And in loving her, he could love everything about her, whether he liked it or not. He knew then that he needed to be with her and if that meant not being single and not being able to make a groundbreaking film about looking for Romance, then so be it.

As the cries of Romance fell away, the blond girl started the next record. The fader of the Romance deck was hidden beneath the tip of her middle finger and its polished nail and she eased it down before stopping the deck. Her fingertips then combined to gently lift the record from the deck and slide it inside the waiting sleeve.

The delicacy of her movements went unnoticed by the

Chinaman, but he could appreciate a pretty face when he saw one. He knew nothing about rubbish, mainstream soul music, let alone quality northern soul, and the beauty of the music was as lost on him as the beauty of the blond girl's inner being, but the sound check had caught his attention. This girl behind the decks added some cheeky glamour to his bar/club. She was certainly different from the dreary male youths who approached him daily offering their dreary DJing services. Now his hopes for the evening were high too and they were only somewhat lessened by the arrival of a tall, big-footed, rosy-cheeked, shiny-headed older man carrying a record box.

'Hello!' he boomed to the Chinaman. 'I'm here for the dead Greek!'

Thankfully, Romance had seen him arrive and no response was needed.

'And now, let us pray,' Romance said over the mic. to attract his attention. The vicar turned and smiled, put down his record box, looked up and held out his arms to the Lord.

'This is a good place,' the vicar said, approaching the decks. 'Yes, this'll do, won't it?'

It was a good place, although the vicar would have thought, and said, that it was a good place whatever it had been like.

Romance was pleased with the venue. He had spent a long time looking. The venue had to be not too big and not too small, available on a Saturday night, affordable, central, have a pleasing and intimate ambience, draft beer and, crucially, a smooth wooden floor. Demetrios Demetriou had been a dancer and this was all for him. He would want people to dance. His spirit might not have needed a wooden floor and if he was merged with the ether (or nowhere at all) the floor would be of no use to him either, but that was beside the point – it was a memorial do.

'Not so easy to find for a yokel like me,' the vicar continued to the blond girl, who was standing with Romance behind the decks. ' "Head for the Post Office Tower," I thought. "You can do worse than that." Ended up parking on the pavement outside the Mozambiquan Embassy. Well, they can't be very busy, can they? What do you think they get up to in London anyway?' Then he paused and listened. 'Ah yes, Darrell Banks,' he said, looking at the record going round. *What it was, I can't explain… my life was not the same…*' He wanted to sing along but couldn't remember the words. 'So you liked the tape?' he asked Romance.

Romance smiled. The vicar had sent him a tape called *Blue*. All the records featured had blue labels.

'I did. Now I'm making you one. *Heartbreak*. Every record has *heartbreak* in the title.'

'Oh that sounds a barrel of laughs. Is the Tripp gonna be here?'

'Yep. He'll be here. I'm hoping he'll do a picture.'

'Oh good. I need to talk to him. *Ohhh, what a beautiful feeling…!*'

He left Romance behind the decks, shuffled his big feet

in time to the music and sashayed over to the bar, leaving Romance to continue playing his Demetrios Demetriou-friendly selection of records. The uptempo northern was on its way, which wasn't what Romance would normally play, especially at this time of the evening, but if his friend wasn't dancing he could be listening and even if he wasn't that was beside the point – it was a memorial do.

## 130

Sam Cooke had two funerals; Demetrios Demetriou had one funeral and one memorial do. The heavenly-voiced womaniser who made the move from gospel to secular music, and in doing so contributed so much to the birth of soul, had two religious ceremonies. (His son, who drowned in the family swimming pool before he was old enough to talk – let alone sing, womanise or be religious – had one religious one, a year before his father's two.) Demetrios Demetriou had never been religious, and he had one religious ceremony and one secular one. At both of his funerals, Sam Cooke's body was on view. At Demetrios Demetriou's funeral all present had to accept the fact that his body was in the coffin, and as if to assuage any doubt the young man's photograph was propped up on it. For want of a body, or even a coffin, it was this photograph that the soul folk were to use as a reference for the lost life and Romance and the blond girl had propped it up on a little table at the entrance to the venue, next to a bucket for cancer money and what was to be a varying number of pints of beer with varying amounts of beer in them.

'He was a goodlooking chap,' thought the vicar, as he wondered if he had ever crossed paths with the deceased.

'Fuckin' 'ell, it's Demetrios,' said Lainie, when she arrived with Lee, little Jimmy and Hippy John.

'Oh, he looks lovely,' the blond girl had said, when she saw the photo earlier in the evening. 'That's a nice picture, isn't it?' It was at Cleethorpes, before the cancer, and he was happy.

'All right, mate?' said little Jimmy, wistfully.

'You didn't even know him, you twat,' said Lainie.

'Yeah I did.'

'No you didn't.'

'We grew up together. We were mods together in west London.'

'But you're from Bognor.'

'No I'm not.'

'Why the fuck do you live there then?'

'Dunno really.'

'Fuckin' 'ell,' said Lainie, shaking her head.

'You should fuckin' marry that girl, she's fuckin' gorgeous,' Lainie said to Romance, once she was inside.

Romance was somewhat taken aback. Seeing Hippy John provided a distraction.

'Bloody hell, the hippy!'

Romance motioned for him to approach the decks.

'You OK, mate? Good to see you.'

Hippy John recognised Romance too and was happy to

say hello.

'I wanted to pay my respects,' he said, looking at the record go round with a childlike wonder. He had heard Lee play the occasional record but not this loud, and he hadn't seen two decks in use before.

Romance smiled. 'You're all right, for a hippy.' And then there was a voice from behind.

'It's gonna be all right. The sound's pretty good.' It was Solomon, who had arrived without Romance noticing. 'It's gonna be a good night.'

'And you're OK to go on later?'

'Yeah, looking forward to it.'

'I think we've done the right thing.'

'Definitely. That funeral was bonkers. Talking of bonkers, I saw JBP the other day.' Romance gave him a questioning look. 'She turned up at the alldayer in Brighton. She's all right, you know. Still not drinking. And she was with a fella. It was good. They both seemed to be enjoying themselves. She looked OK. Some guy she met through AA.'

Good old Solomon. News that at another time would have been hurtful for Romance was delivered thoughtfully and well, and Solomon paused to allow the news to settle. It was difficult for Romance to hear but it was good for him to hear it. For a long time, Romance hadn't liked the thought of JBP being with someone else, but since their separation there had been enough inspired, electrical activity in his brain (enough water under the Itchen Bridge) for that dislike to be overridden by a profounder love, and he wanted her to be happy. In fact, her being OK helped him. It helped him be OK. Now his own happiness need not be hindered by the thought of her unhappiness, and if they could both love again then their own love could continue in some settled, distant and supportive role.

He was wise, Solomon, even though sometimes he said ridiculous things and even though the reason he was called Solomon had nothing to do with him being wise. Romance knew that much. Solomon's workmates had called him 'soul man' and, from that, 'Soul' and 'Sol' and 'Solomon'. Romance had forgotten Solomon's real name, and he had forgotten what his job was too, if he had ever known. But then few of them knew what any of the others did for a living. Such details seemed trivial when there was so much soul to listen to and so much bollocks to talk.

Romance had let *I Thought You Were Mine* come to an end. The Rotations was going round but there was no music. He was thinking. And he was looking at the blond girl who was chatting to little Jimmy. Lee took advantage of the silence to approach the vicar, who was at the bar and was the one among them with a standout profession.

'Have you heard the news about Soul Sam?'

'No.'

'He's fucking pegged out, hasn't he? Died!'

'Has he? Oh my God, that's awful. When? How?'

'Dunno.'

The lack of music didn't matter, because the memorial do hadn't officially started. Romance was playing to the other

DJs, the blond girl and Lee's entourage and to himself. But having given Romance some precise, arbitrary amount of space-time for his news to settle, Solomon decided to bring him back.

'After silence, that which comes nearest to expressing the inexpressible is music.'

'Soul is the answer!' exclaimed a gleeful Romance.

He settled the needle. After some amplified crackles, the music blasted out.

'You know what that means, don't you? I'll be the next to go!' exclaimed the vicar. 'As long as he was still around, I knew I'd be all right. This isn't good at all.'

The vicar wasn't afraid of death and the feeling of exhilaration as he sped towards the light was still a fundamental part of him, but since that experience he had acquired so much to live for. He was thinking about all the tapes he had yet to make. Suddenly, life was feeling short and precarious.

'Makes you think, doesn't it?'

'You'll be all right. You'll go straight to heaven, you jammy bastard.'

'I think I'm probably gay,' the vicar said.

Lee looked at him. 'Of course you're fuckin' gay.'

By the time Spaghetti arrived in London, Lee had found out that the human Soul Sam was alive and as well as could be expected for a DJ of his age, the vicar had attempted to flirt with the blond girl as a way of putting his new theory of gayness to the test, the little venue was filling and Hippy John had gravitated to the entrance and gone a long way towards adopting the role of meeter, greeter and keeper of the bucket. By the time the vicar was at the decks and playing *Wade in the Water*, the Chinaman behind the bar, who insisted his name was Dave, was regretting having booked just the one lazy student to help him. (She was pretty but she was no Bettye and Romance wasn't interested anyway.) As there had been at the funeral, there was a solid soul turnout. The bucket had also filled satisfactorily.

'You could buy a half-decent record with that lot,' said Spaghetti to Hippy John as he dropped in a fiver. He looked at the photo of Demetrios Demetriou and wondered if he should kiss it.

'It's lymphoma,' said the hippy.

'Eh?' said Spaghetti.

'You fuckwit,' said Lee, approaching from the bar. 'You lying fucking Brummie twat.'

Spaghetti smiled. He was already glad he had come.

And then Romance saw Spaghetti.

'For fuck's sake,' he said to blond girl. 'He's come anyway.'

She looked about. 'Spaghetti.'

'Oh yes. And no dead dog. Now what's he come as?'

'He seems to have come as some kind of an idiot.'

'Hmm. It's very convincing.'

The blond girl followed Romance to the dogless Brummie.

'Your Grace,' said Romance, interrupting Lee's own abusive tirade.

Spaghetti looked at him.

'Have you brought your records?'

'No mate. I couldn't.'

'You couldn't?'

'Not so soon after the funeral. It didn't feel right. Showing off like that. I'm in mourning.'

'Right.'

Romance and Lee looked at each other.

'I understand,' said the blond girl. Romance looked at her. 'Well it's good that you've come.'

'I wasn't going to come, you know. It's only been a few days. But I was watching *The Antiques Roadshow* today and it got me thinking. Life should be celebrated, shouldn't it? It's a precious thing. I should be grateful for having had Soul Sam in my life. I mean, I know he was just a dog and everything, but he had soul, didn't he? He must have done, otherwise I wouldn't feel like this.'

'I think he did. He sounds like a wonderful dog.'

'And Demetrios Demetriou was a top bloke. I know he was a human and everything and had more life and more soul or whatever, but they might be all part of the same thing now, mightn't they? Even if the levels are different. So I thought I should come for the two of them. I mean, I know it's for Demetrios Demetriou and everything and I'm not suggesting this is for Soul Sam too or, like, making out that Soul Sam was as important or anything but, like, the nearness of the death means the feeling is more concentrated, don't it? So there's one human death spread over quite a long time and then there's one dog death spread over just a few days.'

'Yeah, it's like washing up liquid,' said Deptford Dave, who had crept up from somewhere. 'You can get more of the cheap stuff or less of the concentrated stuff and they finish about the same time.'

'I don't think it's exactly like washing up liquid,' said Romance.

'Or would you rather have a few brilliant records or a lot of good records?'

'Or, in your case, a pile of crap ones?'

'I know exactly what you mean,' the blond girl said to Spaghetti. 'And I think it's wonderful you're here.'

Romance looked at the blond girl. She did think it was wonderful that Spaghetti was there. She was so nice that she would have said something like that anyway. But then she was so, so nice that she would never not have genuinely thought the nice thought.

'Did you know Eric Knowles was into northern?' said Spaghetti.

'Oh really? Well, now, there's a thing. I always thought he was a lovely man.'

'Probably more Marlena than this though. *I'm like a ship in a stormy sea, so wade in the water daddy rescue me!*' [23]

Spaghetti was looking at Hippy John. He had been struck by him as soon as he had seen him. Hippy John was lost but content with it, and to Spaghetti this relaxed, wide-eyed look seemed other-worldly and spiritual. He was reminded of the Greek priest at the funeral. Spaghetti sneaked up on the hippy from behind.

'Are you a priest?' Spaghetti asked the suddenly even wider-eyed Hippy John.

'No.'

'Oh.'

Spaghetti was disappointed. But then he remembered that there were many wise and saintly men who weren't priests and who found their wisdom and saintliness outside established religion. Jesus, for example.

'Are you here for the music?' asked Spaghetti.

'Not really.'

'Oh. But you knew Demetrios Demetriou, did you?'

'No.'

This was interesting to Spaghetti. His social life was the northern scene and he wasn't used to meeting anyone socially who wasn't a part of it. It was, in fact, very odd that there should be someone at a northern soul do who wasn't into northern soul. And surely it was even odder that there should be someone at a memorial do who never knew the deceased. This added to the strangeness of Hippy John, and so to his other-worldliness. Spaghetti came close to wondering if he was a spiritual messenger of some kind and if he was visible to anyone else.

'I would like to have known him,' continued Hippy John, wondering at the preponderance of Brummies on the soul scene. 'Did you know him?'

'Demetrios Demetriou? Yes. Top bloke. Good records too. It feels strange him not being here... I mean, you know, in body like.'

'For our time is a very shadow that passeth away,' said Hippy John, and now it was Spaghetti with the wider eyes. Those were the words the man on the phone had uttered – the man who talked about the nostrils. He struggled to find the words to reply. He felt as if he were a spy meeting another spy and exchanging coded sentences.

'The breath in our nostrils is as smoke,' Spaghetti stuttered.

Hippy John looked at him, surprised there was another familiar with the words. 'What?'

'The breath in our nostrils is as smoke.'

'Is it?'

'I think so. Isn't it?'

There was a pause as the two men looked at each other. Spaghetti saw Hippy John's surprise as confusion, and he was confused that he was confused. It seemed that Hippy John wasn't the person/mystical being to ask what it meant after all. Hippy John was contemplating being in the midst of such a spiritual and learned gathering. 'You wouldn't have thought it, by looking at them,' he said to himself.

And then Spaghetti remembered that Sam Cooke's two funerals attracted tens of thousands of people and Sam can't have known them all. In fact, he probably only knew a handful of them.

'This nutter could be anyone,' he said to himself.

*Folks don't understand what we got going.*
*No matter, make waves, come on, let's keep the stream flowing!*

'I found the bloody Romance Watson!'

Spaghetti looked confused. He turned to see Romance.

'It was in there. In one of the boxes. Well, blond girl found it.'

'Oh.' He was still looking confused. 'So it's not in the coffin?'

'No.'

'Unless there's two of 'em!' Spaghetti suggested, as if he were a detective with a spark of genius.

'No, you twit, there's not two of them. There's one of them. And I have it. I'm going to buy it myself.'

'We must have missed it, mate,' was Spaghetti's next spark of genius.

'Yep.'

'It could have been me, you know. Whenever I see anything on Tamla, I think about Tamla and get a bit upset about our unjust justice system, and I remember he did have that Virgil Henry in there. And then I was worrying about poor old Sammy boy being stuck downstairs with Mrs Demetriou. I mean, she's very nice, in't she? But I thought maybe all that mourning was freaking him out. He was very aware that he was getting on a bit. I was thinking about it on my way here. We're only about five in dog years.

He was much older than us, you know.'

'Yeah, right, well anyway I've got it. I've got it here. So no one has to go digging the grave up.'

'But we don't know what else is down there,' said Spaghetti. 'Could be one of these,' he said, eyes widening, referring to the record that was just starting. 'What a voice. Fookin' 'ell. 27, weren't she? Linda Jones. What a loss. Is the vicar 'ere?'

'Yeah, he's playing now.'

'Oh yeah.'

Spaghetti wanted to talk to the vicar. But it was an important matter, so he thought to wait until the vicar had stopped DJing.

'Oh look. It's the Tripp.'

It was the Tripp. The Tripp had arrived. And he had arrived, as usual, with a large artist's pad and an assortment of charcoals.

# 131

'The breath in our nostrils is as smoke.'

'I beg your pardon?'

'The breath in our nostrils is as smoke. That's it, isn't it? Something like that.'

'What are you on about?'

'It's from the Bible, init? I wanted to ask you about it.'

Lee was DJing, the vicar was at the bar and Spaghetti was seizing the moment.

'Oh. Oh dear. The Bible, yes, well, it's a big book. I don't remember anything about nostrils.'

'For our time is but a verrieth shadow that passieth away.'

'Oh yeah. Solomon. Well, you don't want to believe everything he says.'

Solomon? What had Solomon to do with it? He hadn't said it. Had he? It was the kind of thing he would say, but the hippy had said it was from the Bible. Anyway, Spaghetti looked disappointed.

'Beware then of useless murmuring. I like that bit. I always say it to Johnny Dells when he's wittering away on the mic between tracks.'

'But what about the nostrils bit, for a gravestone?'

'The breath in our nostrils is like smoke? Did the poor bugger burn to death?'

'No.'

'Oh, lung cancer, was it? Heavy smoker, was he? Is it for the dead Greek? They do smoke out there, don't they?'

'No. It's for Soul Sam.'

The vicar was confused. Was this Brummie twit really responsible for what was to be inscribed on the great Soul Sam's gravestone? Soul Sam didn't even smoke. He decided Spaghetti must be mad.

'I like *Here lies the body of Margaret Gwyn, who was so very pure within. She lived to the age of three score and ten, and gave to the worms what she refused to men.*'

Spaghetti was beginning to doubt the spiritual or practical assistance on offer from this particular vicar. He didn't seem to be grasping Spaghetti's depth of spirit. And he appeared to be drunk, as did Deptford Dave (but it was difficult to tell with him), who was now at the bar beside them. He was waving the barman to him.

'You're called Dave?'

'Yes. Why not?'

'You're not from Deptford though, are you?'

'No.'

'Ha! I knew it!'

For Deptford Dave, this was argument won. For Chinese Dave from Hounslow, this was confusing exchange of the evening number thirty-eight.

Receiving unsatisfactory advice and guidance from a vicar might have led a person of less spiritual depth to cast a broader doubt on the purpose of the church, but Spaghetti was not one for such easy dismissiveness. Rather, the conversation served to affirm his own deep sense of spirituality. If a professional vicar wasn't as deep and spiritual as he was himself then where did that leave him? Even the Greek priest, with whom he had felt a spiritual connection, had shown himself unable to appreciate the goodness of dog. Spaghetti was feeling a calling again, but it was to something greater than established religion. It was nothing to do with dogs per se, but, as far as Soul Sam was concerned, the simplicity of *In Dog We Trust* was now looking like the way to go.

Thelonius Tripp had positioned himself in the corner of the raised area to the side of the DJ, overlooking the dancefloor. He had started sketching before he had bought a drink. From the bar the vicar caught the Tripp's eye, nodded a hello and then seized his own moment and extricated himself from Spaghetti.

'I have to talk to Thelonius. It's a matter of great artistic importance.'

And he took his big feet across the dancefloor, up and behind Thelonius.

'Thelonius! I need to talk to you!'
'What?'

(It hadn't taken long for Lee to whack up the volume.)

'I want to talk to you! Come outside!'

He motioned Thelonius to follow him and led him to the little entrance hall that already held within it the hippy, the table, the photo and the bucket.

'Oh, hello,' the vicar said, cursorily, to Hippy John, and Hippy John smiled and nodded and Thelonius smiled and nodded at Hippy John.

'We need another mural, Thelonius.'

'Another? Excellent. To go where?'

Hippy John was standing directly behind the table, as he thought someone minding the door should. This meant that the vicar and Thelonius found themselves looking across the table at each other with Hippy John in the middle. His head turned as they spoke as if he were at a tennis match, struggling to keep pace with the action.

'In the same place.' Thelonius looked confused. 'Yes. In the same place. The other one isn't there anymore.'

'Where's it gone?'

'Well, it is there, but it's underneath a load of white paint, and now we need another one to go on top of the white paint.'

Thelonius thought this sounded radical. He didn't mind that the mural had been painted over. For him, it was the communal act of painting it that had mattered. Painting white over it must have been a further brave artistic statement and he was impressed. He hadn't put the vicar down as such a modernist. And now a new mural over that!

This could be a continuous process!

'There's no more money but I can give you a record or two.' Thelonius raised his eyebrows in interest. 'We need to think of something else – another idea – another good subject for it that would be good for outreach.'

'What about some kind of celebration of the soul?'

'What do you mean?'

'Well, something that has some life to it. Someone doing something as an act of celebration.'

'What, you mean like dancing?'

'Yes!'

'But that's what the last one was.'

'Yes, but that was dancing as an act of worship. This would be dancing as an act of celebration.'

'Hmm, well, I did like the last one anyway. What kind of dancing?'

'I like the way that blond girl dances. It's like she was born to do it.'

'Yes, she does look rather good.' The vicar thought for a moment. 'The thing is that Gerald has disappeared. And Oli and Caitlin aren't around now either or, if they are, they're avoiding me. I gave them each a copy of my *Surrender To Love* tape and haven't seen either of them since.' Thelonius contemplated and the vicar realised that he should offer some excuse as to why he couldn't help with the mural himself. 'I can't think of anyone else who can help out. I don't have time, really, what with all these tapes I'm making.'

Thelonius thought. He could do it all himself. It was feasible. It wouldn't be as much fun and there would be no one to hold the ladder. But no, he couldn't. He wouldn't. Because then it wouldn't be a community effort.

'We only had the one village idiot in Gerald, and he wasn't even a proper idiot. In fact, he was about the cleverest person in the village. Like the court jester. He'll probably reappear once he's sobered up but I imagine it will be a struggle just with him. And everyone else in the village is too bloody up their own arses to get their hands dirty. We need some fool with nothing better to do, who doesn't mind working all day for nothing and for virtually no gratitude whatsoever. Just for the sake of… doing it. For the soul of the thing.'

Hippy John had been listening intently, and now, as the two men either side of him paused for thought and he had no one in particular to look to, he succumbed to the urge to speak.

'I'll do it. If you like.'

The vicar looked at Hippy John. He hadn't taken any notice of the bearded man until this moment – he had been too busy enjoying the company of the young soul men. Who was this scruffy, lanky, long-haired one? The vicar was reminded of someone, and when he suddenly realised that the someone of whom he was reminded was the saviour of humanity (the son of God), he felt unable to question his identity or his motives.

So that was that. They made the arrangements there and then. Hippy John would travel up for a few days a week and stay at the vicarage, returning to Littlehampton to do his voluntary work in Bognor. The vicar would pay for Hippy John's expenses out of his own pocket. Thelonius Tripp didn't seem bothered that his helper wasn't from the particular community of the village. Presumably, he was still part of one community or another. And when Thelonius returned to his sketch and reviewed it, he saw the makings of a mural already in progress, with the blond girl taking centre stage.

'Do you think someone should say something?'

Romance had been approached by Bird's Nest Woman, and when she looked up at him the height of her hair lowered to a neat right angle behind her. It was odd seeing her without seeing Nutty Casper too, somewhere, making a nuisance of himself.

'What do you mean?'

'You know. Say a few words. About Demetrios.'

Romance thought for a moment. Perhaps she was right. Perhaps someone should say something. It was a memorial do, after all. And nothing had been said at the funeral that was specifically about Demetrios Demetriou. But just trying to think of an appropriate introduction to the *Where Does That Leave Me* had left him floundering.

'Yeah, maybe. Not bloody me though.'

'Casper was planning on saying something.'

'Was he? Where is Casper?'

'Oh I thought you knew. He's inside again, isn't he.'

Romance looked at her, noticeably surprised and somewhat relieved. 'Oh? What's he done?'

'Grave-robbing or something. Grave desecration, I think they said. He didn't mean any harm in it but the family's making a right old fuss about it. He says he didn't mean it to be that grave anyway.' She paused, not to allow the news to sink in but because she had said all she had to say. 'Maybe the vicar should say something.'

'Good idea.'

The vicar seemed happy to oblige.

'Yes, of course. Good idea. A few words about... the deceased. It's not like I've never done that before! That's work though, isn't it? What's the rate? Ha! Buy me a drink and we're off.'

Lee was DJing and he wasn't used to being interrupted.

'What? What the fuck for? Why can't he say something during his own crappy set? Oh for fuck's sake. After this one then.'

Hippy John was pleased to be helping with the mural. He didn't fully understand what it was to be, where it was to be or even why it was to be, but then that was no longer the point of things. These two men seemed to be two decent men and they clearly had a mission that was important to them and if it was anything to do with the soul that inspired Lee and Lainie to be as they were (and it seemed to be) then he was keen to support it.

The music was nothing. He wasn't offended by the little

he had heard – at Lee and Lainie's house and in their car – but it meant nothing to him. In the venue, the music was loud and he didn't like it. It was a racket. He was pleased to be at the door where it was a little quieter. But he could see that these people were united in their love of it and he wouldn't think badly of anything that encouraged such happy togetherness. It didn't bother him that he didn't understand their love of it. He sensed that they didn't understand it either and it clearly didn't bother them. He would revel in the not understanding as they did.

And the vicar's heart was warmed by the hippy's gesture. It reaffirmed his faith in his faith. He had no reason to think that this Christ-like figure was religious in any way, but that wasn't the point. He thought of his faith as a flawed representation of something more general. It was the best that could be believed in the circumstances. It was a limited manifestation of a more general wonder. He looked forward to welcoming the hippy into his life. He sensed they could do some not understanding and wondering together. And he might talk to him about being gay, too. (It was about time he talked to someone about that.)

'One two, one two,' began the vicar in traditional style. 'Now, if we were in church, I'd now say "and please be seated". Was he buried, or the other one? Right. We are here to celebrate the life of… a fellow soul traveller – a long-haired Greek – and to give thanks for the joy he brought into all our lives and to express our grief publicly and together in the way that he would have liked. A life, cruelly cut short by nymphomania. Wasn't it? Something like that. I am reminded of the Greek playwright Aeschylus, even though he had short hair because it was the Persians who had long hair back then. Anyway, he wrote, "In our sleep pain which cannot forget falls drop by drop upon the heart until, in our own despair, against our will, comes wisdom through the awful grace of God." Although what god he was talking about, I'm not too sure. Sometime after that he was killed by a tortoise. But the point is, I think, that we can become wiser through our loss, and soul is about loss too. And whenever you're feeling the loss is too great, open up your heart! Stretch out your arms! Remember somebody else somewhere, somebody, somewhere, remember somebody else somewhere, needs you, right now, they need you, right now. Actually, that's more about the loss of a lover, but you could say that God is there for Demetrios Demetriou to provide his loving embrace. The point is to take what life throws at you and to welcome the opportunity to learn from it and to keep your heart open, as long as you're not dead. But this evening is about our departed friend and we share and delight in the wonder that was his life and the wonder that is life, so give generously to the nymphomania people, and have a drink, have a dance, in the memory of… him. Soul lives on, and his soul will live on with us. Music, Lee, music! We lift up our hearts!'

Lee wasn't ready. He hadn't lined up the next record. He had been listening with delight and wonder.

'Oh, hang on a bit,' said the vicar, continuing with the mic. 'I hope it's something fitting, Lee. Not *Nothing Can Help You Now*.'

It was OK. That wasn't the kind of record Lee played anyway. The music that instantaneously engulfed the venue was something from the seventies that the vicar didn't know. It was uplifting enough and this little collection of humanity started moving, together, and the confines of the room served to confirm their togetherness.

'That was lovely. You are good,' said the blond girl to the vicar.

Romance gave Lee a thumbs up.

# 132

*Even though you've touched my hand*
*I can't believe you are real*
*I can't believe the things I feel*
*I'm wide awake in a dream.* [24]

'They should blast this one to the Taliban,' Deptford Dave shouted to Romance. 'If they don't like soul, this'd drive 'em to pack it in!'

Romance couldn't do anything but smile. Deptford Dave was no doubt right. The Taliban would not approve of *Wide Awake in a Dream*. And they would probably take particular umbrage, as Lyn Collins went by the name of *The Female Preacher*. But then there wasn't much about the evening that would appeal to them. All this drinking and rejoicing in music. Heads would roll. And maybe they were right. Maybe it was an affront to the divine. Maybe, Romance considered, his feelings of exaltation should be reserved for the Almighty. Maybe music was immoral.

But probably not.

The blond girl saw him thinking and wasn't one not to interrupt.

'The vicar told me he'd never even met Demetrios Demetriou.'

'That would explain a thing or two. Well you've never met him either!'

'No but I haven't given a speech at his memorial do. Maybe I can then. Can I? I'd give a good speech.'

'No.'

'If we were to get married, I think the vicar would be a good person to

do it.' Romance smiled.

*Wide awake in a dream*
*Looking at you.*
*Wide awake in a dream*
*The sound of music begins with the magic you do.*

'But we won't, will we? I mean, I'm not even sure if we're an official couple yet.'

'What do you mean?'

'Well, are we? Are you committed to me, Mr Romance? You don't seem like the commitment type. Apart from to your records, of course.'

Romance thought about this. He was committed to his records. That was true. But he wanted this woman. Looking at her, he knew that he couldn't bear to lose her. She was nuts and he knew he would never meet anyone else like her.

'I want you,' he said. 'I want to be with you. I want us to be a proper couple.'

'Well, I shall have to think about it,' she said. 'I mean, there are other things going on in my life at the moment.'

There were? Romance didn't know of any.

'Yes. I mean, it all sounds like a jolly good idea. But there will probably have to be conditions.'

Romance didn't like it. Conditions sounded bad. And they usually meant something to do with records and soul music.

'Yes,' she continued. 'I shall agree to be your partner in love, life and everything on one condition. You have to give me your records, whichever ones I want, for an evening of my choosing, no questions asked.'

Romance was filled with panic. Why was she asking this? Why did she want them? What would she do with them? No one ever asked to borrow another's records. They just didn't. It was unheard of. How could he possibly agree to that? But he couldn't ask her why – even if she hadn't said that he couldn't, he knew that he couldn't – as it would betray his hesitation and he knew she wouldn't have told him anyway.

It was Faustian! It was like asking for someone's soul. She was asking for his soul. How could she expect him to agree to that? For him to hand over whatever she wanted, no questions asked. She knew he would have to say no, and so that's why she was asking: to make him say no so that she could then blame him for the break up of their relationship. But why did she want to finish it? Just when it was all looking so lovely.

'OK,' he was shocked to hear himself say. And he felt the approval of Demetrios Demetriou, divorced from the physicality of his records but forever soulful, and of Romance Watson too – the living embodiment of soul – and he felt also the approving presence of the recordless hippy.

'Oh good,' said the blond girl. 'Cos he's asked me to DJ!'

'Who?'

'Dave! Chinese Dave!' She was brimming with excitement. 'He wants me to DJ! Here!'

'When?'

'Whenever I want! He said he thought I was very good and would be a good DJ to have in his club. Of course, you can help me choose the records and then you can come and be with me and help me. And if it goes well, it might be a regular thing!'

Romance grinned. She was beautiful. It was unorthodox, and it wasn't the way of the soul scene, but he loved her then more than ever, and the fact that she seemed more excited at the prospect of playing records than of being his partner in love and life just made him love her even more.

# 133

Romance was sad about having to give up on *Looking for Romance (with Steve Davis)*. He couldn't see how it would work without his looking for romance. It would be too one-dimensional. There wouldn't even be a double-meaning in the title, which was a prerequisite for a groundbreaking documentary. The idea might still have been good enough BBC1 or ITV, even without his looking for romance, but it wasn't up to Channel 4 level and he doubted that it would be artistic enough to interest arts bodies. Steve Davis would be disappointed, but he couldn't help that. It would have been wonderful to honour Romance Watson on the screen, but then it was Romance Watson who was so insistent that Romance be true to his heart and embrace love. So in devoting himself to the blond girl, perhaps Romance was honouring Romance Watson in a very personal way. There would be no public recognition of Romance Watson's contribution to world culture, but soul was about love and by embracing love maybe Romance would be contributing to a pool of soulfulness and loveliness that was more important than the public recognition of any individual, however soulful. The public were twats anyway. One look at the charts and any fool could see that. Perhaps anything for the good of love was for the good of soul – for the good of the music.

Honouring Van McCoy would have been gratifying, and soulful too. Romance had been thinking that he could incorporate something about Van into *Looking for Romance (with Steve Davis)*. Looking for Van might have been a good idea in itself (although *Looking for Van* sounded particularly unromantic, with or without Steve Davis.) The act of looking for someone was a handy trick in documentaries, providing an easy and neat narrative. But Van being dead was a problem and the fact that he had become so famous meant that it was probably fairly well known that he was dead, so it wouldn't work finding out that he was dead and then being sad about it as a part of the documentary. Meeting Van's family and his professional associates would have been interesting, and delving deeply into his soulful past would have provided some interesting juxtaposition between commercial soul and real soul. Van himself could have been a metaphor for that relationship. But *Looking for Van (with Steve Davis)...* there was no humour to it. There was no reason for it. There was no incendiary mix. It just wasn't soulful.

## 134

So neither the man who gave the speech nor the man manning the door had known the deceased. Romance thought Demetrios Demetriou would have liked that. It would have made him laugh. Perhaps he was laughing and, if he was, he was no doubt laughing too at the subject of Thelonius Tripp's memorial sketch never having met the deceased either, and now the memorial sketch was to be a mural celebrating something (not him) and the man manning the door was going to help with it. Romance had designed none of it, but he smiled in acknowledgement at the imagined spirit of his lost friend. Ha! You weren't expecting that! Now how about I usurp the occasion for the benefit of my own love? Bring it on, he heard. Do your best. Nothing can beat my stoned priest.

Romance and the blond girl were standing together facing the vicar. They had two witnesses: Hippy John and Spaghetti Weston. Romance had chosen Hippy John because he seemed relatively sensible and because he seemed to have played some part in bringing Romance and the blond girl together. Spaghetti had just seemed to present himself; he had sniffed a spiritual going-on and was there. Hippy John and Spaghetti were standing either side of Romance and the blond girl, and they were waiting for the vicar to speak.

'Do you, Romance whatever, take thingamy – lovely girl with excellent hair…'

The blond girl sniggered. If there had been a congregation, it would have sniggered too. But the only other people present were Hippy John and Spaghetti Weston, and they were listening earnestly. Neither of them had ever before been asked to officiate at such an occasion and they were both feeling the responsibility. Spaghetti could hear that beyond the bins, back inside the venue, Solomon was on the decks. Spaghetti knew there was no one else there that evening who owned a copy of *Stop Hurting Me Baby*. It was a painfully beautiful record and he desperately wanted one and he had looked into the possibility of selling a kidney to raise the necessary funds (easiest in Iran), but he had to listen to the vicar for the sake of his friend and for the sake of his calling.

'… to be your proper grown up girlfriend and to treat her lovelily as a boyfriend should?'

'I do.'

'And do you, thingamy, lovely girl with excellent hair, take Romance whatever-his-name-is to be your proper boyfriend and to be nice to him and as understanding as you can be under what will no doubt be very trying circumstances.'

'I do.'

'And so, with no authority at all but with soul music as my witness and these two whatevers as yours, I now pronounce you bloke and bird. You may kiss the bird.'

Romance kissed his bird. They hugged.

'That'll do me,' whispered the blond girl.

Romance closed his eyes and, holding his woman, exchanged smiles with his dead friend.

The hippy smiled too.

'Alleluia,' said Spaghetti.

Spaghetti Weston was happy to be a part of this loving scene. He was glad he had come. Soul Sam had gone and Demetrios Demetriou had gone, but something of their spirit was alive here and it felt right to Spaghetti that he was contributing to the continuation of that spirit. And the experience confirmed for him that he wished to contribute further, in some deeper way. Established religion might suit this batty soul vicar, but it wasn't for him. He was an outsider and, as such, was drawn more to prophets than to priests. Jesus, Rasputin, Obi-Wan Kenobi. It occurred to him then that they all had beards, and standing beside the hippy he began to wonder if he should grow a beard too. He probably should. He had already decided that the hippy was either a prophet or a nutter, but maybe he was both, in a Sam Cooke/Marvin Gaye kind of way – a nutty channel for something wonderful that was beyond him. Spaghetti decided to stick to Hippy John for the rest of the evening, to try to gain more of an understanding of him. After all, they had already been brought together as a couple. And he decided to ask Annie if she could think of any prophets who didn't have beards.

It was a coupling that Hippy John was curious about too. Hearing those words about breath and nostrils was a surprise, and hearing them in that Brummie accent took him home and made him think of the lightness of life and the grounding that was family and, for him, the grounding that was his family – his parents. His mother had gone and he had removed himself from his father. He had taken that grounding away and, if it wasn't for Lee, he would have fallen to nothing. These people were a kind of family and he loved them but he wasn't one of them. (He didn't even like the music.) And they had all come together for their dead friend as a family would (or, in the case of a hippy falling from a bridge, as a family wouldn't). It was a good thing. It was a tribute to love. It was respectful of their own lives as well as the life that had been Demetrios Demetriou. It was a tribute to life and he had failed to give his own mother that tribute. An awareness had been building in Hippy John over the course of the evening and it was an awareness that he was going to phone home. He was going to phone his father. He was going to let his father know that he was OK and he was going to ask his father how he was. The conversation needn't go much further. He didn't like the thought of it but, beyond that, it warmed and excited him. And he was going to shave and get his hair cut.

Normally, at any gathering of the soul clan, Demetrios

Demetriou was the only one with long hair. But he wasn't at his memorial do – at least, not physically – because, at that time, he was dead. But Hippy John was there, with his hair, and as Romance hugged the blond girl and the two witnesses witnessed it, Romance felt the presence of the hair and the benignity of the hair-wearer and a warm shiver came over him. It was a wave of love that passed through the blond girl and it was a pure, musical wave. He surrendered to it and he was right to do so. It was heavenly.

'OK, soul-dier,' he said, silently, to his friend. 'OK.'

Romance opened his eyes and instead of Demetrios Demetriou he saw the Brummie twit standing there. Spaghetti had something of Eric Knowles about him. A more idiotic, scruffy version. Romance hadn't noticed it before, but that foppish hair and that upper lip where a moustache would happily sit.

Until Spaghetti had mentioned it, Romance hadn't known that Eric Knowles was into northern. He remembered hearing somewhere that someone from *The Antiques Roadshow* had been a soul boy, and he remembered suspecting that it wasn't Arthur Negus, but he hadn't thought any more about it than that. But the Eric Knowles revelation had taken root in his brain and was itching away in there. It hadn't been at the forefront of his brain all evening – when he was agreeing to be the bloke of the blond girl that was most certainly of primary concern – but it had been in there, wriggling, niggling, and, now that the whole blond girl/being a couple business seemed to have come to a conclusion and he was holding her and looking over her shoulder to Spaghetti Weston, Eric Knowles was beginning to make himself known. Eric Knowles. Antiques. Antiques were old and often valuable, like soul records. There was a connoisseurs' market and great skill was often needed in telling an original from a bootleg. And there was an even broader issue: taste. Quality versus mass-produced rubbish. Eric Knowles could go to America in search of quality soul records and Romance could go with him, with a camera. Eric could talk about the history and the culture behind the music as they travelled about, and he could explain how real soul music was different from the rubbish that made the charts. They could meet soul people too. They could even meet Romance Watson. Romance Watson could sing *Where Does That Leave Me* to Eric Knowles. And Hemel Hector could no doubt line up some other soulful contributors, as it would all be for the good of the music. The beauty of it was that the idea didn't depend on Romance being single, and furthermore he wouldn't have to worry about Hemel Hector reporting him to Ofcom or *Right to Reply*.

Comparing soul records to antiques gave an 'in' to a celebrity, and antiques were all the rage on telly. It wouldn't work with Steve Davis but it would with Eric Knowles. But it needed a good title and an extra, clever dimension if it was to rise above primetime and become original and groundbreaking.

And then it came to him. Why not go in search of the real Van McCoy as well? As part of the same trip, Eric could investigate the history and background of one of his all-time heroes, Van McCoy. (Van was bound to be one of his heroes, and if he wasn't he would surely go along with that, for the sake of the music.) Eric would look beyond the public image of the man, as he would look beyond the public image of soul. Yes, he was dead, but it wouldn't be a 'looking for' documentary in that sense. It would be a 'looking beyond', which in many ways was even deeper. It would be looking beyond the chart nonsense to the soul music. It would be looking beyond the individual artist to the culture. It would be looking beyond the man to the depths of the collective soul of humanity. Suddenly, the idea was original, groundbreaking and multi-layered, without the need for romance. And then a lightning flash of inspiration: *Searching for the Real McCoy (with Eric Knowles)*. It was brilliant. And by the time he was walking back into the venue, hand in hand with the blond girl, smiling uncontrollably as if in cahoots with the Almighty, he was already, in his head, composing the letter to Channel 4.

# LYRICS

1. Try My Love - Troy Dodds (Lewis-Dodds-Appling)

2. What Have I Done - Billy Stewart (C.McCormick-F.Cash)

3. Somebody (Somewhere) Needs You - Darrell Banks (Wilson-Gordon)

4. Open the Door to Your Heart - Darrell Banks (Banks)

5. If This Is Love - The Precisions (Bassoline-Coleman-Valvano)

6. Steppin' out of the Picture - Johnny Maestro (Raleigh-Barkan)

7. Heartburn - Johnny Maestro (Martin-Jackson)

8. My Heart's Not in It Anymore - The Steinways (Randell-Linzer)

9. Emperor of My Baby's Heart - Kurt Harris (Raleigh-Barkan)

10. Love Is the Answer - Jay Player (Butler-Harris)

11. The Drifter - Ray Pollard (Feldman-Goldstein-Gottehrer)

12. Where Does That Leave Me - Romance Watson (Van McCoy)

13. If It's All the Same to You Babe - Luther Ingram (R.Wylie)

14. That's No Way to Treat a Girl - Marie Knight (Elgin-Millrose-Bruno-Spina)

15. I Was Born to Love You - Herbert Hunter (M.Gayden)

16. You Don't Want Me No More - Major Lance (W.E.Butler-C.H.Davis)
17. Precious Lord Take My Hand - Thomas A. Dorsey (Thomas A. Dorsey)
18. Never Will I - The Magnificent 7 (Archie Himon)
19. Just My Imagination - The Temptations (N.Whitfield-B.Strong)
20. Come On Children Let's Sing - Mahalia Jackson (Harold Smith)
21. People Get Ready - The Impressions (C.Mayfield)
22. You've Been Cheatin' - The Impressions (C.Mayfield)
23. Let's Wade in the Water - Marlena Shaw (Shaw-Magid)
24. Wide Awake in a Dream - Lyn Collins (L.Campbell-J.Phillips)

Printed in Poland
by Amazon Fulfillment
Poland Sp. z o.o., Wrocław